DANCING SHADOWS

DANCING SHADOWS

TALES OF THE SUPERNATURAL BY BERNARD CAPES

COACHWHIP PUBLICATIONS
Landisville, Pennsylvania

Dancing Shadows: Tales of the Supernatural by Bernard Capes

Bernard Capes (1854-1918)

ISBN 1-61646-093-8
ISBN-13 978-1-61646-093-8

Cover Image: Dancer © Franck Camhi

CoachwhipBooks.com

CONTENTS

THE MOON STRICKEN
(1896)

It so fell that one dark evening in the month of June I was belated in the Bernese Oberland. Dusk overtook me toiling along the great Chamounix Road, and in the heart of a most desolate gorge, whose towering snow-flung walls seemed—as the day sucked inwards to a point secret as a leech's mouth—to close about me like a monstrous amphitheatre of ghosts. The rutted road, dipping and climbing toilfully against the shouldering of great tumbled boulders, or winning for itself but narrow foothold over slippery ridges, was thawed clear of snow; but the cold soft peril yet lay upon its flanks thick enough for a wintry plunge of ten feet, or may be fifty where the edge of the causeway fell over to the lower furrows of the ravine. It was a matter of policy to go with caution, and a thing of some moment to hear the thud and splintering of little distant icefalls about one in the darkness. Now and again a cold arrow of wind would sing down from the frosty peaks above or jerk with a squiggle of laughter among the fallen slabs in the valley. And these were the only voices to prick me on through a dreariness lonely as death.

I knew the road, but not its night terrors. Passing along it some days before in the glory of sunshine, broad paddocks and islands of green had comforted the shattered white ruin of the place, and I had traversed it merely as a magnificent episode in the indifferent history of my life. Now, as it seemed, I became one with it—an awful waif of solemnity, a thing apart from mankind and its warm intercourse and ruddy inn doors, a spectral anomaly, whose austere epitaph was once writ upon the snow coating some fallen slab of those glimmering about me. I thought the whole gorge smelt of tombs, like the vault of a cathedral. I thought, in the incomprehensible low moaning sound that ever and again seemed to eddy about me when the wind had swooped and passed, that I recognised the forlorn voices of brother spirits long since dead and forgotten of the world.

Suddenly I felt the sweat cold under the knapsack that swung upon my back; stopped, faced about and became human again. Ridge over ridge to my right the mountain summits fell away against a fathomless sky; and topping the furthermost was a little paring of silver light, the coronet of the rising moon. But the glory of the full orb was in the retrospect; for, closing the savage vista of the ravine, stood up far away a cluster of jagged pinnacles—opal, translucent, lustrous as the peaks of icebergs that are the frozen music of the sea.

It was the toothed summit of the Aiguille Verte, now prosaically bathed in the light of the full moon; but to me, looking from that grim and passionless hollow, it stood for the white hand of God lifted in menace to the evil spirits of the glen.

I drank my fill of the good sight, and then turned me to my tramp again with a freshness in my throat as though it had gulped a glass of champagne. Presently I knew myself descending, leaving, as I felt rather than saw, the stark horror of the gorge and its glimmering snow patches above me. Puffs of a warmer air purred past my face with little friendly sighs of welcome, and the hum of a far-off torrent struck like a wedge into the indurated fibre of the night. As I dropped, however, the mountain heads grew up against the moon, and withheld the comfort of her radiance; and it was not until the whimper of the torrent had quickened about me to a plunging roar, and my foot was on the striding bridge that took its waters at a step, that her light broke through a topmost cleft in the hills, and made glory of the leaping thunder that crashed beneath my feet.

Thereafter all was peace. The road led downwards into a broadening valley, where the smell of flowers came about me, and the mountain walls withdrew and were no longer overwhelming. The slope eased off, dipping and rising no more than a ground swell; and by-and-by I was on a level track that ran straight as a stretched ribbon and was reasonable to my tired feet.

Now the first dusky châlets of the hamlet of Bel-Oiseau straggled towards me, and it was music in my ears to hear the cattle blow and rattle in their stalls under the sleeping lofts as I passed outside in the moonlight. Five minutes more, and the great zinc onion on the spire of the church glistened towards me, and I was in the heart of the silent village.

From the deep green shadow cast by the graveyard wall, heavily buttressed against avalanches, a form wriggled out into the moonlight and fell with a dusty thud at my feet, mowing and chopping at the air with its aimless claws. I started back with a sudden jerk of my pulses. The thing was horrible by reason of its inarticulate voice, which issued from the shapeless folds of its writhings like the wet gutturizing of a back-broken horse. Instinct with repulsion, I stood a moment dismayed, when light flashed from an open doorway a dozen yards further down the street, and a woman ran across to the prostrate form.

"Up, graceless one!" she cried; "and carry thy seven devils within doors!"

The figure gathered itself together at her voice, and stood in an angle of the buttresses quaking and shielding its eyes with two gaunt arms.

"Can I not exchange a word with Mère Pettit," scolded the woman, "but thou must sneak from behind my back on thy crazed moon-hunting?"

"Pity, pity," moaned the figure; and then the woman noticed me, and dropped a curtsy.

"Pardon," she said; "but he has been affronting Monsieur with his antics?"

"He is stricken, Madame?"

"Ah, yes, Monsieur. Holy Mother, but how stricken!"

"It is sad."

"Monsieur knows not how sad. It is so always, but most a great deal when the moon is full. He was a good lad once."

Monsieur puts his hand in his pocket. Madame hears the clink of coin and touches the enclosed fingers with her own delicately. Monsieur withdraws his hand empty.

"Pardon, Madame."

"Monsieur has the courage of a gentleman. Come, Camille, little fool! a sweet good-night to Monsieur."

"Stay, Madame. I have walked far and am weary. Is there an hotel in Bel-Oiseau?"

"Monsieur is jesting. We are but a hundred of poor châlets."

"An auberge, then—a cabaret—anything?"

"*Les Trois Chèvres*. It is not for such as you."

"Is it, then, that I must toil onwards to Châtelard?"

"Monsieur does not know? The *Hôtel Royal* was burned to the walls six months since."

"It follows that I must lie in the fields."

Madame hesitates, ponders, and makes up her mind.

"I keep Monsieur talking, and the night wind is sharp from the snow. It is ill for a heated skin, and one should be indoors. I have a bedroom that is at Monsieur's disposition, if Monsieur will condescend?"

Monsieur will condescend. Monsieur would condescend to a loft and a truss of straw, in default of the neat little chilly chamber that is allotted him, so sick are his very limbs with long tramping, and so uninviting figures the further stretch in the moonlight to Châtelard, with its burnt-out carcase of an hotel.

This is how I came to quarter myself on Madame Barbière and her idiot son, and how I ultimately learned from the lips of the latter the strange story of his own immediate fall from reason and the dear light of intellect.

By day Camille Barbière proved to be a young man, some five and twenty years of age, of a handsome and impressive exterior. His dark hair lay close about his well-shaped head; his features were regular and cut bold as an Etruscan cameo; his limbs were elastic and moulded into the supple finish of one whose life has not been set upon level roads. At a speculative distance he appeared a straight specimen of a Burgundian youth—sinewy, clean-formed, and graceful, though slender to gauntness; and it was only on nearer contact that one marvelled to see the soul die out of him, as a face set in the shadow of leafage resolves itself into some accident of twisted branches as one approaches the billowing tree that presented it.

The soul of Camille, the idiot, had warped long after its earthly tabernacle had grown firm and fair to look upon. Cause and effect were not one from birth in him; and the result was a most wistful expression, as though the lost intellect were for ever struggling and failing to recall its ancient mastery. Mostly he was a gentle young man, noteworthy for nothing but the uncomplaining patience with which he daily observed the monotonous routine of simple duties that were now all-sufficient for the poor life that had "crept so long on a broken wing." He milked the big, red, barrel-bodied cow, and churned industriously for butter; he kept the little vegetable garden in order and nursed the Savoys into fatness like plumping babies; he drove the goats to pasture on the mountain slopes, and all day sat among the rhododendrons, the forgotten soul behind his eyes conning the dead language of fate, as a foreigner vainly interrogates the abstruse complexity of an idiom.

By-and-by I made it an irregular habit to accompany him on these shepherdings; to join him in his simple midday meal of sour brown bread and goat-milk cheese; to talk with him desultorily, and study him the while, inasmuch as he wakened an interest in me that was full of speculation. For his was not an imbecility either hereditary or constitutional. From the first there had appeared to me something abnormal in it—a suspension of intelligence only, a frost-bite in the brain that presently some April breath of memory might thaw out. This was not merely conjectural, of course. I had the story of his mental collapse from his mother in the early days of my sojourn in Bel-Oiseau; for it came to pass that a fitful caprice induced me to prolong my stay in the swart little village far into the gracious Swiss summer.

The "story" I have called it; but it was none. He was out on the hills one moonlight night, and came home in the early morning mad. That was all.

This had happened some eight years before, when he was a lad of seventeen—a strong, beautiful lad, his mother told me; and with a dreamy "poet's corner" in his brain, she added, but in her own better way of putting it. She had no shame that her shepherd should be an Endymion. In Switzerland they still look upon Nature as a respectable pursuit for a young man.

Well, they had thought him possessed of a devil; and his father had at first sought to exorcise it with a chamois-hide thong, as Munchausen flogged the black fox out of his skin. But the counter-irritant failed of its purpose. The devil clung deep, and rent poor Camille with periodic convulsions of insanity.

It was noted that his derangement waxed and waned with the monthly moon; that it assumed a virulent character with the passing of the second quarter, and culminated, as the orb reached its fulness, in a species of delirium, during which it was necessary to carefully watch him; that it diminished with the lessening crescent until it fell away into a quiet abeyance of faculties that was but a step apart from the normal intelligence of his kind. At his worst he was a stricken madman acutely sensitive to impressions; at his best an inoffensive peasant who said nothing foolish and nothing wise.

When he was twenty, his father died, and Camille and his mother had to make out existence in company.

Now, the veil, in my first knowledge of him, was never rent; yet occasionally it seemed to me to gape in a manner that let a little momentary finger of light through, in the flashing of which a soul kindled and shut in his eyes, like a hard-dying spark in ashes. I wished to know what gave life to the spark, and I set to pondering the problem.

"He was not always thus?" I would say to Madame Barbière.

"But no, Monsieur, truly. This place—bah! we are here imbeciles all to the great world, without doubt; but Camille!—*he* was by nature of those who make the history of cities—a rose in the wilderness. Monsieur smiles?"

"By no means. A scholar, Madame?"

"A scholar of nature, Monsieur; a dreamer of dreams such as they become who walk much with the spirits on the lonely mountains."

"Torrents, and avalanches, and the good material forces of nature, Madame means."

"Ah! Monsieur may talk, but he knows. He has heard the *föhn* sweep down from the hills and spin the great stones off the house-roofs. And one may look and see nothing, yet the stones go. It is the wind that runs before the avalanche that snaps the pine trees; and the wind is the spirit that calls down the great snow-slips."

"But how may Madame who sees nothing, know then a spirit to be abroad?"

"My faith; one may know one's foot is on the wild mint without shifting one's sole to look."

"Madame will pardon me. No doubt also one may know a spirit by the smell of sulphur?"

"Monsieur is a sceptic. It comes with the knowledge of cities. There are even such in little Bel-Oiseau, since the evil time when they took to engrossing the contracts of good citizens on the skins of the poor jew-beards that give us flesh and milk. It is horrible as the Tannery of Meudon. In my young days, Monsieur, such agreements were inscribed upon wood."

"Quite so, Madame, and entirely to the point. Also one may see from whom Camille inherited his wandering propensities. But for his fall—it was always unaccountable?"

"Monsieur, as one trips on the edge of a crevasse and disappears. His soul dropped into the frozen cleft that one cannot fathom."

"Madame will forgive my curiosity."

"But surely. There was no dark secret in my Camille's life. If the little head held pictures beyond the ken of us simple women, the angels painted them of a certainty. Moreover, it is that I willingly recount this grief to the wise friend that may know a solution."

"At least the little-wise can seek for one."

"Ah, if Monsieur would only find the remedy!"

"It is in the hands of fate."

Madame crossed herself.

"Of the *Bon Dieu*, Monsieur."

At another time Madame Barbière said:—

"It was in such a parched summer as this threatens to be that my Camille came home in the mists of the morning possessed. He was often out on the sweet hills all night—that was nothing. It had been a full moon, and the whiteness of it was on his face like leprosy, but his hands were hot with fever. Ah, the dreadful summer! The milk turned sour in the cows' udders and the tufts of the stone pines on the mountains fell into ashes like Dead Sea fruit. The springs were dried, and the great cascade of Buet fell to half its volume."

"This cascade; I have never seen it. Is it in the neighbourhood?"

"Of a surety. Monsieur must have passed the rocky ravine that vomits the torrent, on his way hither."

"I remember. I will explore it. Camille shall be my guide."

"Never."

"And why?"

Madame shrugged her plump shoulders.

"Who may say? The ways of the afflicted are not our ways. Only I know that Camille will never drive his flock to pasture near the lip of that dark valley."

"That is strange. Can the place have associations for him connected with his malady?"

"It is possible. Only the good God knows."

But *I* was to know later on, with a little reeling of the reason also.

"Camille, I want to see the Cascade de Buet."

The hunted eyes of the stricken looked into mine with a piercing glance of fear.

"Monsieur must not," he said, in a low voice.

"And why not?"

"The waters are bad—bad—haunted!"

"I fear no ghosts. Wilt thou show me the way, Camille?"

"I!" The idiot fell upon the grass with a sort of gobbling cry. I thought it the prelude to a fit of some sort, and was stepping towards him, when he rose to his feet, waved me off and hurried away down the slope homewards.

Here was food for reflection, which I mumbled in secret.

A day or two afterwards I joined Camille at midday on the heights where he was pasturing his flocks. He had shifted his ground a little distance westwards, and I could not find him at once. At last I spied him, his back to a rock, his hand dabbled for coolness in a little runnel that trickled at his side. He looked up and greeted me with a smile. He had conceived an affection for me, this poor lost soul.

"It will go soon," he said, referring to the miniature streamlet. "It is safe in the woods; but to-morrow or next day the sun will lap it up ere it can reach the skirt of the shadow above there. A farewell kiss to you, little stream!"

He bent and sipped a mouthful of the clear water. He was in a more reasonable state than he had shown for long, though it was now close on the moon's final quarter, a period that should have marked a more general tenor of placidity in him. The summer solstice, was, however, at hand, and the weather sultry to a degree—as it had been, I did not fail to remember, the year of his seizure.

"Camille," I said, "why to-day hast thou shifted thy ground a little in the direction of the Buet ravine?"

He sat up at once, with a curious, eager look in his face.

"Monsieur has asked it," he said. "It was to impel Monsieur to ask it that I moved. Does Monsieur seek a guide?"

"Wilt thou lead me, Camille?"

"Monsieur, last night I dreamed and one came to me. Was it my father? I know not, I know not. But he put my forehead to his breast, and the evil left it, and I remembered without terror. 'Reveal the secret to the stranger,' he said; 'that he may share thy burden and comfort thee; for he is strong where thou art weak, and the vision shall not scare him.' Monsieur, wilt thou come?"

He leaped to his feet, and I to mine.

"Lead on, Camille. I follow."

He called to the leader of his flock: "Petitjean! stray not, my little one. I shall be back sooner than the daisies close." Then he turned to me again. I noticed a pallid, desperate look in his face, as though he were strung to great effort; but it was the face of a mindless one still.

"Do you not fear?" he said, in a whisper; and the apple in his throat seemed all choking core.

"I fear nothing," I answered with a smile; yet the still sombreness of the woods found a little tremor in my breast.

"It is good," he answered, regarding me. "The angel spoke truth. Follow, Monsieur."

He went off through the trees of a sudden, and I had much ado to keep pace with him. He ran as one urged on by a sure sense of doom, looking neither to right nor left. His mountain instincts had remained with him when memory itself had closed around like a fog, leaving him face to face and isolated with his one unconfessed point of terror. Swiftly we made our way, ever slightly climbing, along the rugged hillside, and soon broke into country very wild and dismal. The pastoral character of the scene lessened and altogether disappeared. The trees grew matted and grotesquely gnarled, huddling together in menacing battalions—save where some plunging rock had burst like a shell, forcing a clearing and strewing the black moss with a jagged wreck of splinters. Here no flowers crept for warmth, no sentinel marmot turned his little scut with a whistle of alarm to vanish like a red shadow. All was melancholy and silence and the massed defiance of ever-impending ruin. Storm, and avalanche, and the bitter snap of frost had wrought their havoc year by year, till an uncrippled branch was a rare distinction. The very saplings, of stunted growth, bore the air of thieves reared in a rookery of crime.

We strode with difficulty in an inhuman twilight through this great dark quickset of Nature, and had paused a moment where the thronging trunks thinned somewhat, when a little mouthing moan came towards us on the crest of a ripple of wind. My companion stopped on the instant, and clutched my arm, his face twisting with panic.

"The Cascade, Monsieur!" he shook out in a terrified whisper.

"Courage, my friend! It is that we come to seek."

"Ah! My God, yes—it is that! I dare not—I dare not!"

He drew back livid with fear, but I urged him on.

"Remember the dream, Camille!" I cried.

"Yes, yes—it was good. Help me, Monsieur, and I will try—yes, I will try!"

I drew his arm within mine, and together we stumbled on. The undergrowth grew denser and more fantastic; the murmur filled out, increased and resolved itself into a sound of falling water that ever took shape, and volume, and depth, till its crash shook the ground at our feet. Then in a moment a white blaze of sky came at us through the trunks, and we burst through the fringe of the wood to find ourselves facing the opposite side of a long cleft in the mountain and the blade's edge of a roaring cataract.

It shot out over the lip of the fall, twenty feet above us, in a curve like a scimitar, passed in one sheet the spot where we stood, and dived into a sunless pool thirty feet below with a thunderous boom. What it may have been in full phases of the stream, I know not; yet even now it was sufficiently magnificent to give pause to a dying soul eager to shake off the restless horror of the world. The flat of its broad blade divided the lofty black walls of a deep and savage ravine, on whose jagged shelves some starved clumps of rhododendron shook in the wind of the torrent. Far down the narrow gully we could see the passion of water tossing, champed white with the ravening of its jaws, until it took a bend of the cliffs at a leap and rushed from sight.

We stood upon a little platform of coarse grass and bramble, whose fringe dipped and nodded fitfully as the sprinkle caught it. Beyond, the sliding sheet of water looked like a great strap of steel, reeled ceaselessly off a whirling drum pivoted between the hills. The midday sun shot like a piston down the shaft of the valley, painting purple spears and angles behind its abutting rocks, and hitting full upon the upper curve of the fall; but half-way down the cataract slipped into shadow.

My brain sickened with the endless gliding and turmoil of descent, and I turned aside to speak to my companion. He was kneeling upon the grass, his eyes fixed and staring, his white lips mumbling some crippled memory of a prayer. He started and cowered down as I touched him on the shoulder.

"I cannot go, Monsieur; I shall die!"

"What next, Camille? I will go alone,"

"My God, Monsieur! the cave under the fall! It is there the horror is."

He pointed to a little gap in the fringing bushes with shaking finger. I stole gingerly in the direction he indicated. With every step I took the awful fascination of the descending water increased upon me. It seemed hideous and abnormal to stand mid-way against a perpendicularly-rushing torrent. Above or below the effect would have been different; but here, to look up was to feel one's feet dragging towards the unseen—to look down and pass from vision of the lip of the fall was to become the waif of a force that was unaccountable.

I had a battle with my nerves, and triumphed. As I approached the opening in the brambles I became conscious of a certain relief. At a little distance the cataract had seemed to actually wash in its descent the edge of the platform. Now I found it to be further away than I had imagined, the ground dropping in a sharp slope to a sort of rocky buttress which lay obliquely on the slant of the ravine, and was the true margin of the torrent. Before I essayed the descent, I glanced back at my companion. He was kneeling where I had left him, his hands pressed to his face, his features hidden; but looking back once again, when I had with infinite caution accomplished the downward climb, I saw that he had crept to the edge of the slope, and was watching me with wide, terrified eyes. I waved my hand to him and turned to the wonderful vision of water that now passed almost within reach of my arm. I stood near the point where the whole glassy breadth glided at once from sunlight into shadow. It fell silently, without a break, for only its feet far below trod the thunder.

Now, as I peered about, I noticed a little cleft in the rocky margin, a minute's climb above me. I was attracted to this by an appearance of smoke or steam that incessantly emerged from it, as though some witch's caldron were simmering alongside the fall. Spray it might be, or the condensing of water splashed on the granite; but of this I might not be sure. Therefore I determined to investigate, and straightway began climbing the rocks—with my heart in my mouth, it must be confessed, for the foothold was undesirable and the way perilous. And all the time I was conscious that the white face of Camille watched me from above. As I reached the cleft I fancied I heard a queer sort of gasping sob issue from his lips, but to this I could give no heed in the sudden wonder that broke upon me. For, lo! it appeared that the cleft led straight to a narrow platform or ledge of rock right underneath the fall itself, but extending how far I could not see, by reason of the steam that filled the passage, and for which I was unable to account. Footing it carefully and groping my way, I set step in the little water-curtained chamber and advanced a pace or two. Suddenly, light grew about me, and a beautiful rose of fire appeared on the wall of the passage in the midst of what seemed a vitrified scoop in the rock.

Marvelling, I put out my hand to touch it, and fell back on the narrow floor with a scream of anguish. An inch farther, and these lines had not been written. As it was, the fall caught me by the fingers with the suck of a cat-fish, and it was only a gigantic wrench that saved me from slipping off the ledge. The jerk brought my head against the rock with a stunning blow, and for some moments I lay dizzy and confused, daring hardly to breathe, and conscious only of a burning and blistering agony in my right hand.

At length I summoned courage to gather my limbs together and crawl out the way I had entered. The distance was but a few paces, yet to traverse these seemed an interminable nightmare of swaying and stumbling. I know only one other occasion upon which the liberal atmosphere of the open earth seemed sweeter to my senses when I reached it than it did on this.

I tumbled somehow through the cleft, and sat down, shaking, upon the grass of the slope beyond; but, happening to throw myself backwards in the reeling faintness induced by my fright and the pain of my head, my eyes encountered a sight that woke me at once to full activity.

Balanced upon the very verge of the slope, his face and neck craned forward, his jaw dropped, a sick, tranced look upon his features, stood Camille. I saw him topple, and shouted to him; but before my voice was well out, he swayed, collapsed, and came down with a running thud that shook the ground. Once he wheeled over, like a shot rabbit, and, bounding thwack with his head against a flat boulder not a dozen yards from me, lay stunned and motionless.

I scrambled to him, quaking all over. His breath came quick, and a spirt of blood jerked from a sliced cut in his forehead at every pump of his heart.

I kicked out a wad of cool moist turf, and clapped it in a pad over the wound, my handkerchief under. For his body, he was shaken and bruised, but otherwise not seriously hurt.

Presently he came to himself; to himself in the best sense of the word—for Camille was sane.

I have no explanation to offer. Only I know that, as a fall will set a long-stopped watch pulsing again, the blow here seemed to have restored the misplaced intellect to its normal balance.

When he woke, there was a new soft light of sanity in his eyes that was pathetic in the extreme.

"Monsieur," he whispered, "the terror has passed."

"God be thanked! Camille," I answered, much moved.

He jerked his poor battered head in reverence.

"A little while," he said, "and I shall know. The punishment was just."

"What punishment, my poor Camille?"

"Hush! The cloud has rolled away. I stand naked before *le bon Dieu*. Monsieur, lift me up; I am strong."

I winced as I complied. The palm of my hand was scorched and blistered in a dozen places. He noticed at once, and kissed and fondled the wounded limb as softly as a woman might.

"Ah, the poor hand!" he murmured. "Monsieur has touched the disc of fire."

"Camille," I whispered, "what is it?"

"Monsieur shall know—ah! yes, he shall know; but not now. Monsieur, my mother."

"Thou art right, good son."

I bound up his bruised forehead and my own burnt hand as well as I was able, and helped him to his feet. He stood upon them staggering; but in a minute could essay to stumble on the homeward journey with assistance. It was a long and toilsome progress; but in time we accomplished it. Often we had to sit down in the blasted woods and rest awhile; often moisten our parched mouths at the runnels of snow-water that thridded the undergrowth. The shadows were slanting eastwards as we reached the clearing we had quitted some hours earlier, and the goats had disappeared. Petitjean was leading his charges homewards in default of a human commander, and presently we overtook them browsingly loitering and desirous of definite instructions.

I pass over Camille's meeting with his mother, and the wonder, and fear, and pity of it all. Our hurts were attended to, and the battery of questions met with the best armour of tact at command. For myself, I said that I had scorched my hand against a red-hot rock, which was strictly true; for Camille, that it were wisest to take no early advantage of the reason that God had restored to him. She was voluble, tearful, half-hysterical with joy and the ecstasy of gratitude.

"That a blow should effect the marvel! Monsieur, but it passes comprehension."

All night long I heard her stirring and sobbing softly outside his door, for I slept little, owing to pain and the wonder in my mind. But towards morning I dozed, and my dreams were feverish and full of terror.

The next day Camille kept his bed and I my room. By this I at least escaped the first onset of local curiosity, for the villagers naturally made of Camille's restoration a nine-days' wonder. But towards evening Madame Barbière brought a message from him that he would like to see Monsieur alone, if Monsieur would condescend to visit him in his room. I went at once, and found him, as Haydon found Keats, lying in a white bed, hectic, and on his back. He greeted me with a smile peculiarly sweet and restful.

"Does Monsieur wish to know?" he said in a low voice.

"If it will not hurt thee, Camille."

"Not now—not now; the good God has made me sound. I remember, and am not terrified."

I closed the door and took a seat by his bedside. There, with my hand shading my eyes from the level glory of sunset that flamed into the room, I listened to the strange tale of Camille's seizure.

"Once, Monsieur, I lived in myself and was exultant with a loneliness of fancied knowledge. My youth was my excuse; but God could not pardon me all. I read where I could find books, and chance put an evil choice in my way, for I learned to sneer at His name, His heaven, His hell. Each man has his god in self-will, I thought in my pride, and through it alone he accepts the responsibility of life and death. He is his own curse or blessing here and hereafter, inheriting no sin and earning no doom but such as he himself inflicts upon himself. I interpret this from the world about me, and knowing it, I have no fear and own no tyrant but my own passions. Monsieur, it was through fear the most terrible that God asserted Himself to me."

The light was fading in the west, and a lance of shadow fell upon the white bed, as though the hushed day were putting a finger to its lips as it withdrew.

"I was no coward then, Monsieur—that at least I may say. I lived among the mountains, and on their ledges the feet of my own goats were not surer. Often, in summer, I spent the night among the woods and hills, reading in them the story of the ages, and exploring, exploring till my feet were wearier than my brain. Strangers came from far to see the great cascade; but none but I—and you, too, Monsieur, now—know the track through the thicket that leads to the cave under the waters. I found it by chance, and, like you, was scorched by the fire, though not badly."

"Camille—the cause?"

"Monsieur, I will tell you a wonderful thing. The falling waters there make a monstrous burning glass, when the hot sun is upon them, which has melted the rock behind like wax."

"Can that be so?"

"It is true—dear Jesus, I have fearful reason to know it."

He half rose on his elbow, his face, crossed by the bandage, grey as stone in the gathering dusk. Hereafter he spoke in an awed whisper.

"When the knowledge broke upon me, I grew great to myself in the possession of a wonderful secret. Day after day I visited the cave and examined this phenomenon—and yet another more marvellous in its connection with the first. The huge lens was a simple accident of curved rocks and convex water, planed smooth as crystal. In other than a droughty summer it would probably not exist; the spouting torrent would overwhelm it—but I know not. Was not this astonishing enough? Yet Nature had worked a second miracle to mock in anticipation the self-sufficient plagiarism of little man. I noticed that the rays of the sun concentrated in the lens only during the half-hour of the orb's apparent crossing of the ravine. Then the light smote upon a strange curved little fan of water, that spouted from a high crevice at the mouth of the shallow vitrified tunnel, and devoured it, and played upon the rocks behind, that hissed and sputtered like pitch, and the place was blind with steam. But when the tooth of fire was withdrawn, the tiny inner cascade fell again and wrought coolness with its sprinkling.

"I did not discover this all at once, for at first fright took me, and it was enough to watch for the moment of the light's appearance and then flee with a little laughter. But one day I ventured back into the cave after the sun had crossed the valley, and the steam had died away, and the rock cooled behind the miniature cascade.

"I looked through the lens, and it seemed full of a great white light that blazed into my eyes, so that I fell back through the inner fan of water and was well soused by it; but my sight presently recovering, I stood forward in the scoop of rock admiring the dainty hollow curve the fan took in its fall. By-and-by I became aware that I was looking out through a smaller lens upon the great one, and that strange whirling mists seemed to be sweeping across a huge disc, within touch of my hand almost.

"It was long before I grasped the meaning of this; but, in a flash, it came upon me. The great lens formed the object glass, the small, the eyeglass, of a natural telescope of tremendous power, that drew the high summer clouds down within seeming touch and opened out the heavens before my staring eyes.

"Monsieur, when this dawned upon me I was wild. That so astonishing a discovery should have been reserved for a poor ignorant Swiss peasant filled me with pride wicked in proportion with its absence of gratitude to the mighty dispenser of good. I came even to think my individuality part of the wonder and necessary to its existence. 'Were it not for my courage and enterprise,' I cried, 'this phenomenon would have remained a secret of the Nature that gave birth to it. She yields her treasures to such only as fear not.'

"I had read in a book of Huyghens, Guinand, Newton, Herschel—the great high-priests of science who had striven through patient years to read the hieroglyphics of the heavens. 'The wise imbeciles,' I thought. 'They toiled and died, and Nature held no mirror up to them. For me, the poor Camille, she has worked in secret while they grew old and passed unsatisfied.'

"Brilliant projects of astronomy whirled in my brain. The evening of my last discovery I remained out on the hills, and entered the cave as it grew dusk. A feeling of awe surged in me as dark fell over the valley, and the first stars glistened faintly. I dipped under the fan of water and took my stand in the hollow behind it. There was no moon, but my telescope was inclined, as it were, at a generous angle, and a section of the firmament was open before me. My heart beat fast as I looked through the lens.

"Shall I tell you what I saw then and many nights after? Rings and crosses in the heavens of golden mist, spangled, as it seemed, with jewels; stars as big as cart-wheels, twinkling points no longer, but round, like great bosses of molten fire; things shadowy, luminous, of strange colours and stranger forms, that seemed to brush the waters as they passed, but were in reality vast distances away.

"Sometimes the thrust of wind up the ravine would produce a tremulous motion in the image at the focus of the mirror; but this was seldom. For the most part the wonderful lenses presented a steady curvature, not flawless, but of magnificent capacity.

"Now it flashed upon me that, when the moon was at the full, she would top the valley in the direct path of my telescope's range of view. At the thought I grew exultant. I—I, little Camille, should first read aright the history of this strange satellite. The instrument that could give shape to the stars would interpret to me the composition of that lonely orb as clearly as though I stood upon her surface.

"As the time of her fulness drew near I grew feverish with excitement. I was sickening, as it were, to my madness, for never more should I look upon her willingly, with eyes either speculative or insane."

At this point Camille broke off for a little space, and lay back on his pillow. When he spoke again it was out of the darkness, with his face turned to the wall.

"Monsieur, I cannot dwell upon it—I must hasten. We have no right to peer beyond the boundary God has drawn for us. I saw His hell—I saw His hell, I tell you. It is peopled with the damned—silent, horrible, distorted in the midst of ashes and desolation. It was a memory that, like the snake of Aaron, devoured all others till yesterday—till yesterday, by Christ's mercy."

It seemed to me, as the days wore on, that Camille had but recovered his reason at the expense of his life; that the long rest deemed necessary for him after his bitter period of brain exhaustion might in the end prove an everlasting one. Possibly the blow to his head had, in expelling the seven devils, wounded beyond cure the vital function that had fostered them. He lay white, patient, and sweet-tempered to all, but moved by no inclination to rise and re-assume the many-coloured garment of life.

His description of the dreadful desert in the sky I looked upon, merely, as an abiding memory of the brain phantasm that had finally overthrown a reason, already tottering under the tremendous excitement induced by his discovery of the lenses, and the magnified images they had presented to him. That there was truth in the asserted fact of the existence of these, my own experience convinced me; and curiosity as to this alone impelled me to the determination of investigating further, when my hand should be sufficiently recovered to act as no hindrance to me in forcing my way once more through the dense woods that bounded the waterfall. Moreover, the dispassionate enquiry of a mind less sensitive to impressions might, in the result, do more towards restoring the warped imagination of my friend to its normal state than any amount of spoken scepticism.

To Camille I said nothing of my resolve; but waited on, chafing at the slow healing of my wounds. In the meantime the period of the full moon approached, and I decided, at whatever cost, to make the venture on the evening she topped her orbit, if circumstances at the worst should prevent my doing so sooner—and thus it turned out.

On the eve of my enterprise, the first fair spring of rain in a drought of two months fell, to my disappointment, among the hills; for I feared an increase of the torrent and the effacement of the mighty lens. I set off, however, on the afternoon of the following day, in hot sunshine, mentally prognosticating a favourable termination to my expedition, and telling Madame Barbière not to expect me back till late.

In leisurely fashion I made my way along the track we had previously traversed, risking no divergence through overhaste, and carefully examining all landmarks before deciding on any direction. Thus slowly proceeding, I had the good fortune to come within sound of the cataract as the sun was sinking behind the mountain ridges to my front; and presently emerged from the woods at the very spot we had struck in our former journey together.

A chilly twilight reigned in the ravine, and the noise that came up from the ruin of the torrent seemed doubly accented by reason of it. The sound of water moving in darkness has always conveyed to me an impression of something horrible and deadly, be it nothing of more moment than the drip and hollow tinkle of a gutter pipe. But the crash in this echoing gorge was appalling indeed.

For some moments I stood on the brink of the slope, looking across at the great knife of the fall, with a little shiver of fear. Then I shook myself, laughed, and without further ado took my courage in hand, and scrambled down the declivity and up again towards the cleft in the rocks.

Here the chill of heart gripped me again—the watery sliding tunnel looked so evil in the contracting gloom. A false step in that humid chamber, and my bones would pound and crackle on the rocks forty feet below. It must be gone through with now, however; and, taking a long breath, I set foot in the passage under the curving downpour that seemed taut as an arched muscle.

Reaching the burnt recess, a few moments sufficed to restore my self-confidence; and without further hesitation I dived under the inner little fan-shaped fall—which was there, indeed, as Camille had described it—and recovered my balance with pulses drumming thicker than I could have desired.

In a moment I became conscious that some great power was before me. Across a vast, irregular disc filled with the ashy whiteness of the outer twilight, strange, unaccountable forms, misty and undefined, passed, and repassed, and vanished. Cirrus they might have been, or the shadows flung by homing flights of birds; but of this I could not be certain. As the dusk deepened they showed no more, and presently I gazed only into a violet fathomless darkness.

My own excitement now was great; and I found some difficulty in keeping it under control. But for the moment, it seemed to me, I pined greatly for free commune with the liberal atmosphere of earth. Therefore, I dipped under the little fall and made my cautious way to the margin of the cataract.

I was surprised to find for how long a time the phenomenon had absorbed me. The moon was already high in the heavens, and making towards the ravine with rapid steps. Far below, the tumbling waters flashed in her rays, and on all sides great tiers of solemn, trees stood up at attention to salute her.

When her disc silvered the inner rim of the slope I had descended, I returned to my post of observation with tingling nerves. The field of the great object lens was already suffused with the radiance of her approach.

Suddenly my pupils shrank before the apparition of a ghastly grey light, and all in a moment I was face to face with a segment of desolation more horrible than any desert. Monstrous growths of leprosy that had bubbled up and stiffened; fields of ashen slime—the sloughing of a world of corruption; hills of demon fungus swollen with the fatness of putrefaction; and, in the midst of all, dim, convulsed shapes wallowing, protruding, or stumbling aimlessly onwards, till they sank and disappeared.

Madame Barbière threw up her hands when she let me in at the door. My appearance, no doubt, was ghastly. I knew not the hour nor the lapse of time covered by my wanderings about the hills, my face hidden in my palms, a drawn feeling about my heart, my lips muttering—muttering fragments of prayers, and my throat jerking with horrible laughter.

For hours I lay face downwards on my bed.

"Monsieur has seen it?"

"I have seen it."

"I heard the rain on the hills. The lens will have been blurred. Monsieur has been spared much."

"God, in His mercy, pity thee! And me—oh, Camille, and me too!"

"He has held out His white hand to me. I go, when I go, with a safe conduct."

He went before the week was out. The drought had broken and for five days the thunder crashed and the wild rain swept the mountains. On the morning of the sixth a drenched shepherd reported in the village that a landslip had choked the fall of Buet, and completely altered its shape. Madame Barbière broke into the room where I was sitting with Camille, big with the news. She little guessed how it affected her listeners.

"The *bon Dieu*" said Camille, when she had gone, "has thundered His curse on Nature for revealing His secrets. I, who have penetrated into the forbidden, must perish."

"And I, Camille?"

He turned to me with a melancholy sweet smile, and answered, paraphrasing the dying words of certain noble lips,—

"Be good, Monsieur; be good."

DARK DIGNUM
(1897)

"I'd not go higher, sir," said my landlady's father. I made out his warning through the shrill piping of the wind; and stopped and took in the plunging seascape from where I stood. The boom of the waves came up from a vast distance beneath; sky and the horizon of running water seemed hurrying upon us over the lip of the rearing cliff.

"It crumbles!" he cried. "It crumbles near the edge like as frosted mortar. I've seen a noble sheep, sir, eighty pound of mutton, browsing here one moment, and seen it go down the next in a puff of white dust. Hark to that! Do you hear it?"

Through the tumult of the wind in that high place came a liquid vibrant sound, like the muffled stroke of iron on an anvil. I thought it the gobble of water in clanging caves deep down below.

"It might be a bell," I said.

The old man chuckled joyously. He was my cicerone for the nonce; had come out of his chair by the ingle-nook to taste a little the salt of life. The north-easter flashed in the white cataracts of his eyes and woke a feeble activity in his scrannel limbs. When the wind blew loud, his daughter had told me, he was always restless, like an imprisoned sea-gull. He would be up and out. He would rise and flap his old draggled pinions, as if the great air fanned an expiring spark into flame.

"It *is* a bell!" he cried— "the bell of old St. Dunstan's, that was swallowed by the waters in the dark times."

"Ah," I said. "That is the legend hereabouts."

"No legend, sir—no legend. Where be the tombstones of drownded mariners to prove it such? Not one to forty that they has in other sea-board parishes. For why? Dunstan bell sounds its warning, and not a craft will put out."

"There is the storm cone," I suggested.

He did not hear me. He was punching with his staff at one of a number of little green mounds that lay about us.

"I could tell you a story of these," he said. "Do you know where we stand?"

"On the site of the old churchyard?"

"Ay, sir; though it still bore the name of the *new* yard in my first memory of it."

"Is that so? And what is the story?"

He dwelt a minute, dense with introspection. Suddenly he sat himself down upon a mossy bulge in the turf, and waved me imperiously to a place beside him.

"The old order changeth," he said. "The only lasting foundations of men's works shall be godliness and law-biding. Long ago they builded a new church—here, high up on the cliffs, where the waters could not reach; and, lo! the waters wrought beneath and sapped the foundations, and the church fell into the sea."

"So I understand," I said.

"The godless are fools," he chattered knowingly. "Look here at these bents—thirty of 'em, may be. Tombstones, sir; perished like man his works, and the decayed stumps of them coated with salt grass."

He pointed to the ragged edge of the cliff a score paces away.

"They raised it out there," he said, "and further—a temple of bonded stone. They thought to bribe the Lord to a partnership in their corruption, and He answered by casting down the fair mansion into the waves."

I said, "Who—who, my friend?"

"They that builded the church," he answered.

"Well," I said. "It seems a certain foolishness to set the edifice so close to the margin."

Again he chuckled.

"It was close, close, as you say; yet none so close as you might think nowadays. Time hath gnawed here like a rat on a cheese. But the foolishness appeared in setting the brave mansion between the winds and its own graveyard. Let the dead lie seawards, one had thought, and the church inland where we stand. So had the bell rung to this day; and only the charnel bones flaked piecemeal into the sea."

"Certainly, to have done so would show the better providence."

"Sir, I said the foolishness *appeared*. But, I tell you, there was foresight in the disposition—in neighbouring the building to the cliff path. *For so they could the easier enter unobserved, and store their kegs of Nantes brandy in the belly of the organ.*"

"They? Who were they?"

"Why, who—but two-thirds of all Dunburgh?"

"Smugglers?"'

"It was a nest of 'em—traffickers in the eternal fire o' week-days, and on the Sabbath, who so sanctimonious? But honesty comes not from the washing, like a clean shirt, nor can the piety of one day purge the evil of six. They built their church anigh the margin, forasmuch as it was handy, and that they thought, 'Surely the Lord will not undermine His own?' A rare community o' blasphemers, fro' the parson that took his regular toll of the organ-loft, to him that sounded the keys and pulled out the joyous stops as if they was so many spigots to what lay behind."

"Of when do you speak?"

"I speak of nigh a century and a half ago. I speak of the time o' the Seven Years' War and of Exciseman Jones, that, twenty year after he were buried, took his revenge on the cliff side of the man that done him to death."

"And who was that?"

"They called him Dark Dignum, sir—a great feat smuggler, and as wicked as he was bold."

"Is your story about him?"

"Ay, it is; and of my grandfather, that were a boy when they laid, and was glad to lay, the exciseman deep as they could dig; for the sight of his sooty face in his coffin was worse than a bad dream."

"Why was that?"

The old man edged closer to me, and spoke in a sibilant voice.

"He were murdered, sir, foully and horribly, for all they could never bring it home to the culprit."

"Will you tell me about it?"

He was nothing loth. The wind, the place of perished tombs, the very wild-blown locks of this 'withered apple-john,' were eerie accompaniments to the tale he piped in my ear:—

"When my grandfather were a boy," he said, "there lighted in Dunburgh Exciseman Jones. P'r'aps the village had gained an ill reputation. P'r'aps Exciseman Jones's predecessor had failed to secure the confidence o' the exekitive. At any rate, the new man was little to the fancy of the village. He was a grim, sour-looking, brass-bound galloot; and incorruptible—which was the worst. The keg o' brandy left on his doorstep o' New Year's Eve had been better unspiled and run into the gutter; for it led him somehow to the identification of the innocent that done it, and he had him by the heels in a twinkling. The squire snorted at the man, and the parson looked askance; but Dark Dignum, he swore he'd be even with him, if he swung for it. They was hurt and surprised, that was the truth, over the scrupulosity of certain people; and feelin' ran high against Exciseman Jones.

"At that time Dark Dignum was a young man with a reputation above his years for profaneness and audacity. Ugly things there were said about him; and amongst many wicked he was feared for his wickedness. Exciseman Jones had his eye on him; and that was bad for Exciseman Jones.

"Now one murk December night Exciseman Jones staggered home with a bloody long slice down his scalp, and the red drip from it spotting the cobble-stones.

"'Summut fell on him from a winder,' said Dark Dignum, a little later, as he were drinkin' hisself hoarse in the Black Boy. 'Summut fell on him retributive, as you might call it. For, would you believe it, the man had at the moment been threatenin' me? He did. He said, "I know damn well about you, Dignum; and for all your damn ingenuity, I'll bring you with a crack to the ground yet."'

"What had happened? Nobody knew, sir. But Exciseman Jones was in his bed for a fortnight; and when he got on his legs again, it was pretty evident there was a hate between the two men that only blood-spillin' could satisfy.

"So far as is known, they never spoke to one another again. They played their game of death in silence—the lawful, cold and unfathomable; the unlawful, swaggerin' and crool—and twenty year separated the first move and the last.

"This were the first, sir—as Dark Dignum leaked it out long after in his cups. This were the first; and it brought Exciseman Jones to his grave on the cliff here.

"It were a deep soft summer night; and the young smuggler sat by hisself in the long room of the Black Boy. Now, I tell you he were a fox-ship intriguer—grand, I should call him, in the aloneness of his villainy. He would play his dark games out of his own hand; and sure, of all his wickedness, this game must have seemed the sum.

"I say he sat by hisself; and I hear the listening ghost of him call me a liar. For there were another body present, though invisible to mortal eye; and that second party were Exciseman Jones, who was hidden up the chimney.

"How had he inveigled him there? Ah, they've met and worried that point out since. No other will ever know the truth this side the grave. But reports come to be whispered; and reports said as how Dignum had made an appointment with a bodiless master of a smack as never floated, to meet him in the Black Boy and arrange for to run a cargo as would never be shipped; and that somehow he managed to acquent Exciseman Jones o' this dissembling appointment, and to secure his presence in hidin' to witness it.

"That's conjecture; for Dignum never let on so far. But what *is* known for certain is that Exciseman Jones, who were as daring and determined as his enemy—p'r'aps more so—for some reason was in the chimney, on to a grating in which he had managed to lower hisself from the roof; and that he could, if given time, have scrambled up again with difficulty, but was debarred from going lower. And, further, this is known—that, as Dignum sat on, pretendin' to yawn and huggin' his black intent, a little sut plopped down the chimney and scattered on the coals of the laid fire beneath.

"At that— 'Curse this waitin'!' said he. 'The room's as chill as a belfry'; and he got to his feet, with a secret grin, and strolled to the hearthstone.

"'I wonder,' said he, 'will the landlord object if I ventur' upon a glint of fire for comfort's sake?' and he pulled out his flint and steel, struck a spark, and with no more feelin' than he'd express in lighting a pipe, set the flame to the sticks.

"The trapt rat above never stirred or give tongue. My God! what a man! Sich a nature could afford to bide and bide—ay, for twenty year, if need be.

"Dignum would have enjoyed the sound of a cry; but he never got it. He listened with the grin fixed on his face; and of a sudden he heard a scrambling struggle, like as a dog with the colic jumping at a wall; and presently, as the sticks blazed and the smoke rose denser, a thick coughin', as of a consumptive man under bedclothes. Still no cry, nor any appeal for mercy; no, not from the time he lit the fire till a horrible rattle come down, which was the last twitches of somethin' that choked and died on the sooty gratin' above.

"When all was quiet, Dignum he knocks with his foot on the floor and sits hisself down before the hearth, with a face like a pillow for innocence.

"'I were chilled and lit it,' says he to the landlord. 'You don't mind?'

"Mind? Who would have ventur'd to cross Dark Dignum's fancies?

"He give a boisterous laugh, and ordered in a double noggin of humming stuff.

"'Here,' he says, when it comes, 'is to the health of Exciseman Jones, that swore to bring me to the ground.'

"'To the ground,' mutters a thick voice from the chimney.

"'My God!' says the landlord— 'there's something up there!'

"Something there was; and terrible to look upon when they brought it to light. The creature's struggles had ground the sut into its face, and its nails were black below the quick.

"Were those words the last of its death-throe, or an echo from beyond? Ah! we may question; but they were heard by two men.

"Dignum went free. What could they prove agen him? Not that he knew there was aught in the chimney when he lit the fire. The other would scarcely have acquent him of his plans. And Exciseman Jones was hurried into his grave alongside the church up here.

"And therein he lay for twenty year, despite that, not a twelvemonth after his coming, the sacrilegious house itself sunk roaring into the waters. For the Lord would have none of it, and, biding His time, struck through a fortnight of deluge, and hurled church and cliff into ruin. But the yard remained, and, nighest the seaward edge of it, Exciseman Jones slept in his fearful winding sheet and bided *his* time.

"It came when my grandfather were a young man of thirty, and mighty close and confidential with Dark Dignum. God forgive him! Doubtless he were led away by the older smuggler, that had a grace of villainy about him, 'tis said, and used Lord Chesterfield's printed letters for wadding to his bullets.

"By then he was a ramping, roaring devil; but, for all his bold hands were stained with crime, the memory of Exciseman Jones and of his promise dwelled with him and darkened him ever more and more, and never left him. So those that knew him said.

"Now all these years the cliff edge agen the graveyard, where it was broke off, was scabbing into the sea below. But still they used this way of ascent for their ungodly traffic; and over the ruin of the cliff they had drove a new path for to carry up their kegs.

"It was a cloudy night in March, with scud and a fitful moon, and there was a sloop in the offing, and under the shore a loaded boat that had just pulled in with muffled rowlocks. Out of this Dark Dignum was the first to sling hisself a brace of rundlets; and my grandfather followed with two more. They made softly for the cliff path—began the ascent—was half-way up.

"Whiz!—a stone of chalk went by them with a skirl, and slapped into the rubble below.

"'Some more of St. Dunstan's gravel!' cried Dignum, pantin' out a reckless laugh under his load; and on they went again.

"Hwish!—a bigger lump came like a thunderbolt, and the wind of it took the bloody smuggler's hat and sent it swooping into the darkness like a bird.

"'Thunder!' said Dignum; 'the cliff's breaking away!'

"The words was hardly out of his mouth, when there flew such a volley of chalk stones as made my grandfather, though none had touched him, fall upon the path where he stood, and begin to gabble out what he could call to mind of the prayers for the dying. He was in the midst of it, when he heard a scream come from his companion as froze the very marrow in his bones. He looked up, thinkin' his hour had come.

"My God! What a sight he saw! The moon had shone out of a sudden, and the light of it struck down on Dignum's face, and that was the colour of dirty parchment. And he looked higher, and give a sort of sob.

"For there, stickin' out of the cliff side, was half the body of Exciseman Jones, with its arms stretched abroad, *and it was clawin' out lumps of chalk and hurling them down at Dignum*!

"And even as he took this in through his terror, a great ball of white came hurtling, and went full on to the man's face with a splash—and he were spun down into the deep night below, a nameless thing."

The old creature came to a stop, his eyes glinting with a febrile excitement.

"And so," I said, "Exciseman Jones was true to his word?"

The tension of memory was giving—the spring slowly uncoiling itself.

"Ay," he said doubtfully. "The cliff had flaked away by degrees to his very grave. They found his skelington stickin' out of the chalk."

"His *skeleton?*" said I, with the emphasis of disappointment.

"The first, sir, the first. Ay, his was the first. There've been a many exposed since. The work of decay goes on, and the bones they fall into the sea. Sometimes, sailing off shore, you may see a shank or an arm protrudin' like a pigeon's leg from a pie. But the wind or the weather takes it and it goes. There's more to follow yet. Look at 'em! look at these bents! Every one a grave, with a skelington in it. The wear and tear from the edge will reach each one in turn, and then the last of the ungodly will have ceased from the earth."

"And what became of your grandfather?"

"My grandfather? There were something happened made him renounce the devil. He died one of the elect. His youth were heedless and unregenerate; but, 'tis said, after he were turned thirty he never smiled agen. There was a reason. Did I ever tell you the story of Dark Dignum and Exciseman Jones?"

THE VANISHING HOUSE
(1898)

"My grandfather," said the banjo, "drank 'dog's-nose,' my father drank 'dog's-nose,' and I drink 'dog's-nose.' If that ain't heredity, there's no virtue in the board schools."

"Ah!" said the piccolo, "you're always a-boasting of your science. And so, I suppose, your son'll drink 'dog's-nose,' too?"

"No," retorted the banjo, with a rumbling laugh, like wind in the bung-hole of an empty cask; "for I ain't got none. The family ends with me; which is a pity, for I'm a full-stop to be proud on."

He was an enormous, tun-bellied person—a mere mound of expressionless flesh, whose size alone was an investment that paid a perpetual dividend of laughter. When, as with the rest of his company, his face was blackened, it looked like a specimen coal on a pedestal in a museum.

There was Christmas company in the Good Intent, and the sanded tap-room, with its trestle tables and sprigs of holly stuck under sooty beams reeked with smoke and the steam of hot gin and water.

"How much could you put down of a night, Jack?" said a little grinning man by the door.

"Why," said the banjo, "enough to lay the dustiest ghost as ever walked."

"*Could* you, now?" said the little man.

"Ah!" said the banjo, chuckling. "There's nothing like settin' one sperit to lay another; and there I could give you proof number two of heredity."

"What! Don't you go for to say you ever see'd a ghost!"

"Haven't I? What are you whisperin' about, you blushful chap there by the winder?"

"I was only remarking sir, 'twere snawin' like the devil."

"*Is* it? Then the devil has been misjudged these eighteen hundred and ninety odd years."

"But *did* you ever see a ghost?" said the little grinning man, pursuing his subject.

"No, I didn't, sir," mimicked the banjo, "saving in coffee grounds. But my grandfather in *his* cups see'd one; which brings us to number three in the matter of heredity."

"Give us the story, Jack," said the "bones," whose agued shins were extemporizing a rattle on their own account before the fire.

"Well, I don't mind," said the fat man. "It's seasonable; and I'm seasonable, like the blessed plum-pudden, I am; and the more burnt brandy you set about me, the richer and headier I'll go down."

"You'd be a jolly old pudden to digest," said the piccolo.

"You blow your aggrawation into your pipe and sealing-wax the stops," said his friend.

He drew critically at his "churchwarden" a moment or so, leaned forward, emptied his glass into his capacious receptacles, and, giving his stomach a shift, as if to accommodate it to its new burden, proceeded as follows:—

"Music and malt is my nat'ral inheritance. My grandfather blew his 'dog's-nose,' and drank his clarinet like a artist and my father—"

"What did you say your grandfather did?" asked the piccolo.

"He played the clarinet."

"You said he blew his 'dog's-nose.'"

"Don't be a ass, Fred!" said the banjo, aggrieved. "How the blazes could a man blow his dog's nose, unless he muzzled it with a handkercher, and then twisted its tail? He played the clarinet, I say; and my father played the musical glasses, which was a form of harmony pertiklerly genial to him. Amongst us we've piped out a good long century—ah! we have, for all I look sich a babby bursting on sops and spoon meat."

"What!" said the little man by the door. "You don't include them cockt hatses in your expeerunce?"

"My grandfather wore 'em, sir. He wore a play-actin' coat, too, and buckles to his shoes, when he'd got any; and he and a friend or two made a permanency of 'waits' (only they called 'em according to the season), and got their profit goin' from house to house, principally in the country, and discoursin' music at the low rate of whatever they could get for it."

"Ain't you comin' to the ghost, Jack?" said the little man hungrily.

"All in course, sir. Well, gentlemen, it was hard times pretty often with my grandfather and his friends, as you may suppose; and never so much as when they had to trudge it across country, with the nor'-easter buzzin' in their teeth and the snow piled on their cockt hats like lemon sponge on entry dishes. The rewards, I've heard him say—for he lived to be ninety, nevertheless—was poor compensation for the drifts, and the inflienza, and the broken chilblains; but now and again they'd get a fair skinful of liquor from a jolly squire, as 'd set 'em up like boggarts mended wi' new broom-sticks."

"Ho-haw!" broke in a hurdle-maker in a corner; and then, regretting the publicity of his merriment, put his fingers bashfully to his stubble lips.

"Now," said the banjo, "it's of a pertikler night and a pertikler skinful that I'm a-going to tell you; and that night fell dark, and that skinful were took a hundred years ago this December, as I'm a Jack-pudden!"

He paused a moment for effect, before he went on:—

"They were down in the sou'-west country, which they little knew; and were anighing Winchester city, or should 'a' been. But they got muzzed on the ungodly downs, and before they guessed, they was off the track. My good hat! there they was, as lost in the snow as three nutshells a-sinkin' into a hasty pudden. Well, they wandered round; pretty confident at first, but getting madder and madder as every sense of their bearings slipped from them. And the bitter cold took their vitals, so as they saw nothing but a great winding sheet stretched abroad for to wrap their dead carcasses in.

"At last my grandfather he stopt and pulled hisself together with an awful face, and says he: 'We're Christmas pie for the carrying-on crows if we don't prove ourselves human. Let's fetch out our pipes and blow our trouble into 'em.' So they stood together, like as if they was before a house, and they played 'Kate of Aberdare' mighty dismal and flat, for their fingers froze to the keys.

"Now, I tell you, they hadn't climbed over the first stave, when there come a skirl of wind and spindrift of snow as almost took them off of their feet; and, on the going down of it, Jem Sloke, as played the hautboy, dropped the reed from his mouth, and called out, 'Sakes alive! if we fools ain't been standin' outside a gentleman's gate all the time, and not knowin' it!'

"You might 'a' knocked the three of 'em down wi' a barley straw, as they stared and stared, and then fell into a low, enjoyin' laugh. For they was standin' not six fut from a tall iron gate in a stone wall, and behind these was a great house showin' out dim, with the winders all lighted up.

"'Lord!' chuckled my grandfather, 'to think o' the tricks o' this vagarious country! But, as we're here, we'll go on and give 'em a taste of our quality.'

"They put new heart into the next movement, as you may guess; and they hadn't fair started on it, when the door of the house swung open, and down the shaft of light that shot out as far as the gate there come a smiling young gal, with a tray of glasses in her hands.

"Now she come to the bars; and she took and put a glass through, not sayin' nothin', but invitin' some one to drink with a silent laugh.

"Did any one take that glass? Of course he did, you'll be thinkin'; and you'll be thinkin' wrong. Not a man of the three moved. They was struck like as stone, and their lips was gone the colour of sloe berries. Not a man took the glass. For why? The moment the gal presented it, each saw the face of a thing lookin' out of the winder over the porch, and the face was hidjus beyond words, and the shadder of it, with the light behind, stretched out and reached to the gal, and made her hidjus, too.

"At last my grandfather give a groan and put out his hand; and, as he did it, the face went, and the gal was beautiful to see agen.

"'Death and the devil!' said he. 'It's one or both, either way; and I prefer 'em hot to cold!'

"He drank off half the glass, smacked his lips, and stood staring a moment.

"'Dear, dear!' said the gal, in a voice like falling water, 'you've drunk blood, sir!'

"My grandfather gave a yell, slapped the rest of the liquor in the faces of his friends, and threw the cup agen the bars. It broke with a noise like thunder, and at that he up'd with his hands and fell full length into the snow."

There was a pause. The little man by the door was twisting nervously in his chair.

"He came to—of course, he came to?" said he at length.

"He come to," said the banjo solemnly, "in the bitter break of dawn; that is, he come to as much of hisself as he ever was after. He give a squiggle and lifted his head; and there was he and his friends a-lyin' on the snow of the high downs."

"And the house and the gal?"

"Narry a sign of either, sir, but just the sky and the white stretch; and one other thing."

"And what was that?"

"A stain of red sunk in where the cup had spilt."

There was a second pause, and the banjo blew into the bowl of his pipe.

"They cleared out of that neighbourhood double quick, you'll bet," said he. "But my grandfather was never the same man agen. His face took purple, while his friends' only remained splashed with red, same as birth marks; and, I tell you, if he ever ventur'd upon 'Kate of Aberdare,' his cheeks swelled up to the reed of his clarinet, like as a blue plum on a stalk. And forty year after, he died of what they call solution of blood to the brain."

"And you can't have better proof than that," said the little man.

"That's what *I* say," said the banjo. "Next player, gentlemen, please."

A VOICE FROM THE PIT
(1899)

"Signor, we are arrived," whispered the old man in my ear; and he put out a sudden cold hand, corded like melon rind, to stay me in the stumbling darkness.

We were on a tilted table-land of the mountain; and, looking forth and below, the far indigo crescent of the bay, where it swept towards Castellamare, seemed to rise up at me, as if it were a perpendicular wall, across which the white crests of the waves flew like ghost moths.

We skirted a boulder, and came upon a field of sleek purple lava sown all over with little lemon jets of silent smoke, which in their wan and melancholy glow might have been the corpse lights of those innumerable dead whose tombstone was the mountain itself.

Far away to the right the great projecting socket of the crater flickered intermittently with a nerve of fire. It was like the glinting of the watchful eye of some vast Crustacean, and in that harsh and stupendous desolation seemed the final crown and expression of utter inhumanity.

I started upon hearing the low whisper of my companion at my ear.

"In the bay yesterday the Signor saved my life. I give the Signor, in return, my life's secret."

He seized my right hand in his left with a sinewy clutch, and pointed a stiff finger at the luminous blots.

"See there, and there, and there," he shrilled. "One floats and wavers like a spineless ribbon of seaweed in the water; another burns with a steady radiance; a third blares from its fissure like a flame driven by the blowpipe. It is all a question of the under-draught, and some may feel it a little, and some a little more or a little less. Ah! but I will show you one that feels it not at all—a hole, a narrow shaft that goes straight down into the pit of the great hell, and is cold as the mouth of a barbel."

The bones of his face stood out like rocks against sand, and the pupils of his maniac eyes were glazed or fell into shadow as the volcano lightnings fluttered.

Suddenly he drew me to a broken pile of sulphur rock lying tumbled against a ridge of the mountain that ran towards the crater. It lay heaped, a fused and fantastic ruin; and in a moment the old man leapt from me, and was tugging by main strength a vast fragment from its place.

I leaned over his shoulder, and looked down upon the hollow revealed by the displaced boulder. It was like the bell of a mighty trumpet, and in the middle a puckered opening seemed to suck inwards, as it were the mouth of some subterranean monster risen to the surface of the world for air.

"Quick! quick!" muttered Paolo. "The Signor must place his ear to the hole."

With a little odd stir at my heart, I dropped upon my knees and leaned my head deep into the cup. I must have stayed thus for a full minute before I drew myself back and looked up at the old mountaineer. His eyes gazed down into mine with mad intensity.

"*Si! si!*" he whispered. "What didst thou hear?"

"I heard a long surging thunder, Paolo, and the deep shrill screaming of many gas jets."

He bent down, with livid face.

"Signor, it is the booming of the everlasting fire, and thou hast heard the voices of the damned."

"No, my friend, no. But it is a marvellous transmission of the uproar of hidden forces."

He leapt to the shallow pit.

"Listen and believe!" he cried; and funnelling his hands about his lips, he stooped over the central hole.

"Marco! Marco!" he screeched, in a piercing voice.

Something answered back. What was it? A malformed and twisted echo? A whistle of imprisoned steam tricked into some horrible caricature of a human voice?

"Paolo!" it seemed to wail, weak and faint with agony. "*L'arqua, l'arqua*, Paolo!"

The old man sprang to his feet and, looking down upon me in a sort of terrible triumph, unslung a water-flask from his belt, and, pulling out the cork, poured the cold liquid down into the puckered orifice. Then I felt his clutch on my arm again.

"He drinks!" he cried. "Listen and thou wilt understand."

I rose with a ghost of a laugh, and once more addressed my ear to the opening.

From unthinkable depths came up a strange, gloating sound, as from a ravenous throat made vibrant with ecstasy.

"Paolo," I cried, as I rose and stood before him—and there was an admonitory note in my voice— "a feather may decide the balance. Beware meddling with hidden thunders, or thou mayst set rolling such another tombstone as that on which these corpse fires are yet flaming."

And he only answered me, set and deathly,—

"We of the mountains, Signor, know more things than we may tell of."

AN EDDY ON THE FLOOR
(1899)

PART I OF POLYHISTOR'S NARRATIVE

WRITTEN FOR, BUT NEVER INSERTED IN, THE — FAMILY MAGAZINE

The eyes of Polyhistor—as he sat before the fire at night—took in the tawdry surroundings of his lodging-house room with nothing of that apathy of resignation to his personal *áíÜãêç* which of all moods is to Fortune, the goddess of spontaneity, the most antipathetic. Indeed, he felt his wit, like Romeo's, to be of cheveril; and his conviction that it needed only the pull of circumstance to stretch it "from an inch narrow to an ell broad" expressed but the very wooing quality of a constitutional optimism.

Now this inherent optimism is at least a serviceable weapon when it takes the form of self-reliance. It is always at hand in an emergency—a guard of honour to the soul. The loneliness of individual life must learn self-respect from within, not without; and were all creeds to be mixed, that truism should be found their precipitate.

Therefore Polyhistor was content to draw grass-green rep curtains across window-panes sloughed with wintry sleet; to place his feet upon a rug flayed of colour to it dusty sinews; to admit to his close fellowship—and find a familiar comfort in them, too—three separate lithographs of affected babies inviting any canine confidences but the bite one desired for them, and a dismal daguerreotype of his landlady's deceased husband, slowly perishing in pegtops and a yellow fog of despondency, out of which only his boots and a very tall hat frowned insistent, the tabernacles of enduring respectability:—he was content, because he knew these were only incidents in his career—the slums to be first traversed on a journey before the rounding breadths of open country were reached,—and the station in life he purposed stopping at eventually was the terminus of prosperity, intellectual and material.

With no present good fortune but the capacity for desiring it; with the right to affix a letter or so—like grace after skilly—to his name; with the consciousness that, having overcome theoretical pharmaceutics masterfully, he was now combatting practical dispensing slavishly; with full confidence in his social position (he stood under the shadow of "high connections," like the little winged "Victory" in a conqueror's hand, he chose to think) to help him to eventual distinction, he toasted his toes that sour winter evening and reviewed in comfort an army of prospects.

Also his thoughts reverted indulgently to the incidents and experiences of the previous night.

He had had the pleasure of an invitation to one of those reunions or séances at the house, in a fashionable quarter, of his distant connection, Lady Barbara Grille, whereat it was his hostess's humour to gather together those many birds of alien feather and incongruous habit that will flock from the hedgerows to the least little flattering crumb of attention. And scarce one of them but thinks the simple feast is spread for him alone. And with so cheap a bait may a title lure.

Lady Barbara, to do her justice, trades upon her position only in so far as it shapes itself the straight road to her desires. She is a carpet adventurer—an explorer amongst the nerves of moral sensation, to whom the discovery of an untrodden mental tract is a pure delight, and the more delightful the more ephemeral. She flits from guest to guest, shooting out to each a little proboscis, as it were, and happy if its point touches a speck of honey. She gathers from all, and stores the sweet agglomerate, let us hope, to feed upon it in the winter of her life, when the hive of her busy brain shall be thatched with snow.

That reference to so charming a personality should be in this place a digression is Polyhistor's unhappiness. She affects his narrative only inasmuch as he happened to meet at her house a gentleman who for a time exerted a considerable influence over his fortunes.

Here Polyhistor's narrative must give place to certain editorial marginalia by Miss Lucy —, who "runs" the — Family Magazine:—

"Polyhistor, indeed!" she writes. "The conceit of some people! He seems to take himself for a sort of *Admirable Crichton*, and all because his chance meeting with the gentleman referred to (a very *interesting* person, who is, I understand, reforming our prisons) brought him the offer of an appointment quite beyond his deserts. I was very glad to hear of it, however, and I asked the creature to contribute a paper recording his first impressions of *this notable man*; instead of which he begins with an opinionated rigmarole about himself, and goes on from bad to worse by describing a long conversation he had about prison reform with that horrid, masculine Mrs. C—, whom all the officers call 'Charlie,' and who thinks that for men to grow humane is a sign of their *decadence. Of course* I shall 'cut' the whole of their talk together (it is a blessed privilege to be an editor), and jump to the part where *Polyhistor* (!) describes the *notable person's* visit to him, which was due to his (the N.P.'s) having the night before overheard some of the conversation *between those two*."

POLYHISTOR'S NARRATIVE (*continued*).

Now as Polyhistor sat, he humoured his recollection (in the intervals of scribbling verses to the *beaux yeux* of a certain Miss L—) with some of "Charlie's" characteristic last-night utterances.

She had dated man's decadence from the moment when he began to "poor-fellow" irreclaimable savagery on the score of heredity.

She had repudiated the old humbug of sex superiority because she had seen it fall on its face to howl over a trodden worm, with the result that it discovered itself hollow behind, like the elf-maiden.

She had said: "Once you taught us divinely—*argumentum baculinum*," said she; "(for you are the sons of God, you know). But you have since so insisted upon the Rights of Humanity that we have learned ourselves in the phrase, and that the earthy have the best right to precedence on the earth."

And thereupon Charlie had launched into abuse of what she called the latest masculine fad—prison reform, to wit—and a heated discussion between her and Polyhistor had ensued, in the midst of which she had happened to glance behind her, to find that very notable person who is the subject of this narrative vouchsafing a silent attention to her diatribe. And then—

But at this period to his cogitations Polyhistor's landlady entered with a card, which she presented to his consideration:—

MAJOR JAMES SHRIKE,
H.M. PRISON, D—.

All astonishment, Polyhistor bade his visitor up.

He entered briskly, fur-collared, hat in hand, and bowed as he stood on the threshold. He was a very short man—snub-nosed; rusty-whiskered; indubitably and unimpressively a cockney in appearance. He might have walked out of a Cruikshank etching.

Polyhistor was beginning, "May I inquire—" when the other took him up with a vehement frankness that he found engaging at once.

"This is a great intrusion. Will you pardon me? I heard some remarks of yours last night that deeply interested me. I obtained your name and address of our hostess, and took the liberty of—"

"Oh! pray be seated. Say no more. My kinswoman's introduction is all-sufficient. I am happy in having caught your attention in so motley a crowd."

"She doesn't—forgive the impertinence—take herself seriously enough."

"Lady Barbara? Then you've found her out?"

"Ah!—you're not offended?"

"Not in the least."

"Good. It was a motley assemblage, as you say. Yet I'm inclined to think I found my pearl in the oyster. I'm afraid I interrupted—eh?"

"No, no, not at all. Only some idle scribbling. I'd finished."

"You are a poet?"

"Only a lunatic. I haven't taken my degree."

"Ah! it's a noble gift—the gift of song; precious through its rarity."

Polyhistor caught a note of emotion in his visitor's voice, and glanced at him curiously.

"Surely," he thought, "that vulgar, ruddy little face is transfigured."

"But," said the stranger, coming to earth, "I am lingering beside the mark. I must try to justify my solecism in manners by a straight reference to the object of my visit. That is, in the first instance, a matter of business."

"Business!"

"I am a man with a purpose, seeking the hopefullest means to an end. Plainly: if I could procure you the post of resident doctor at D— gaol, would you be disposed to accept it?"

Polyhistor looked his utter astonishment.

"I can affect no surprise at yours," said the visitor, attentively regarding Polyhistor. "It is perfectly natural. Let me forestall some unnecessary expression of it. My offer seems unaccountable to you, seeing that we never met until last night. But I don't move entirely in the dark. I have ventured in the interval to inform myself as to the details of your career. I was entirely one with much of your expression of opinion as to the treatment of criminals, in which you controverted the crude and unpleasant scepticism of the lady you talked with." (Poor New Charlie!) "Combining the two, I come to the immediate conclusion that you are the man for my purpose."

"You have dumbfounded me. I don't know what to answer. You have views, I know, as to prison treatment. Will you sketch them? Will you talk on, while I try to bring my scattered wits to a focus?"

"Certainly I will. Let me, in the first instance, recall to you a few words of your own. They ran somewhat in this fashion: Is not the man of practical genius the man who is most apt at solving the little problems of resourcefulness in life? Do you remember them?"

"Perhaps I do, in a cruder form."

"They attracted me at once. It is upon such a postulate I base my practice. Their moral is this: To know the antidote the moment the snake bites. That is to have the intuition of divinity. We shall rise to it some day, no doubt, and climb the hither side of the new Olympus. Who knows? Over the crest the spirit of creation may be ours."

Polyhistor nodded, still at sea, and the other went on with a smile:—

"I once knew a world-famous engineer with whom I used to breakfast occasionally. He had a patent egg-boiler on the table, with a little double-sided ladle underneath to hold the spirit. He complained that his egg was always undercooked. I said, 'Why not reverse the ladle so as to bring the deeper cup uppermost?' He was charmed with my perspicacity. The solution had never occurred to him. You remember, too, no doubt, the story of Coleridge and the horse collar. We aim too much at great developments. If we cultivate resourcefulness, the rest will follow. Shall I state my system *in nuce*? It is to encourage this spirit of resourcefulness."

"Surely the habitual criminal has it in a marked degree?"

"Yes; but abnormally developed in a single direction. His one object is to out-manoeuvre in a game of desperate and immoral chances. The tactical spirit in him has none of the higher ambition. It has felt itself in the degree only that stops at defiance."

"That is perfectly true."

"It is half self-conscious of an individuality that instinctively assumes the hopelessness of a recognition by duller intellects. Leaning to resentment through misguided vanity, it falls 'all oblique.' What is the cure for this? I answer, the teaching of a divine egotism. The subject must be led to a pure devotion to self. What he wishes to respect he must be taught to make beautiful and interesting. The policy of sacrifice to others has so long stunted his moral nature because it is an hypocritical policy. We are responsible to ourselves in the first instance; and to argue an eternal system of blind self-sacrifice is to undervalue the fine gift of individuality. In such he sees but an indefensible policy of force applied to the advantage of the community. He is told to be good—not that he may morally profit, but that others may not suffer inconvenience."

Polyhistor was beginning to grasp, through his confusion, a certain clue of meaning in his visitor's rapid utterance. The stranger spoke fluently, but in the dry, positive voice that characterizes men of will.

"Pray go on," Polyhistor said; "I am digesting in silence."

"We must endeavour to lead him to respect of self by showing him what his mind is capable of. I argue on no sectarian, no religious grounds even. Is it possible to make a man's self his most precious possession? Anyhow, I work to that end. A doctor purges before building up with a tonic. I eliminate cant and hypocrisy, and then introduce self-respect. It isn't enough to employ a man's hands only. Initiation in some labour that should prove wholesome and remunerative is a redeeming factor, but it isn't all. His mind must work also, and awaken to its capacities. If it rusts, the body reverts to inhuman instincts."

"May I ask how you—?"

"By intercourse—in my own person or through my officials. I wish to have only those about me who are willing to contribute to my designs, and with whom I can work in absolute harmony. All my officers are chosen to that end. No doubt a dash of constitutional sentimentalism gives colour to my theories. I get it from a human tract in me that circumstances have obliged me to put a hoarding round."

"I begin to gather daylight."

"Quite so. My patients are invited to exchange views with their guardians in a spirit of perfect friendliness; to solve little problems of practical moment; to acquire the pride of self-reliance. We have competitions, such as certain newspapers open to their readers, in a simple form. I draw up the questions myself. The answers give me insight into the mental conditions of the competitors. Upon insight I proceed. I am fortunate in private means, and I am in a position to offer modest prizes to the winners. Whenever such an one is discharged, he finds awaiting him the tools most handy to his vocation. I bid him go forth in no pharisaical spirit, and invite him to communicate with me. I wish the shadow of the gaol to extend no further than the road whereon it lies. Henceforth, we are acquaintances with a common interest at heart. Isn't it monstrous that a state-fixed degree of misconduct should earn a man social ostracism? Parents are generally inclined to rule extra tenderness towards a child whose peccadilloes have brought him a whipping. For myself, I have no faith in police supervision. Give a culprit his term and have done with it. I find the majority who come back to me are ticket-of-leave men.

"Have I said enough? I offer you the reversion of the post. The present holder of it leaves in a month's time. Please to determine here and at once."

"Very good. I have decided."

"You will accept?"

"Yes."

So far wrote Polyhistor in the bonny days of early manhood—an attempt made in a spasm of enthusiasm inspired in him and humoured by his most engaging Mentor, to record his first impressions of a notable personality not many days after its introduction to him. He has never taken up the tale again until now, when an insistent sense, as of a task left unfinished, compels him to the effort. Over his sweet Mentor the grass lies thick, and flowers of aged stalk bloom perennially, and "Oh, the difference to me!"

To *me*, for it is time to drop the poor conceit, the pseudonym that once served its little purpose to awaken tender derision.

I take up the old and stained manuscript, with its marginalia, that are like the dim call from a far-away voice, and I know that, so I am driven to record the sequel to that gay introduction, it must be in a spirit of sombreness most deadly by contrast. I look at the faded opening words. The fire of the first line of the narrative is long out; the grate is cold some forty years—forty years!—and I think I have been a little chill during all that time. But, though the room rustle with phantoms and menace stalk in the retrospect, I shall acquit my conscience of its burden, refusing to be bullied by the counsel of a destiny that subpoena'd me entirely against my will.

PART II OF POLYHISTOR'S NARRATIVE
CONTINUED AND FINISHED AFTER A LAPSE OF FORTY YEARS

With my unexpected appointment as doctor to D— gaol, I seemed to have put on the seven-league boots of success. No doubt it was an extraordinary degree of good fortune, even to one who had looked forward with a broad view of confidence; yet, I think, perhaps on account of the very casual nature of my promotion, I never took the post entirely seriously.

At the same time I was fully bent on justifying my little cockney patron's choice by a resolute subscription to his theories of prison management.

Major James Shrike inspired me with a curious conceit of impertinent respect. In person the very embodiment of that insignificant vulgarity, without extenuating circumstances, which is the type in caricature of the ultimate cockney, he possessed a force of mind and an earnestness of purpose that absolutely redeemed him on close acquaintanceship. I found him all he had stated himself to be, and something more.

He had a noble object always in view—the employment of sane and humanitarian methods in the treatment of redeemable criminals, and he strove towards it with completely untiring devotion. He was of those who never insist beyond the limits of their own understanding, clear-sighted in discipline, frank in relaxation, an altruist in the larger sense.

His undaunted persistence, as I learned, received ample illustration some few years prior to my acquaintance with him, when—his system being experimental rather than mature—a devastating endemic of typhoid in the prison had for the time stultified his efforts. He stuck to his post; but so virulent was the outbreak that the prison commissioners judged a complete evacuation of the building and overhauling of the drainage to be necessary. As a consequence, for some eighteen months—during thirteen of which the Governor and his household remained sole inmates of the solitary pile (so sluggishly do we redeem our condemned social boglands)—the "system" stood still for lack of material to mould. At the end of over a year of stagnation, a contract was accepted and workmen put in, and another five months saw the prison reordered for practical purposes.

The interval of forced inactivity must have sorely tried the patience of the Governor. Practical theorists condemned to rust too often eat out their own hearts. Major Shrike never referred to this period, and, indeed, laboriously snubbed any allusion to it.

He was, I have a shrewd notion, something of an officially petted reformer. Anyhow, to his abolition of the insensate barbarism of crank and treadmill in favour of civilizing methods no opposition was offered. Solitary confinement—a punishment outside all nature to a gregarious race—found no advocate in him. "A man's own suffering mind," he argued, "must be, of all moral food, the most poisonous for him to feed on. Surround a scorpion with fire and he stings himself to death, they say. Throw a diseased soul entirely upon its own resources and moral suicide results."

To sum up: his nature embodied humanity without sentimentalism, firmness without obstinacy, individuality without selfishness; his activity was boundless, his devotion to his system so real as to admit no utilitarian sophistries into his scheme of personal benevolence. Before I had been with him a week, I respected him as I had never respected man before.

One evening (it was during the second month of my appointment) we were sitting in his private study—a dark, comfortable room lined with books. It was an occasion on which a new characteristic of the man was offered to my inspection.

A prisoner of a somewhat unusual type had come in that day—a spiritualistic medium, convicted of imposture. To this person I casually referred.

"May I ask how you propose dealing with the new-comer?"

"On the familiar lines."

"But, surely—here we have a man of superior education, of imagination even?"

"No, no, no! A hawker's opportuneness; that describes it. These fellows would make death itself a vulgarity."

"You've no faith in their—"

"Not a tittle. Heaven forfend! A sheet and a turnip are poetry to their manifestations. It's as crude and sour soil for us to work on as any I know. We'll cart it wholesale."

"I take you—excuse my saying so—for a supremely sceptical man."

"As to what?"

"The supernatural."

There was no answer during a considerable interval. Presently it came, with deliberate insistence:—

"It is a principle with me to oppose bullying. We are here for a definite purpose—his duty plain to any man who *wills* to read it. There may be disembodied spirits who seek to distress or annoy where they can no longer control. If there are, mine, which is not yet divorced from its means to material action, declines to be influenced by any irresponsible whimsy, emanating from a place whose denizens appear to be actuated by a mere frivolous antagonism to all human order and progress."

"But supposing you, a murderer, to be haunted by the presentment of your victim?"

"I will imagine that to be my case. Well, it makes no difference. My interest is with the great human system, in one of whose veins I am a circulating drop. It is my business to help to keep the system sound, to do my duty without fear or favour. If disease—say a fouled conscience—contaminates me, it is for me to throw off the incubus, not accept it, and transmit the poison. Whatever my lapses of nature, I owe it to the entire system to work for purity in my allotted sphere, and not to allow any microbe bugbear to ride me roughshod, to the detriment of my fellow drops."

I laughed.

"It should be for you," I said, "to learn to shiver, like the boy in the fairy tale."

"I cannot," he answered, with a peculiar quiet smile; "and yet prisons, above all places, should be haunted."

Very shortly after his arrival I was called to the cell of the medium, F—. He suffered, by his own statement, from severe pains in the head.

I found the man to be nervous, anemic; his manner characterized by a sort of hysterical effrontery.

"Send me to the infirmary," he begged. "This isn't punishment, but torture."

"What are your symptoms?"

"I see things; my case has no comparison with others. To a man of my super-sensitiveness close confinement is mere cruelty."

I made a short examination. He was restless under my hands.

"You'll stay where you are," I said.

He broke out into violent abuse, and I left him.

Later in the day I visited him again. He was then white and sullen; but under his mood I could read real excitement of some sort.

"Now, confess to me, my man," I said, "what do you see?"

He eyed me narrowly, with his lips a little shaky.

"Will you have me moved if I tell you?"

"I can give no promise till I know."

He made up his mind after an interval of silence.

"There's something uncanny in my neighbourhood. Who's confined in the next cell—there, to the left?"

"To my knowledge it's empty."

He shook his head incredulously.

"Very well," I said, "I don't mean to bandy words with you"; and I turned to go.

At that he came after me with a frightened choke.

"Doctor, your mission's a merciful one. I'm not trying to sauce you. For God's sake have me moved! I can see further than most, I tell you!"

The fellow's manner gave me pause. He was patently and beyond the pride of concealment terrified.

"What do you see?" I repeated stubbornly.

"It isn't that I see, but I know. The cell's not empty!"

I stared at him in considerable wonderment.

"I will make inquiries," I said. "You may take that for a promise. If the cell proves empty, you stop where you are."

I noticed that he dropped his hands with a lost gesture as I left him. I was sufficiently moved to accost the warder who awaited me on the spot.

"Johnson," I said, "is that cell—"

"Empty, sir," answered the man sharply and at once.

Before I could respond, F— came suddenly to the door, which I still held open.

"You lying cur!" he shouted. "You damned lying cur!"

The warder thrust the man back with violence.

"Now you, 49," he said, "dry up, and none of your sauce!" and he banged to the door with a sounding slap, and turned to me with a lowering face. The prisoner inside yelped and stormed at the studded panels.

"That cell's empty, sir," repeated Johnson.

"Will you, as a matter of conscience, let me convince myself? I promised the man."

"No, I can't."

"You can't?"

"No, sir."

"This is a piece of stupid discourtesy. You can have no reason, of course?"

"I can't open it—that's all."

"Oh, Johnson! Then I must go to the fountain-head."

"Very well, sir."

Quite baffled by the man's obstinacy, I said no more, but walked off. If my anger was roused, my curiosity was piqued in proportion.

I had no opportunity of interviewing the Governor all day, but at night I visited him by invitation to play a game of piquet.

He was a man without "incumbrances"—as a severe conservatism designates the *lares* of the cottage—and, at home, lived at his ease and indulged his amusements without comment.

I found him "tasting" his books, with which the room was well lined, and drawing with relish at an excellent cigar in the intervals of the courses.

He nodded to me, and held out an open volume in his left hand.

"Listen to this fellow," he said, tapping the page with his fingers:—

"'*The most tolerable sort of Revenge, is for those wrongs which there is no Law to remedy: But then, let a man take heed, the Revenge be such, as there is no law to punish: Else, a man's Enemy, is still before hand, and it is two for one. Some, when they take Revenge, are Desirous the party should know, whence it cometh. This is the more Generous. For the Delight seemeth to be, not so much in doing the Hurt, as in making the Party repent: But Base and Crafty Cowards are like the Arrow that flyeth in the Dark. Cosmus, Duke of Florence, had a Desperate Saying against Perfidious or Neglecting Friends, as if these wrongs were unpardonable. You shall reade (saith he) that we are commanded to forgive our Enemies: But you never read, that we are commanded, to forgive our Friends.*'

"Is he not a rare fellow?"

"Who?" said I.

"Francis Bacon, who screwed his wit to his philosophy, like a hammer-head to its handle, and knocked a nail in at every blow. How many of our friends round about here would be picking oakum now if they had made a gospel of that quotation?"

"You mean they take no heed that the Law may punish for that for which it gives no remedy?"

"Precisely; and specifically as to revenge. The criminal, from the murderer to the petty pilferer, is actuated solely by the spirit of vengeance—vengeance blind and speechless—towards a system that forces him into a position quite outside his natural instincts."

"As to that, we have left Nature in the thicket. It is hopeless hunting for her now."

"We hear her breathing sometimes, my friend. Otherwise Her Majesty's prison locks would rust. But, I grant you, we have grown so unfamiliar with her that we call her simplest manifestations *super*natural nowadays."

"That reminds me. I visited F— this afternoon. The man was in a queer way—not foxing, in my opinion. Hysteria, probably."

"Oh! What was the matter with him?"

"The form it took was some absurd prejudice about the next cell—number 47, He swore it was not empty—was quite upset about it—said there was some infernal influence at work in his neighbourhood. Nerves, he finds, I suppose, may revenge themselves on one who has made a habit of playing tricks with them. To satisfy him, I asked Johnson to open the door of the next cell—"

"Well?"

"He refused."

"It is closed by my orders."

"That settles it, of course. The manner of Johnson's refusal was a bit uncivil, but—"

He had been looking at me intently all this time—so intently that I was conscious of a little embarrassment and confusion. His mouth was set like a dash between brackets, and his eyes glistened. Now his features relaxed, and he gave a short high neigh of a laugh.

"My dear fellow, you must make allowances for the rough old lurcher. He was a soldier. He is all cut and measured out to the regimental pattern. With him Major Shrike, like the king, can do no wrong. Did I ever tell you he served under me in India? He did; and, moreover, I saved his life there."

"In an engagement?"

"Worse—from the bite of a snake. It was a mere question of will. I told him to wake and walk, and he did. They had thought him already in *rigor mortis*; and, as for him—well, his devotion to me since has been single to the last degree."

"That's as it should be."

"To be sure. And he's quite in my confidence. You must pass over the old beggar's churlishness."

I laughed an assent. And then an odd thing happened. As I spoke, I had walked over to a bookcase on the opposite side of the room to that on which my host stood. Near this bookcase hung a mirror—an oblong affair, set in brass *repoussé* work—on the wall; and, happening to glance into it as I approached, I caught sight of the Major's reflection as he turned his face to follow my movement.

I say "turned his face"—a formal description only. What met my startled gaze was an image of some nameless horror—of features grooved, and battered, and shapeless, as if they had been torn by a wild beast.

I gave a little indrawn gasp and turned about. There stood the Major, plainly himself, with a pleasant smile on his face.

"What's up?" said he.

He spoke abstractedly, pulling at his cigar; and I answered rudely, "That's a damned bad looking-glass of yours!"

"I didn't know there was anything wrong with it," he said, still abstracted and apart. And, indeed, when by sheer mental effort I forced myself to look again, there stood my companion as he stood in the room.

I gave a tremulous laugh, muttered something or nothing, and fell to examining the books in the case. But my fingers shook a trifle as I aimlessly pulled out one volume after another.

"Am *I* getting fanciful?" I thought— "I whose business it is to give practical account of every bugbear of the nerves. Bah! My liver must be out of order. A speck of bile in one's eye may look a flying dragon."

I dismissed the folly from my mind, and set myself resolutely to inspecting the books marshalled before me. Roving amongst them, I pulled out, entirely at random, a thin, worn duodecimo, that was thrust well back at a shelf end, as if it shrank from comparison with its prosperous and portly neighbours. Nothing but chance impelled me to the choice; and I don't know to this day what the ragged volume was about. It opened naturally at a marker that lay in it—a folded slip of paper, yellow with age; and glancing at this, a printed name caught my eye.

With some stir of curiosity, I spread the slip out. It was a title-page to a volume, of poems, presumably; and the author was James Shrike.

I uttered an exclamation, and turned, book in hand.

"An author!" I said. "*You* an author, Major Shrike!"

To my surprise, he snapped round upon me with something like a glare of fury on his face. This the more startled me as I believed I had reason to regard him as a man whose principles of conduct had long disciplined a temper that was naturally hasty enough.

Before I could speak to explain, he had come hurriedly across the room and had rudely snatched the paper out of my hand.

"How did this get—" he began; then in a moment came to himself, and apologized for his ill manners.

"I thought every scrap of the stuff had been destroyed," he said, and tore the page into fragments. "It is an ancient effusion, doctor—perhaps the greatest folly of my life; but it's something of a sore subject with me, and I shall be obliged if you'll not refer to it again."

He courted my forgiveness so frankly that the matter passed without embarrassment; and we had our game and spent a genial evening together. But memory of the queer little scene stuck in my mind, and I could not forbear pondering it fitfully.

Surely here was a new side-light that played upon my friend and superior a little fantastically.

Conscious of a certain vague wonder in my mind, I was traversing the prison, lost in thought, after my sociable evening with the Governor, when the fact that dim light was issuing from the open door of cell number 49 brought me to myself and to a pause in the corridor outside.

Then I saw that something was wrong with the cell's inmate, and that my services were required.

The medium was struggling on the floor, in what looked like an epileptic fit, and Johnson and another warder were holding him from doing an injury to himself.

The younger man welcomed my appearance with relief.

"Heerd him guggling," he said, "and thought as something were up. You come timely, sir."

More assistance was procured, and I ordered the prisoner's removal to the infirmary. For a minute, before following him, I was left alone with Johnson.

"It came to a climax, then?" I said, looking the man steadily in the face.

"He may be subject to 'em, sir," he replied, evasively.

I walked deliberately up to the closed door of the adjoining cell, which was the last on that side of the corridor. Huddled against the massive end wall, and half imbedded in it, as it seemed, it lay in a certain shadow, and bore every sign of dust and disuse. Looking closely, I saw that the trap in the door was not only firmly bolted, but *screwed into its socket.*

I turned and said to the warder quietly,—

"Is it long since this cell was in use?"

"You're very fond of asking questions," he answered doggedly.

It was evident he would baffle me by impertinence rather than yield a confidence. A queer insistence had seized me—a strange desire to know more about this mysterious chamber. But, for all my curiosity, I flushed at the man's tone.

"You have your orders," I said sternly, "and do well to hold by them. I doubt, nevertheless, if they include impertinence to your superiors."

"I look straight on my duty, sir," he said, a little abashed. "I don't wish to give offence."

He did not, I feel sure. He followed his instinct to throw me off the scent, that was all.

I strode off in a fume, and after attending F— in the infirmary, went promptly to my own quarters.

I was in an odd frame of mind, and for long tramped my sitting-room to and fro, too restless to go to bed, or, as an alternative, to settle down to a book. There was a welling up in my heart of some emotion that I could neither trace nor define. It seemed neighbour to terror, neighbour to an intense fainting pity, yet was not distinctly either of these. Indeed, where was cause for one, or the subject of the other? F— might have endured mental sufferings which it was only human to help to end, yet F— was a swindling rogue, who, once relieved, merited no further consideration.

It was not on him my sentiments were wasted. Who, then, was responsible for them?

There is a very plain line of demarcation between the legitimate spirit of inquiry and mere apish curiosity. I could recognise it, I have no doubt, as a rule, yet in my then mood, under the influence of a kind of morbid seizure, inquisitiveness took me by the throat. I could not whistle my mind from the chase of a certain graveyard will-o'-the-wisp; and on it went stumbling and floundering through bog and mire, until it fell into a state of collapse, and was useful for nothing else.

I went to bed and to sleep without difficulty, but I was conscious of myself all the time, and of a shadowless horror that seemed to come stealthily out of corners and to bend over and look at me, and to be nothing but a curtain or a hanging coat when I started and stared.

Over and over again this happened, and my temperature rose by leaps, and suddenly I saw that if I failed to assert myself, and promptly, fever would lap me in a consuming fire. Then in a moment I broke into a profuse perspiration, and sank exhausted into delicious unconsciousness.

Morning found me restored to vigour, but still with the maggot of curiosity boring in my brain. It worked there all day, and for many subsequent days, and at last it seemed as if my every faculty were honeycombed with its ramifications. Then "this will not do," I thought, but still the tunnelling process went on.

At first I would not acknowledge to myself what all this mental to-do was about. I was ashamed of my new development, in fact, and nervous, too, in a degree of what it might reveal in the matter of moral degeneration; but gradually, as the curious devil mastered me, I grew into such harmony with it that I could shut my eyes no longer to the true purpose of its insistence. It was the *closed cell* about which my thoughts hovered like crows circling round carrion.

"In the dead waste and middle" of a certain night I awoke with a strange, quick recovery of consciousness. There was the passing of a single expiration, and I had been asleep and was awake. I had gone to bed with no sense of premonition or of resolve in a particular direction; I sat up a monomaniac. It was as if, swelling in the silent hours, the tumour of curiosity had come to a head, and in a moment it was necessary to operate upon it.

I make no excuse for my then condition. I am convinced I was the victim of some undistinguishable force, that I was an agent under the control of the supernatural, if you like. Some thought had been in my mind of late that in my position it was my duty to unriddle the mystery of the closed cell. This was a sop timidly held out to and rejected by my better reason. I sought—and I knew it in my heart—solution of the puzzle, because it was a puzzle with an atmosphere that vitiated my moral fibre. Now, suddenly, I knew I must act, or, by forcing self-control, imperil my mind's stability.

All strung to a sort of exaltation, I rose noiselessly and dressed myself with rapid, nervous hands. My every faculty was focused upon a solitary point. Without and around there was nothing but shadow and uncertainty. I seemed conscious only of a shaft of light, as it were, traversing the darkness and globing itself in a steady disc of radiance on a lonely door.

Slipping out into the great echoing vault of the prison in stockinged feet, I sped with no hesitation of purpose in the direction of the corridor that was my goal. Surely some resolute Providence guided and encompassed me, for no meeting with the night patrol occurred at any point to embarrass or deter me. Like a ghost myself, I flitted along the stone flags of the passages, hardly waking a murmur from them in my progress.

Without, I knew, a wild and stormy wind thundered on the walls of the prison. Within, where the very atmosphere was self-contained, a cold and solemn peace held like an irrevocable judgment.

I found myself as if in a dream before the sealed door that had for days harassed my waking thoughts. Dim light from a distant gas jet made a patch of yellow upon one of its panels; the rest was buttressed with shadow.

A sense of fear and constriction was upon me as I drew softly from my pocket a screwdriver I had brought with me. It never occurred to me, I swear, that the quest was no business of mine, and that even now I could withdraw from it, and no one be the wiser. But I was afraid—I was afraid. And there was not even the negative comfort of knowing that the neighbouring cell was tenanted. It gaped like a ghostly garret next door to a deserted house.

What reason had I to be there at all, or, being there, to fear? I can no more explain than tell how it was that I, an impartial follower of my vocation, had allowed myself to be tricked by that in the nerves I had made it my interest to study and combat in others.

My hand that held the tool was cold and wet. The stiff little shriek of the first screw, as it turned at first uneasily in its socket, sent a jarring thrill through me. But I persevered, and it came out readily by-and-by, as did the four or five others that held the trap secure.

Then I paused a moment; and, I confess, the quick pant of fear seemed to come grey from my lips. There were sounds about me—the deep breathing of imprisoned men; and I envied the sleepers their hard-wrung repose.

At last, in one access of determination, I put out my hand, and sliding back the bolt, hurriedly flung open the trap. An acrid whiff of dust assailed my nostrils as I stepped back a pace and stood expectant of anything—or nothing. What did I wish, or dread, or foresee? The complete absurdity of my behaviour was revealed to me in a moment. I could shake off the incubus here and now, and be a sane man again.

I giggled, with an actual ring of self-contempt in my voice, as I made a forward movement to close the aperture. I advanced my face to it, and inhaled the sluggish air that stole forth, and—God in heaven!

I had staggered back with that cry in my throat, when I felt fingers like iron clamps close on my arm and hold it. The grip, more than the face I turned to look upon in my surging terror, was forcibly human.

It was the warder Johnson who had seized me, and my heart bounded as I met the cold fury of his eyes.

"Prying!" he said, in a hoarse, savage whisper. "So you will, will you? And now let the devil help you!"

It was not this fellow I feared, though his white face was set like a demon's; and in the thick of my terror I made a feeble attempt to assert my authority.

"Let me go!" I muttered. "What! you dare?"

In his frenzy he shook my arm as a terrier shakes a rat, and, like a dog, he held on, daring me to release myself.

For the moment an instinct half-murderous leapt in me. It sank and was overwhelmed in a slough of some more secret emotion.

"Oh!" I whispered, collapsing, as it were, to the man's fury, even pitifully deprecating it. "What is it? What's there? It drew me—something unnameable."

He gave a snapping laugh like a cough. His rage waxed second by second. There was a maniacal suggestiveness in it; and not much longer, it was evident, could he have it under control. I saw it run and congest in his eyes; and, on the instant of its accumulation, he tore at me with a sudden wild strength, and drove me up against the very door of the secret cell.

The action, the necessity of self-defence, restored me to some measure of dignity and sanity.

"Let me go, you ruffian!" I cried, struggling to free myself from his grasp.

It was useless. He held me madly. There was no beating him off: and, so holding me, he managed to produce a single key from one of his pockets, and to slip it with a rusty clang into the lock of the door.

"You dirty, prying civilian!" he panted at me, as he swayed this way and that with the pull of my body. "You shall have your wish, by G—! You want to see inside, do you? Look, then!"

He dashed open the door as he spoke, and pulled me violently into the opening. A great waft of the cold, dank air came at us, and with it—what?

The warder had jerked his dark lantern from his belt, and now—an arm of his still clasped about one of mine—snapped the slide open.

"Where is it?" he muttered, directing the disc of light round and about the floor of the cell. I ceased struggling. Some counter influence was raising an odd curiosity in me.

"Ah!" he cried, in a stifled voice, "there you are, my friend!"

He was setting the light slowly travelling along the stone flags close by the wall over against us, and now, so guiding it, looked askance at me with a small, greedy smile.

"Follow the light, sir," he whispered jeeringly.

I looked, and saw twirling on the floor, in the patch of radiance cast by the lamp, *a little eddy of dust*, it seemed. This eddy was never still, but went circling in that stagnant place without apparent cause or influence; and, as it circled, it moved slowly on by wall and corner, so that presently in its progress it must reach us where we stood.

Now, draughts will play queer freaks in quiet places, and of this trifling phenomenon I should have taken little note ordinarily. But, I must say at once, that as I gazed upon the odd moving thing my heart seemed to fall in upon itself like a drained artery.

"Johnson!" I cried, "I must get out of this. I don't know what's the matter, or— Why do you hold me? D—n it! man, let me go; let me go, I say!"

As I grappled with him he dropped the lantern with a crash and flung his arms violently about me.

"You don't!" he panted, the muscles of his bent and rigid neck seeming actually to cut into my shoulder-blade. "You don't, by G—! You came of your own accord, and now you shall take your bellyful!"

It was a struggle for life or death, or, worse, for life and reason. But I was young and wiry, and held my own, if I could do little more. Yet there was something to combat beyond the mere brute strength of the man I struggled with, for I fought in an atmosphere of horror unexplainable, and I knew that inch by inch the *thing* on the floor was circling round in our direction.

Suddenly in the breathing darkness I felt it close upon us, gave one mortal yell of fear, and, with a last despairing fury, tore myself from the encircling arms, and sprang into the corridor without. As I plunged and leapt, the warder clutched at me, missed, caught a foot on the edge of the door, and, as the latter whirled to with a clap, fell heavily at my feet in a fit. Then, as I stood staring down upon him, steps sounded along the corridor and the voices of scared men hurrying up.

Ill and shaken, and, for the time, little in love with life, yet fearing death as I had never dreaded it before, I spent the rest of that horrible night huddled between my crumpled sheets, fearing to look forth, fearing to think, wild only to be far away, to be housed in some green and innocent hamlet, where I might forget the madness and the terror in learning to walk the unvext paths of placid souls. I had not fairly knocked under until alone with my new dread familiar. That unction I could lay to my heart, at least. I had done the manly part by the stricken warder, whom I had attended to his own home, in a row of little tenements that stood south of the prison walls. I had replied to all inquiries with some dignity and spirit, attributing my ruffled condition to an assault on the part of Johnson, when he was already under the shadow of his seizure. I had directed his removal, and grudged him no professional attention that it was in my power to bestow. But afterwards, locked into my room, my whole nervous system broke up like a trodden anthill, leaving me conscious of nothing but an aimless scurrying terror and the black swarm of thoughts, so that I verily fancied my reason would give under the strain.

Yet I had more to endure and to triumph over.

Near morning I fell into a troubled sleep, throughout which the drawn twitch of muscle seemed an accent on every word of ill-omen I had ever spelt out of the alphabet of fear. If my body rested, my brain was an open chamber for any toad of ugliness that listed to "sit at squat" in.

Suddenly I woke to the fact that there was a knocking at my door—that there had been for some little time.

I cried, "Come in!" finding a weak restorative in the mere sound of my own human voice; then, remembering the key was turned, bade the visitor wait until I could come to him.

Scrambling, feeling dazed and white-livered, out of bed, I opened the door, and met one of the warders on the threshold. The man looked scared, and his lips, I noticed, were set in a somewhat boding fashion.

"Can you come at once, sir?" he said. "There's summat wrong with the Governor."

"Wrong? What's the matter with him?"

"Why,"—he looked down, rubbed an imaginary protuberance smooth with his foot, and glanced up at me again with a quick, furtive expression,— "he's got his face set in the grating of 47, and danged if a man Jack of us can get him to move or speak."

I turned away, feeling sick. I hurriedly pulled on coat and trousers, and hurriedly went off with my summoner. Reason was all absorbed in a wildest phantasy of apprehension.

"Who found him?" I muttered, as we sped on.

"Vokins see him go down the corridor about half after eight, sir, and see him give a start like when he noticed the trap open. It's never been so before in my time. Johnson must ha' done it last night, before he were took."

"Yes, yes."

"The man said the Governor went to shut it, it seemed, and to draw his face to'ards the bars in so doin'. Then he see him a-lookin' through, as he thought; but nat'rally it weren't no business of his'n, and he went off about his work. But when he come anigh agen, fifteen minutes later, there were the Governor in the same position; and he got scared over it, and called out to one or two of us."

"Why didn't one of you ask the Major if anything was wrong?"

"Bless you! we did; and no answer. And we pulled him, compatible with discipline, but—"

"But what?"

"He's stuck."

"Stuck!"

"See for yourself, sir. That's all I ask."

I did, a moment later. A little group was collected about the door of cell 47, and the members of it spoke together in whispers, as if they were frightened men. One young fellow, with a face white in patches, as if it had been floured, slid from them as I approached, and accosted me tremulously.

"Don't go anigh, sir. There's something wrong about the place."

I pulled myself together, forcibly beating down the excitement reawakened by the associations of the spot. In the discomfiture of others' nerves I found my own restoration.

"Don't be an ass!" I said, in a determined voice, "There's nothing here that can't be explained. Make way for me, please!"

They parted and let me through, and I saw him. He stood, spruce, frock-coated, dapper, as he always was, with his face pressed against and *into* the grill, and either hand raised and clenched tightly round a bar of the trap. His posture was as of one caught and striving frantically to release himself; yet the narrowness of the interval between the rails precluded so extravagant an idea. He stood quite motionless—taut and on the strain, as it were—and nothing of his face was visible but the back ridges of his jawbones, showing white through a bush of red whiskers.

"Major Shrike!" I rapped out, and, allowing myself no hesitation, reached forth my hand and grasped his shoulder. The body vibrated under my touch, but he neither answered nor made sign of hearing me. Then I pulled at him forcibly, and ever with increasing strength. His fingers held like steel braces. He seemed glued to the trap, like Theseus to the rock.

Hastily I peered round, to see if I could get glimpse of his face. I noticed enough to send me back with a little stagger.

"Has none of you got a key to this door?" I asked, reviewing the scared faces about me, than which my own was no less troubled, I feel sure.

"Only the Governor, sir," said the warder who had fetched me. "There's not a man but him amongst us that ever seen this opened."

He was wrong there, I could have told him; but held my tongue, for obvious reasons.

"I want it opened. Will one of you feel in his pockets?"

Not a soul stirred. Even had not sense of discipline precluded, that of a certain inhuman atmosphere made fearful creatures of them all.

"Then," said I, "I must do it myself."

I turned once more to the stiff-strung figure, had actually put hand on it, when an exclamation from Vokins arrested me.

"There's a key—there, sir!" he said— "stickin' out yonder between its feet."

Sure enough there was—Johnson's, no doubt, that had been shot from its socket by the clapping to of the door, and afterwards kicked aside by the warder in his convulsive struggles.

I stooped, only too thankful for the respite, and drew it forth. I had seen it but once before, yet I recognised it at a glance.

Now, I confess, my heart felt ill as I slipped the key into the wards, and a sickness of resentment at the tyranny of Fate in making me its helpless minister surged up in my veins. Once, with my fingers on the iron loop, I paused, and ventured a fearful side glance at the figure whose crookt elbow almost touched my face; then, strung to the high pitch of inevitability, I shot the lock, pushed at the door, and in the act, made a back leap into the corridor.

Scarcely, in doing so, did I look for the totter and collapse outwards of the rigid form. I had expected to see it fall away, face down, into the cell, as its support swung from it. Yet it was, I swear, as if *something* from within had relaxed its grasp and given the fearful dead man a swingeing push outwards as the door opened.

It went on its back, with a dusty slap on the stone flags, and from all its spectators—me included—came a sudden drawn sound, like wind in a keyhole.

What can I say, or how describe it? A dead thing it was—but the face!

Barred with livid scars where the grating rails had crossed it, the rest seemed to have been worked and kneaded into a mere featureless plate of yellow and expressionless flesh.

And it was this I had seen in the glass!

There was an interval following the experience above narrated, during which a certain personality that had once been mine was effaced or suspended, and I seemed a passive creature, innocent of the least desire of independence. It was not that I was actually ill or actually insane. A merciful Providence set my finer wits slumbering, that was all, leaving me a sufficiency of the grosser faculties that were necessary to the right ordering of my behaviour.

I kept to my room, it is true, and even lay a good deal in bed; but this was more to satisfy the busy scruples of a *locum tenens*—a practitioner of the neighbourhood, who came daily to the prison to officiate in my absence—than to cosset a complaint that in its inactivity was purely negative. I could review what had happened with a calmness as profound as if I had read of it in a book. I could have wished to continue my duties, indeed, had the power of insistence remained to me. But the saner medicus was acute where I had gone blunt, and bade me to the restful course. He was right. I was mentally stunned, and had I not slept off my lethargy, I should have gone mad in an hour—leapt at a bound, probably, from inertia to flaming lunacy.

I remembered everything, but through a fluffy atmosphere, so to speak. It was as if I looked on bygone pictures through ground glass that softened the ugly outlines.

Sometimes I referred to these to my substitute, who was wise to answer me according to my mood; for the truth left me unruffled, whereas an obvious evasion of it would have distressed me.

"Hammond," I said one day, "I have never yet asked you. How did I give my evidence at the inquest?"

"Like a doctor and a sane man."

"That's good. But it was a difficult course to steer. You conducted the *post-mortem*. Did any peculiarity in the dead man's face strike you?"

"Nothing but this: that the excessive contraction of the bicipital muscles had brought the features into such forcible contact with the bars as to cause bruising and actual abrasion. He must have been dead some little time when you found him."

"And nothing else? You noticed nothing else in his face—a sort of obliteration of what makes one human, I mean?"

"Oh, dear, no! nothing but the painful constriction that marks any ordinary fatal attack of *angina pectoris*.—There's a rum breach of promise case in the paper to-day. You should read it; it'll make you laugh."

I had no more inclination to laugh than to sigh; but I accepted the change of subject with an equanimity now habitual to me.

One morning I sat up in bed, and knew that consciousness was wide awake in me once more. It had slept, and now rose refreshed, but trembling. Looking back, all in a flutter of new responsibility, along the misty path by way of which I had recently loitered, I shook with an awful thankfulness at sight of the pitfalls I had skirted and escaped—of the demons my witlessness had baffled.

The joy of life was in my heart again, but chastened and made pitiful by experience.

Hammond noticed the change in me directly he entered, and congratulated me upon it.

"Go slow at first, old man," he said. "You've fairly sloughed the old skin; but give the sun time to toughen the new one. Walk in it at present, and be content."

I was, in great measure, and I followed his advice. I got leave of absence, and ran down for a month in the country to a certain house we wot of, where kindly ministration to my convalescence was only one of the many blisses to be put to an account of rosy days.

"*Then did my love awake,*
Most like a lily-flower,
And as the lovely queene of heaven,
So shone shee in her bower."

Ah, me! ah, me! when was it? A year ago, or two-thirds of a lifetime? Alas! "Age with stealing steps hath clawde me with his crowch." And will the yews root in *my* heart, I wonder?

I was well, sane, recovered, when one morning, towards the end of my visit, I received a letter from Hammond, enclosing a packet addressed to me, and jealously sealed and fastened. My friend's communication ran as follows:—

"There died here yesterday afternoon a warder, Johnson—he who had that apoplectic seizure, you will remember, the night before poor Shrike's exit. I attended him to the end, and, being alone with him an hour before the finish, he took the enclosed from under his pillow, and a solemn oath from me that I would forward it direct to you, sealed as you will find it, and permit no other soul to examine or even touch it. I acquit myself of the charge, but, my dear fellow, with an uneasy sense of the responsibility I incur in thus possibly suggesting to you a retrospect of events which you had much best consign to the limbo of the—not unexplainable, but not worth trying to explain. It was patent from what I have gathered that you were in an overstrung and excitable condition at that time, and that your temporary collapse was purely nervous in its character. It seems there was some nonsense abroad in the prison about a certain cell, and that there were fools who thought fit to associate Johnson's attack and the other's death with the opening of that cell's door. I have given the new Governor a tip, and he has stopped all that. We have examined the cell in company, and found it, as one might suppose, a very ordinary chamber. The two men died perfectly natural deaths, and there is the last to be said on the subject. I mention it only from the fear that enclosed may contain some allusion to the rubbish, a perusal of which might check the wholesome convalescence of your thoughts. If you take my advice, you will throw the packet into the fire unread. At least, if you *do* examine it, postpone the duty till you feel yourself absolutely impervious to any mental trickery, and—bear in mind that you are a worthy member of a particularly matter-of-fact and unemotional profession."

I smiled at the last clause, for I was now in a condition to feel a rather warm shame over my erst weak-knee'd collapse before a sheet and an illuminated turnip. I took the packet to my bedroom, shut the door, and sat myself down by the open window. The garden lay below me, and the dewy meadows beyond. In the one, bees were busy ruffling the ruddy gillyflowers and April stocks; in the other, the hedge twigs were all frosted with Mary buds, as if Spring had brushed them with the fleece of her wings in passing.

I fetched a sigh of content as I broke the seal of the packet and brought out the enclosure. Somewhere in the garden a little sardonic laugh was clipt to silence. It came from groom or maid, no doubt; yet it thrilled me with an odd feeling of uncanniness, and I shivered slightly.

"Bah!" I said to myself determinedly. "There is a shrewd nip in the wind, for all the show of sunlight;" and I rose, pulled down the window, and resumed my seat.

Then in the closed room, that had become deathly quiet by contrast, I opened and read the dead man's letter.

"Sir,—I hope you will read what I here put down. I lay it on you as a solemn injunction, for I am a dying man, and I know it. And to who is my death due, and the Governor's death, if not to you, for your pryin' and curiosity, as surely as if you had drove a nife through our harts? Therefore, I say, Read this, and take my burden from me, for it has been a burden; and now it is right that you that interfered should have it on your own mortal shoulders. The Major is dead and I am dying, and in the first of my fit it went on in my head like cimbells that the trap was left open, and that if he passed he would look in and *it* would get him. For he knew not fear, neither would he submit to bullying by God or devil.

"Now I will tell you the truth, and Heaven quit you of your responsibility in our destruction.

"There wasn't another man to me like the Governor in all the countries of the world. Once he brought me to life after doctors had given me up for dead; but he willed it, and I lived; and ever afterwards I loved him as a dog loves its master. That was in the Punjab; and I came home to England with him, and was his servant when he got his appointment to the jail here. I tell you he was a proud and fierce man, but under control and tender to those he favoured; and I will tell you also a strange thing about him. Though he was a soldier and an officer, and strict in discipline as made men fear and admire him, his heart at bottom was all for books, and literature, and such-like gentle crafts. I had his confidence, as a man gives his confidence to his dog, and before me sometimes he unbent as he never would before others. In this way I learnt the bitter sorrow of his life. He had once hoped to be a poet, acknowledged as such before the world. He was by natur' an idelist, as they call it, and God knows what it meant to him to come out of the woods, so to speak, and sweat in the dust of cities; but he did it, for his will was of tempered steel. He buried his dreams in the clouds and came down to earth greatly resolved, but with one undying hate. It is not good to hate as he could, and worse to be hated by such as him; and I will tell you the story, and what it led to.

"It was when he was a subaltern that he made up his mind to the plunge. For years he had placed all his hopes and confidents in a book of verses he had wrote, and added to, and improved during that time. A little encouragement, a little word of praise, was all he looked for, and then he was ready to buckle to again, profitin' by advice, and do better. He put all the love and beauty of his heart into that book, and at last, after doubt, and anguish, and much diffidents, he published it and give it to the world. Sir, it fell what they call still-born from the press. It was like a green leaf flutterin' down in a dead wood. To a proud and hopeful man, bubblin' with music, the pain of neglect, when he come to realize it, was terrible. But nothing was said, and there was nothing to say. In silence he had to endure and suffer.

"But one day, during maneuvers, there came to the camp a grey-faced man, a newspaper correspondent, and young Shrike knocked up a friendship with him. Now how it come about I cannot tell, but so it did that this skip-kennel wormed the lad's sorrow out of him, and his confidents, swore he'd been damnabilly used, and that when he got back he'd crack up the book himself in his own paper. He was a fool for his pains, and a serpent in his cruelty. The notice come out as promised, and, my God! the author was laughed and mocked at from beginning to end. Even confidentses he had given to the creature was twisted to his ridicule, and his very appearance joked over. And the mess got wind of it, and made a rare story for the dog days.

"He bore it like a soldier, and that he became heart and liver from the moment. But he put something to the account of the grey-faced man and locked it up in his breast.

"He come across him again years afterwards in India, and told him very politely that he hadn't forgotten him, and didn't intend to. But he was anigh losin' sight of him there for ever and a day, for the creature took cholera, or what looked like it, and rubbed shoulders with death and the devil before he pulled through. And he come across him again over here, and that was the last of him, as you shall see presently.

"Once, after I knew the Major (he were Captain then), I was a-brushin' his coat, and he stood a long while before the glass. Then he twisted upon me, with a smile on his mouth, and says he,—

"'The dog was right, Johnson: this isn't the face of a poet. I was a presumtious ass, and born to cast up figgers with a pen behind my ear.'

"'Captain,' I says, 'if you was skinned, you'd look like any other man without his. The quality of a soul isn't expressed by a coat.'

"'Well,' he answers, 'my soul's pretty clean-swept, I think, save for one Bluebeard chamber in it that's been kep' locked ever so many years. It's nice and dirty by this time, I expect,' he says. Then the grin comes on his mouth again. 'I'll open it some day,' he says, 'and look. There's something in it about comparing me to a dancing dervish, with the wind in my petticuts. Perhaps I'll get the chance to set somebody else dancing by-and-by.'

"He did, and took it, and the Bluebeard chamber come to be opened in this very jail.

"It was when the system was lying fallow, so to speak, and the prison was deserted. Nobody was there but him and me and the echoes from the empty courts. The contract for restoration hadn't been signed, and for months, and more than a year, we lay idle, nothing bein' done.

"Near the beginnin' of this period, one day comes, for the third time of the Major's seein' him, the grey-faced man. 'Let bygones be bygones,' he says. 'I was a good friend to you, though you didn't know it; and now, I expect, you're in the way to thank me.'

"'I am,' says the Major.

"'Of course,' he answers. 'Where would be your fame and reputation as one of the leadin' prison reformers of the day if you had kep' on in that riming nonsense?'

"'Have you come for my thanks?' says the Governor.

"'I've come,' says the grey-faced man, 'to examine and report upon your system.'

"'For your paper?'

"'Possibly; but to satisfy myself of its efficacy, in the first instance.'

"'You aren't commissioned, then?'

"'No; I come on my own responsibility.'

"'Without consultation with any one?'

"'Absolutely without. I haven't even a wife to advise me,' he says, with a yellow grin. What once passed for cholera had set the bile on his skin like paint, and he had caught a manner of coughing behind his hand like a toast-master.

"'I know,' says the Major, looking him steady in the face, 'that what you say about me and my affairs is sure to be actuated by conscientious motives.'

"'Ah,' he answers. 'You're sore about that review still, I see.'

"'Not at all,' says the Major; 'and, in proof, I invite you to be my guest for the night, and to-morrow I'll show you over the prison and explain my system.'

"The creature cried, 'Done!' and they set to and discussed jail matters in great earnestness. I couldn't guess the Governor's intentions, but, somehow, his manner troubled me. And yet I can remember only one point of his talk. He were always dead against making public show of his birds. 'They're there for reformation, not ignimony,' he'd say. Prisons in the old days were often, with the asylum and the work'us, made the holiday show-places of towns. I've heard of one Justice of the Peace, up North, who, to save himself trouble, used to sign a lot of blank orders for leave to view, so that applicants needn't bother him when they wanted to go over. They've changed all that, and the Governor were instrumental in the change.

"'It's against my rule,' he said that night, 'to exhibit to a stranger without a Government permit; but, seein' the place is empty, and for old remembrance' sake, I'll make an exception in your favour, and you shall learn all I can show you of the inside of a prison.'

"Now this was natural enough; but I was uneasy.

"He treated his guest royally; so much that when we assembled the next mornin' for the inspection, the grey-faced man were shaky as a wet dog. But the Major were all set prim and dry, like the soldier he was.

"We went straight away down corridor B, and at cell 47 we stopped.

"'We will begin our inspection here,' said the Governor. 'Johnson, open the door.'

"I had the keys of the row; fitted in the right one, and pushed open the door.

"'After you, sir,' said the Major; and the creature walked in, and he shut the door on him.

"I think he smelt a rat at once, for he began beating on the wood and calling out to us. But the Major only turned round to me with his face like a stone.

"'Take that key from the bunch,' he said, 'and give it to me.'

"I obeyed, all in a tremble, and he took and put it in his pocket.

"'My God, Major!' I whispered, 'what are you going to do with him?'

"'Silence, sir!' he said. 'How dare you question your superior officer!'

"And the noise inside grew louder.

"The Governor, he listened to it a moment like music; then he unbolted and flung open the trap, and the creature's face came at it like a wild beast's.

"'Sir,' said the Major to it, 'you can't better understand my system than by experiencing it. What an article for your paper you could write already—almost as pungint a one as that in which you ruined the hopes and prospects of a young cockney poet.'

"The man mouthed at the bars. He was half-mad, I think, in that one minute.

"'Let me out!' he screamed. 'This is a hideous joke! Let me out!'

"'When you are quite quiet—deathly quiet,' said the Major, 'you shall come out. Not before;' and he shut the trap in its face very softly.

"'Come, Johnson, march!' he said, and took the lead, and we walked out of the prison.

"I was like to faint, but I dared not disobey, and the man's screeching followed us all down the empty corridors and halls, until we shut the first great door on it.

"It may have gone on for hours, alone in that awful emptiness. The creature was a reptile, but the thought sickened my heart.

"And from that hour till his death, five months later, he rotted and maddened in his dreadful tomb."

There was more, but I pushed the ghastly confession from me at this point in uncontrollable loathing and terror. Was it possible—possible, that injured vanity could so falsify its victim's every tradition of decency?

"Oh!" I muttered, "what a disease is ambition! Who takes one step towards it puts his foot on Alsirat!"

It was minutes before my shocked nerves were equal to a resumption of the task; but at last I took it up again, with a groan.

"I don't think at first I realized the full mischief the Governor intended to do. At least, I hoped he only meant to give the man a good fright and then let him go. I might have known better. How could he ever release him without ruining himself?

"The next morning he summoned me to attend him. There was a strange new look of triumph in his face, and in his hand he held a heavy hunting-crop. I pray to God he acted in madness, but my duty and obedience was to him.

"'There is sport toward, Johnson,' he said. 'My dervish has got to dance.'

"I followed him quiet. We listened when I opened the jail door, but the place was silent as the grave. But from the cell, when we reached it, came a low, whispering sound.

"The Governor slipped the trap and looked through.

"'All right,' he said, and put the key in the door and flung it open.

"He were sittin' crouched on the ground, and he looked up at us vacant-like. His face were all fallen down, as it were, and his mouth never ceased to shake and whisper.

"The Major shut the door and posted me in a corner. Then he moved to the creature with his whip.

"'Up!' he cried. 'Up, you dervish, and dance to us!' and he brought the thong with a smack across his shoulders.

"The creature leapt under the blow, and then to his feet with a cry, and the Major whipped him till he danced. All round the cell he drove him, lashing and cutting—and again, and many times again, until the poor thing rolled on the floor whimpering and sobbing. I shall have to give an account of this some day. I shall have to whip my master with a red-hot serpent round the blazing furnace of the pit, and I shall do it with agony, because here my love and my obedience was to him.

"When it was finished, he bade me put down food and drink that I had brought with me, and come away with him; and we went, leaving him rolling on the floor of the cell, and shut him alone in the empty prison until we should come again at the same time tomorrow.

"So day by day this went on, and the dancing three or four times a week, until at last the whip could be left behind, for the man would scream and begin to dance at the mere turning of the key in the lock. And he danced for four months, but not the fifth.

"Nobody official came near us all this time. The prison stood lonely as a deserted ruin where dark things have been done.

"Once, with fear and trembling, I asked my master how he would account for the inmate of 47 if he was suddenly called upon by authority to open the cell; and he answered, smiling,—

"I should say it was my mad brother. By his own account, he showed me a brother's love, you know. It would be thought a liberty; but the authorities, I think, would stretch a point for me. But if I got sufficient notice, I should clear out the cell.'

"I asked him how, with my eyes rather than my lips, and he answered me only with a look.

"And all this time he was, outside the prison, living the life of a good man—helping the needy, ministering to the poor. He even entertained occasionally, and had more than one noisy party in his house.

"But the fifth month the creature danced no more. He was a dumb, silent animal then, with matted hair and beard; and when one entered he would only look up at one pitifully, as if he said, 'My long punishment is nearly ended.' How it came that no inquiry was ever made about him I know not, but none ever was. Perhaps he was one of the wandering gentry that nobody ever knows where they are next. He was unmarried, and had apparently not told of his intended journey to a soul.

"And at the last he died in the night. We found him lying stiff and stark in the morning, and scratched with a piece of black crust on a stone of the wall these strange words: 'An Eddy on the Floor.' Just that—nothing else.

"Then the Governor came and looked down, and was silent. Suddenly he caught me by the shoulder.

"'Johnson,' he cried, 'if it was to do again, I would do it! I repent of nothing. But he has paid the penalty, and we call quits. May he rest in peace!'

"'Amen!' I answered low. Yet I knew our turn must come for this.

"We buried him in quicklime under the wall where the murderers lie, and I made the cell trim and rubbed out the writing, and the Governor locked all up and took away the key. But he locked in more than he bargained for.

"For months the place was left to itself, and neither of us went anigh 47. Then one day the workmen was to be put in, and the Major he took me round with him for a last examination of the place before they come.

"He hesitated a bit outside a particular cell; but at last he drove in the key and kicked open the door.

"'My God!' he says, 'he's dancing still!'

"My heart was thumpin', I tell you, as I looked over his shoulder. What did we see? What you well understand, sir; but, for all it was no more than that, we knew as well as if it was shouted in our ears that it was him, dancin'. It went round by the walls and drew towards us, and as it stole near I screamed out, 'An Eddy on the Floor!' and seized and dragged the Major out and clapped to the door behind us.

"'Oh!' I said, 'in another moment it would have had us.'

"He looked at me gloomily.

"'Johnson,' he said, 'I'm not to be frighted or coerced. He may dance, but he shall dance alone. Get a screwdriver and some screws and fasten up this trap. No one from this time looks into this cell.'

"I did as he bid me, sweatin'; and I swear all the time I wrought I dreaded a hand would come through the trap and clutch mine.

"On one pretex' or another, from that day till the night you meddled with it, he kep' that cell as close shut as a tomb. And he went his ways, discardin' the past from that time forth. Now and again a over-sensitive prisoner in the next cell would complain of feelin' uncomfortable. If possible, he would be removed to another; if not, he was damd for his fancies. And so it might be goin' on to now, if you hadn't pried and interfered. I don't blame you at this moment, sir. Likely you were an instrument in the hands of Providence; only, as the instrument, you must now take the burden of the truth on your own shoulders. I am a dying man, but I cannot die till I have confessed. Per'aps you may find it in your hart some day to give up a prayer for me—but it must be for the Major as well.

"Your obedient servant,
"J. Johnson."

What comment of my own can I append to this wild narrative? Professionally, and apart from personal experiences, I should rule it the composition of an epileptic. That a noted journalist, nameless as he was and is to me, however nomadic in habit, could disappear from human ken, and his fellows rest content to leave him unaccounted for, seems a tax upon credulity so stupendous that I cannot seriously endorse the statement.

Yet, also—there *is* that little matter of my personal experience.

THE BLACK REAPER
(1899)

Proem
Heaven's Nursery

"Sinner, sinner, whence do you come?"
  "From the bitter earth they called my home."
"Sinner, sinner, why do you wait?"
  "I fear to knock at the golden gate:
"My crimes were heavy; my doom is sure,
  And I dread the anguish I must endure."
"Had you ever a child down there?"
  "One—but it died, and I learnt despair."
"Here you will find it, behind the gate."
  "God forbid! for it felt my hate—
"Shrunk in the frost of my cruelties.
  More than the Judge's I fear its eyes."
"Hist! At the keyhole place your ear.
  Sinner, what is the sound you hear?
"Is it ten thousand babes at play?
  Heaven's nursery lies that way.
"Through it to judgment all must fare
  It was God's pity placed it there."
 The gate swung open; the sinner past;
  Little hands caught and held him fast.
"While you wait the call of the Nameless One,
  There's time for a game at 'Touch-and-Run'!"

He played with them there in that shining place,
With the hot tears scorching his furrowed face—
Played, till the voice rang dread and clear:
"Where is the sinner? I wait him here!"
Then shouting with laughter one and all
They pushed him on to the Judgment Hall;
Stood by him; swarmed to the daïs steps,
A jumble of gleeful eyes and lips.
The Judge leaned stern from His Judgment Throne:
"*I gave thee—where is thy little one?*"
Wildly the culprit caught his breath:
"Lord, I have sinned. My doom be death."
He hung his head with a broken sob.
There sprang a child from the rosy mob—
"Daddy!" it cried, with a joyful shriek;
Leapt to his arms and kissed his cheek.
But he put it from him with bursting sighs,
And looked on the Judge with swimming eyes;
Stood abashed in his bitter shame,
Waiting the sentence that never came.
From the Throne spoke out the thundered Word:
"*This be thy doom!*" No more he heard,
For a chime of laughter from baby throats
Took up those crashing organ notes,
Mixed with; silenced them; made them void—
And the children's laughter was unalloyed,
"This be thy doom," came a little squeak,
"To play with us here at 'hide-and-seek'!"
Thrice did the Judge essay to frown;
Thrice did the children laugh Him down—
Till at the last, He caught and kissed
The maddest of all and the merriest;
Turned to the sinner, with smiling face:
"These render futile the Judgment Place.
"Sunniest rascals, imp and elf,
Who think they can better the Judge Himself.

"Sinner—whatever thy sins may be,
Theirs is the sentence—go from Me!"

THE BLACK REAPER

Taken from the Q— Register of Local Events,
as Compiled from Authentic Narratives

I

Now I am to tell you of a thing that befell in the year 1665 of the Great Plague, when the hearts of certain amongst men, grown callous in wickedness upon that rebound from an inhuman austerity, were opened to the vision of a terror that moved and spoke not in the silent places of the fields. Forasmuch as, however, in the recovery from delirium a patient may marvel over the incredulity of neighbours who refuse to give credence to the presentments that have been *ipso facto* to him, so, the nation being sound again, and its constitution hale, I expect little but a laugh for my piety in relating of the following incident; which, nevertheless, is as essential true as that he who shall look through the knot-hole in the plank of a coffin shall acquire the evil eye.

For, indeed, in those days of a wild fear and confusion, when every condition that maketh for reason was set wandering by a devious path, and all men sitting as in a theatre of death looked to see the curtain rise upon God knows what horrors, it was vouchsafed to many to witness sights and sounds beyond the compass of Nature, and that as if the devil and his minions had profited by the anarchy to slip unobserved into the world. And I know that this is so, for all the insolence of a recovered scepticism; and, as to the unseen, we are like one that traverseth the dark with a lanthorn, himself the skipper of a little moving blot of light, but a positive mark for any secret foe without the circumference of its radiance.

Be that as it may, and whether it was our particular ill-fortune, or, as some asserted, our particular wickedness, that made of our village an inviting back-door of entrance to the Prince of Darkness, I know not; but so it is that disease and contagion are ever inclined to penetrate by way of flaws or humours where the veil of the flesh is already perforated, as a kite circleth round its quarry, looking for the weak place to strike: and, without doubt, in that land of corruption we were a very foul blot indeed.

How this came about it were idle to speculate; yet no man shall have the hardihood to affirm that it was otherwise. Nor do I seek to extenuate myself, who was in truth no better than my neighbours in most that made us a community of drunkards and forswearers both lewd and abominable. For in that village a depravity that was like madness had come to possess the heads of the people, and no man durst take his stand on honesty or even common decency, for fear he should be set upon by his comrades and drummed out of his government on a pint pot. Yet for myself I will say was one only redeeming quality, and that was the pure love I bore to my solitary orphaned child, the little Margery.

Now, our Vicar—a patient and God-fearing man, for all his predial tithes were impropriated by his lord, that was an absentee and a sheriff in London—did little to stem that current of lewdness that had set in strong with the Restoration. And this was from no lack of virtue in himself, but rather from a natural invertebracy, as one may say, and an order of mind that, yet being no order, is made the sport of any sophister with a wit for paragram. Thus it always is that mere example is of little avail without precept,—of which, however, it is an important condition,—and that the successful directors of men be not those who go to the van and lead, unconscious of the gibes and mockery in their rear, but such rather as drive the mob before them with a smiting hand and no infirmity of purpose. So, if a certain affection for our pastor dwelt in our hearts, no title of respect was there to leaven it and justify his high office before Him that consigned the trust; and ever deeper and deeper we sank in the slough of corruption, until was brought about this pass—that naught but some scourging despotism of the Church should acquit us of the fate of Sodom. That such, at the eleventh hour, was vouchsafed us of God's mercy, it is my purpose to show; and, doubtless, this offering of a loop-hole was to account by reason of the devil's having debarked his reserves, as it were, in our port; and so quartering upon us a soldiery that we were, at no invitation of our own, to maintain, stood us a certain extenuation.

It was late in the order of things before in our village so much as a rumour of the plague reached us. Newspapers were not in those days, and reports, being by word of mouth, travelled slowly, and were often spent bullets by the time they fell amongst us. Yet, by May, some gossip there was of the distemper having gotten a hold in certain quarters of London and increasing, and this alarmed our people, though it made no abatement of their profligacy. But presently the reports coming thicker, with confirmation of the terror and panic that was enlarging on all sides, we must take measures for our safety; though into June and July, when the pestilence was raging, none infected had come our way, and that from our remote and isolated position. Yet it needs but fear for the crown to that wickedness that is self-indulgence; and forasmuch as this fear fattens like a toadstool on the decomposition it springs from, it grew with us to the proportions that we were set to kill or destroy any that should approach us from the stricken districts.

And then suddenly there appeared in our midst *he* that was appointed to be our scourge and our cautery.

Whence he came, or how, no man of us could say. Only one day we were a community of roysterers and scoffers, impious and abominable, and the next he was amongst us smiting and thundering.

Some would have it that he was an old collegiate of our Vicar's, but at last one of those wandering Dissenters that found never as now the times opportune to their teachings—a theory to which our minister's treatment of the stranger gave colour. For from the moment of his appearance he took the reins of government, as it were, appropriating the pulpit and launching his bolts therefrom, with the full consent and encouragement of the other. There were those, again, who were resolved that his commission was from a high place, whither news of our infamy had reached, and that we had best give him a respectful hearing, lest we should run a chance of having our hearing stopped altogether. A few were convinced he was no man at all, but rather a fiend sent to thresh us with the scourge of our own contriving, that we might be tender, like steak, for the cooking; and yet other few regarded him with terror, as an actual figure or embodiment of the distemper.

But, generally, after the first surprise, the feeling of resentment at his intrusion woke and gained ground, and we were much put about that he should have thus assumed the pastorship without invitation, quartering with our Vicar; who kept himself aloof and was little seen, and seeking to drive us by terror, and amazement, and a great menace of retribution. For, in truth, this was not the method to which we were wont, and it both angered and disturbed us.

This feeling would have enlarged the sooner, perhaps, were it not for a certain restraining influence possessed of the new-comer, which neighboured him with darkness and mystery. For he was above the common tall, and ever appeared in public with a slouched hat, that concealed all the upper part of his face and showed little otherwise but the dense black beard that dropped upon his breast like a shadow.

Now with August came a fresh burst of panic, how the desolation increased and the land was overrun with swarms of infected persons seeking an asylum from the city; and our anger rose high against the stranger, who yet dwelt with us and encouraged the distemper of our minds by furious denunciations of our guilt.

Thus far, for all the corruption of our hearts, we had maintained the practice of church-going, thinking, maybe, poor fools! to hoodwink the Almighty with a show of reverence; but now, as by a common consent, we neglected the observances and loitered of a Sabbath in the fields, and thither at the last the strange man pursued us and ended the matter.

For so it fell that at the time of the harvest's ripening a goodish body of us males was gathered one Sunday for coolness about the neighbourhood of the dripping well, whose waters were a tradition, for they had long gone dry. This well was situate in a sort of cave or deep scoop at the foot of a cliff of limestone, to which the cultivated ground that led up to it fell somewhat. High above, the cliff broke away into a wide stretch of pasture land, but the face of the rock itself was all patched with bramble and little starved birch-trees clutching for foothold; and in like manner the excavation beneath was half-stifled and gloomed over with undergrowth, so that it looked a place very dismal and uninviting, save in the ardour of the dog-days.

Within, where had been the basin, was a great shattered hole going down to unknown depths; and this no man had thought to explore, for a mystery held about the spot that was doubtless the foster-child of ignorance.

But to the front of the well and of the cliff stretched a noble field of corn, and this field was of an uncommon shape, being, roughly, a vast circle and a little one joined by a neck and in suggestion not unlike an hour-glass; and into the crop thereof, which was of goodly weight and condition, were the first sickles to be put on the morrow.

Now as we stood or lay around, idly discussing of the news, and congratulating ourselves that we were featly quit of our incubus, to us along the meadow path, his shadow jumping on the corn, came the very subject of our gossip.

He strode up, looking neither to right nor left, and with the first word that fell, low and damnatory, from his lips, we knew that the moment had come when, whether for good or evil, he intended to cast us from him and acquit himself of further responsibility in our direction.

"Behold!" he cried, pausing over against us, "I go from among ye! Behold, ye that have not obeyed nor inclined your ear, but have walked every one in the imagination of his evil heart! Saith the Lord, 'I will bring evil upon them, which they shall not be able to escape; and though they shall cry unto Me, I will not hearken unto them.'"

His voice rang out, and a dark silence fell among us. It was pregnant, but with little of humility. We had had enough of this interloper and his abuse. Then, like Jeremiah, he went to prophesy:—

"I read ye, men of Anathoth, and the murder in your hearts. Ye that have worshipped the shameful thing and burned incense to

Baal—shall I cringe that ye devise against me, or not rather pray to the Lord of Hosts, 'Let me see Thy vengeance on them'? And He answereth, 'I will bring evil upon the men of Anathoth, even the year of their visitation.'"

Now, though I was no participator in that direful thing that followed, I stood by, nor interfered, and so must share the blame. For there were men risen all about, and their faces lowering, and it seemed that it would go hard with the stranger were he not more particular.

But he moved forward, with a stately and commanding gesture, and stood with his back to the well-scoop and threatened us and spoke.

"Lo!" he shrieked, "your hour is upon you! Ye shall be mowed down like ripe corn, and the shadow of your name shall be swept from the earth! The glass of your iniquity is turned, and when its sand is run through, not a man of ye shall be!"

He raised his arm aloft, and in a moment he was overborne. Even then, as all say, none got sight of his face; but he fought with lowered head, and his black beard flapped like a wounded crow. But suddenly a boy-child ran forward of the bystanders, crying and screaming,—

"Hurt him not! They are hurting him—oh, me! oh, me!"

And from the sweat and struggle came his voice, gasping, "I spare the little children!"

Then only I know of the surge and the crash towards the well-mouth, of an instant cessation of motion, and immediately of men toiling hither and thither with boulders and huge blocks, which they piled over the rent, and so sealed it with a cromlech of stone.

II

That, in the heat of rage and of terror, we had gone farther than we had at first designed, our gloom and our silence on the morrow attested. True we were quit of our incubus, but on such terms as not even the severity of the times could excuse. For the man had but chastised us to our improvement; and to destroy the scourge is not to condone the offence. For myself, as I bore up the little Margery to my shoulder on my way to the reaping, I felt the burden of guilt so great as that I found myself muttering of an apology to the Lord that I durst put myself into touch with innocence. "But the walk would fatigue her otherwise," I murmured; and, when we were come to the field, I took and carried her into the upper or little meadow, out of reach of the scythes, and placed her to sleep amongst the corn, and so left her with a groan.

But when I was come anew to my comrades, who stood at the lower extremity of the field—and this was the bottom of the hourglass, so to speak—I was aware of a stir amongst them, and, advancing closer, that they were all intent upon the neighbourhood of the field I had left, staring like distraught creatures, and holding well together, as if in a panic. Therefore, following the direction of their eyes, and of one that pointed with rigid finger, I turned me about, and looked whence I had come; and my heart went with a somersault, and in a moment I was all sick and dazed.

For I saw, at the upper curve of the meadow, where the well lay in gloom, that a man had sprung out of the earth, as it seemed, and was started reaping; and the face of this man was all in shadow, from which his beard ran out and down like a stream of gall.

He reaped swiftly and steadily, swinging like a pendulum; but, though the sheaves fell to him right and left, no swish of the scythe came to us, nor any sound but the beating of our own hearts.

Now, from the first moment of my looking, no doubt was in my lost soul but that this was him we had destroyed come back to verify his prophecy in ministering to the vengeance of the Lord of Hosts; and at the thought a deep groan rent my bosom, and was echoed by those about me. But scarcely was it issued when a second terror smote me as that I near reeled. Margery—my babe! put to sleep there in the path of the Black Reaper!

At that, though they called to me, I sprang forward like a madman, and running along the meadow, through the neck of the glass, reached the little thing, and stooped and snatched her into my arms. She was sound and unfrighted, as I felt with a burst of thankfulness; but, looking about me, as I turned again to fly, I had near dropped in my tracks for the sickness and horror I experienced in the nearer neighbourhood of the apparition. For, though it never raised its head, or changed the steady swing of its shoulders, I knew that it was aware of and was *reaping at me*. Now, I tell you, it was ten yards away, yet the point of the scythe came gliding upon me silently, like a snake, through the stalks, and at that I screamed out and ran for my life.

I escaped, sweating with terror; but when I was sped back to the men, there was all the village collected, and our Vicar to the front, praying from a throat that rattled like a dead leaf in a draught. I know not what he said, for the low cries of the women filled the air; but his face was white as a smock, and his fingers writhed in one another like a knot of worms.

"The plague is upon us!" they wailed. "We shall be mowed down like ripe corn!"

And even as they shrieked the Black Reaper paused, and, putting away his scythe, stooped and gathered up a sheaf in his arms and stood it on end. And, with the very act, a man—one that had been forward in yesterday's business—fell down amongst us yelling and foaming; and he rent his breast in his frenzy, revealing the purple blot thereon, and he passed blaspheming. And the reaper stooped and stooped again, and with every sheaf he gathered together one of us fell stricken and rolled in his agony, while the rest stood by palsied.

But, when at length all that was cut was accounted for, and a dozen of us were gone each to his judgment, and he had taken up his scythe to reap anew, a wild fury woke in the breasts of some of the more abandoned and reckless amongst us.

"It is not to be tolerated!" they cried. "Let us at once fire the corn and burn this sorcerer!"

And with that, some fire or six of them, emboldened by despair, ran up into the little field, and, separating, had out each his flint and fired the crop in his own place, and retreated to the narrow part for safety.

Now the reaper rested on his scythe, as if unexpectedly acquitted of a part of his labour; but the corn flamed up in these five or six directions, and was consumed in each to the compass of a single sheaf: whereat the fire died away. And with its dying the faces of those that had ventured went black as coal; and they flung up their arms, screaming, and fell prone where they stood, and were hidden from our view.

Then, indeed, despair seized upon all of us that survived, and we made no doubt but that we were to be exterminated and wiped from the earth for our sins, as were the men of Anathoth. And for an hour the Black Reaper mowed and trussed, till he had cut all from the little upper field and was approached to the neck of juncture with the lower and larger. And before us that remained, and who were drawn back amongst the trees, weeping and praying, a fifth of our comrades lay foul, and dead, and sweltering, and all blotched over with the dreadful mark of the pestilence.

Now, as I say, the reaper was nearing the neck of juncture; and so we knew that if he should once pass into the great field towards us and continue his mowing, not one of us should be left to give earnest of our repentance.

Then, as it seemed, our Vicar came to a resolution, moving forward with a face all wrapt and entranced; and he strode up the meadow path and approached the apparition, and stretched out his arms to it entreating. And we saw the other pause, awaiting him; and, as he came near, put forth his hand, and so, gently, on the good old head. But as we looked, catching at our breaths with a little pathos of hope, the priestly face was thrown back radiant, and the figure of him that would give his life for us sank amongst the yet standing corn and disappeared from our sight.

So at last we yielded ourselves fully to our despair; for if our pastor should find no mercy, what possibility of it could be for us!

It was in this moment of an uttermost grief and horror, when each stood apart from his neighbour, fearing the contamination of his presence, that there was vouchsafed to me, of God's pity, a wild and sudden inspiration. Still to my neck fastened the little Margery—not frighted, it seemed, but mazed—and other babes there were in plenty, that clung to their mothers' skirts and peeped out, wondering at the strange show.

I ran to the front and shrieked: "The children! the children! He will not touch the little children! Bring them and set them in his path!" And so crying I sped to the neck of meadow, and loosened the soft arms from my throat, and put the little one down within the corn.

Now at once the women saw what I would be at, and full a score of them snatched up their babes and followed me. And here we were reckless for ourselves; but we knelt the innocents in one close line across the neck of land, so that the Black Reaper should not find space between any of them to swing his scythe. And having done this, we fell back with our hearts bubbling in our breasts, and we stood panting and watched.

He had paused over that one full sheaf of his reaping; but now, with the sound of the women's running, he seized his weapon again and set to upon the narrow belt of corn that yet separated him from the children. But presently, coming out upon the tender array, his scythe stopped and trailed in his hand, and for a full minute he stood like a figure of stone. Then thrice he walked slowly backwards and forwards along the line, seeking for an interval whereby he might pass; and the children laughed at him like silver bells, showing no fear, and perchance meeting that of love in his eyes that was hidden from us.

Then of a sudden he came to before the midmost of the line, and, while we drew our breath like dying souls, stooped and snapped his blade across his knee, and, holding the two parts in his hand, turned and strode back into the shadow of the dripping well. There arrived, he paused once more, and, twisting him about, waved his hand once to us and vanished into the blackness. But there were those who affirmed that in that instant of his turning, his face was revealed, and that it was a face radiant and beautiful as an angel's.

Such is the history of the wild judgment that befell us, and by grace of the little children was foregone; and such was the stranger whose name no man ever heard tell, but whom many have since sought to identify with that spirit of the pestilence that entered into men's hearts and confounded them, so that they saw visions and were afterwards confused in their memories.

But this I may say, that when at last our courage would fetch us to that little field of death, we found it to be all blackened and blasted, so as nothing would take root there then or ever since; and it was as if, after all the golden sand of the hour-glass was run away and the lives of the most impious with it, the destroyer saw fit to stay his hand for sake of the babes that he had pronounced innocent, and for such as were spared to witness to His judgment. And this I do here, with a heart as contrite as if it were the morrow of the visitation, the which with me it ever has remained.

THE SWORD OF CORPORAL LACOSTE
(1899)

"'Tis many a wise Man's hap, while he is providing against one Danger, to fall into another: And for his very Providence to turn his Destruction."

Corporal Lacoste—cuirassier in the following of Murat, the Rupert of an Imperial army—had had a long dream, chiefly of a roaring thunder of surf bursting upon jagged rocks. And, as the storm of water thrashed the very pinnacles that toppled into mist, he had seen the ribs of cliff laid bare and bleeding—as it were the laceration of a living land that he looked on. Then, "*Corne et tonnerre!*" he had seemed to cry to himself, "the very world is torn by some inhuman power, and flows to the sea in rivers of purple!" and he heard the bells of the ocean, receding innumerably, choke at their moorings, muffled and congested with the floating scum of carnage that no wind might ruffle and only God's fire cleanse.

Now, in a moment, he saw that what he had taken for land was in truth a great cliff built up of human bodies—a vast reserve of human force accumulated by, and for the use of, a single dominant will. And this cliff was washed by the waves of an ocean of blood, to which its life contributed in a thousand spouting rivulets. And it was compact of limitless pain; and the cry of torture never ceased within it. And suddenly the dreamer—as in the way of dreams—felt himself to be a constituent agony of that he gazed upon—a pulp of suffering self-contained, yet partaking of the wretchedness of all.

Suddenly there was a faint stir and pushing here and there into the mound, a quiet soft heaving such as a mole makes; and whenever this ceased a moment, a shriek, thin as a needle, pierced the very nerve of the mass. And, with horror indescribable, the dreamer felt the approach of the thing, testing and feeling at one point or another, until it reached and entered his breast. "Hideous and unnameable!" he would have screamed, but clinched his teeth upon the cry; for, lo! it was but a little familiar hand, plump and white, that groped within his ribs, seeking to find and snap the tendons that held his heart in place.

Then he found voice, and whispered in his extremity, "Spare me, my Emperor!" but the hand neither shook nor hurried, severing his chords of being one by one, until it could lift the heart from its socket and fling it to the waves that leapt like wolves beneath. And, at the instant of the lifting, it was as if a tooth of flame were thrust into him and withdrawn; and thereafter he fell cold—colder, waxing blithe and painless, until he was moved to laugh to himself with a secret ecstasy of applause.

"A good soldier has no heart. Of a truth *le p'tit caporal* must now as always have his way. And he has done it so deftly that I scarce feel a wound."

The very association of the word seemed to open his eyes, morally and physically. Immediately he was conscious of a slit of blinding daylight; of the grip upon some exposed parts of his body of a frost sharp enough to hold him by the legs like a man-trap. Yet, save for these partial seizures, he appeared to be reclining under a blanket so suffocatingly thick that he could not account for his certain conviction that the heat was slowly retiring from it.

All in a moment he had comprehended, and was struggling to relieve himself of his incubus. It rolled from him as he emerged from under it. It fell ridiculously into the caricature of a dead dragoon. Corporal Lacoste knew the thing for a mess-sergeant of his late acquaintance. He nodded to the body as he sat himself down in the snow.

"Thou never servedst a comrade so well before, sergeant," said he; and, indeed, he would surely have died of the frost in his wound had not this unconscious trooper given him of the heat of his own vitality.

"But, what made the man delay his going till the sun rose?" thought Corporal Lacoste.

He looked again, and started.

The dragoon's throat had been pierced by a sword-thrust. A thread of vermilion yet crawled from it down his swarthy neck, like the awkward tracing by a schoolboy of a river on a map.

Corporal Lacoste screwed his eyes, intuitively and obliquely, to get glimpse of his own right shoulder. There was a sensation of wet numbness thereabouts. Something had pricked him pretty deeply—possibly the point of the very murderous weapon that had finished off the dragoon.

"It was when I dreamt of the tooth of flame," thought Corporal Lacoste. "There have been vampires here amongst the wounded."

It hardly troubled him, this familiar experience. Those of Murat's hated *beaux sabreurs* who fell alive and had the misfortune to be left for dead, must always run the risk of mutilation. It was enough for him that the blow that had prostrated him had failed of its deadliness; that his senseless condition had not been made by the frost everlasting; that he owed his salvation to the accidental superimposition of a wounded dragoon.

He took his dazed head between his hands, as he sat, and indulged a little retrospect of the events that had preceded his downfall, as he dwelt upon the scene before him.

That was marvellous enough to a Gascon. He crouched in the bed of a precipitous defile that joined higher and lower terraces of the Amstetten forest. Beneath him, the gully went down with a rush of trampled snow, in the swirl of which dead horses and men and the wreck of accoutrements, half-buried in a foam of white, seemed the very freebooty of a frost-stricken waterfall. It was a strange picture of furious motion held in suspension—the more wonderful for its framing. For all the trees, great and small, that over-stooped the lip, and sprouted from the sides, of the pass were hung with monstrous lustres of ice, up which millions of little reflected suns travelled like beads of champagne rising in specimen-glasses.

Of the stunning effectiveness of these icicles, as a species of natural artillery, Corporal Lacoste had had a recent demonstration. His mind now was slowly electrotyping, in the midst of a clearing obscurity, certain images impressed upon it during the moments antecedent to his collapse. He recalled the weird long ride through forest vaults so roofed with snow that the world had seemed one vast tent propped by countless poles. He recalled how here and there a sluice of sunlight pouring through a rift overhead had reminded him of that strange Roman Pantheon that he had once seen when serving in the military suite of M. Barthollet, the appraiser of works of art to the Directory. He recalled how, jingling blithely in his saddle, in the wake of his swashbuckler general, with all the glory of the late capitulation of Ulm tingling in his careless heart, he had started to the sudden shout, the recoiling shock of ambush; and had seen and heard the outlet of this very glen, down which Murat and his advance-guard were riding, clank to the wheel of an Austrian regiment, that shut upon it like a gate of steel. He remembered the thunderous rush that succeeded—the charge of the *beaux sabreurs* down the defile—the crash, the retreat, the rally; and again he saw the young artillery officer—some *cadet inconnu*—gallop his two pieces into position, and, at the critical moment, discharge his buzzing canisters of grape into the welter of the enemy.

Corne et tonnerre! what a clearing of the pass! It had been like cleaning a pipe-stem with a fizz of gunpowder. But, at the same time, a catastrophe quite unexpected had resulted. For the explosion had brought down a very avalanche of snow and icicles from the weighted branches a hundred feet above; and these terrific bolts, bursting as it were in a cloud of smoke, had salvoed on helmet and breastplate of friend and foe alike, with a sound like the clanging of enormous cymbals, and had hurled horses and men in one shouting ruin to the ground.

And it was precisely at this point that Corporal Lacoste's perceptions had been severed, and so left for the night as clean-ended as a pack of straw in a chaff-cutter.

But destiny—his particular Atropos—was now to turn at the knife again—for a time.

"To be floored by an icicle!" he muttered, twirling his fierce moustache. "*Corne et tonnerre!* it is after all a weapon unknown to courage and passion. This Queen of the snow is a barbarous fighter. Yet all night she kisses the wounds of her victims that they may not bleed. She woos to her embraces by the twin snares of hurt and pity. It is an amiable artifice, not unfamiliar to the experience of us that ply the sword. Whom a woman strikes she loves. My faith—but she was a chill bed-fellow, nevertheless!"

He was feeling now very sick. His wounds, opening to his returned vitality, were beginning to run afresh. He rose and looked about for his helmet. It lay, a mere crushed tin kettle, under the dead dragoon. But his sword was flung aside uninjured, and this he recovered and slipped back into its scabbard.

"It retires with a hiss. *Mon Dieu*, what a poisonous snake!" he said; and then he took off his neckcloth and fastened it about his battered head.

It was while he was thus engaged that his vision, wandering afield, rested on a figure that moved at the far end of the glen. This figure—that appeared to be the only thing living in all the length of the pass—had an odd appearance to the dim eyes of the corporal. It was squat, and of fantastic garb and gesture; and to his weak exalted perceptives it presented itself as a gnome, crept, like a hound from the womb of sin, out of some icy dark crypt of the forest. Now and again it would stoop; now and again fling a goblin dance; and then all of a sudden it seemed to catch sight of the tall shape standing high in the lift of the defile, and stopped motionless and shaded its forehead with horizontal palm.

Now, in a moment it appeared to set an extinguisher on its head, literally, as if subduing an unholy flame; and immediately it came up the glen with a quick elastic step, the cone standing back at a rakish angle.

The creature drew near.

"*Beaucoup de bruit pour rien!*" muttered Corporal Lacoste, with a rallying twinge of self-contempt, for the thing had resolved itself into nothing more formidable than a little fat monk in a cowl; and "*Bénédicité, mon père*," he added, as a concession to a certain traditional superstition that yet affected him.

"My cap is already doffed, or I would pull it off to your reverence," he said, leavening his grace with a pinch of mockery. "But—*corne et tonnerre!* I am forgetting. You will only converse in your own detestable tongue."

"I know a little French," said the monk, promptly.

"*C'est bien*," cried the soldier, but without surprise; for, indeed, he could not comprehend how one could speak any other language from choice.

"And what was my father doing down there?" he asked. "And why did he dance?"

The monk had steady little brown eyes, of the shape and fulness of a rabbit's. His face was round, ruddy, and extremely dirty; his chin peaked and under-hung; his stomach shaped like a case-bottle, but a hogshead in capacity. He had on a hooded cassock, the original black of which had paid a fine interest of coppery blotches to the investors of *trinkgeld* in that hallowed paunch; and he was altogether a very typical example, it must be admitted, of a filthy little Bavarian priest.

"I looked," he said— "yes, I looked for one or two yet in the state to receive the *viaticum*."

"And that was a good thought, *mon père*; but the frost-demon had an earlier and a better. Still, it does not explain why you danced."

The monk kept each of his hands thrust up the wide sleeve of the opposite arm. He seemed to hug himself over some nameless jest—the physical condition of what was thus concealed, perhaps. But he was more ostentatious of his teeth, the under-row of which broke up his conscious smile into unlovely intervals, and were like little dilapidated gravestones to the memory of deceased appetites.

"I danced because the cold bit my feet," he said.

"Oh!" said Corporal Lacoste. "And is not the cold, like the sunlight, a dispensation of Providence?"

"Of Providence, assuredly—yes, of Providence."

The soldier smacked his chest, consequentially but feebly.

"Behold a Providence, then, that favours its recreant children at the expense of its ministers! That which is your chastisement hath been my salvation. So it rebukes the arrogance of priestcraft, and demonstrates it more an honour to be a soldier than a monk."

The stranger lifted his elbows and embraced himself, drawing in his breath.

"Sometimes," he said, suddenly giggling and voluble, "it sanctifies, we understand, the double gift. The Bishop of Beauvais, he was soldier and divine: the Archbishop of Canterbury also. It is good to be either in its season—very good to be both. To know to put one you slay on the road to heaven, eh?"

"If there is time. But, *mon père*, do you always stop to show him the way?"

He took the monk invitingly by a sleeve, and led him to the dead dragoon.

"He is passed before I come," said the *curé*.

"It is all a question of tenses," said the corporal. "Come or came: which is it? And who killed him, my father?"

"How,—do you say?"

"Why, dead men do not bleed if you stick them through the neck."

"Doubtless that is so."

"And he hath lain on me all night like a toast; yet I wake to find him with the fresh blood running."

"It must be, then, that the sun-warmth broke anew his wound that the frost had closed."

"*Corne et tonnerre!* It was a fine lance of sun-warmth to go clean through his neck and into my shoulder."

The priest rolled his eyes, so as to show little parings of white at their edges. His fingers seemed to twitch within the sleeves. Suddenly he burst out, sputtering—

"You damned devil, if you think that I, a servant of God, killed this man!"

Corporal Lacoste was inexpressibly shocked—as much to hear this snake of profanity hiss from an anointed vessel, as to find that he had been understood to suggest a charge so execrable. At the same time his instincts as a soldier were hard set to discount a truism.

"I ask only for information," he cried, dismayed. "A dead man struck does not bleed. If you are priest only, there may be those of the flock abroad who would give their pastor an opportunity to exercise his office."

The monk mumbled to himself, like any angry layman.

"Those and those! But, it is you that empty the land—that desolate the hearths—that convert the innocuous hind into a beast of desperation!"

He was gesticulating violently with his shoulders.

"They crashed down the defile!" he yelled, wheeling himself about: "they carried all before them with atrocious glee—the hopes, the happiness, the innocent life of the poor jocund foresters. Follow, you, down the glen! Track the storm by its litter! Go, rejoin your comrades of blood, that the measure of your iniquity may be theirs."

Corporal Lacoste stood amazed.

"My father," he said, "the rebuke may be just; but the long night and many leagues by now stretch between me and mine. And I am a wounded and famished man."

Perhaps he was discreetly humble in his realisation of the fact that he was abandoned alone to the perils of a hostile country.

"*Confiteor Deo omnipotenti*" he began to murmur, jogging a drowsy memory. He bowed his head and struck his dinted breastplate, his expression studiously set to the very formula of deprecation.

The rabbit eyes seemed all pupil in their searching watchfulness of him.

"God forbid!" said the priest at last, "that I deny succour to the worst of His erring sons. But what is this courage that, in its aggregate, roars down the world, and, disintegrated, cries for help, abasing itself before the least of its would-be victims?"

His tone and speech, to the common hearing, were sufficiently fraught with a sarcastic bitterness. But, in moments of excitement, he would relapse into his native Low German, the barbarous gutturals of which, shouldering their way amongst the crisp bowing idioms of the more courtly tongue, would confound the intelligibility they sought to emphasise. Therefore Corporal Lacoste—whose hearing, indeed, was at the moment a diffuse faculty—took no umbrage of the affront, and recognised only that the priest—as he pushed by him to pass on his way—was pattering *aves* innumerable in expiation of his late verbal transgression.

At what number he ceased, having squared his account with Heaven, it did not appear; and in the meanwhile he was going with his dancing step up the glen, having first signed to the wounded soldier to follow him.

Before Corporal Lacoste's eyes the goblin figure rose from terrace to terrace of the pass, mounting to the chill black portico, as it were, of the forest above. Reaching this, it turned, beckoned, and faced about—and immediately darkness took it at a gulp.

Instinctive mockery, some old-worn rags of reverence, contempt, and trepidation were all confused in the soldier's mind with an ever-present consciousness of suffering. His skull—as he reeled in pursuit of the gnomish thing by endless corridors of trunks, stark and silent, above which the roof, like slabs of stone, let in slits and blotches of piercing light—seemed to sway to the roll of a shifting cargo of quicksilver, his legs to move independent of any will to control them. But through all he never lost sight of the fact that he was a *beau sabreur*. His sword, flapping against his thigh, was a link long enough to connect any apparent discrepancies in mind or matter. He longed very ardently, nevertheless, for a period to be put to his pain and fatigue.

Still the priest went on before, flitting and hopping like some ungainly lob of the underworld, by glades of thronging gloom as voiceless and sightless as the streets of an excavated city. Once or twice only he turned about sharply as he sped.

"It pleases you," he would demand, "to know how your comrades left you without thought or care where you fell?"

"*Mon père*," the cuirassier would cry, answering, "it pleases me in that my abandonment means their success. Pity is, in truth, a flower; but one cannot stop to pick flowers during a pursuit."

Again, to emphasise a final inquiry, the monk had fallen back a little.

"What is this emperor, then, to you?"

"He is my god!" Corporal Lacoste had answered promptly.

"Be the measure of his mercy thy judgment," had been the reply; and thereat they had come into a sudden mist of twilight, that broadened and increased until it broke into the blinding glare of day beating upon a little house set in the flat of a snowy clearing.

Corporal Lacoste started, hung fire, and dropped his hand to his sword-hilt.

"A tavern!" he exclaimed.

The priest wheeled round and faced him, his head cocked derisively in the shadow of his cowl.

"And what better house of rest and entertainment to a brave *chasseur* of the Emperor?" said he.

"But the people, my father! It is to lead a blind man into a nest of hornets!"

"Truly, if you fear the stings of beauty. There is no peril other than that."

The frost was in the trooper's blood, and sickness in his brain.

"Lead on!" he cried. "A gallant soldier dreads neither man nor devil."

They went forward to the house. It was a mean enough little shanty, sloughing piecemeal its skin of rough-cast. From the thatched lean-to of the porch, that went up to the broken shingles of the roof above, a pole, with a withered fardel of heather tied to its end, stuck out like an ironical fingerpost to signify to the convivial wanderer any direction but that immediately behind it.

Nevertheless, the two men passed under, walking straight into a ramshackle kitchen, where only the figure of a solitary wench moved in a world of disorder.

She was busying herself desultorily near a great open hearth, above which projected a wedge-shaped chimney-hood of battered plaster, with an iron chain and hook pendulous from its sooty maw. A crazy wooden partition cut the room at a third of its length; and over this appeared the top of a ladder, on whose highest rung a squatting hen reposed. Some steaming dish-cloths drooped from a line; parings and foul greasy scraps littered the corners into which they had been kicked; and the brick floor was everywhere sodden, as from the precipitated atmosphere of much unsqueamish revelry.

"Wilma, *mein mädchen*," said the priest, softly.

The girl glanced round and up, as she stooped. The gallant Corporal's heart seemed to fill to so great an extent as to ease the throbbing of his wounds. This composed, this actually stolid-looking jade in her stone-grey petticoat and striped corset and degraded slippers—*corne et tonnerre!* she was a very Hebe, a wall-peach, a china-rose of prettiness. One might wish to cull her face at its slender neck like a flower, and put it in a vase of fragrant water to watch the blue eyes bud and open.

"Here," said Corporal Lacoste, "I may divest myself of all fear save that this love is plighted to another."

The girl expressed no surprise, no concern, very little interest. Indeed she did not understand a word that he spoke. But the priest interpreted.

"He would swear his heart to you at the outset. He is a wounded enemy that had not the courage to enter until I assured him that you were alone. Now he would willingly value his life at the price of your favour. Wilt thou minister to him, Wilma?"

"Ask him," said the girl, in a low dull voice, "why the peril lies here when all our manhood is flown to Vienna?"

The soldier stood smiling, and desperately catching himself from an inclination to faint.

"But it is right, is it not, Wilma," continued the priest, without heeding her answer, "to forgive our enemies, though they come like the wolves at night into a peaceful fold, wantonly harrying and destroying? '*Et dimitte nobis debita nostra.*' Yet we must trespass to be forgiven; and heaven loves a repentant sinner, Wilma."

"Where is my father?" said the girl (they seemed to talk at cross-purposes). "Hast thou left him down there?"

"I saw him watching us from ambush. Be assured he will follow soon."

The girl turned away.

"The stranger, like any other," she said coldly, "can share, for the paying, in whatever he and his devil-comrades have left us;" and with that she went to feel her drying dish-clouts.

The priest turned upon the Corporal.

"It is the custom in our Bavarian inns," said he, "for the guest to bring his own food. Wine, you will understand, is another matter."

"*S'il ne tient qu'à Ça!*" cried Corporal Lacoste jovially. "I have meat in my haversack and louis-d'ors in my pouch. We will make a feast, my father!"

He was so direfully in need of stimulant that he would do nothing till he had drunk.

"Here!" he shouted arrogantly, conscious of the hesitation of the other; and he fetched out and clapped upon a plank-table hard by a fistful of jangling pieces.

"Put them away," said the priest, his eyes quite rigid in their sockets. "My profession is one of faith."

He profited by demonstration, however, to give an entirely generous order. Wilma attended to it with the cold tranquillity that seemed to characterise all her actions. She was like a beautiful cataleptic.

The hole in Corporal Lacoste's head served as no vent, apparently, to the heady Steinwein. The core of heat it represented appeared rather to aggravate the potency of the fumes. He reddened, he sang, he rattled; by the time he had put down his share of the first bottle he was clamorous with good-fellowship and braggadocio.

"*Oh, mon Dieu Jésus!*" he cried; "to accuse us of stripping you when, in this chance corner, I find such wine and such beauty!"

The monk was no coy tosspot. He pledged the other glass for glass, till his heated face glared forward of its cowl like a great opening nasturtium bud. He showed, moreover, a tendency to coarseness and violence of speech that effectively counter-buffed the soldier's insolence.

Corporal Lacoste's veins were flushed to their remotest channels. They made up in fever what they had lost in measure. Once he suddenly leapt to his feet.

"To pluck the fruit that will not fall!" he shouted—and staggered away from the table.

In a moment the priest had risen and thrown himself upon him. He was little and underweighted; but he held the cuirassier in a clutch as crippling as that of a "scavenger's daughter."

"You go to insult the maid!" he shrieked. "My God, I will tear your heart out!"

Corporal Lacoste vainly struggled, shaken with crapulous laughter.

"But for dessert to the feast!" he protested: "my lips only to the warm side of the peach!"

The part profile of Wilma, seated knitting against the farther lintel of a rough opening in the partition, seemed unruffled by the least interest or apprehension. It did not even turn towards the wrestling men.

At the instant, as it happened, that these came to the floor, the priest uppermost, the house-door was flung open, and a man ran into the room.

"Hold his hands from his neck, my father!" cried this newcomer, in a small biting voice; and, flicking a thin knife from his sleeve, he dropped quickly upon his knees at the head of the labouring soldier and raised his arm.

The monk uttered a stifled oath.

"Down, down!" he cried in fury, as if to a dog. "Don't you see the girl?"

The man leapt to his feet, springing straight from his soles backwards with an odd nimble movement. There he stood watching the soldier—his eyes as sharp as flint-stones—as the latter, released by the monk, scrambled upright, staggering.

The trooper, the instant he felt himself free, swept his blade from its sheath.

"The sword of Corporal Lacoste!" he shouted, the wild tipsy Gascon. "Is there a wolf here will set his tooth against that?"

The word might have been haphazard—or vinously inspired. For, indeed, the face and attitude of the man opposite him were curiously wolfish in character—the temples wide, the forehead sweeping downwards and forth into a pinched snout, the projecting underjaw spiked with savage teeth and hung with tangs of brindled hair. If, for the rest, the creature was phenomenally small and lithe and active for a Bavarian peasant, still it was a peasant patently and clothed as such, from its close-bodied homespun tunic belted by a crimson sash, and its rusty cloak buckled under the right arm, to its cap of mangy fur from which a flock of coarse hair fell upon its shoulders.

"The sword of Corporal Lacoste!" howled the soldier again, and spun his weapon so that it whistled, making an arc of light.

The stranger stood rigidly set, the hilt of his long lancet clutched against his shoulder, his head thrust forward like a pointing hound's. There could be no least doubt as to which would prove the deadlier adversary.

Now, as they stood a moment, watchful of each other, the apple in the peasant's throat flickered of a sudden; and immediately a rising moan, a very strange little ululation, began to make itself audible, and the man lifted his chin, as if to give some voice in him freer passage. At once the priest, in an ecstasy of haste, flung himself between the two.

"On the threshold of the Church!" he screamed; "and the girl looking on!"

For the first time, indeed, Wilma was alert.

The peasant relaxed from his rigid pose. Corporal Lacoste saw the man's tongue, curling like a red leaf, pass over and across his upper lip. The movement gave him a little thrilling shock, as if of terror.

"What am I to do, my father?" asked the creature.

The priest pushed back his cowl and passed a trembling hand across his forehead.

"The cards," he muttered confusedly, affecting an impossible laugh. "Let us reconcile all over a bout at ombre."

He suddenly bethought himself, and repeated his proposal in French. The soldier threw his sword into the air, recovered it by the hilt, and returned it to its sheath.

"At bottle or pasteboard!" he cried: "*c'la m'est égal*—I am a match for the devil!"

He seemed, at least, a match for these commoner spirits. Luck stood at his shoulder, as was befitting when a *beau sabreur* of Murat staked against a clown and a Friar-Rush.

The three played and drank and wrangled up to midday of the blessed bright morn. Not a soul came in to disturb them. The neighbourhood, it appeared, was depopulated by conscription—stunned by fear. Only the girl moved staidly in the background of the reeking kitchen, quite silent over her simple duties, even when from time to time she brought a fresh bottle to the table and came under fire of the reckless trooper's badinage.

The play waxed fast and furious. Oaths and execrations, flying from fecund lips, seemed to swarm obscenely under the very rafters overhead. The monk, educated perhaps to the rich vocabulary of anathema, was peculiarly apt at fulminating expletive. He bawled and he cursed from the conscious standpoint of privilege. He never damned but to hell, or failed to translate his most consuming maledictions for the soldier's benefit.

Now it chanced that once during the morning Corporal Lacoste, happening to glance up as Wilma fetched an empty jug from their midst in order to the replenishing of it, saw the girl's strange eyes fixed upon him in a curious stare. She looked away immediately; but he rose, took the jug from her with a "*permettez-moi, mam'selle*," and followed her to the rear of the premises.

The lip of the dog-man lifted. The priest caught his hand in a warning clinch.

"Between Angelus and Angelus, Wolfzahn," he muttered.

"What does he with the girl, then, my father?"

"What does he? The wine consumes his nerve. He is a man of gingerbread. Let him be."

"How came we to miss him down there? Between Angelus and Angelus, say'st thou? So! I will whet my tooth. But beware, my father! the dark in these days is an early guest. How came we to miss him—him and his fat gold pieces?"

"Hush! *Der Herr Jesus* recompenses otherwise the agents of

His vengeance. Little Wolfzahn, the gold shall pay for masses to his soul—his, and the others. Not here, before the girl! The devil, I think, has commerce with her nowadays. Often I see him peep from the windows of her eyes. Between Angelus and Angelus: one snap of thy tooth—and there are twenty fresh indulgences to quit thee of thy purgatory."

"But, here, in the forest! Ah, *mein Vater!* when will thy indulgences quit me of this in the forest?"

The strange creature gave a sort of sob, a bay, and buried his face in his hands.

In the meanwhile Corporal Lacoste followed Wilma to the cellar. She neither invited nor repulsed him. She went down a flight of humid steps, through a square aperture in the floor, into a little musty cavern, the walls of which seemed all eyes. These were the "kicks" of bottles whose long snouts were thrust into wooden racks. Elsewhere a cask or two lolled on its belly, its tap run into purple like a drowsy drunken nose; and the tracks of snails went all over the ceiling.

The girl struck light from a flint, kindled a greasy dip, and, holding it in her hand, turned suddenly round on her escort. Her face was alive with some secret emotion. The soldier, in whose brain a wanton fever flared, swayed himself steady, endeavouring to return her gaze.

"Ludwig!" she whispered hurriedly— "my Ludwig that went with Wimpffen's dragoons to defend the pass,—my Ludwigchen that would have taken me out of hell. When I caught thy face against the light, *ach, mein Gott!* I could have cried in pain. Thou art so like him."

She held the candle nearer the fuddled stupid eyes. Her own glittered to them like sparks through a curtain of smoke. She drew back with a quick hopeless movement.

"But I forget," she murmured. "Thou canst not understand—nor would, nor would, though we spoke in one language."

She filled the jug, and went hastily past him. Then, at a thought, she turned, with her foot on the first step, and spoke back into his very ear, "*Hüten Sie sich vor dem Wehrwolf!*"

"Wilma!" howled her father from above.

Corporal Lacoste reeled back to his cards, with an obfuscated impression that something of moment had been spoken to him. His soul, pregnantly engaged in hatching wind-eggs, squatted in a little private dark-house of cunning, from which it looked forth as full of self-importance as a monkey in a cage.

Now, again, play being resumed, the fetid air of the kitchen blattered with oaths. It was as if, approaching a dunghill, the returned gambler had disturbed a settled cloud of flies.

Howl, and uproar, and the jangle of unbridled tongues! A knife was drawn; the soldier staggered to his feet, and his chair crashed on the floor. At the moment a timepiece tinkled out midday from some attic above. The priest flung up his arm and yelled, "Angelus, Angelus, ye swine of the Gadarenes!"

He fell upon his knees. "*Angelus Domini nuntiavit Mariæ*," he began to gabble.

"*Et concepit de Spiritu Sancto*," responded the peasant, who, at the word, had pulled from his breast a little leaden image of St Christopher carrying a baby Christ, and prostrated himself before it.

But as to Corporal Lacoste, it was for him to drop upon the floor and asleep simultaneously.

Something—it might have been a savagely restrained kick—aroused the slumbering man. He started up, sitting, and beat away a red-hot film of cobwebs that seemed to stretch and flicker before his eyes. Slowly at first, then by sickening leaps, consciousness returned to him. He looked vacantly from point to point of the frowsy kitchen. Wilma sat knitting as though she had never moved; the doglike peasant crouched on the hearth, his red eyes glinting back the ember-glow; and whenever he yawned a little singing whine issued from his throat. The priest, his hands as heretofore vanished up the meeting cuffs of his cassock, his cowl pulled forward over his eyes, stood a yard withdrawn from and looking down upon him. At the sound of the first word between them the creature before the fire flashed alert.

"The noon draws on," said the monk. "If you wish to track your comrades in safety you must be out of the forest before dusk."

The trooper got to his feet. He was steady enough on them now. It was his head that seemed to roll and totter.

"I have delayed too long already," he cried peevishly. "What does the sword of Corporal Lacoste in this ignoble den? To death or victory, my father—if I but knew the way!"

The monk whistled to the man on the hearth.

"Up!" he cried; "he would have us show him the way—to victory or death. The issue is his."

He turned to the soldier.

"It is the will of God that shall be wrought at the hands of His agents."

"Meaning thyself, my father?"

"Surely, and Wolfzahn here. Arise, and we will put thee on thy road."

"Thou wear'st His livery, at least. *Corne et tonnerre!* it is true a priest must not be judged out of his own mouth. To refute the devil one must speak the devil's tongue. And, after all, thy face rounds as jovial as an English rennet."

"Hasten!" cried the peasant from the door, to which he had run. "I can hear far off the dusk striking amongst the trees like a wood-reeve."

"A moment, Wolfzahn!" exclaimed the priest. "One parting dram of brandy for a lock to the stomach!"

As Corporal Lacoste took his *petit-verre* from Wilma he was troubled by a desperately elusive thought of some confidence that had passed between him and her. Then he remembered that they had no word in common. It could not be. As for any temptation to gallantry, the nausea following debauch had robbed him of all inclination to it.

But glancing back once, when he had swaggered from the house into the shuddering chillness of the snow without, it startled him to see, as he thought, the white face of the girl pressed against the lattice. The sight, the shadow, gave him a momentary thrill of uneasiness—something like a strange swerve of the heart that was surely inexplicable in a *sabreur* of the great army.

After the turn of noon a sombreness of cloud had usurped the happy throne of morning. The forest had fallen into deathly silence. The trees were ranked stiffly, each seeming to edge into each in terror of some nameless oppression. From the hollows came trooping grey spectres of mist that climbed the branches to overlook the travellers, or peered stealthily from behind enormous trunks. Not a voice, not a sound but the squeaking crunch of the wayfarers' feet as they trod the beds of snow that had silted through the openings in the roof above, broke the vast quiet.

This was a matter of concern to the swashbuckler Corporal, who rose many times from the deep waters of his dejection to clutch at some straw of comfort in the shape of a monosyllabic utterance by one or other of his guides. It was of no use. The straw would sink with him, leaving him again submerged.

Suddenly light grew upon them—light wan and grudging, but still a beacon of hope. At the same moment their ears were aware of a long quarrelling moan—a diffuse liquid snarl uttered and echoed from a score of points on the ground below them on their left. The peasant, who led, sprang at the instant behind a tree, from the covert of which he looked forth and down into a narrow sloping defile—that very riven pass in which the wounded soldier had spent the night.

The priest stood stricken, petrified, where he had halted at the top of the glen, in a wedge of white slanting mist. The wondering trooper hurried to join him.

"*Mon Dieu Jésus!*" cried the latter, dumfounded; "is it that way we must go?"

The gorge was dotted with wolves—ravenous, unclean. Wherever a shapeless bulge of cloth, a hooped flank of man or charger projected, there a bloody snout burrowed and tore, spattering the white with red.

Corporal Lacoste drew and whirled aloft his sabre.

"Forward, comrades!" he shouted. "It is the sword of Corporal Lacoste!"

He was a man again—a *beau sabreur* of the wild Murat in face of immediate danger. He ran down into the glen alone and slashed at the first brute he reached. It fled screaming, a near-severed ear flapping against its jaw as it galloped.

He paused a moment, turned, and beckoned to the two above him. They were drawn together, and the priest, it appeared, was frantically beating back the other from descending.

"*Canaille!*" hissed Corporal Lacoste between his teeth, and he faced about once more to his business of aggression.

The alarm was gone abroad. The beasts, converging from their isolated positions, were forming into a compact body.

To the tactician, the moment of rally offers as full opportunity for assault as the moment of retreat. Either is the twilight of disorder. Corporal Lacoste snatched a flung cloak from the ground, wrapped it about his left arm, and with a screaming *huée!* charged down upon the foe.

At the very outset the wings of the dastard troop folded back before the furious onrush, leaving the formation a wedge. The point of this the soldier crumpled up, thrusting and threshing. His blade flung aloft a spray of crimson; the whole hotch-potch of writhing shapes seemed to boil into hideous jangle; he shrieked again and again as he drove his way into it. Then in a moment the pass was won. The pack, recoiling upon its rear to escape the swinging flail, fell into demoralisation, showed its panic tail, and went off in a wind of uproar down the glen.

The instant they were vanished, the monk and his companion descended from their coign of "reserve." The soldier held out his dripping weapon mutely, and with a stare of scorn.

"It is, in truth, a blade worthy of the arm that wields it," cried the priest cringingly. His voice shook. He kept glancing furtively at the peasant by his side. This man's eyes had a strange glare in them, and his mouth was dribbling.

Corporal Lacoste cleansed his sword scrupulously on the cloak he had appropriated.

"Dishonouring blood," he said, "for the imbruing of a noble weapon! But—*corne et tonnerre!*—a king must take tribute of chief and villain alike. At least, now, the stain is wiped away."

He ran the sword back into its scabbard with a clank.

"*En avant!*" he cried disdainfully, and swaggered off down the defile.

Perhaps for a mile they proceeded in this order, the *beau sabreur* indulging his fancy with a priest and a peasant for lackeys. Now and again he would turn and cry "Which way?"—but, for the rest, he condescended to no familiarity with cravens.

By-and-by the dead air lightened, the trees thinning so as to make but a ragged canopy of the snow overhead. Then the toiling monk quavered out a "halt!" to him that strode in front.

"Monsieur," he panted, "it necessitates that we part at the cross-track."

"How, then!" exclaimed Corporal Lacoste, facing about.

The two men advanced. The peasant passed the trooper a half-dozen paces, and wheeled round softly. They were all by then come into a little open dell, drowsy with snow, into which the fog drooped from above, like smoke in the down-draught of a chimney. Not a twig of all the laden bushes stirred. The very heart of nature, frozen and constricted, had ceased of its audible beating.

The priest pulled his cowl farther over his eyes.

"My God, the cold!" he muttered. Then he appeared to shudder himself into fury.

"Have we not brought you far enough? Thither goes the road to St. Pölten and Wien. *Mein Gott*, the assurance, the assurance—!"

He leapt back. The point of the wolf's tooth had almost pricked him as it shot through Corporal Lacoste's throat.

"*Stehen sie auf!* ah, you devil!" he sobbed, as the dog-man threw himself upon the quivering tumbled body, snarling and quarrelling with the knife that would not be withdrawn.

Suddenly a terrible lust overtook the onlooker. He tore the trooper's sword from its sheath and slashed at the senseless face till the blade streamed.

"The blood of a wolf!" he screeched,— "of a ravisher and despoiler! Unbuckle me the scabbard. It shall stay here—the red shall stay, and mingle presently, for all his boasting, with that of the beasts to which he was kin!"

For long the winged flakes had fallen, the huddled labyrinths of the forest been dense as with the myriad settling of ghost-moths. Here, indeed, was the spinning-mill of Fate, drawing steadily, relentlessly, from the loaded distaff of the clouds, working an impenetrable warp for the snaring of forfeited lives.

Lost, gasping, and horrorstricken, the monk stumbled aimlessly onward, the trooper's sheathed sword clasped convulsively—half unconsciously—under his arm, the trooper's gold clinking in his mendicant pouch. He beat his way anywhither among the glimmering trunks, and the terror of hell was in his soul.

For, not a hundred paces of their return journey had the murderers traversed, when the blinding hood of the snow-wraith shut upon the shameful scene—upon all the woodlands of Amstetten, blotting out the voiceless passes, obscuring and confusing the familiar avenues of retreat. Too well then these men realised, out of their knowledge of it, the menace of the dumb eclipse—of the trackless silence that no instinct might interpret. But the fulness of dismay was for one only of the two.

In a minute they were astray; at the end of an hour, two hours, they were still ice-bound wanderers—white spectres of the living death. And so at last the natural dusk, weaving weft into warp of darkness, had crept upon them; and a greater fear, long-foreshadowed, had knocked at the priest's heart—a sickening thud to every step he took. Then his eyes, straining in the inhuman blackness, would seek frantically to resolve the character of that that pattered at his side; and he had jibbed as he walked, daring neither to question nor to touch.

Suddenly an attenuated whimper, that swelled to a piercing yaup, had sounded at his very ear, and something had leapt from his neighbourhood and gone scurrying into the darkness.

Then he knew that what he had dreaded had befallen, and the utter ecstasy of horror entered into and possessed his soul.

Now, all in a moment, he broke from the thronged terrorism of trees into a little ghastly glen. A bursting sigh, compound of a dozen clashing emotions, issued from his lungs. He could faintly see here once more; and he knew himself to have happened upon that very pass wherein he had been busy in the morning imbruing his hands, by wolfish proxy, in the blood of the wounded.

But he had not climbed a score of yards up the slope in a whirl of flakes when a guttural sound, that seemed to come from almost under his feet, shocked him to a pause. He stood, forcibly striving to constrict his heart lest the thud of it knocking on his ribs should betray him. For the wolves were in the glen again. His every nerve jumped to the consciousness of their neighbourhood.

The swinish sound went on. Suddenly the ticking wheel of Life touched off its alarum. Wrought to the topping-pitch of endurance, he gave way, uttering scream after scream in a mere paralysis of fright. The whole glen seemed to howl in echo: there came a snarling rush.

Who had shouted it?— "The sword of Corporal Lacoste!" The cry, he could have sworn, clanged in his frantic ears. It rallied him to recollection of what he held in his hand. The sword! At least, in his despair, he could endeavour to do with it as he had seen done.

A score of rabid snouts budded through the gloom before him. He clutched at the hilt. Some latent memory, perhaps, of the stinging thrash of the weapon it looked upon kept the pack at bay a moment. But clutch and tear as the priest might, the blade would not come forth. The lust of hatred that had sheathed it, wet with the life of its victim, had recoiled upon itself. Corporal Lacoste still claimed his sword—claimed it by testimony of his blood, that had dried upon it, gluing it within its scabbard.

A low laugh issued from the thick of the pack—an unearthly bark confusedly blended of the utterance of beast and man. It was as if some one brute, intelligent above his fellows, had realised the humour of the situation.

A grey snout, grinning and slavering from a single long tooth, came nozzling itself through the herd.

The priest screamed and fell upon his knees.

WILLIAM TYRWHITT'S "COPY"
(1899)

This is the story of William Tyrwhitt, who went to King's Cobb for rest and change, and, with the latter, at least, was so far accommodated as for a time to get beyond himself and into regions foreign to his experiences or his desires. And for this condition of his I hold myself something responsible, inasmuch as it was my inquisitiveness was the means of inducing him to an exploration, of which the result, with its measure of weirdness, was for him alone. But, it seems, I was appointed an agent of the unexplainable without my knowledge, and it was simply my misfortune to find my first unwitting commission in the selling of a friend.

I was for a few days, about the end of a particular July, lodged in that little old seaboard town of Dorset that is called King's Cobb. Thither there came to me one morning a letter from William Tyrwhitt, the polemical journalist (a queer fish, like the cuttle, with an ink-bag for the confusion of enemies), complaining that he was fagged and used up, and desiring me to say that nowhere could complete rest be obtained as in King's Cobb.

I wrote and assured him on this point. The town, I said, lay wrapped in the hills as in blankets, its head only, winking a sleepy eye, projecting from the top of the broad steep gully in which it was stretched at ease. Thither few came to the droning coast; and such as did, looked up at the High Street baking in the sun, and, thinking of Jacob's ladder, composed them to slumber upon the sand and left the climbing to the angels. Here, I said, the air and the sea were so still that one could hear the oysters snoring in their beds; and the little frizzle of surf on the beach was like to the sound to dreaming ears of bacon frying in the kitchens of the blest.

William Tyrwhitt came, and I met him at the station, six or seven miles away. He was all strained and springless, like a broken child's toy— "not like that William who, with lance in rest, shot through the lists in Fleet Street." A disputative galley-puller could have triumphed over him morally; a child physically.

The drive in the inn brake, by undulating roads and scented valleys, shamed his cheek to a little flush of self-assertion.

"I will sleep under the vines," he said, "and the grapes shall drop into my mouth."

"Beware," I answered, "lest in King's Cobb your repose should be everlasting. The air of that hamlet has matured like old port in the bin of its hills, till to drink of it is to swoon."

We alighted at the crown of the High Street, purposing to descend on foot the remaining distance to the shore.

"Behold," I exclaimed, "how the gulls float in the shimmer, like ashes tossed aloft by the white draught of a fire! Behold these ancient buildings nodding to the everlasting lullaby of the bay waters! The cliffs are black with the heat apoplexy; the lobster is drawn scarlet to the surface. You shall be like an addled egg put into an incubator."

"So," he said, "I shall rest and not hatch. The very thought is like sweet oil on a burn."

He stayed with me a week, and his body waxed wondrous round and rosy, while his eye acquired a foolish and vacant expression. So it was with me. We rolled together, by shore and by road of this sluggard place, like spent billiard balls; and if by chance we cannoned, we swerved sleepily apart, until, perhaps, one would fall into a pocket of the sand, and the other bring up against a cushion of sea-wall.

Yet, for all its enervating atmosphere, King's Cobb has its fine traditions of a sturdy independence, and a slashing history withal; and its aspect is as picturesque as that of an opera bouffe fishing-harbour. Then, too, its High Street, as well as its meandering rivulets of low streets, is rich in buildings, venerable and antique.

We took an irresponsible, smiling pleasure in noting these advantages—particularly after lunch; and sometimes, where an old house was empty, we would go over it, and stare at beams and chimneypieces and hear the haunted tale of its fortunes, with a faint half-memory in our breasts of that one-time bugbear we had known as "copy." But though more than once a flaccid instinct would move us to have out our pencils, we would only end by bunging our foolish mouths with them, as if they were cigarettes, and then vaguely wondering at them for that, being pencils, they would not draw.

By then we were so sinewless and demoralized that we could hear in the distant strains of the European Concert nothing but an orchestra of sweet sounds, and would have given ourselves away in any situation with a pound of tea. Therefore, perhaps, it was well for us that, a peremptory summons to town reaching me after seven days of comradeship with William, I must make shift to collect my faculties with my effects, and return to the more bracing climate of Fleet Street.

And here, you will note, begins the story of William Tyrwhitt, who would linger yet a few days in that hanging garden of the south coast, and who would pull himself together and collect matter for "copy."

He found a very good subject that first evening of his solitude.

I was to leave in the afternoon, and the morning we spent in aimlessly rambling about the town. Towards mid-day, a slight shower drove us to shelter under the green verandah of a house, standing up from the lower fall of the High Street, that we had often observed in our wanderings. This house—or rather houses, for it was a block of two—was very tall and odd-looking, being all built of clean squares of a whitish granite; and the double porch in the middle base—led up to by side-going steps behind thin iron railings—roofed with green-painted zinc. In some of the windows were jalousies, but the general aspect of the exterior was gaunt and rigid; and the whole block bore a dismal, deserted look, as if it had not been lived in for years.

Now we had taken refuge in the porch of that half that lay uppermost on the slope; and here we noticed that, at a late date, the building was seemingly in process of repair, painters' pots and brushes lying on a window-sill, and a pair of steps showing within through the glass.

"They have gone to dinner," said I. "Supposing we seize the opportunity to explore?"

We pushed at the door; it yielded. We entered, shut ourselves in, and paused to the sound of our own footsteps echoing and laughing from corners and high places. On the ground floor were two or three good-sized rooms with modern grates, but cornices, chimney-pieces, embrasures finely Jacobean. There were innumerable under-stair and over-head cupboards, too, and pantries, and closets, and passages going off darkly into the unknown.

We clomb the stairway—to the first floor—to the second. Here was all pure Jacobean; but the walls were crumbling, the paper peeling, the windows dim and foul with dirt.

I have never known a place with such echoes. They shook from a footstep like nuts rattling out of a bag; a mouse behind the skirting led a whole camp-following of them; to ask a question was, as in that other House, to awaken the derisive shouts of an Opposition. Yet, in the intervals of silence, there fell a deadliness of quiet that was quite appalling by force of contrast.

"Let us go down," I said. "I am feeling creepy."

"Pooh!" said William Tyrwhitt; "I could take up my abode here with a feather bed."

We descended, nevertheless. Arrived at the ground floor, "I am going to the back," said William.

I followed him—a little reluctantly, I confess. Gloom and shadow had fallen upon the town, and this old deserted hulk of an abode was ghostly to a degree. There was no film of dust on its every shelf or sill that did not seem to me to bear the impress of some phantom finger feeling its way along. A glint of stealthy eyes would look from dark uncertain corners; a thin evil vapour appear to rise through the cracks of the boards from the unvisited cellars in the basement.

And here, too, we came suddenly upon an eccentricity of outbuilding that wrought upon our souls with wonder. For, penetrating to the rear through what might have been a cloak-closet or butler's pantry, we found a supplementary wing, or rather tail of rooms, loosely knocked together, to proceed from the back, forming a sort of skilling to the main building. These rooms led direct into one another, and, consisting of little more than timber and plaster, were in a woeful state of dilapidation. Everywhere the laths grinned through torn gaps in the ceilings and walls; everywhere the latter were blotched and mildewed with damp, and the floorboards rotting in their tracks. Fallen mortar, rusty tins, yellow teeth of glass, whitened soot—all the decay and rubbish of a generation of neglect littered the place and filled it with an acrid odour. From one of the rooms we looked forth through a little discoloured window upon a patch of forlorn weedy garden, where the very cats glowered in a depression that no surfeit of mice could assuage.

We went on, our nervous feet apologetic to the grit they crunched; and, when we were come to near the end of this dreary annexe, turned off to the left into a short gloom of passage that led to a closed door.

Pushing this open, we found a drop of some half-dozen steps, and, going gingerly down these, stopped with a common exclamation of surprise on our lips.

Perhaps our wonder was justified, for we were in the stern cabin of an ancient West Indiaman.

Some twenty feet long by twelve wide—there it all was, from the deck transoms above, to the side lockers and great curved window, sloping outwards to the floor and glazed with little panes in galleries, that filled the whole end of the room. Thereout we looked, over the degraded garden, to the lower quarters of the town—as if, indeed, we were perched high up on waves—and even to a segment of the broad bay that swept by them.

But the room itself! What phantasy of old sea-dog or master-mariner had conceived it? What palsied spirit, condemned to rust in inactivity, had found solace in this burlesque of shipcraft? To renew the past in such a fixture, to work oneself up to the old glow of flight and action, and then, while one stamped and rocked maniacally, to feel the refusal of so much as a timber to respond to one's fervour of animation! It was a grotesque picture.

Now, this cherished chamber had shared the fate of the rest. The paint and gilding were all cracked and blistered away; much of the glass of the stern-frame was gone or hung loose in its sashes; the elaborately carved lockers mouldered on the walls.

These were but dummies when we came to examine them—mere slabs attached to the brickwork, and decaying with it.

"There should be a case-bottle and rummers in one, at least," said William Tyrwhitt.

"There are, sir, at your service," said a voice behind us.

We started and turned.

It had been such a little strained voice that it was with something like astonishment I looked upon the speaker. Whence he had issued I could not guess; but there he stood behind us, nodding and smiling—a squab, thick-set old fellow with a great bald head, and, for all the hair on his face, a tuft like a teasel sprouting from his under lip.

He was in his shirt-sleeves, without coat or vest; and I noticed that his dirty lawn was oddly plaited in front, and that about his ample paunch was buckled a broad belt of leather. Greased hip-boots encased his lower limbs, and the heels of these were drawn together as he bowed.

William Tyrwhitt—a master of nervous English—muttered "Great Scott!" under his breath.

"Permit me," said the stranger—and he held out to us a tin pannikin (produced from Heaven knows where) that swam with fragrance.

I shook my head. William Tyrwhitt, that fated man, did otherwise. He accepted the vessel and drained it.

"It smacks of all Castille," he said, handing it back with a sigh of ecstasy. "Who the devil are you, sir?"

The stranger gave a little crow.

"Peregrine Iron, sir, at your service—Captain Peregrine Iron, of the *Raven* sloop amongst others. You are very welcome to the run of my poor abode."

"Yours?" I murmured in confusion. "We owe you a thousand apologies."

"Not at all," he said, addressing all his courtesy to William. Me, since my rejection of his beaker, he took pains to ignore.

"Not at all," he said. "Your intrusion was quite natural under the circumstances. I take a pleasure in being your cicerone. This cabin (he waved his hand pompously)—a fancy of mine, sir, a fancy of mine. The actual material of the latest of my commands brought hither and adapted to the exigencies of shore life. It enables me to live eternally in the past—a most satisfying illusion. Come to-night and have a pipe and a glass with me."

I thought William Tyrwhitt mad.

"I will come, by all means," he said.

The stranger bowed us out of the room.

"That is right," he exclaimed. "You will find me here. Good-bye for the present."

As we plunged like dazed men into the street, now grown sunny, I turned on my friend.

"William," I said, "did you happen to look back as we left the cabin?"

"No."

"I did."

"Well?"

"There was no stranger there at all. The place was empty."

"Well?"

"You will not go to-night?"

"You bet I do."

I shrugged my shoulders. We walked on a little way in silence. Suddenly my companion turned on me, a most truculent expression on his face.

"For an independent thinker," he said, "you are rather a pusillanimous jackass. A man of your convictions to shy at a shadow! Fie, sir, fie! What if the room *were* empty? The place was full enough of traps to permit of Captain Iron's immediate withdrawal."

Much may be expressed in a sniff. I sniffed.

That afternoon I went back to town, and left the offensive William to his fate.

It found him at once.

The very day following that of my retreat, I was polishing phrases by gaslight in the dull sitting-room of my lodgings in the Lambeth Road, when he staggered in upon me. His face was like a sheep's, white and vacant; his hands had caught a trick of groping blindly along the backs of chairs.

"You have obtained your 'copy'?" I said.

I made him out to murmur "yes" in a shaking under-voice. He was so patently nervous that I put him in a chair and poured him out a wine-glassful of London brandy. This generally is a powerful emetic, but it had no more effect upon him than water. Then I was about to lower the gas, to save his eyes, but he stopped me with a thin shriek.

"Light, light!" he whispered. "It cannot be too light for me!"

"Now, William Tyrwhitt," I said, by-and-by, watchful of him, and marking a faint effusion of colour soak to his cheek, "you would not accept my warning, and you were extremely rude to me. Therefore you have had an experience—"

"An awful one," he murmured.

"An awful one, no doubt; and to obtain surcease of the haunting memory of it, you must confide its processes to me. But, first, I must put it to you, which is the more pusillanimous—to refuse to submit one's manliness to the tyranny of the unlawful, or to rush into situations you have not the nerve to adapt yourself to?"

"I could not foresee, I could not foresee."

"Neither could I. And that was my very reason for declining the invitation. Now proceed."

It was long before he could. But presently he essayed, and gathered voice with the advance of his narrative, and even unconsciously threw it into something the form of "copy." And here it is as he murmured it, but with a gasp for every full-stop.

"I confess I was so far moved by the tone of your protest as, after your departure, to make some cautious inquiries about the house we had visited. I could discover nothing to satisfy my curiosity. It was known to have been untenanted for a great number of years; but as to who was the landlord, whether Captain Iron or another, no one could inform me; and the agent for the property was of the adjacent town where you met me. I was not fortunate, indeed, in finding that any one even knew of the oddly appointed room; but considering that, owing to the time the house had remained vacant, the existence of this eccentricity could be a tradition only with some casual few, my failure did not strike me as being at all bodeful. On the contrary, it only whetted my desire to investigate further in person, and penetrate to the heart of a very captivating little mystery. But probably, I thought, it is quite simple of solution, and the fact of the repairers and the landlord being in evidence at one time, a natural coincidence.

"I dined well, and sallied forth about nine o'clock. It was a night pregnant with possibilities. The lower strata of air were calm, but overhead the wind went down the sea with a noise of baggage-wagons, and there was an ominous hurrying and gathering together of forces under the bellying standards of the clouds.

"As I went up the steps of the lonely building, the High Street seemed to turn all its staring eyes of lamps in my direction. 'What a droll fellow!' they appeared to be saying; 'and how will he look when he reissues?'

"'There ain't nubbudy in that house,' croaked a small boy, who had paused below, squinting up at me.

"'How do you know?' said I. 'Move on, my little man.'

"He went; and at once it occurred to me that, as no notice was taken of my repeated knockings, I might as well try the handle. I did, found the door unlatched, as it had been in the morning, pushed it open, entered, and swung it to behind me.

"I found myself in the most profound darkness—that darkness, if I may use the paradox, of a peopled desolation that men of but little nerve or resolution find insupportable. To me, trained to a serenity of stoicism, it could make no demoralizing appeal. I had out my matchbox, opened it at leisure, and, while the whole vaulting blackness seemed to tick and rustle with secret movement, took a half-dozen vestas into my hand, struck one alight, and, by its dim radiance, made my way through the building by the passages we had penetrated in the morning. If at all I shrank or perspired on my spectral journey, I swear I was not conscious of doing so.

"I came to the door of the cabin. All was black and silent.

"'Ah!' I thought, 'the rogue has played me false.'

"Not to subscribe to an uncertainty, I pushed at the door, saw only swimming dead vacancy before me, and tripping at the instant on the sill, stumbled crashing into the room below and slid my length on the floor.

"Now, I must tell you, it was here my heart gave its first somersault. I had fallen, as I say, into a black vault of emptiness; yet, as I rose, bruised and dazed, to my feet, there was the cabin all alight from a great lanthorn that swung from the ceiling, and our friend of the morning seated at a table, with a case-bottle of rum and glasses before him.

"I stared incredulous. Yes, there could be no doubt it was he, and pretty flushed with drink, too, by his appearance.

"'Incandescent light in a West Indiaman!' I muttered; for not otherwise could I account for the sudden illumination. 'What the deuce!'

"'Belay that!' he growled. He seemed to observe me for the first time.

"'A handsome manner of boarding a craft you've got, sir,' said he, glooming at me.

"I was hastening to apologize, but he stopped me coarsely.

"'Oh, curse the long jaw of him! Fill your cheek with that, you Barbary ape, and wag your tail if you can, but burn your tongue.'

"He pointed to the case-bottle with a forefinger that was like a dirty parsnip. What induced me to swallow the insult, and even some of the pungent liquor of his rude offering? The itch for 'copy' was, no doubt, at the bottom of it.

"I sat down opposite my host, filled and drained a bumper. The fire ran to my brain, so that the whole room seemed to pitch and courtesy.

"'This is an odd fancy of yours,' I said.

"'What is?' said he.

"'This,' I answered, waving my hand around— 'this freak of turning a back room into a cabin.'

"He stared at me, and then burst into a malevolent laugh.

"'Back room, by thunder!' said he. 'Why, of course—just a step into the garden where the roses and the buttercupses be agrowing.'

"Now I pricked my ears.

"'Has the night turned foul?' I muttered. 'What a noise the rain makes beating on the window!'

"'It's like to be a foul one for you, at least,' said he. 'But, as for the rain, it's blazing moonlight.'

"I turned to the broad casement in astonishment. My God! what did I see? Oh, my friend, my friend! will you believe me? By the melancholy glow that spread therethrough I saw that the whole room was rising and sinking in rhythmical motion; that the lights of King's Cobb had disappeared, and that in their place was revealed a world of pale and tossing water, the pursuing waves of which leapt and clutched at the glass with innocuous fingers.

"I started to my feet, mad in an instant.

"'Look, look!' I shrieked. 'They follow us—they struggle to get at you, you bloody murderer!'

"They came rising on the crests of the billows; they hurried fast in our wake, tumbling and swaying, their stretched, drowned faces now lifted to the moonlight, now over-washed in the long trenches of water. They were rolled against the galleries of glass, on which their hair slapped like ribbons of seaweed—a score of ghastly white corpses, with strained black eyes and pointed stiff elbows crookt up in vain for air.

"I was mad, but I knew it all now. This was no house, but the good, ill-fated vessel *Rayo,* once bound for Jamaica, but on the voyage fallen into the hands of the bloody buccaneer, Paul Hardman, and her crew made to walk the plank, and most of her passengers. I knew that the dark scoundrel had boarded and mastered her, and—having first fired and sunk his own sloop—had steered her straight for the Cuban coast, making disposition of what remained of the passengers on the way, and I knew that my great-grandfather had been one of these doomed survivors, and that he had been shot and murdered under orders of the ruffian that now sat before me. All this, as retailed by one who sailed for a season under Hardman to save his skin, is matter of old private history; and of common report was it that the monster buccaneer, after years of successful trading in the ship he had stolen, went into secret and prosperous retirement under an assumed name, and was never heard of more on the high seas. But, it seemed, it was for the great-grandson of one of his victims to play yet a sympathetic part in the grey old tragedy.

"How did this come to me in a moment—or, rather, what was that dream buzzing in my brain of 'proof' and 'copy' and all the tame stagnation of a long delirium of order? I had nothing in common with the latter. In some telepathic way—influenced by these past-dated surroundings—dropped into the very den of this Procrustes of the seas, I was there to re-enact the fearful scene that had found its climax in the brain of my ancestor.

"I rushed to the window, thence back to within a yard of the glowering buccaneer, before whom I stood, with tost arms, wild and menacing.

"'They follow you!' I screamed. 'Passive, relentless, and deadly, they follow in your wake and will not be denied. The strong, the helpless, the coarse and the beautiful—all you have killed and mutilated in your wanton devilry—they are on your heels like a pack of spectre-hounds, and sooner or later they will have you in their cold arms and hale you down to the secret places of terror. Look at Beston, who leads, with a fearful smile on his mouth! Look at that pale girl you tortured, whose hair writhes and lengthens—a swarm of snakes nosing the hull for some open port-hole to enter by! Dog and devil, you are betrayed by your own hideous cruelty!'

"He rose and struck at me blindly; staggered, and found his filthy voice in a shriek of rage.

"'Jorinder! make hell of the galley-fire! Heat some irons red and fetch out a bucket of pitch. We'll learn this dandy galloot his manners!'

"Wrought to the snapping-point of desperation, I sprang at and closed with him; and we went down on the floor together with a heavy crash. I was weaponless, but I would choke and strangle him with my hands. I had him under, my fingers crookt in his throat. His eyeballs slipped forward, like banana ends squeezed from their skins; he could not speak or cry, but he put up one feeble hand and flapped it aimlessly. At that, in the midst of my fury, I glanced above me, and saw a press of dim faces crowding a dusk hatch; and from them a shadowy arm came through, pointing a weapon; and all my soul reeled sick, and I only longed to be left time to destroy the venomous horror beneath me before I passed.

"It was not to be. Something, a physical sensation like the jerk of a hiccup, shook my frame; and immediately the waters of being seemed to burst their dam and flow out peaceably into a valley of rest."

William Tyrwhitt paused, and "Well?" said I.

"You see me here," he said. "I woke this morning, and found myself lying on the floor of that shattered and battered closet, and a starved demon of a cat licking up something from the boards. When I drove her away, there was a patch there like ancient dried blood."

"And how about your head?"

"My head? Why, the bullet seemed stuck in it between the temples; and there I am afraid it is still."

"Just so. Now, William Tyrwhitt, you must take a Turkish, bath and some cooling salts, and then come and tell me all about it again."

"Ah! you don't believe me, I see. I never supposed you would. Good-night!"

But, when he was gone, I sat ruminating.

"That Captain Iron," I thought, "walked over the great rent in the floor without falling through. Well, well!"

THE ACCURSED CORDONNIER
(1900)

I

"Poor Chrymelus, I remember, arose from the diversion of a card-table, and dropped into the dwellings of darkness."—*Hervey*

It must be confessed that Amos Rose was considerably out of his element in the smoking-room off Portland Place. All the hour he remained there he was conscious of a vague rising nausea, due not in the least to the visible atmosphere—to which, indeed, he himself contributed languorously from a crackling spilliken of South American tobacco rolled in a maize leaf and strongly tinctured with opium—but to the almost brutal post-prandial fecundity of its occupants.

Rose was patently a degenerate. Nature, in scheduling his characteristics, had pruned all superlatives. The rude armour of the flesh, under which the spiritual, like a hide-bound chrysalis, should develop secret and self-contained, was perished in his case, as it were, to a semi-opaque suit, through which his soul gazed dimly and fearfully on its monstrous arbitrary surroundings. Not the mantle of the poet, philosopher, or artist fallen upon such, can still its shiverings, or give the comfort that Nature denies.

Yet he was a little bit of each—poet, philosopher, and artist; a nerveless and self-deprecatory stalker of ideals, in the pursuit of which he would wear patent leather shoes and all the apologetic graces. The grandson of a "three-bottle" J.P., who had upheld the dignity of the State constitution while abusing his own in the best spirit of squirearchy; the son of a petulant dyspeptic, who alternated seizures of long moroseness with fits of abject moral helplessness, Amos found his inheritance in the reversion of a dissipated constitution, and an imagination as sensitive as an exposed nerve. Before he was thirty he was a neurasthenic so practised, as to have learned a sense of luxury in the very consciousness of his own suffering. It was a negative evolution from the instinct of self-protection—self-protection, as designed in this case, against the attacks of the unspeakable. Another evolution, only less negative, was of a certain desperate pugnacity, that derived from a sense of the inhuman injustice conveyed in the fact that temperamental debility not only debarred him from that bold and healthy expression of self that it was his nature to wish, but made him actually appear to act in contradiction to his own really sweet and sound predilections.

So he sat (in the present instance, listening and revolting) in a travesty of resignation between the stools of submission and defiance.

The neurotic youth of to-day renews no ante-existent type. You will look in vain for a face like Amos's amongst the busts of the recovered past. The same weakness of outline you may point to—the sheep-like features falling to a blunt prow; the lax jaw and pinched temples—but not to that which expresses a consciousness that combative effort in a world of fruitless results is a lost desire.

Superficially, the figure in the smoking-room was that of a long, weedy young man—hairless as to his face; scalped with a fine lank fleece of neutral tint; pale-eyed, and slave to a bored and languid expression, over which he had little control, though it frequently misrepresented his mood. He was dressed scrupulously, though not obtrusively, in the mode, and was smoking a pungent cigarette with an air that seemed balanced between a genuine effort at self-abstraction and a fear of giving offence by a too pronounced show of it. In this state, flying bubbles of conversation broke upon him as he sat a little apart and alone.

"Johnny, here's Callander preaching a divine egotism."

"Is he? Tell him to beg a lock of the Henbery's hair. Ain't she the dog that bit him?"

"Once bit, twice shy."

"Rot!—In the case of a woman? I'm covered with their scars."

"What," thought Rose, "induced me to accept an invitation to this person's house?"

"A divine egotism, eh? It jumps with the dear Sarah's humour. The beggar is an imitative beggar."

"Let the beggar speak for himself. He's in earnest. Haven't we been bred on the principle of self-sacrifice, till we've come to think a man's self is his uncleanest possession?"

"There's no thinking about it. We've long been alarmed on your account, I can assure you."

"Oh! I'm no saint."

"Not you. *Your* ecstasies are all of the flesh."

"Don't be gross. I—"

"Oh! take a whisky and seltzer."

"If I could escape without exciting observation," thought Rose.

Lady Sarah Henbery was his hostess, and the inspired projector of a new scheme of existence (that was, in effect, the repudiation of any scheme) that had become quite the "thing." She had found life an arbitrary design—a coil of days (like fancy pebbles, dull or sparkling) set in the form of a main-spring, and each gem responsible to the design. Then she had said, "To-day shall not follow yesterday or precede to-morrow"; and she had taken her pebbles from their setting and mixed them higgledy-piggledy, and so was in the way to wear or spend one or the other as caprice moved her. And she became without design and responsibility, and was thus able to indulge a natural bent towards capriciousness to the extent that—having a face for each and every form of social hypocrisy and licence—she was presently hardly to be put out of countenance by the extremest expression of either.

It followed that her reunions were popular with worldlings of a certain order.

By-and-by Amos saw his opportunity, and slipped out into a cold and foggy night.

II

"De savoir votr' grand âge,
Nous serions curieux;
A voir votre visage,
Vous paraissez fort vieux;
Vous avez bien cent ans,
Vous montrez bien autant?"

A stranger, tall, closely wrapped and buttoned to the chin, had issued from the house at the same moment, and now followed in Rose's footsteps as he hurried away over the frozen pavement.

Suddenly this individual overtook and accosted him.

"Pardon," he said. "This fog baffles. We have been fellow-guests, it seems. You are walking? May I be your companion? You look a little lost yourself."

He spoke in a rather high, mellow voice—too frank for irony.

At another time Rose might have met such a request with some slightly agitated temporising. Now, fevered with disgust of his late company, the astringency of nerve that came to him at odd moments, in the exaltation of which he felt himself ordinarily manly and human, braced him to an attitude at once modest and collected.

"I shall be quite happy," he said. "Only, don't blame me if you find you are entertaining a fool unawares."

"You were out of your element, and are piqued. I saw you there, but wasn't introduced."

"The loss is mine. I didn't observe you—yes, I did!"

He shot the last words out hurriedly—as they came within the radiance of a street lamp—and his pace lessened a moment with a little bewildered jerk.

He had noticed this person, indeed—his presence and his manner. They had arrested his languid review of the frivolous forces about him. He had seen a figure, strange and lofty, pass from group to group; exchange with one a word or two, with another a grave smile; move on and listen; move on and speak; always statelily restless; never anything but an incongruous apparition in a company of which every individual was eager to assert and expound the doctrines of self.

This man had been of curious expression, too—so curious that Amos remembered to have marvelled at the little comment his presence seemed to excite. His face was absolutely hairless—as, to all evidence, was his head, upon which he wore a brown silk handkerchief loosely rolled and knotted. The features were presumably of a Jewish type—though their entire lack of accent in the form of beard or eyebrow made identification difficult—and were minutely covered, like delicate cracklin, with a network of flattened wrinkles. Ludicrous though the description, the lofty individuality of the man so surmounted all disadvantages of appearance as to overawe frivolous criticism. Partly, also, the full transparent olive of his complexion, and the pools of purple shadow in which his eyes seemed to swim like blots of resin, neutralised the superficial barrenness of his face. Forcibly, he impelled the conviction that here was one who ruled his own being arbitrarily through entire fearlessness of death.

"You saw me?" he said, noticing with a smile his companion's involuntary hesitation. "Then let us consider the introduction made, without further words. We will even expand to the familiarity of old acquaintanceship, if you like to fall in with the momentary humour."

"I can see," said Rose, "that years are nothing to you."

"No more than this gold piece, which I fling into the night. They are made and lost and made again."

"You have knowledge and the gift of tongues."

The young man spoke bewildered, but with a strange warm feeling of confidence flushing up through his habitual reserve. He had no thought why, nor did he choose his words or inquire of himself their source of inspiration.

"I have these," said the stranger. "The first is my excuse for addressing you."

"You are going to ask me something."

"What attraction—"

"Drew me to Lady Sarah's house? I am young, rich, presumably a desirable *parti*. Also, I am neurotic, and without the nerve to resist."

"Yet you knew your taste would take alarm—as it did."

"I have an acute sense of delicacy. Naturally I am prejudiced in favour of virtue."

"Then—excuse me—why put yours to a demoralising test?"

"I am not my own master. Any formless apprehension—any shadowy fear enslaves my will. I go to many places from the simple dread of being called upon to explain my reasons for refusing. For the same cause I may appear to acquiesce in indecencies my soul abhors; to give countenance to opinions innately distasteful to me. I am a quite colourless personality."

"Without force or object in life?"

"Life, I think, I live for its isolated moments—the first half-dozen pulls at a cigarette, for instance, after a generous meal."

"You take the view, then—"

"Pardon me. I take no views. I am not strong enough to take anything—not even myself—seriously."

"Yet you know that the trail of such volitionary ineptitude reaches backwards under and beyond the closed door you once issued from?"

"Do I? I know at least that the ineptitude intensifies with every step of constitutional decadence. It may be that I am wearing down to the nerve of life. How shall I find that? diseased? Then it is no happiness to me to think it imperishable."

"Young man, do you believe in a creative divinity?"

"Yes."

"And believe without resentment?"

"I think God hands over to His apprentices the moulding of vessels that don't interest Him."

The stranger twitched himself erect.

"I beg you not to be profane," he said.

"I am not," said Rose. "I don't know why I confide in you, or what concern I have to know. I can only say my instincts, through bewildering mental suffering, remain religious. You take me out of myself and judge me unfairly on the result."

"Stay. You argue that a perishing of the bodily veil reveals the soul. Then the outlook of the latter should be the cleaner."

"It gazes through a blind of corruption. It was never designed to stand naked in the world's marketplaces."

"And whose the fault that it does?"

"I don't know. I only feel that I am utterly lonely and helpless."

The stranger laughed scornfully.

"You can feel no sympathy with my state?" said Rose.

"Not a grain. To be conscious of a soul, yet to remain a craven under the temporal tyranny of the flesh; fearful of revolting, though the least imaginative flight of the spirit carries it at once beyond any bodily influence! Oh, sir! Fortune favours the brave."

"She favours the fortunate," said the young man, with a melancholy smile. "Like a banker, she charges a commission on small accounts. At trifling deposits she turns up her nose. If you would escape her tax, you must keep a fine large balance at her house."

"I dislike parables," said the stranger drily.

"Then, here is a fact in illustration. I have an acquaintance, an impoverished author, who anchored his ark of hope on Mount Olympus twenty years ago. During all that time he has never ceased to send forth his doves; only to have them return empty-beaked with persistent regularity. Three days ago the olive branch—a mere sprouting twig—came home. For the first time a magazine—an indifferent one—accepted a story of his and offered him a pound for it. He acquiesced; and the same night was returned to him from an important American firm an understamped MS., on which he had to pay excess postage, half a crown. That was Fortune's commission."

"Bully the jade, and she will love you."

"Your wisdom has not learned to confute that barbarism?"

The stranger glanced at his companion with some expression of dislike.

"The sex figures in your ideals, I see," said he. "Believe my long experience that its mere animal fools constitute its only excuse for existing—though" (he added under his breath) "even they annoy one by their monogamous prejudices."

"I won't hear that with patience," said Rose. "Each sex in its degree. Each is wearifully peevish over the hateful rivalry between mind and matter; but the male only has the advantage of distractions."

"This," said the stranger softly, as if to himself, "is the woeful proof, indeed, of decadence. Man waives his prerogative of lordship over the irreclaimable savagery of earth. He has warmed his temperate house of clay to be a hot-house to his imagination, till the very walls are frail and eaten with fever."

"Christ spoke of no spiritual division between the sexes."

There followed a brief silence. Preoccupied, the two moved slowly through the fog, that was dashed ever and anon with cloudy blooms of lamplight.

"I wish to ask you," said the stranger at length, "in what has the teaching of Christ proved otherwise than so impotent to reform mankind, as to make one sceptical as to the divinity of the teacher?"

"Why, what is your age?" asked Rose in a tone of surprise.

"I am a hundred to-night."

The astounded young man jumped in his walk.

"A hundred!" he exclaimed. "And you cannot answer that question yourself?"

"I asked you to answer it. But never mind. I see faith in you like a garden of everlastings—as it should be—as of course it should be. Yet disbelievers point to inconsistencies. There was a reviling Jew, for instance, to whom Christ is reported to have shown resentment quite incompatible with His teaching."

"Whom do you mean?"

"Cartaphilus; who was said to be condemned to perpetual wandering."

"A legend," cried Amos scornfully. "Bracket it with Nero's fiddling and the hymning of Memnon."

A second silence fell. They seemed to move in a dead and stagnant world. Presently said the stranger suddenly—

"I am quite lost; and so, I suppose, are you?"

"I haven't an idea where we are."

"It is two o'clock. There isn't a soul or a mark to guide us. We had best part, and each seek his own way."

He stopped and held out his hand.

"Two pieces of advice I should like to give you before we separate. Fall in love and take plenty of exercise."

"Must we part?" said Amos. "Frankly, I don't think I like you. That sounds strange and discourteous after my ingenuous confidences. But you exhale an odd atmosphere of witchery; and your scorn braces me like a tonic. The pupils of your eyes, when I got a glimpse of them, looked like the heads of little black devils peeping out of windows. But you can't touch my soul on the raw when my nerves are quiescent; and then I would strike any man that called me coward."

The stranger uttered a quick, chirping laugh, like the sound of a stone on ice.

"What do you propose?" he said.

"I have an idea you are not so lost as you pretend. If we are anywhere near shelter that you know, take me in and I will be a good listener. It is one of my negative virtues."

"I don't know that any addition to my last good counsel would not be an anti-climax."

He stood musing and rubbing his hairless chin.

"Exercise—certainly. It is the golden demephitizer of the mind. I am seldom off my feet."

"You walk much—and alone?"

"Not always alone. Periodically I am accompanied by one or another. At this time I have a companion who has tramped with me for some nine months."

Again he pondered apart. The darkness and the fog hid his face, but he spoke his thoughts aloud.

"What matter if it does come about? To-morrow I have the world—the mother of many daughters. And to redeem this soul—a dog of a Christian—a friend at Court!"

He turned quickly to the young man.

"Come!" he said. "It shall be as you wish."

"Do you know where we are?"

"We are at the entrance to Wardour Street."

He gave a gesture of impatience, whipped a hand at his companion's sleeve, and once more they trod down the icy echoes, going onwards.

The narrow lane reverberated to their footsteps; the drooping fog swayed sluggishly; the dead blank windows and high-shouldered doors frowned in stubborn progression and vanished behind them.

The stranger stopped in a moment where a screen of iron bars protected a shop front. From behind them shot leaden glints from old clasped book-covers, hanging tongues of Toledo steel, croziers rich in nielli—innumerable and antique curios gathered from the lumber-rooms of history.

A door to one side he opened with a latch-key. A pillar of light, seeming to smoke as the fog obscured it, was formed of the aperture.

Obeying a gesture, Rose set foot on the threshold. As he was entering, he found himself unable to forbear a thrill of effrontery.

"Tell me," said he. "It was not only to point a moral that you flung away that coin?"

The stranger, going before, grinned back sourly over his shoulder.

"Not only," he said. "It was a bad one."

III

. . . *"La Belle Dame sans merci*
Hath thee in thrall!"

All down the dimly luminous passage that led from the door straight into the heart of the building, Amos was aware, as he followed his companion over the densely piled carpet, of the floating sweet scent of amber-seed. Still his own latter exaltation of nerve burned with a steady radiance. He seemed to himself bewitched—

translated; a consciousness apart from yesterday; its material fibres responsive to the least or utmost shock of adventure. As he trod in the other's footsteps, he marvelled that so lavish a display of force, so elastic a gait, could be in a centenarian.

"Are you ever tired?" he whispered curiously.

"Never. Sometimes I long for weariness as other men desire rest."

As the stranger spoke, he pulled aside a curtain of stately black velvet, and softly opening a door in a recess, beckoned the young man into the room beyond.

He saw a chamber, broad and low, designed, in its every rich stain of picture and slumberous hanging, to appeal to the sensuous. And here the scent was thick and motionless. Costly marqueterie; Palissy candlesticks reflected in half-concealed mirrors framed in embossed silver; antique Nankin vases brimming with pot-pourri; in one corner a suit of Milanese armour, fluted, damasquinée, by Felippo Negroli; in another a tripod table of porphyry, spectrally repeating in its polished surface the opal hues of a vessel of old Venetian glass half filled with some topaz-coloured liqueur—such and many more tokens of a luxurious aestheticism wrought in the observer an immediate sense of pleasurable enervation. He noticed, with a swaying thrill of delight, that his feet were on a padded rug of Astrakhan—one of many, disposed eccentrically about the yellow tessellated-marble floor; and he noticed that the sole light in the chamber came from an iridescent globed lamp, fed with some fragrant oil, that hung near an alcove traversed by a veil of dark violet silk.

The door behind him swung gently to: his eyes half closed in a dreamy surrender of will: the voice of the stranger speaking to him sounded far away as the cry of some lost unhappiness.

"Welcome!" it said only.

Amos broke through his trance with a cry.

"What does it mean—all this? We step out of the fog, and here—I think it is the guest-parlour of Hell!"

"You flatter me," said the stranger, smiling. "Its rarest antiquity goes no further back, I think, than the eighth century. The skeleton of the place is Jacobite and comparatively modern."

"But you—the shop!"

"Contains a little of the fruit of my wanderings."

"You are a dealer?"

"A casual collector only. If through a representative I work my accumulations of costly lumber to a profit—say thousands per cent.—it is only because utility is the first principle of Art. As to myself, here I but pitch my tent—periodically, and at long intervals."

"An unsupervised agent must find it a lucrative post."

"Come—there shows a little knowledge of human nature. For the first time I applaud you. But the appointment is conditional on many things. At the moment the berth is vacant. Would you like it?"

"My (paradoxically) Christian name was bestowed in compliment to a godfather, sir. I am no Jew. I have already enough to know the curse of having more."

"I have no idea how you are called. I spoke jestingly, of course; but your answer quenches the flicker of respect I felt for you. As a matter of fact, the other's successor is not only nominated, but is actually present in this room."

"Indeed? You propose to fill the post yourself?"

"Not by any means. The mere suggestion is an insult to one who can trace his descent backwards at least two thousand years."

"Yes, indeed. I meant no disparagement, but—"

"I tell you, sir," interrupted the stranger irritably, "my visits are periodic. I could not live in a town. I could not settle anywhere. I must always be moving. A prolonged constitutional—that is my theory of health."

"You are always on your feet—at your age—"

"I am a hundred to-night. But—mark you—*I have eaten of the Tree of Life*."

As the stranger uttered these words, he seized Rose by the wrist in a soft, firm grasp. His captive, staring at him amazed, gave out a little involuntary shriek.

"Hadn't I better leave? There is something—nameless—I don't know; but I should never have come in here. Let me go!"

The other, heedless, half pulled the troubled and bewildered young man across the room, and drew him to within a foot of the curtain closing the alcove.

"Here," he said quietly, "is my fellow-traveller of the last nine months, fast, I believe, in sleep—unless your jarring outcry has broken it."

Rose struggled feebly.

"Not anything shameful," he whimpered— "I have a dread of your manifestations."

For answer, the other put out a hand, and swiftly and silently withdrew the curtain. A deepish recess was revealed, into which the soft glow of the lamp penetrated like moonlight. It fell in the first instance upon a couch littered with pale, uncertain shadows, and upon a crucifix that hung upon the wall within.

In the throb of his emotions, it was something a relief to Amos to see his companion, releasing his hold of him, clasp his hands and bow his head reverently to this pathetic symbol. The cross on which the Christ hung was of ebony a foot high; the figure itself was chryselephantine and purely exquisite as a work of art.

"It is early seventeenth century," said the stranger suddenly, after a moment of devout silence, seeing the other's eyes absorbed in contemplation. "It is by Duquesnoy." (Then, behind the back of his hand) The rogue couldn't forget his bacchanals even here."

"It is a Christ of infidels," said Amos, with repugnance. He was adding involuntarily (his *savoir faire* seemed suddenly to have deserted him)— "But fit for an unbelieving—" when his host took him up with fury—

"Dog of a Gentile!—if you dare to call me Jew!"

The dismayed start of the young man at this outburst blinded him to its paradoxical absurdity. He fell back with his heart thumping. The eyes of the stranger flickered, but in an instant he had recovered his urbanity.

"Look!" he whispered impatiently. "The Calvary is not alone in the alcove."

Mechanically Rose's glance shifted to the couch; and in that moment shame and apprehension and the sickness of being were precipitated in him as in golden flakes of rapture.

Something, that in the instant of revelation had seemed part only of the soft tinted shadows, resolved itself into a presentment of loveliness so pure, and so pathetic in its innocent self-surrender to the passionate tyranny of his gaze, that the manhood it him was abashed in the very flood of its exaltation. He put a hand to his face before he looked a second time, to discipline his dazzled eyes. They were turned only upon his soul, and found it a reflected glory. Had the vision passed? His eyes, in a panic, leaped for it once more.

Yes, it was there—dreaming upon its silken pillow; a grotesque carved dragon in ivory looking down, from a corner of the fluted couch, upon its supernal beauty—a fate that, at a glance, could fill the vague desire of a suffering, lonely heart—spirit informing matter with all the flush and essence of some flower of the lost garden of Eden.

And this expressed in the form of one simple slumbering girl; in its stately sweet curves of cheek and mouth and throat; in its drifted heap of hair, bronze as copper-beech leaves in spring; in the very pulsing of its half-hidden bosom, and in its happy morning lips, like Psyche's, night-parted by Love and so remaining entranced.

A long light robe, sulphur-coloured, clung to the sleeper from low throat to ankle; bands of narrow nolana-blue ribbon crossed her breast and were brought together in a loose cincture about her waist; her white, smooth feet were sandalled; one arm was curved beneath her lustrous head; the other lay relaxed and drooping. Chrysoberyls, the sea-virgins of stones, sparkled in her hair and lay in the bosom of her gown like dewdrops in an evening primrose.

The gazer turned with a deep sigh, and then a sputter of fury—

"Why do you show me this? You cruel beast, was not my life barren enough before?"

"Can it ever be so henceforward? Look again."

"Does the devil enter? Something roars in me! Have you no fear that I shall kill you?"

"None. I cannot die."

Amos broke into a mocking, fierce laugh. Then, his blood shooting in his veins, he seized the sleeper roughly by her hand.

"Wake!" he cried, "and end it!"

With a sigh she lifted her head. Drowsiness and startled wonderment struggled in her eyes; but in a moment they caught the vision of the stranger standing aside, and smiled and softened. She held out her long, white arms to him.

"You have come, dear love," she said, in a happy, low voice, "and I was not awake to greet you." Rose fell on his knees.

"Oh, God in Heaven!" he cried, "bear witness that this is monstrous and unnatural! Let me die rather than see it."

The stranger moved forward.

"Do honour, Adnah, to this our guest; and minister to him of thy pleasure."

The white arms dropped. The girl's face was turned, and her eyes, solemn and witch-like, looked into Amos's. He saw them, their irises golden-brown shot with little spars of blue; and the soul in his own seemed to rush towards them and to recoil, baffled and sobbing.

Could she have understood? He thought he saw a faint smile, a gentle shake of the head, as she slid from the couch and her sandals tapped on the marble floor.

She stooped and took him by the hand.

"Rise, I pray you," she said, "and I will be your handmaiden."

She led him unresisting to a chair, and bade him sweetly to be seated. She took from him his hat and overcoat, and brought him rare wine in a cup of crystal.

"My lord will drink," she murmured, "and forget all but the night and Adnah."

"You I can never forget," said the young man, in a broken voice.

As he drank, half choking, the girl turned to the other, who still stood apart, silent and watchful.

"Was this wise?" she breathed. "To summon a witness on this night of all—was this wise, beloved?"

Amos dashed the cup on the floor. The red liquid stained the marble like blood.

"No, no!" he shrieked, springing to his feet. "Not that! It cannot be!"

In an ecstasy of passion he flung his arms about the girl, and crushed all her warm loveliness against his breast. She remained quite passive—unstartled even. Only she turned her head and whispered:

"Is this thy will?"

Amos fell back, drooping, as if he had received a blow.

"Be merciful and kill me," he muttered. "I—even I can feel at last the nobility of death."

Then the voice of the stranger broke, lofty and passionless.

"Tell him what you see in me."

She answered, low and without pause, like one repeating a cherished lesson—

"I see—I have seen it for the nine months I have wandered with you—the supreme triumph of the living will. I see that this triumph, of its very essence, could not be unless you had surmounted the tyranny of any, the least, gross desire. I see that it is incompatible with sin; with offence given to oneself or others; that passion cannot live in its serene atmosphere; that it illustrates the enchantment of the flesh by the intellect; that it is happiness for evermore redeemed."

"How do you feel this?"

"I see it reflected in myself—I, the poor visionary you took from the Northern Island. Week by week I have known it sweetening and refining in my nature. None can taste the bliss of happiness that has not you for master—none can teach it save you, whose composure is unshadowed by any terror of death."

"And love that is passion, Adnah?"

"I hear it spoken as in a dream. It is a wicked whisper from far away. You, the lord of time and of tongues, I worship—you, only you, who are my God."

"Hush! But the man of Nazareth?"

"Ah! His name is an echo. What divine egotism taught He?"

Where lately had Amos heard this phrase? His memory of all things real seemed suspended.

"He was a man, and He died," said Adnah simply.

The stranger threw back his head, with an odd expression of triumph; and almost in the same moment abased it to the crucifix on the wall.

Amos stood breathing quickly, his ears drinking in every accent of the low musical voice. Now, as she paused, he moved forward a hurried step, and addressed himself to the shadowy figure by the couch—

"Who are you, in the name of the Christ you mock and adore in a breath, that has wrought this miracle of high worship in a breathing woman?"

"I am he that has eaten of the Tree of Life."

"Oh, forego your fables! I am not a child."

"It could not of its nature perish" (the voice went on evenly, ignoring the interruption). "It breathes its immortal fragrance in no transplanted garden, invisible to sinful eyes, as some suppose. When the curse fell, the angel of the flaming sword bore it to the central desert; and the garden withered, for its soul was withdrawn. Now, in the heart of the waste place that is called Tiah-Bani-Israïl, it waits in its loveliness the coming of the Son of God."

"He has come and passed."

It might have been an imperceptible shrug of the shoulders that twitched the tall figure by the couch. If so, it converted the gesture into a bow of reverence.

"Is He not to be revealed again in His glory? But there, set as in the crater of a mountain of sand, and inaccessible to mortal footstep, stands unperishing the glory of the earth. And its fragrance is drawn up to heaven, as through a wide chimney; and from its branches hangs the undying fruit, lustrous and opalescent; and in each shining globe the world and its starry system are reflected in miniature, moving westwards; but at night they glow, a cluster of tender moons."

"And whence came *your* power to scale that which is inaccessible?"

"From Death, that, still denying me immortality, is unable to encompass my destruction."

The young man burst into a harsh and grating laugh.

"Here is some inconsistency!" he cried. "By your own showing you were not immortal till you ate of the fruit!"

Could it be that this simple deductive snip cut the thread of coherence? A scowl appeared to contract the lofty brow for an instant. The next, a gay chirrup intervened, like a little spark struck from the cloud.

"The pounding logic of the steam engine!" cried the stranger, coming forward at last with an open smile. "But we pace in an altitude refined above sensuous comprehension. Perhaps before long you will see and believe. In the meantime let us be men and women enjoying the warm gifts of Fortune!"

IV

"Nous pensions comme un songe
Le récit de vos maux;
Nous traitions de mensonge
Tous vos plus grands travaux!"

In that one night of an unreality that seemed either an enchanted dream or a wilfully fantastic travesty of conventions, Amos alternated between fits of delirious self-surrender and a rage of resignation, from which now and again he would awake to flourish an angry little bodkin of irony.

Now, at this stage, it appeared a matter for passive acquiescence that he should be one of a trio seated at a bronze table, that might have been recovered from Herculaneum, playing three-handed cribbage with a pack of fifteenth-century cards—limned, perhaps, by some Franceso Bachiacca—and an ivory board inlaid with gold and mother-of-pearl. To one side a smaller "occasional" table held the wine, to which the young man resorted at the least invitation from Adnah.

In this connexion (of cards), it would fitfully perturb him to find that he who had renounced sin with mortality, had not only a proneness to avail himself of every oversight on the part of his adversaries, but frequently to peg-up more holes than his hand entitled him to. Moreover, at such times, when the culprit's attention was drawn to this by his guest at first gently; later, with a little scorn—he justified his action on the assumption that it was an essential interest of all games to attempt abuse of the confidence of one's antagonist, whose skill in checkmating any movement of this nature was in right ratio with his capacity as a player; and finally he rose, the sole winner of a sum respectable enough to allow him some ingenuous expression of satisfaction.

Thereafter conversation ensued; and it must be remarked that nothing was further from Rose's mind than to apologise for his long intrusion and make a decent exit. Indeed, there seemed some thrill of vague expectation in the air, to the realisation of which his presence sought to contribute; and already—so rapidly grows the assurance of love—his heart claimed some protective right over the pure, beautiful creature at his feet.

For there, at a gesture from the other, had Adnah seated herself, leaning her elbow, quite innocently and simply, on the young man's knee.

The sweet strong Moldavian wine buzzed in his head; love and sorrow and intense yearning went with flow and shock through his veins. At one moment elated by the thought that, whatever his understanding of the ethical sympathy existing between these two, their connexion was, by their own acknowledgment, platonic; at another, cruelly conscious of the icy crevasse that must gape between so perfectly proportioned an organism and his own atrabilarious personality, he dreaded to avail himself of a situation that was at once an invitation and a trust; and ended by subsiding, with characteristic lameness, into mere conversational commonplace.

"You must have got over a great deal of ground," said he to his host, "on that constitutional hobbyhorse of yours?"

"A great deal of ground."

"In all weathers?"

"In all weathers; at all times; in every country."

"How do you manage—pardon my inquisitiveness—the little necessities of dress and boots and such things?"

"Adnah," said the stranger, "go fetch my walking suit and show it to our guest."

The girl rose, went silently from the room, and returned in a moment with a single garment, which she laid in Rose's hands.

He examined it curiously. It was a marvel of sartorial tact and ingenuity; so fashioned that it would have appeared scarcely a solecism on taste in any age. Built in one piece to resemble many, and of the most particularly chosen material, it was contrived and ventilated for any exigencies of weather and of climate, and could be doffed or assumed at the shortest notice. About it were cunningly distributed a number of strong pockets or purses for the reception of divers articles, from a comb to a sandwich-box; and the position of these was so calculated as not to interfere with the symmetry of the whole.

"It is indeed an excellent piece of work," said Amos, with considerable appreciation; for he held no contempt for the art which sometimes alone seemed to justify his right of existence.

"Your praise is deserved," said the stranger, smiling, "seeing that it was contrived for me by one whose portrait, by Giambattista Moroni, now hangs in your National Gallery."

"I have heard of it, I think. Is the fellow still in business?"

"The tailor or the artist? The first died bankrupt in prison—about the year 1560, it must have been. It was fortunate for me, inasmuch as I acquired the garment for nothing, the man disappearing before I had settled his claim."

Rose's jaw dropped. He looked at the beautiful face reclining against him. It expressed no doubt, no surprise, no least sense of the ludicrous.

"Oh, my God!" he muttered, and ploughed his forehead with his hands. Then he looked up again with a pallid grin.

"I see," he said. "You play upon my fancied credulity. And how did the garment serve you in the central desert?"

"I had it not then, by many centuries. No garment would avail against the wicked Samiel—the poisonous wind that is the breath of the eternal dead sand. Who faces that feels, pace by pace, his body wither and stiffen. His clothes crackle like paper, and so fall to fragments. From his eyeballs the moist vision flakes and flies in powder. His tongue shrinks into his throat, as though fire had writhed and consumed it to a little scarlet spur. His furrowed skin peels like the cerements of an ancient mummy. He falls, breaking in his fall—there is a puff of acrid dust, dissipated in a moment—and he is gone."

"And this you met unscathed?"

"Yes; for it was preordained that Death should hunt, but never overtake me—that I might testify to the truth of the first Scriptures."

Even as he spoke, Rose sprang to his feet with a gesture of uncontrollable repulsion; and in the same instant was aware of a horrible change that was taking place in the features of the man before him.

V

> "Trahentibus autem Judaeis Jesum extra praetorium cum venisset ad ostium, Cartaphilus praetorii ostiarius et Pontii Pilati, cum per ostium exiret Jesus, pepulit Eum pugno contemptibiliter post tergum, et irridens dixit, 'Vade, Jesu citius, vade, quid moraris?' Et Jesus severo vultu et oculo respiciens in eum, dixit: 'Ego vado, et expectabis donec veniam!' Itaque juxta verbum Domini expectat adhuc Cartaphilus ille, qui tempore Dominicae passionis—erat quasi triginta annorum, et semper cum usque ad centum attigerit aetatem redeuntium annorum redit redivivus ad illum aetatis statum, quo fuit anno quand passus est Dominus."—Matthew of Paris, *Historia Major*.

The girl—from whose cheek Rose, in his rough rising, had seemed to brush the bloom, so keenly had its colour deepened—sank from the stool upon her knees, her hands pressed to her bosom, her lungs working quickly under the pressure of some powerful excitement.

"It comes, beloved!" she said, in a voice half terror, half ecstasy.

"It comes, Adnah," the stranger echoed, struggling— "this periodic self-renewal—this sloughing of the veil of flesh that I warned you of."

His soul seemed to pant grey from his lips; his face was bloodless and like stone; the devils in his eyes were awake and busy as maggots in a wound. Amos knew him now for wickedness personified and immortal, and fell upon his knees beside the girl and seized one of her hands in both his.

"Look!" he shrieked. "Can you believe in him longer? believe that any code or system of his can profit you in the end?"

She made no resistance, but her eyes still dwelt on the contorted face with an expression of divine pity.

"Oh, thou sufferest!" she breathed; "but thy reward is near!"

"Adnah!" wailed the young man, in a heartbroken voice. "Turn from him to me! Take refuge in my love. Oh, it is natural, I swear. It asks nothing of you but to accept the gift—to renew Yourself in it, if you will; to deny it, if you will, and chain it for your slave. Only to save you and die for you, Adnah!"

He felt the hand in his shudder slightly; but no least knowledge of him did she otherwise evince.

He clasped her convulsively, released her, mumbled her slack white fingers with his lips. He might have addressed the dead.

In the midst, the figure before them swayed with a rising throe—turned—staggered across to the couch, and cast itself down before the crucifix on the wall.

"Jesu, Son of God," it implored, through a hurry of piercing groans, "forbear Thy hand: Christ, register my atonement! My punishment—eternal—and oh, my mortal feet already weary to death! Jesu, spare me! Thy justice, Lawgiver—let it not be vindictive, oh, in Thy sacred name! lest men proclaim it for a baser thing than theirs. For a fault of ignorance—for a word of scorn where all reviled, would *they* have singled *one* out, have made him, most wretched, the scapegoat of the ages? Ah, most holy, forgive me! In mine agony I know not what I say. A moment ago I could have pronounced it something seeming less than divine that Thou couldst so have stultified with a curse Thy supreme hour of self-sacrifice—a moment ago, when the rising madness prevailed. Now, sane once more—Nazarene, oh, Nazarene! not only retribution for my deserts, but pity for my suffering—Nazarene, that Thy slanderers, the men of little schisms, be refuted, hearing me, the very witness to Thy mercy, testify how the justice of the Lord triumphs supreme through that His superhuman prerogative,—that they may not say, He can destroy, even as we; but can He redeem? The sacrifice—the yearling lamb;—it awaits Thee, Master, the proof of my abjectness and my sincerity. I, more curst than Abraham, lift my eyes to Heaven, the terror in my heart, the knife in my hand. Jesu—Jesu!"

He cried and grovelled. His words were frenzied, his abasement fulsome to look upon. Yet it was impressed upon one of the listeners, with a great horror, how unspeakable blasphemy breathed between the lines of the prayer—the blasphemy of secret disbelief in the Power it invoked, and sought, with its tongue in its cheek, to conciliate.

Bitter indignation in the face of nameless outrage transfigured Rose at this moment into something nobler than himself. He feared, but he upheld his manhood. Conscious that the monstrous situation was none of his choosing, he had no thought to evade its consequences so long as the unquestioning credulity of his co-witness seemed to call for his protection. Nerveless, sensitive natures, such as his, not infrequently give the lie to themselves by accesses of an altruism that is little less than self-effacement.

"This is all bad," he struggled to articulate. "You are hipped by some devilish cantrip. Oh, come—come!—in Christ's name I dare to implore you—and learn the truth of love!"

As he spoke, he saw that the apparition was on its feet again—that it had returned, and was standing, its face ghastly and inhuman, with one hand leaned upon the marble table.

"Adnah!" it cried, in a strained and hollow voice. "The moment for which I prepared you approaches. Even now I labour. I had thought to take up the thread on the further side; but it is ordained otherwise, and we must part."

"Part!" The word burst from her in a sigh of lost amazement.

"The holocaust, Adnah!" he groaned— "the holocaust with which every seventieth year my expiation must be punctuated! This time the cross is on thy breast, beloved; and to-morrow—oh! thou must be content to tread on lowlier altitudes than those I have striven to guide thee by."

"I cannot—I cannot. I should die in the mists. Oh, heart of my heart, forsake me not!"

"Adnah—my selma, my beautiful—to propitiate—"

"Whom? Thou hast eaten of the Tree, and art a God!"

"Hush!" He glanced round with an awed visage at the dim hanging Calvary; then went on in a harsher tone, "It is enough—it must be." (His shifting face, addressed to Rose, was convulsed into an expression of bitter scorn.) "I command thee, go with him. The sacrifice—oh, my heart, the sacrifice! And I cry to Jehovah, and He makes no sign; and. into thy sweet breast the knife must enter."

Amos sprang to his feet with a loud cry.

"I take no gift from you. I will win or lose her by right of manhood!"

The girl's face was white with despair.

"I do not understand," she cried in a piteous voice.

"Nor I," said the young man, and he took a threatening step forward. "We have no part in this—this lady and I. Man or devil you may be; but—"

"Neither!"

The stranger, as he uttered the word, drew himself erect with a tortured smile. The action seemed to kilt the skin of his face into hideous plaits.

"I am Cartaphilus," he said, "who denied the Nazarene shelter."

"The *Wandering Jew!*"

The name of the old strange legend broke involuntarily from Rose's lips.

"Now you know him!" he shrieked then. "Adnah, I am here! Come to me!"

Tears were running down the girl's cheeks. She lifted her hands with an impassioned gesture; then covered her face with them.

But Cartaphilus, penetrating the veil with eyes no longer human, cried suddenly, so that the room vibrated with his voice, "Bismillah! Wilt thou dare the Son of Heaven, questioning if His sentence upon the Jew—to renew, with his every hundredth year, his manhood's prime—was not rather a forestalling, through His infinite penetration, of the consequences of that Jew's finding and eating of the Tree of Life? Is it Cartaphilus first, or Christ?"

The girl flung herself forward, crushing her bosom upon the marble floor, and lay blindly groping with her hands.

"He was a God and vindictive!" she moaned. "He was a man and He died. The cross—the cross!"

The lost cry pierced Rose's breast like a knife. Sorrow, rage, and love inflamed his passion to madness. With one bound he met and grappled with the stranger.

He had no thought of the resistance he should encounter. In a moment the Jew, despite his age and seizure, had him broken and powerless. The fury of blood blazed down upon him from the unearthly eyes.

"Beast! that I might tear you! But the Nameless is your refuge. You must be chained—you must be chained. Come!"

Half dragging, half bearing, he forced his captive across the room to the corner where the flask of topaz liquid stood.

"Sleep!" he shrieked, and caught up the glass vessel and dashed it down upon Rose's mouth.

The blow was a stunning one. A jagged splinter tore the victim's lip and brought a gush of blood; the yellow fluid drowned his eyes and suffocated his throat. Struggling to hold his faculties, a startled shock passed through him, and he dropped insensible on the floor.

VI

"Wandering stars, to whom is reserved the blackness of darkness for ever."

Where had he read these words before? Now he saw them as scrolled in lightning upon a dead sheet of night.

There was a sound of feet going on and on.

Light soaked into the gloom, faster—faster; and he saw—

The figure of a man moved endlessly forward by town and pasture and the waste places of the world. But though he, the dreamer, longed to outstrip and stay the figure and look searchingly in its face, he could not, following, close upon the intervening space; and its back was ever towards him.

And always as the figure passed by populous places, there rose long murmurs of blasphemy to either side, and bestial cries: "We are weary! the farce is played out! He reveals Himself not, nor ever will! Lead us—lead us, against Heaven, against hell; against any other, or against ourselves! The cancer of life spreads, and we cannot enjoy nor can we think cleanly. The sins of the fathers have accumulated to one vast mound of putrefaction. Lead us, and we follow!"

And, uttering these cries, swarms of hideous half-human shapes would emerge from holes and corners and rotting burrows, and stumble a little way with the figure, cursing and jangling, and so drop behind, one by one, like glutted flies shaken from a horse.

And the dreamer saw in him, who went ever on before, the sole existent type of a lost racial glory, a marvellous survival, a prince over monstrosities; and he knew him to have reached, through long ages of evil introspection, a terrible belief in his own self-acquired immortality and lordship over all abased peoples that must die and pass; and the seed of his blasphemy he sowed broadcast in triumph as he went; and the ravenous horrors of the earth ran forth in broods and devoured it like birds, and trod one another underfoot in their gluttony.

And he came to a vast desolate plain, and took his stand upon a barren drift of sand; and the face the dreamer longed and feared to see was yet turned from him.

And the figure cried in a voice that grated down the winds of space: "Lo! I am he that cannot die! Lo! I am he that has eaten of the Tree of Life; who am the Lord of Time and of the races of the earth that shall flock to my standard!"

And again: "Lo! I am he that God was impotent to destroy because I had eaten of the fruit! He cannot control that which He hath created. He hath builded His temple upon His impotence, and it shall fall and crush Him. The children of His misrule cry out against Him. There is no God but Antichrist!"

Then from all sides came hurrying across the plain vast multitudes of the degenerate children of men, naked and unsightly; and they leaped and mouthed about the figure on the hillock, like hounds baying a dead fox held aloft; and from their swollen throats came one cry:

"There is no God but Antichrist!"

And thereat the figure turned about—and it was Cartaphilus the Jew.

VII

"There is no death! What seems so is transition."

Uttering an incoherent cry, Rose came to himself with a shock of agony and staggered to his feet. In the act he traversed no neutral ground of insentient purposelessness. He caught the thread of being where he had dropped it—grasped it with an awful and sublime resolve that admitted no least thought of self-interest.

If his senses were for the moment amazed at their surroundings—the silence, the perfumed languor, the beauty and voluptuousness of the room—his soul, notwithstanding, stood intent, unfaltering—waiting merely the physical capacity for action.

The fragments of the broken vessel were scattered at his feet; the blood of his wound had hardened upon his face. He took a dizzy step forward, and another. The girl lay as he had seen her cast herself down—breathing, he could see; her hair in disorder; her hands clenched together in terror or misery beyond words.

Where was the other?

Suddenly his vision cleared. He saw that the silken curtains of the alcove were closed.

A poniard in a jewelled sheath lay, with other costly trifles, on a settle hard by. He seized and, drawing it, cast the scabbard clattering on the floor. His hands would have done; but this would work quicker.

Exhaling a quick sigh of satisfaction, he went forward with a noiseless rush and tore apart the curtains.

Yes—he was there—the Jew—the breathing enormity, stretched silent and motionless. The shadow of the young man's lifted arm ran across his white shirt front like a bar sinister.

To rid the world of something monstrous and abnormal—that was all Rose's purpose and desire. He leaned over to strike. The face, stiff and waxen as a corpse's, looked up into his with a calm impenetrable smile—looked up, for all its eyes were closed. And this was a horrible thing, that, though the features remained fixed in that one inexorable expression, something beneath them seemed alive and moving—something that clouded or revealed them, as when a sheet of paper glowing in the fire wavers between ashes and flame. Almost he could have thought that the soul, detached from its envelope, struggled to burst its way to the light.

An instant he dashed his left palm across his eyes; then shrieking, "Let the fruit avail you now!" drove the steel deep into its neck with a snarl.

In the act, for all his frenzy, he had a horror of the spurting blood that he knew must foul his hand obscenely, and sprinkle his face, perhaps, as when a finger half plugs a flowing water-tap.

None came! The fearful white wound seemed to suck at the steel, making a puckered mouth of derision.

A thin sound, like the whinny of a dog, issued from Rose's lips. He pulled out the blade—it came with a crackling noise, as if it had been drawn through parchment. Incredulous—mad—in an ecstasy of horror, he stabbed again and again. He might as fruitfully have struck at water. The slashed and gaping wounds closed up so soon as he withdrew the steel, leaving not a scar.

With a scream he dashed the unstained weapon on the floor and sprang back into the room. He stumbled and almost fell over the prostrate figure of the girl.

A strength as of delirium stung and prickled in his arms. He stooped and forcibly raised her—held her against his breast—addressed her in a hurried passion of entreaty.

"In the name of God, come with me! In the name of God, divorce yourself from this horror! He is the abnormal—the deathless—the Antichrist!"

Her lids were closed; but she listened.

"Adnah, you have given me myself. My reason cannot endure the gift alone. Have mercy and be pitiful, and share the burden!"

At last she turned on him her swimming gaze. "Oh! I am numbed and lost! What would you do with me?"

With a sob of triumph he wrapped his arms hard about her, and sought her lips with his. In the very moment of their meeting, she drew herself away, and stood panting and gazing with wide eyes over his shoulder. He turned.

A young man of elegant appearance was standing by the table where *he* had lately leaned.

In the face of the new-comer the animal and the fanatic were mingled, characteristics inseparable in pseudo-revelation.

He was unmistakably a Jew, of the finest primitive type—such as might have existed in preneurotic days. His complexion was of a smooth golden russet; his nose and lips were cut rather in the lines of sensuous cynicism; the look in his polished brown eyes was of defiant self-confidence, capable of the extremes of devotion or of obstinacy. Short curling black hair covered his scalp, and his moustache and small crisp beard were of the same hue.

"Thanks, stranger," he said, in a somewhat nasal but musical voice. "Your attack—a little cowardly, perhaps, for all its provocation—has served to release me before my time. Thanks—thanks indeed!"

Amos sent a sick and groping glance towards the alcove. The curtain was pulled back—the couch was empty. His vision returning, caught sight of Adnah still standing motionless.

"No, no!" he screeched in a suffocated voice, and clasped his hands convulsively.

There was an adoring expression in her wet eyes that grew and grew. In another moment she had thrown herself at the stranger's feet.

"Master," she cried, in a rich and swooning voice: "O Lord and Master—as blind love foreshadowed thee in these long months!"

He smiled down upon her.

"A tender welcome on the threshold," he said softly, "that I had almost renounced. The young spirit is weak to confirm the self-sacrifice of the old. But this ardent modern, Adnah, who, it seems, has slipped his opportunity?"

Passionately clasping the hands of the young Jew, she turned her face reluctant.

"He has blood on him," she whispered. "His lip is swollen like a schoolboy's with fighting. He is not a man, sane, self-reliant and glorious—like you, O my heart!"

The Jew gave a high, loud laugh, which he checked in mid-career.

"Sir," he said derisively, "we will wish you a very pleasant good-morning."

How—under what pressure or by what process of self-effacement—he reached the street, Amos could never remember. His first sense of reality was in the stinging cold, which made him feel, by reaction, preposterously human.

It was perhaps six o'clock of a February morning, and the fog had thinned considerably, giving place to a wan and livid glow that was but half-measure of dawn. He found himself going down the ringing pavement that was talcous with a sooty skin of ice, a single engrossing resolve hammering time in his brain to his footsteps.

The artificial glamour was all past and gone—beaten and frozen out of him. The rest was to do—his plain duty as a Christian, as a citizen—above all, as a gentleman. He was, unhypnotized, a law-abiding young man, with a hatred of notoriety and a detestation of the abnormal. Unquestionably his forebears had made a huge muddle of his inheritance.

About a quarter to seven he walked (rather unsteadily) into Vine Street Police Station and accosted the inspector on duty.

"I want to lay an information."

The officer scrutinised him, professionally, from the under side, and took up a pen.

"What's the charge?"

"Administering a narcotic, attempted murder, abduction, profanity, trading under false pretences, wandering at large—great heavens! what isn't it?"

"Perhaps you'll say. Name of accused?"

"Cartaphilus."

"Any other?"

"The Wandering Jew."

The Inspector laid down his pen and leaned forward, bridging his finger-tips under his chin.

"If you take my advice," he said, "you'll go and have a Turkish bath."

The young man gasped and frowned.

"You won't take my information?"

"Not in that form. Come again by-and-by."

Amos walked straight out of the building and retraced his steps to Wardour Street.

"I'll watch for his coming out," he thought, "and have him arrested, on one charge only, by the constable on the beat. Where's the place?"

Twice he walked the length of the street and back, with dull increasing amazement. The sunlight had edged its way into the fog by this time, and every door and window stood out sleek and self-evident. But amongst them all was none that corresponded to the door or window of his adventure.

He hung about till day was bright in the air, and until it occurred to him that his woeful and bloodstained appearance was beginning to excite unflattering comment. At that he trudged for the third time the entire length to and fro, and so coming out into Oxford Street stood on the edge of the pavement, as though it were the brink of Cocytus.

"Well, she called me a boy," he muttered; "what does it matter?"

He hailed an early hansom and jumped in.

THE FACE ON THE SHEET
(1900)

This, you may take it, is the true version of a very extraordinary story, a garbled report of which at one time got into the papers. Its *bona fides*, as here written down, I can attest, for I was a native of Compton Martel, and present at the lecture ("Domestic Architecture," with dissolving views), at which the shocking scene took place.

I must premise that, some months before the date of the lecture, which was simply one of a series organised by a local "Literature, Science, and Art Society," Compton Martel had acquired an unenviable notoriety on account of an extremely brutal murder, that had for the once stained its rather boorish records with an ugly blot. The victim of the crime was one Martha Blumenthal, a middle-aged lady of eccentric habits and small popularity, who had lived by herself in an old Jacobean house at the extreme north end of the High Street.

This poor woman—a reputed miser, with, it must be confessed, a detestable misanthropic character had been found one morning murdered in her own hall. The fact that the man, who was in the habit of bringing her her daily milk from a neighbouring farm, had failed for some three or four mornings to procure an answer to his knockings, at length aroused suspicions, with the result that constables forced an entrance, and found the wretched creature lying dead, her skull starred and splintered, in a perfect pond of blood.

There were, of course, a frantic hue and cry, inflated rumour, extravagant speculation, and—a blank full-stop. The fox had run to earth, it seemed, and lay close.

That robbery had been the motive, was sufficiently evident; but only that had been removed from the house which was easy of carriage and concealment.

For long Compton Martel suffered a nightmare of insecurity. Then the vestry elections were to the fore, and interests shifted.

Still, in cottages on rainy days, or in the tap of the "Three Tuns," discussion wavered to the tragedy; and still, fitfully, local labourer and black-boding tramp were pitted one against another as candidates for a grisly distinction.

Now you shall hear how at that lecture the truth came to be known, and in a very awful fashion.

It was in the schoolroom (not "Board," for we hadn't come to that then), and the most of us who were respectable were present. Mr. Cornish, from the neighbouring town, peripatetic archaeologist and photographer, a stiff, dry talker, with a cold, insistent way about him that overawed clownish disrespect, was on the platform against the sheet, and his operator, with the lantern and slides, was posted at the back of the room. To the front, in the place of honour, was Barom Gramshaw of Leets, Lord of the Manor of Compton, President of the Society, and high patron of the interests it represented.

The lecturer had spoken of architecture technically and morally, of cornices, architraves, and columns, both from the structural point of view and from that of their expression of a national character. He would trace the ethical evolution of any race through the processes of its builders, and he would be, and was, most profoundly pedantic over it all, and most monstrously uninteresting.

Still we listened—thinking of the indemnifying pipe and glass before the fire presently, no doubt. But we listened, nevertheless; for I tell you there was something about the man that commanded attention—an atmosphere, rather than a personality, the room being too dark to make out more of him than a black skimp figure and a white blotch of face.

He was no stranger to us, however. Poking about in the neighbourhood with folding stand and camera, snapping at bits of wall, cankered gravestones, half-tumbled byres, and such candle-ends of "auld lichts," so to speak, as men of his kidney take their mental sustenance of, his figure was most familiar to Compton Martel. To secure a negative gave him a sense of possession in its subject, it was said, that was as arrogant as ownership. And he, too, was suspected of being a miser.

Now the dissolving views were our milestones on a dreary road of prolixity; and therefore a rustle of relief went round the room when, after a fifteen-minutes preamble (or pre-maunder) on the subject of the ethical significances of Jacobean architecture, he came to the recurrent stop which was the prelude to something on the sheet.

"You have in your own village," drawled the lecturer, "an elegant example of early Georgian work. I allude to a house that recently gained some unpleasant notoriety. That is nothing to the point. What interests us is the extreme beauty of the porch, and of the lines of the window above it. No earlier than this morning I took a photograph of the subject, which I will now proceed to show you in illustration. John!"

He signed to the man at the back to put in the slide. His speech was commonplace enough, was it not?—little in it to show how it was to "thunder in the index."

On the disc of brilliant light a shadow fell—out of focus—click! and it snapped into place.

There was a moment's dead silence. Then a stir went amongst the audience, that suggested to me, I swear, the shudder of dying limbs under bedclothes. A woman or two shrieked out in a stifled way, and I saw the man next to me lean forward, his eyeballs glinting like porcelain.

What was the matter? Why, this. On the sheet before us was depicted the upper part of the porch of Martha Blumenthal's house, with the window above it, *and through the window was looking a face hateful and ghastly beyond words!*

Remember that, by his own statement, Mr. Cornish had taken the photograph that very morning, and remember that the murder had been committed quite three months before, and that the house had remained ever since shunned and tenantless!

I heard the Hodge next to me fall back in his chair with a straining groan.

"Mawtha Bloomintail herself, by God!" he whispered.

There was menace of a general hysteric collapse, when old Gramshaw struggled to his feet and broke the spell on the nick of the moment.

"Mr. Cornish!" he cried, in a loud, wavering voice, "what does this mean—what does this mean, sir? It is not right nor decent, upon my word—it is in abominably bad taste, sir!"

There was no answer. Suddenly someone turned up the gas, and the horrible face went into a phantom of itself.

But an explanation of the silence was given in the figure of the lecturer, swaying, half-convulsed, his cheeks a sick white, his fingers picking at his collar.

Before a soul could help him, down he went his full length, with a dusty slap—and on the instant the face sunk out of the sheet, and there was only the porch and an empty window.

Then a dozen of us ran up, through the cries and babble of the women, and carried him into the little side room and stretched him on the table.

Now, this is an old story with those of us who received and retained the impression; and that I must say, because many, so it appeared, afterwards professed themselves unconscious of the vision, and as only affected by an unexplainable atmosphere while the photograph was exhibiting. Therefore it was that, in the result, we who both saw and remembered the hideous presentment, decided to lay no emphasis upon the circumstances that induced the murderer to his confession.

For it was Mr. Cornish who had committed the crime. So far, in its bald facts, you may read in certain past-dated newspapers. He was led to it, at once by his monomania for possession, and by the miserly reputation of the dark recluse in the old Jacobean house. In his hauntings of the ancient village he had learned of her habits, of her solitariness, of her conjectural hoards. It was miser cut miser. The lust of avarice came to a head in him, and, stimulated by the sense of security her isolation afforded him, he did the deed. One windy March morning, before the sleep was out of village eyes, he rapped at the door with the plaster shell over it. Martha Blumenthal came to the window above the porch, and looked down upon him. His aspect presented nothing fearful; the loaded stick in his hand might have been a light walking cane. Very possibly she knew him by sight, and had marked his innocuous pursuits. At any rate, she came to his summons and was murdered.

All this he gasped out on the table. What he might not explain was that abnormal development of the acquisitive in him, which could not only triumph over all traditions of culture, but could affect, and apparently feel, a callousness so astonishingly great as to enable him, without emotion, to illustrate an innocent phase of his character with material drawn from that character's most diseased propensities. But the pathology of crime bristles with such paradoxes.

As to the apparition—well, "Death and the sun are not to be looked at steadily," as M. Rochefoucauld says; and I prefer not to think of that face.

And Mr. Cornish died on the table. At the inquest they could find no more definite verdict than "Shock."

But that we had all had.

THE FOOT OF TIME
(1900)

"*How noiseless falls the foot of time.*"—W. R. Spencer.

There was no doubt that Mandrel had outrivalled himself. The doctor, the duchess, the poet, the critic—any typical collectorate of Show Sunday even to the brother artist—must admit that the picture was an indisputable masterpiece. It was not that the technique was superb; that detail and atmosphere were truth represented by one who was her admirable proxy; that here was a work with which one could as completely live a lifetime on terms of intimacy as with a window that framed a noble view. Such qualities, and such sentiments respecting them, were, according to the Mandrel "cult," the accepted creed. This artist was always signal, always whole-hearted, always impressive. He sold that he might live: but he did not live to sell.

Upon this, his last work, however, there lay the glamour of an inspiration that seemed to draw direct, through no construing medium, from the brain of the infinite. It was in the expression of an arrested moment, effortless, unself-conscious, that the power *was*. Here were no scagliola; no "tricky" effects; no art jerry-built to crumble under the usage of a generation. It was just a ray of Nature mirrored by genius and reflected upon a screen.

The subject of the picture was simplicity itself: a wood of vast summer trees and inextricable undergrowth; space in the foreground, dominated by a single dying and near denuded monarch of timber; to the front of all, a presentment of the artist seated upon a log, his back to the spectator, an indescribable expression of fascination in his pose.

And there was this in suggestion (so wonderfully did art administer truth, or truth accredit art) that silence was in the woods; the silence that precedes some change, some advent; the silence that takes the thick pattering of its own heart for the footfall of an unrealised presence. Before the scattering airs of dawn are astir; when the moonlight is dripping like quicksilver from the branches, and making a dull amalgam of the first golden charity of the day; when shrouded things of the forest are stealing reluctant into the deep rayless copses, and every bough throbs like an artery with the excited breathings of birds—here was the moment seized, the impression rendered. No one could doubt that change was imminent; no one could doubt that the figure in the foreground was intent on something that had just withdrawn or was just approaching.

It was an odd tribute to the genius of the picture that those who came up and stood before it fell instinctively quiet, as though they had passed from sunlight and its voices into the hushed solemnity of a church, and were there Catholics all in their sure consciousness of a Presence. One by one they gazed; woke, as from a little chilly trance; shivered, and moved on. But, curiously enough, whatever their undemonstrative homage to his art, to the painter himself—who, reserved, unobtrusive, austere, stood persistently apart from this his work—none seemed moved to proffer congratulation; but each, in taking leave, would murmur some half-intelligible social formula of thanks, and so hurriedly quit the studio. Only the doctor seemed to take exception to the general conduct in a note of somewhat protesting wonder.

"You have succeeded to the inheritance of the lost arts, Mandrel," he said. "It is quite inconceivable to the lay mind how you get your effects."

"Miraculous!" murmured a passing voice.

The doctor, deliberately twirling and vibrating his pince-nez before him on their guard, deliberately conned the artist's face, as he took up the phrase:—

"Miraculous? Nonsense! A cluster of congenital impulses brought to the focus that produces an abnormal degree of heat and light—nothing more."

Mandrel smiled, looking steadily back into the other's eyes. Quite suddenly the doctor held out his hand.

"Good-bye!" he said: "Good-bye!"—and went preoccupied out into the street. There he joined two or three that had immediately preceded him; and they all strolled on together.

"Umph!" grunted the doctor to himself— "umph-umph!" like a very gentlemanly pig; and that was the measure of the general conversation for some moments.

"I didn't like it!" burst out the duchess at length: "I didn't like it at all. There was something—secret, inhuman—*la dessous des cartes*—I don't know how to describe it!"

Her high pretty voice ended the strain—or began it, according to one's rendering of the word. Immediately, one and all—save the doctor—opened upon the subject that was nearest the soul of each.

"To me it was full of an indescribable suggestion," cried the poet, in a rapture of emotion. "I have seen a vision, and I shall be the humbler poet and the truer man for the lesson. I thought I heard the sound of breathing behind the tree, and the doves moaning prettily in their dreams as they listened to the stories of their own hearts.

The critic glanced at the speaker with a shrug of disdain; but his own face fell bewildered, as he said—

"Mandrel has certainly surpassed himself. Technique, Composition, Chiaroscuro—pooh! it is profanation to cite them. The cant falls lame as a wind-galled jade. It is nothing less than a miracle; but—I agree with you, duchess, the atmosphere is haunted."

The tall girl hugged herself into her furs with a shiver and a half-petulant exclamation.

"Haunted! I don't know. I wish I was at San Remo amongst the orange-trees. Isn't it vilely cold? Look at that wretched girl, with a basketful of narcissus!"

She fumbled in her pocket; produced her purse. "Give it to her," she said imperatively to the critic; but he hung fire.

"Please!" she said, turning to the poet. "I have so many arrears to make up."

The poet took the costly "trash," smiled, crossed the road, and executing his commission with aplomb, returned to his companions. The critic—be it marked—forbore to criticise an act so deadlily irrational. They moved on together again.

"What were we talking about?" said the duchess— "the picture? But it was that horrible wrinkled foot, I think, that—"

"Horrible!" struck in the poet; and "wrinkled!" he echoed in astonishment. "Pardon me, duchess. Surely—"

"The point of view," interrupted the critic acidly.

"To me," said the poet, quite amazed, "it was the foot of an ageless dryad. It was fragrant with the crush of flowers. It lay like a smooth white stone in the moss."

"Are you mad?" cried the duchess. "It was clawed and wrinkled, and it gripped the earth. Crushed flowers! Indeed, yes. It looked as heavy as one of those hideous saurian things. The whole wood seemed to cower under its tread."

"Well!" cried the poet. "Can it be possible we mean the same?"

"Behind the tree?"

"Yes; behind the tree. Why, my dear madam, it was the foot of the very bride of earth—white and sweet and welcome."

The critic laughed out on a mirthless note.

"Hear the superlatives of sciolism!" he said; "the extravagance to which undisciplined temperaments are wont!" And, "Believe me" (he went on authoritatively), "the art of the painter was never more signally illustrated than in making this foot a phantom—a suggestion. Claws! Dryad! Oh, be assured it was neither one nor the other such definite conception; but the treatment was intentionally vague, that each might interpret of it his own chimera. For myself—to look at it long was to see it a mere mask, with neither beauty or terror, but only emptiness behind it."

At this point the doctor coming to a sudden stop, the others paused instinctively, as though he had cried halt!

"Would you mind telling me," he said—a sort of protesting desperation on his face— "if you are all possessed of a common devil?"

"Eh?" said the critic drawlingly.

"This foot?" said the doctor: "what foot?"

"What foot!" exclaimed the poet and the duchess.

"Ah!" said the critic. "You go a step further than I, even—"

The doctor, spotless, and groomed to a hair, looked as if he could tear open the bosom of his shirt.

"Please tell me," he said, forcibly pinioning his own reason by the elbows. "A foot, you say? Where was the foot?"

They let the duchess speak.

"Showing from behind the tree. You didn't know what was there; but you worried yourself horribly. It was coming—but it never came. The artist himself was intent on it—fascinated by it. You could see it in his attitude, though his face was hidden. Surely you don't mean to say you never noticed it?"

"I studied the picture minutely, as it claimed to be studied. As I am a sane human being, unemotional, and an F.R.C.S., there was no hint of a foot anywhere on the canvas."

The duchess turned away with a shrug of her shoulders, the poet with a smile.

"Come!" said the former; and that was all. The doctor and the critic were left standing together.

"You go too far—you go too far," said the critic, a little impatient annoyance in his voice. "The interpretation is open to dispute; but it is ridiculous to affirm that the foot is not there in suggestion."

The doctor placed his finger-tips gently on the other's shoulder.

"We have a common profession in this—not to waste words. It is but a little way to go. Will you come back with me to Mandrel's studio and show me this foot?"

Curiously, the critic hesitated. A slight shadow seemed to draw itself over his face. He sighed—and frowned.

"Certainly," he said doggedly.

They returned together. The studio, when they re-entered it, was empty and deathly quiet. A shaft of sunlight struck through the glass in the ceiling, full upon the picture where it rested, solemn and alone, upon its easel.

The critic went straight and stubbornly to resolve the question in dispute. The doctor stepped hastily in the direction of the recess where he had last seen the artist standing.

"Mandrel! Mandrel!" he cried.

His voice rang out in the stillness—snapped suddenly—reeled up to the rafters, and dissipated like smoke. . . .

The critic turned about to a touch on his shoulder. There was a lost expression on his face—of amazement and terror.

"It is gone," he whispered awfully. "The canvas is not wet, and it is gone. There is not a sign of it here."

"Of what?"

"The foot."

The doctor pulled himself up and together, and spoke in his driest tones.

"Oh, the foot! Of course. It had escaped me for the moment. You will acknowledge now your observation was at fault. There is a more serious matter to engage us. Will you brace yourself to something of a shock? I was concerned for his appearance when we parted just now. He looks quite peaceful and happy, but—Mandrel has died suddenly—during these few minutes while we have been walking up the street."

THE LADY-KILLER
(1900)

It was when I was standing before the looking-glass, dressing for dinner, that I first saw the face. To say I was immediately conscious of a shock and a thrill is no more than to admit my premature realisation of the existence within myself of that nameless nerve that in the general case is touched and proved for the first time by Death. I was startled, but not terrified. That a preposterously earnest poodle countenance (so I thought it) should suddenly be reflected as appearing actually between my face and the white bow I was manipulating in the front of my collar (as if, indeed, it were interposing itself, to try the effect of the ornament against its own neck), shocked me on the instant only as a silent dig in the ribs would have done. And, in the same moment, the impression had vanished. The door had opened to admit a belated servant, who murmured an apology, rattled down a can of hot water on the wash-hand-stand, and withdrew.

I was still on the poise of the rebound—my hands petrified at their task—and I did not turn my head. But I was distinctly aware how the girl in her retreat gave a quick little rush and giggle, as though she were evading some playfully proffered embrace. The door shut with a bang.

Then I myself laughed; found a more or less plausible explanation of my fancy; finished my dressing, and descended in order to the dining-room.

Now, here I will not say that I and my digestion were on their usual easy terms, or that a self-consciousness of preoccupation was not jarred upon by the little boisterous habits of speech and manner that in general I might regard as engaging characteristics of my friend and host. He would rally me, after his custom, upon my inattentiveness to my partner; he would ask me what had come between me and my appetite. And, in moments of exalted irritation, I could have wished to cry out, "A poodle's face, you fool! and there it sticks in my gullet yet!"

Was the house, in truth, haunted? George can have been nothing but inimical to a spectral condition of things. His laugh would have shivered the very mirror that produced it. He was one of those men who have an impregnable reverence for their own limitations. It was hopeless to think of approaching his confidence in the matter; and that any phantom itself may have felt. And so my reflections (uneasy word!) would revert to the plausible explanation, and I myself to a slightly hysterical ostentation of sanity. But still I would be fingering my tie.

I paused a minute outside my bedroom door to listen to the cheery sounds of parting fellowship that, at midnight, still pursued me up the stairs. If I had tried to stimulate myself into forgetfulness, mine was a "vaulting ambition." The door might have been a guillotine, for the way in which it severed my vital continuity, and committed my bloodless face to the basket, so to speak.

I left a long candle—two candles—burning, and lay on my pillows gasping in an unnatural ague. But one speck of warmth—a little close range of pride (that my sickness had not idiotically succumbed to its yearning for sympathy)—must serve to medicine my overmastering chill. Little by little it took hold—extended—absorbed and stupefied my brain. I slept like a condemned criminal.

The period put to my trance may have been soon or late. There was no interval but such as is spanned by the shadowy devil's-bridge of dreams. When I awoke with a shock and sat up, I recognised, as surely as the condemned recognises the hangman's step in the corridor, that my fate was upon me.

At the first, in my drugged vision, I must associate the horror with a sort of inhuman travesty of myself. I had flung my trousers—after denuding myself of them—over the back of a chair, so that the legs depended, limp and separate, to within an inch or two of the floor. And on the chair-back—habited in these garments after the spectral fashion by intruding its limbs *behind* rather *into* them—*it* was seated.

It appeared, I could have thought, to be criticising the effect with some complacency. And then in a moment it raised its face, looked at me with a certain intensity, and, finding its feet, came soundlessly towards the bed and leaned its arms akimbo over the foot bar.

"'Twixt saddle and ground Grace he found." So, in legendary doggerel, the Roman Catholic crystallises his faith in the efficacy of the ultimate "act of contrition." I don't know that I had made *any* specifically (emotionally, my instinct may have deprecated the visitation with some such schoolboy's protest as "It wasn't me, sir!"), but I had thought I should die directly the phantom moved. It moved—and on the instant Grace was vouchsafed me. It moved—and the very "nice conduct" of its legs seemed to galvanise me back to reason. Was this because the legs themselves were clothed in pepper-and-salt "pegtops"? Was it because the *poodle* character of the face was due—as I instantly recognised—to long "Dundreary" whiskers? Our apprehensions, it would appear, are only exaggerated conventions of thought. It is said that the man who eats mutton, thinking it to be beef, will experience a difficulty in digesting his meal. I may have gone further than this. My ghostly pabulum hitherto had ranged from cavaliers to cocked hats. I could not even swallow a long-whiskered spectre in pegtops.

It stood dwelling upon my face with haunting eyes. There was something of cockney self-sufficiency—if I may dare the term—in its aspect. But even that was vindicated by the diaphanous propriety of its gestures. It seemed to hold itself with such gentlemanly tact from collapsing into a shapeless blot of mist upon the floor. And its voice—when it spoke at last—might have come, little and distant, from the window-curtains or the wardrobe, as if it would politely accommodate itself to my fancy that I dreamt.

"You haunt this house?" I said at last desperately.

"And this room." (The tone was indescribably *inwardly* shrill and mournful.)

"Why?"

"In life it was mine."

(I thought it particularly mean of George—if he knew—not to have told me this.)

"A senseless self-restriction," I said, "when you are become a very lord of time and space."

At my words it raised and wrung its hands—even posing abstractedly to its own reflection, which it suddenly caught sight of in the looking-glass.

"Senseless!" it cried in protest, adjusting a curl on its forehead, yet not unpleased, I could have thought, with the titular distinction I had conferred upon it. And "Lord of time and space!" it moaned— "but not of one material cure to the transmitted tyranny of the senses!"

I sat trembling on my pillows. Hideously I knew myself to be verging on the confidence of the unnamable.

It wrung its hands again. It seemed to be trying to wash them of the accusation.

"Blind, blind!" it shrilled; "blind and deaf, not to know that to crop a limb is not to cull the cramps and itchings that were incidental to it! not to know that to be quit of life is not to forego one sensation of all that made it actual."

"The House of Death is a house of blind walls," I said, with a shiver. "One may lie all night under its eaves and see nothing and hear nothing. Is there then a physical torture-chamber within? Is the spirit but extended matter—a captive balloon with a nerve for cable? Yet it is written in the very text-book of spectrology that I may throw this candlestick through, and not inconvenience you."

"And may you not kick a wooden leg without hurt to its owner?" mourned the phantom. "Yet shall he feel every tight boot, every twinge of gout that once gave suffering to his vanished limb. Oh, mortal, double-cased in vainglory! hear this! No colic stabbed, no crawling flea tickled me in my material life but the sensation pursues me into this. Shadowy and helpless, I must suffer again, and over again, all the torment, all the aggravation, and no nail to scratch myself or hot compress to apply withal."

My flesh crept. My heart went chill.

"But cannot you," I implored, "re-live these remedial sensations also?"

"No," it cried; "for they were self-indulgent, and only that, in character."

Then, in a moment, I knew what it was to be damned.

"And none," I muttered, "and none can relieve your wretchedness?"

I think it read the undermeaning in my words. A shadow of embarrassment—the shadow of a shadow—flickered in its face. It half-glanced round at my trousers where they hung—then faced me again.

"I only wanted to see," it murmured; then checked itself, and said firmly, "None."

"Then why—" I began.

"In this room," it took me up with, "much of the glory and tragedy of my life were enacted."

"And many of the sensations?"

"It follows," said the ghost.

"Forgive me," I ventured tremulously; "but is not this haunting of it rather wantonly to invite on your part the transmitted tyranny of—say the fleas?"

It did not answer me directly, and then with only a certain irrelevant manner of coxcombry. It was evidently preoccupied by its own thoughts.

"There was Evadne," it murmured, as it seemed retrospectively, "and Maudlin, and the little gloriosa. They came like bees to a dahlia, and one by one they dropped off drunk with love. I entered their names in my book of engagements, and scratched them out in rotation as their hearts broke."

I sprang to my knees in uncontrollable horror.

"Wretch!" I shrieked, "I see it all now! Cursing and accursed, you are condemned to haunt for evermore the scene of your abominations!"

A smile of infinite complacency illumined its features.

"You have said it," it lisped. "Behold, the lady-killer!"

And at that moment the cock crew, and I fell back senseless on the bed.

I had no need to approach my subject with circumlocution. George, it seemed, was prepared for it. The frenzy of rage I felt thereat did something to relieve my nervous tension.

I had come down feeling like a damned soul packed into a battered old trunk and addressed to eternity with the *This side up* disregarded. In such condition I must run the gauntlet of chaff or commiseration. But immediately breakfast was over I took George aside and opened upon him. I began considerately, willing even in the deplorable state of my own feelings to spare his. I said, while he stared at me, that under no circumstances could I ever sleep in that room again; that—

And before I could utter a word further he went into a bellow of laughter.

"What!" says he. "You have seen him, I suppose?"

My jaw dropped. Rage began to boil in my heart. He gave me a sickening thump on the shoulder.

"Why, it's only Uncle John!" he cried, his whole face creasing. "It never occurred to me you'd mind him. He died in '60 and has been here at intervals ever since. Nobody heeds him. The children throw things through him (they've got a special game they call stomach-ball), the cats are always falling downstairs through trying to rub against his legs, the maids are forever on the giggle over his trying to kiss 'em, you know. He's quite harmless."

"Quite!" I managed to choke out in bitter irony; "quite harmless; quite a companion for children; quite an exemplary shadow to hang over servant-girls!—Quite an inhuman devil!" I suddenly shouted, losing my self-control.

George put a hand on the shoulder he had injured, and the skin of his face was all flickering up in little shreds of subdued laughter.

"I see he's been gassing as usual," he said. "Maud and Evadne and all the rest of it, I suppose. Now, I'll tell you, he was the dearest, simplest old fellow that ever staked his honesty against the jockeys. Only, he was vain! my good hat, wasn't he vain! Intrigue! he never had one in his life; and why he sticks to his old room—well, the truth is, I expect, that he can't find such another morally sweet spot in the town. 'Twas all vanity, sir. He loved to be thought irresistible. I've heard him boast of his success in t'other world with Messalina and Ninon de l'Enclos—two pretty rapid young ladies, as I understand. But I don't suppose in point of fact he's done more than bow to 'em. It's reprehensible, of course, but it's just a disease. Dear old boy—how I remember him in life! And as for vanity—why, I don't believe that to this day a new button's invented that he don't know about it. He tries on everything he can get hold of. He can't shed his pegtops, of course, but for all that it's heaven to him, in my opinion, to know the fashions. And if Uncle John wasn't given the chance to choose his own heaven—why, there's reform wanted in the system of rewards; that's all I can say."

"He called himself a lady-killer," I murmured.

"And that he certainly was," said George; "for they used to die with laughter at the figure he cut."

THE DEVIL'S FANTASIA
(1902)

"Signor Marconi," said I, "is confident that in a little while New York and Land's End will be able to talk together without the need of wires."

"The whole world will be one whispering-gallery," said George. "If you sit here, Johnny, and turn a deaf ear to me—as you very often do—I shall only have to show you my back, and speak a matter of twenty-three thousand miles into your other ear."

"Crikey!" said young Bob, in great admiration; "wouldn't Mr. Markham have fits just!"

Nevertheless, Bob was pleased with the fancy; for, though not yet out of Eton jackets—a tailless cub, *qui ne respirait que plaies et bosses*—he had a turn for practical science, and was permeated at that very moment with a wriggling and itching consciousness of proprietorship in one of its most characteristic toys—a phonograph, to wit—which his guardian brother George had presented to him that morning for a New Year's gift, and which was even then gloating sleekly on the sideboard, in anticipation of its opening, and so far unresolved-upon, charge.

"What a wheeze!" said Bobby; "and the old cables'll be pretty sick, I *don't* think. They'll have to reconcile 'emselves to slow freight, you know sermons, and marriages, and poetry, and rot like that."

Crack! went a chestnut in the fire, round which we were all sitting.

"There goes another!" said George. "Take care, Lucy; there's a bit blown on to your dress." Lucy flicked the fragment of shell away.

"I wish it was Signor what's-his-name's theory exploded," said she quite plaintively. "You didn't prick them, George. I must say I think this world is going to be made a detestable place for people who don't want to know everything."

"What don't you want to know, miss?" said Bobby brazenly. "Anything old Sneak's been tryin' to teach you?"

"You infernal young—" began George, roaring; but Lucy hushed him immediately, and addressed the monkey in a quiet enough voice, though her face was white.

"Don't speak about Mr. Schneck again, Bobby. I'm afraid you're particularly inclined to to-night, because you see it annoys me."

George subsided; and both he and I showed, I am sure, some small embarrassment.

"Well, anyhow, you've got to have him, or he you, about that old Philippine nut," muttered the boy mutinously; and then, though I was a little sick in the heart, I came to the rescue of the situation.

Lucy was a china shepherdess and the proudest little virtuosa in one. She was a born musician—so much to her finger-tips, that out of those poured the love and melody that are wont to issue elsewhere from lips. She could teach the old piano a trick or two, Bobby said; and indeed he was right. In taking her hand, one felt that one was half-way to her heart.

But even native gifts must be disciplined; and in Mr. Schneck, a naturalised *musiklehrer*, Lucy had found a professional director and confessor. After her heart? Well, sometimes I was unhappily constrained to think so—and in the double sense.

But he was popular with none other of us—not with George, who felt him, I think, a rather ugly responsibility; not with Bob, who loathed him; not certainly with George's partner, Mr. Markham, because that gentleman, at least, did believe him to be altogether too much after Lucy's own heart.

And then, suddenly, Miss Virtuosa herself, who had for months sat at the man's great feet—Miss Lucy, who had been Spring, froze to him. Why? Had he presumed beyond his engagement? I knew nothing, except that Schneck was a dangerous beast to offend.

The last time I had seen him was when, some evenings before at these Hessels' dinner table, he had secured the half of a double-kernelled nut that Lucy had cracked. That was Bobby's allusion. Pupil and teacher might be estranged (and, indeed, it seemed that they were, as effectually as unaccountably); yet each, by an absurd superstition, held the means to a playful forfeit of the other.

"I quite agree with you, Miss Hessel," said I. "There's too much of this sifting of the grain. What are we going to do, I should like to know, when we've worked out the sum of our own little corner of creation?"

"Kill the scientists and be haunted by their ghosts," said George.

"Yes," said Lucy, "that would be capital. It would be hoisting the creatures with their own—"

She stopped with an uncomfortable look. It had suddenly occurred to her that, not knowing the meaning of the word, she might be committing herself to a quotation from an un-Bowdlerised Shakespeare.

I quoted, in my turn, with a nervous glance at Bobby—

"When Science from Creation's face
  Enchantment's veil withdraws,
What lovely visions yield their place
  To cold material laws!

"Look here," said George hurriedly, for he saw Bobby prepared to explode, "I'll read the three of you a passage from a book I was looking into before dinner. It ought to reconcile you all—science and romance and the rest of it—because it makes poetry out of progress," and he collared the volume and went at it—

"I never hold with those who cry that hollow are delights—that first is but the beginning of last. Life flies before, and the ecstasy is in the chase. Shall man's soul be a lesser thing than his imagination? Shall the hunt end with the running down of the

> quarry? Ah, the glimpses, the vistas, the wild voices, seen and heard in the racing! We have gained upon, we have outstripped them in the rush; but, when we stop, they overtake and pass us, and we must on once more. It is not given to us to rest for ever in quiet pastures. The spirits of those we have slain we must follow, for every sacrifice we make to death robs us of a part of our independence, and always we are ready to yield that part for a song. Forward! forward with every pace the imagination extends its horizon. Forward! forward! and what if over the edge of the world? Does not the sound of horns blown from other stars echo down to us?
>
> "And, should we run the live game to earth? Earth is sweet and lovable—its fields, its flowers, its roads; the warm and hearty tenements compacted of its clay; the wine of its grapes, the fragrant smoke of its leaf, the bread and headstrong drink yielded of its grain. Give me life and a sunny road; good-humour and a cool tavern."

He came to a stop.

"And no phonographs," said Lucy defiantly. Bobby scowled, and turned a superior shoulder on his sister.

"What bally rot, George!" said he. "That's the stuff to go by slow freight."

Lucy smiled, serene and aggravating.

"Well," said she, "I prefer fancy to its imitations; and I wish every phonograph was burnt; and I declare I'd rather be haunted by a voice from the grave, than by one from a walnut-wood box."

The room door had been opened very softly.

"*Bon jour, Philippine!*" said a voice there.

We all started, and Lucy gasped like a frightened bird. Then Bobby gave a great rude laugh.

"Miss Fancy, Miss Fancy," crowed he, clapping his hands; "Mr. Sneak's got you first, and you'll have to pay forfeit!"

George rose, his instinct of hospitality bettering in him some natural restraint. After all, he was without warrant for implying a closure of the intimacy that had often hitherto found this visitor a guest at his fireside. Schneck, being better acquainted with the facts, must be judge of the propriety of his own conduct.

I stole a look at the girl. She was frowning—biting her lip. It was ignoble in me, perhaps, but my heart gave a little skip of exultation to read—or to think that it read—some signs in her face of implacable offence.

Schneck came heavily to the fire, nodding and humming, and smiling a little to himself. He was an unwieldy man, with a face one mask of hair, and a great nose—disgustedly pinched and pommelled out of shape in the modelling—that drew in at the wings, when he filled his chest for laughter. His clothes were like evangelical misfits. His voice tore every decent sentiment to rags. Yet he carried force on his shoulders, and his eyes were burning-glasses. An Englishman and pretty obstinate, I had always felt, up to now, that I had had little chance against this man.

Suddenly he spoke, his bass finding out a wire in the piano, that jarred to it.

"Pravo, Miss Lucy! Boetry from a parrel-organ? Ach Himmel! One would find as soon consistency in a woman. To be py fear, or remorse, or a melody haunted—yes, that is understoot; but py a mechanical hopgoblin! Indeet the world is going to pe made a detestaple blace for beoples who don't want to know everything."

He had no shame, it will be observed, in making this implicit confession of eavesdropping. He intended that it should suggest his knowledge of some personalities, of which he had been the subject long before he revealed himself. There was an air of hardly repressed ferocity about him, under which we all, I am sure, though conscious enough of guilt, found it difficult to regard *les convenances*.

Lucy, leaning back in her chair, took no notice whatever of his address. Her face was set in a studied indifference—pink and hard as china; but it was not the hardness that waits to be courted from its mood.

Schneck put away roughly the cigarette box proffered by George.

"I do not stop here," he said, "not more than a few minutes. I com to my forfeit claim, dat is all."

He nodded and laughed, and pinching out from his bagging waistcoat pocket his bit of a nut, held it up for evidence.

"*Bon jour, Philippine,*" says he, repeating himself. "It shall pe for you the task of all the easiest. Dat is jchost to blay me a little God-speed pefore I am on a long journey brojected."

George alone amongst us had the nerve, or the decency, to murmur something vaguely significative of a polite concern over this intimation of leave-taking. Schneck only growled in response, as if he were wishing to spit, the beast.

But Miss Hessel was on her feet immediately, her eyes expressing a relief that her lips would not acknowledge. It was evident that the question of the nut had been upon her mind (a mind—God bless her!—quite orthodox in its superstitions), and that the indifferent penalty exacted disburdened that of some apprehensions.

"I am ready, Herr Schneck," said she. "What shall it be?"

Perhaps he had hoped against hope for some expression of regret, of protest, at least of surprise over his departure. He looked into the fire a moment, biting at his under-lip till the hair on it rose like the withers of a dog; and then he put a hand into his inner breast-pocket, reluctantly, as if he were robbing his heart, and brought out a single yellow sheet of music.

"It is this," he said, his eyes lowered, while he fidgeted the paper eternally in his hands. "Somthing that has a very strange recollegtion. It was giffen me wonce by a man—a musician—that picked it up corked into a pottle and vloating at sea. I haf it myself never blayed, and he only wonce. He was ill that same night. He was neffer petter. On his death-ped he for me sent, and boot this into my hands. Now, at last, I would hear it. It is to regord a long farewell."

We all, I think, longed to get this unprofitable sentimentality over; yet we couldn't in decency rally Lucy on the situation. She accepted the faded sheet from the hand that held it out to her, and looked at it with some instinctive curiosity.

"It is very old," she said; "a figured bass."

"It is old," said Schneck quietly.

"And incomplete," said the girl wonderingly; "a duet, it seems, with the treble left out."

Schneck did not answer.

"Am I to play it," she asked, "unscored, imperfect, just as it is?"

He bowed, as if he could not trust himself to speak, and withdrawing as she crossed to the piano, halted between her and the door, his arms folded over his chest. As he thus stood motionless, the shaded gaslight, streaming upon his head, seemed to melt his every knot and feature into rivulets of gall, that flowed down and were merged into his beard.

Lucy, as sweet and native a musician as ever perched on a stool, settled herself, and paid out the first notes of her forfeit.

"Good God!" cried George, getting hurriedly to his feet; "not again, Lucy. We've had enough."

I came out of a nightmare, and stared at him. His face was livid. Bobby, crouched down in the chimney-corner, was snivelling. And Schneck was gone—had vanished in the thick of that infernal cacophony as if blown to the winds.

Once, twice, thrice had Lucy gone through the devilish duet—duet! was the girl hideously exalted, inspired, reduplicated?—and now a fourth time she was restarting on it.

"Oh, do stop her!" whimpered Bob.

George, in a loud, shaky voice, asserted his authority.

"That's enough, Lucy. Mr. Schneck's gone, and we don't care about any more. Damn it!" he screamed, "*will* you stop!"

I saw the girl's face peering evilly at us over the top of the piano; but the rush and explosion of notes never ceased. Yet, physically, she did not seem agitated in any degree proportionate with the hell she was raising. Her face looked calm, and shockingly evil—just that.

I felt as sick as a rat in a trap; but in a moment I was across the room and by her side—had put down my hands upon hers as they danced upon the keyboard. As I did so, I heard an appalling little sound through the rest. It was her teeth grinding at me. Then, in pure, unadulterated horror, I snatched my arms away and stood glaring. Her hands were flashing and glancing in the bass. She was responsible for no more than her share of the *duo diabolique.* But, up in the treble, nevertheless, the keys were pitting and pattering in a furious gambade, *though there were no fingers there to work them.*

"Come away, *in God's name!*" I muttered.

A chord so dissonant answered me, that I felt as if a bullet had crashed through my jaws and teeth.

"I can't—I wont!" she whined, her voice hopping in time to her hands. "I've chosen to bind myself, and I must go on—for ever and ever. Please stand away. It's the most wicked and delightful thing—not heavenly, but delightful."

I heard George breathing at my ear.

"What's happened to her? Who is she?"

And in an instant he had thrust me aside, and was making as if to tear her from her seat.

"Ah!" she shrieked hoarsely, crouching aside from him with a hateful look (and it was horrible to see that in her facile memory the *thing* was now so scored that she had no longer need to consult the manuscript). "Ah !—if you dare—if you touch me, I will scream the house down!"

Her fingers never stopped while she spoke—hers, or those others. He staggered back as if she had flung her little fist into his face.

"What are we to do?" he said in a thick, sick voice.

Suddenly he was flinging about, stamping, beating his ears, swearing like a madman.

"That devil!" he screeched. "Someone must go after him, kill him, bring him back at once—you, Markham!"

I turned and seized and held him steady.

"Not I, George. You, you. Leave me alone with her. You know why. It may bring her to herself. Listen, man: it may bring her to herself, I say."

He stared a moment, reeled, and went floundering towards the door. There he stopped and twisted about, fumbling drunkenly behind him for the handle.

"Come, Bobby," he muttered.

The boy edged, sobbing and slinking, by the wall, made a little final rush, and hustled him from the room. The door closed upon them.

With an indescribable desperate feeling of exaltation in my heart, I turned and fell on my knees by the girl. The sweet young bedevilled face had a smile of triumph on it. She laughed softly, with an infamous happiness. In the midst of her ecstasy, her gloating eyes were moved to look into the pain of mine. Immediately something—it was like a breath coming and going very faintly on a mirror pulsed in her cheek.

"I can't help it, you know," she said, in a bewildered, but much gentler voice and I don't think I want to. But I wish you wouldn't look so troubled. If you loved me really" (I had spoken no word to her), "you wouldn't wish to rob me of such a transport."

I put my arms about her waist, and my lips to the little shining band of satin that imprisoned it from me.

"I do love you!" I cried. "Oh, my little girl, with my whole soul of love and sorrow!"

I felt a tremor go through her, and I thought the music rose suddenly in gasps and bounds, as if she were urging herself, or were being urged reluctant, to a new intoxication. Then in an instant she was moaning—

"If I could get rid of it! If someone would take it from me, as I took it from him!"

I scrambled to my feet and snatched (it was inexplicable we had not thought of it sooner) the damned sheet from the stand, and hurrying with it to the fire, threw it and stamped it upon the burning coals. It caught, blazed into a roar and hiss, and went wobbling piecemeal in ashes up the chimney. . . . Still the accursed fantasia went on, and I was back at her side.

"Lucy!" I cried, heart-sick.

She laughed horribly.

"It's no good, unless someone can catch it—take my place—take it from me. And how can they do it, now you've burnt the score?"

Someone! It was all one to me. I knew no more, George knew no more, Bobby knew no more, about music than an organ-grinder. If she should die or go mad at her post! I was desperate now to keep her going till—till when? What would justify us in transmitting the scourge to another—an expert—even if we could find one demented enough to—

My brain crackled. In a frenzy of horror I ran round her, and flogged down with my hands at the hands I could not see.

"Take care!" said Lucy. "It's turning its nails up."

I fell back, and upon an inspiration. In a moment I was across the room, had seized Bobby's new year's gift from the sideboard, had turned the key in the lock. Here at least was such an instrument as I had experimented with and could manipulate. My nerves were strung to snapping. My hands were steady as a hangman's.

The duet leapt to its close. As the little ringing pause, that preluded a renewal of the horror, succeeded, I had all in readiness. Before Lucy's fingers rose for the opening swoop, I had dumped the naked machine down on the piano lid.

Now I set my teeth, and stood, and endured. I had something more than the others to uphold me; but the tension was terrible. As the riot swept on, I felt burning drops trickling down my forehead. The performance was more astounding, more delirious, more shattering than ever. It rose to a pitch, a fury that was scarce endurable. I wanted to outscream it; I took a step forward, and it slammed to an end. Standing rigid, as I had moved, I waited—waited, thinking I should die on my feet. Would the terrible white fingers lift and poise again? A minute passed—crawled into another. Suddenly she was swaying—drooping a little forward. I tore her into my arms, looked into her face, dropped my lips to her shut eyes, to her open mouth, looked again in agony. I had healed that wound—at least, had closed it; and a little smile was come about its corners. For the rest, she did not seem swooning so much as fallen into a deep, exhausted sleep. Murmuring incoherently, I carried her to a sofa, and laid her gently to rest there.

I had but drawn back, panting, regarding her, when the door hurriedly opened, and George reentered the room. His face was like ashes.

"Johnny! my God!" he said.

I signalled silence to him.

"Yes," I whispered, "she's asleep. It's all right; I've managed it," and I told him.

He stared, but was so far from being incredulous that he fell in at once with the practical solution of the problem. This was a demonology that one could understand—the psychical brought accountable to the physical; the supernatural brought up to date.

"That skunk—" he snarled.

"Did you find him—kill him?"

"He was gone—had packed up his luggage (a comb and a sausage, I suppose), and left his lodgings before he came here. He can keep now for a bit."

"And—and that there? what shall we do with it?"

"Why, the thing's got in; it's *taken* it, you know. There's no help for it. We must treat it as they treat infected bed-clothes."

"Burn it?"

He nodded.

"We'll not leave a rivet. We'll sweep the very ashes to the devil. I'll speak to Bobby; go and get rid of the servants. Two of them met me crying just now, and cook is leaving at a moment's notice. We score on that. I notice there's back in the stand a silver-knobbed umbrella that's been missing for months. She wouldn't embezzle goods with the devil's hall-mark on 'em. I expect this is going to be quite an event—a resurrection of unconsidered trifles. I'm looking forward quite touchingly to renewing my acquaintance with a dozen little matters of personal furniture, that from time to time have mysteriously vanished in the very face of large-eyed innocence, leaving not a rack behind. Stay here a moment."

His head was blown with relief, I think. He returned in a few minutes, carrying a lantern.

"Now, Johnny," said he, "you've done much, but, by your own account, you've been rather overpaid than under. I'm not going to be modest about it. Lucy's a plum for any man. You must win her up to the hilt. A deed half done is a deed undone. It's for you to finish—to take up that abomination and carry it downstairs."

I set my mouth. I would sooner have handled an adder. But I would not have had another complete my work. Gingerly I dismembered the mechanism, as I would have unscrewed the cap of a gorged shell; breathlessly I reconsigned all to the box, and, holding that at arm's length, followed George out into the hall and down to the basement. At the door of the kitchen I paused, while he lit the gas. Then, ghost-like, I stalked in. Black beetles—my detestation—exploded beneath my feet. I took no heed. Had I not fairly won my love at last?

Fortunately a great fire was burning. Deliberately, at scorching risk, I placed the box on the top of it, and then we seized upon pokers and fell back.

It was long in catching, but at length, with a jarring bang, it was riven and in full blast. As the case burst and fell asunder, the metal rose writhing from it like a Pharaoh's serpent. The black beetles, I could swear it, stood up on their hind legs and cheered. The chimney was become a hellish trumpet, roaring shrieks and laughter into the night. At last, chord by chord, the turmoil died away and the fire sank into an exhausted glimmer.

Lucy remembered nothing of it all, but that she had dreamed she was mated to the devil. It was for me to disabuse her mind of that extravagance, and I have no reason to suppose that I failed in doing so.

Once upon a time business carried George to Germany. He returned at the end of two or three weeks, sound enough in health, but with a long scar across his temple. He had got it in a fall, he said.

But in the evening he opened quietly upon me—

"I have come across him, Johnny; he is bandmaster in a Bavarian regiment. I had a little talk with him. He treated the whole thing as a joke. It was very true, he said, that the manuscript had come out of a bottle that had been picked up on the seashore by a professional friend of his; that this friend had carried the prize home and had, then and there, in Schneck's presence, played over the piece; that he had been very queerly seized, it appeared as a consequence; that he, Schneck, being a powerful man, had succeeded in dragging his friend away from the piano, but unavailingly, for that the victim had succumbed a few days later to something in the nature of brain fever. 'And *how was I to know,' says he, 'that the resbonsibility was to anything bot the artistic Empfindlichkeit* of my vrent?' But a little pressure brought something else from the brute—that there had been extracted from the flask a second paper, which, being presently examined, was found to relate how the composer of the score had, for some unnamable atrocity, been put overboard from a West-Indiaman (whether marooned or cast adrift, I don't know), and how this accursed conjuration of his, found after his departure, had been bottled and committed to the sea, none daring to destroy it. Schneck, I think, had not meant to tell me that, but his hate got the better of him. Anyhow, he did tell me, and—"

"What?"

"I laid my whip across his face."

I nodded.

"And you met the next morning?"

"His first bullet," said George, "took me here, where you see. I was stunned by the shock and the wind of it, and Schneck thought he had accounted for me. He was unhurt himself, and he cleared out. I was well in a week. I wish I had killed him."

He broke off as his brother entered the room.

"Hullo, Bobby!" said he. "Got tired of poetry and the imaginative arts yet?"

"Oh, rot!" said Bobby.

THE GREEN BOTTLE
(1902)

My knowledge of Sewell was principally of a fox-nosed, weedy, scorbutic youth who wrote four-to-the-pound pars for the *Daily Record*. Further, I bore in mind his flaccid palms, his dropping under-jaw, and the way in which in Fleet Street bars he would hang—looking, indeed, rather like a wet towel—on the words of any Captain Bobadil of his craft who would condescend to wipe his boots on him, or, for the matter of that, his foul mouth. He had no principles, I think. He was born lacking the sentiments of pride and decency. If he was kicked into the mud, he would make, before rising, a little conciliatory gift of mud pie for the kicker. On close terms with the petty ailments of his own body, the secret discoveries that delighted him were of similar weaknesses in others. The prescriptively unmentionable was his humour's best inspiration; his belief in the real approval underlying the affected disgust of his hearers quite genuine. He was, in short, a sort of editors' pimp, with all the taste and the instinct to *procure* "copy," in the detestable sense.

At one time he elected, to my sorrow, to attach himself to me, with this justification (from his point of view) that I then happened to be grinding my literary barrel-organ—always adaptable to the popular need—to the tune of a contemporary interest in the problems of criminology; and the mudlark, being himself of a Newgate complexion of mind, had the assurance in consequence to assume a sympathetic bond between us. Now, the difficulty being to convince Sewell that decency was ever anything but a diplomatic pose, and that one did not pursue vice, as dogs hunt foxes, because of the mere bestial attraction to an abominable scent, but with the sole purpose to reach and end the offence, I was led, more contemptuously than wisely, into allowing the assumption of claim by default, with the result that for some weeks the unsavoury thing stuck to me like a jigger. Then, at the climax of the annoyance, just when I had resolved, as an anthropological economy, upon dissecting my torment or himself as the closest possible illustration of my meaning, of a sudden the creature vanished—disappeared *sans phrase*; and Fleet Street and the *Daily Record* knew him no more.

The fact was that Mr. Sewell had been left a competence, and had retired into private life.

I did not see the fellow again for some eighteen months, when, one afternoon, he visited me quite unexpectedly at my lodgings. He accepted, as of old, the finger I committed to his clasp, and which I then—hardly covertly, under my desk—wrenched dry between my knees. He was scarcely altered in appearance. The only accent of difference that I could observe was in his tie, which was a spotted burglarious-looking token, in place of the rusty-black wisp that had been wont to depend, loosely knotted, from his neck. For the rest, he was the slack, unwholesome figure, with the sniggering and inward manner, of my knowledge. And yet, scanned again, there was something unusual about him after all—a suggestion, it might be, of excited nervousness, such as one might imagine in a very fulsome Paul Pry bursting, while fearing, to retail a ticklish piece of scandal.

"Well," I said, after some indifferent commonplaces, "so you've got your ticket-of-leave? And aren't your fingers itching, in a vacuous freedom, for oakum and the Fleet Street crank again?"

"Oh, Mr. Deering," says he, tittering and twisting, "I like that metaphor. I come to report myself to you, Mr. Deering."

"H'mph!" said I. "Well, when all's said, how *do* you manage to kill time?"

"Why, I kill it," says he, grinning, "and I lay it out. It's only necessary to have an object in life, Mr. Deering. Mine's killing time, that I may lay it out. You'll never guess what I've become."

"I'll make one shot. A body-snatcher."

"Tee-hee! Not so far wrong. A collector, Mr. Deering. I wish you'd come and see my museum. Will you have dinner with me to-night?"

"Not to be thought of. See here and here! In fact, I've already given you longer than I can spare. Good-bye, till our next meeting. If I'm on the jury, I'll try to forget the worst I know of you."

He rose, fidgeted, still lingered.

"I do wish you'd dine with me."

"I tell you I can't. Besides, I'm particular—it's a fad of mine—about my alimentary atmosphere. An unwholesome one balks my digestion."

I began to be annoyed that the fellow would not go. Suddenly he turned upon me, with more decision than he had yet shown.

"The fact is something—something very odd has happened; quite impossible, you'd say. I don't know; if you'd only come and look."

I did look—at him—in some surprise.

"Odd—that concerns me? Why not tell me now, then?"

"You'd never believe unless you saw."

"Saw! Saw what? Why, I'm hanged if, by the jaw of you, you aren't thinking to come the supernatural over me!"

"Yes," he said, fawningly persistent; "I want you to see. It's a case of horrors or nothing. You'll be able to judge, as you've made it your line."

"I've done no such thing. I never raised a banshee yet that would deceive so much as a psychist."

"Well," said he, "that's another inducement. You'd not be pre-disposed to the infection."

"Infection!" I shouted. "What, the devil! You've not been lay-ing-out in earnest!"

He wriggled over a laugh.

"No," said he. "I meant the infection of fear."

"Oh, trust me there!" said I.

This was so far a concession that, under the stimulus of a curiosity the creature had succeeded in arousing in me, I presently accepted, though grudgingly, his invitation. Then he took himself away, and I went on with my work—rather peevishly, for there was a bad taste in my mouth, that I endeavoured unsuccessfully to neutralise with tobacco.

At seven o'clock I packed away and went, depressed, to keep my engagement. It was a July evening of that unsavoury closeness that paints faces with a metallic sweat, and vulgarises out of all picturesqueness the motley concerns of life; an evening when fat women are truculent at omnibus doors; when the brassy twang of piano-organs blends indescribably with the sour stench of the roads; when a dive into a sequestered bar brings no consequence as of virtue refreshed, but rather as of self-indulgence rebuked with an added dyspepsia. And, appropriate to the atmosphere, my goal was in that inferno of dreary unfulfilments, Notting Hill. Thither I made my way, and there in the end house of a stuccoed and lifeless-looking terrace, converted (by an S.A. missionary, one might, from its vulgarity, suppose) into flats, came presently to a stop.

There was a bill "To Let" in the ground-floor window, from which, by inference, my host was engaged to the upper rooms. He himself greeted me at the front door, to which I had mounted by a dozen of ill-laid steps. A second door within, set in a makeshift partition, opened straight upon the stairway that led up to his quarters.

"I hope you won't object to a cold collation, Mr. Deering?" said he.

The stairs were so steep, and he looked so down upon me, twisting about from the height at which he led, that his white face seemed to hang like a clammy stone gargoyle from the gloom.

"I wouldn't suggest it's what you're accustomed to," he said; "but when one's only slavey goes out with the daylight, and doesn't return till the milk, it can't be helped, you know."

"It's all right," I said brusquely, and rudely enough, to be sure. "I never supposed you kept a retinue. You're the only soul in the house, I conclude?"

We had come to a landing, where the stairs gave a wheel and went up, carpetless, steeper than ever. Looking aloft, it was some unmeaning comfort to me to observe that a skylight, obscured by dirt, took the slope of the ceiling with a wan sheen as of phosphorescence.

Two doorways, a step or so apart, faced us entering upon the landing. Through the nearest of these I caught glimpse of a white tablecloth and our meal set upon it. The second, and further, door, that was opposite the turn of the stairs, was shut.

"Eh!" said Sewell, with a curious intonation. "The only soul, eh? Well, upon my word, I won't answer for that."

"What the devil do you mean?" I exclaimed irritably.

"Why," he answered, propitiatory at once, "the rooms below are tenantless, if that's what you refer to."

"What else should I refer to?"

"To be sure, to be sure," he answered. "Oh, yes; I'm the only one in possession! I don't mind. Generally speaking—there may be something now and again that makes a difference, you know—but, generally speaking, I think I've got the collector's love of solitude. We sort of hug ourselves over our finds, don't we? and then it isn't nice to have anybody else by, eh? That's my museum—that second door. I'd like you, if you don't mind, just to go cursorily round it now, before we sit down, and see what sort of an impression it makes on you."

"Is your rotten mystery connected with it?"

"Well, yes, it is."

"Lead on, then, and let's get it over."

He obeyed, opening the door gingerly to its full width before entering, as if he half expected something to be there before him. I uttered an instant grunt. A row of unclean faces, their upper prominences so covered with dust as to give one the impression of their posturing over some infernal kind of footlights, leered down upon us from the top of a high bookcase.

"Yes," said Sewell, though I had not spoken to him, "they're a pretty lot, aren't they, Mr. Deering? I picked 'em up at the Vandal sale—the lunatic specialist, don't you remember, that went mad and cut his own throat in the end? I don't know half their stories; but when I'm in the mood I sit here and try to piece 'em out of their faces. That fellow with the fat wale on his neck, now—"

"Oh, shut your imagination, you anthropophagist! Here, we'll hurry up with this. I see, I see. Absolutely characteristic; and I might have guessed the bent of your virtuosity."

I found a percursory inspection more than sufficient. The creature had only found himself out of independence. He was become logically an Old Bailey curioso. His collection, disposed about the shelves of that same bookless bookcase and on little tables and whatnots, ranged from housebreakers' tools (miracles of vicious elegance) to a slip from a C.C. open spaces seat, on the branch of a tree above which a suicide had hanged himself. There were murderous revolvers, together with the bullets extracted from their victims. There were knives, lengths of Newgate rope, last confessions, photographs, and bloodstains. And, in inviting me to the discussion of this garbage, Sewell, I believe, was actuated by no inhumanity of malevolence. An unnatural appetite is normal to itself, I suppose.

But all the time his manner was *distrait*—spasmodic—watchful, and not of me, I could have thought.

All at once I felt myself constrained to rise from an examination, and to walk to the window. It looked across to the sordid backs of other converted houses; it looked down into a well of a garden, choked with rank grass, from the jungle of which stiff ears of dockweed stood up, as if pricked to the French casement, that I could not see, in the room below. Now the tall buildings so blocked out the sunset that, although day still ruled, the room in which we stood was already appropriated to a livid twilight. I tugged at the window, striving to open it.

"What are you trying?" cried Sewell. "What are you up to? What's the matter with you?"

He hurried across the room. He looked curiously into my face, as if for confirmation of some hope or fear of his own.

"You can't do it," he said. "It's been nailed up. Look here, Mr. Deering, we'll feed, shall we?"

"Yes," I snarled. I was furious with myself. I walked out of the room as stiff as, and bristling like, a baited cat. For the moment I was exalted above the impulse to put my tail between my legs.

Sewell's cold collation was vile. I swear it, though no sybarite, in some explanation of a subsequent nightmare. Macbeth hadn't supped when he saw the ghost of Banquo. How many ghosts he would have seen after a slice of Sewell's steak pie is conjectural. At the fourth mouthful I put down (I might have, dietetically, with scarce more discomfort to myself) my knife and fork.

"Is that beastly door shut?" I said crossly.

He knew, without my explaining, that I meant the door of the museum.

"Yes," he answered, impervious to my rudeness, and offered no further remark. But, perhaps from a like sentiment of oppression, he turned up the gas above the table.

I made another effort at the pie, and finally desisted.

"Look here," I said, falling back in my chair, and streaking down the damp hair on my forehead, "I'm not a fool. D'you hear? I'm not a fool, I say. I want to know, that's all. What the devil's the matter with that bottle?"

"Ah!" he breathed out, with a curious under-inflexion of relief, or triumph. "The bottle; yes; I thought you'd come to it."

"Did you, indeed? So that's your Asian mystery?"

"Yes, that's it," he said quietly. "You've found it out, Mr. Deering, and I wasn't mistaken, it seems."

"Mistaken? I don't know. What's the matter with it? What infernal trick have you been planning? Take care!" I said bullyingly.

"Shall we go and look at it again?"

He only answered with the soft question.

I half rose, fought with myself, yielded, and dropped back.

"I'm damned if I do," I said, "until you've told me."

"Very well," he replied, slinkingly moved to govern and applaud me in a breath. "I'll tell you at once, Mr. Deering."

He felt in his inner breast-pocket, produced a memorandum-book, withdrew a newspaper cutting from it, rose, and crossing to me, placed the slip in my hand. Accepting it sullenly, and taking my reason by the ears, I forced that to focus itself on the lines. They were headed and ran as follows:—

"The Lambeth Tragedy.

"Mr. Hobbins, the south-western district coroner, held an inquest yesterday on the body of Ephraim Ellis, glassblower, who, as has been stated, fell down dead at the very moment that the officers of justice entered the premises of his employers, Messrs. Mackay, to arrest him on suspicion of having caused the death of Francis Riddick, a fellow-workman. Ellis, it will be remembered, was actually engaged in blowing bottles at the moment of his arrest. A verdict of death from syncope, resulting on shock, was returned."

Sewell stood behind me as I read. His long, ropy claw slid over my shoulder, and a finger of it traced along the words "it will be remembered."

"Yes," I muttered, in response to the unspoken query, "I recollect reading something about it. What then?"

Sewell's finger went on five—six letters, and stopped.

"He was 'blowing bottles,'" he said. "He *was*, Mr. Deering. I was standing by him at the time, and he was blowing that very green bottle you saw on the table in the next room. Do you know how they do it? They dip the end of their pipe into the melting-pot that sits in the furnace, and then, having rolled the little knob they've fished up tube-shape on an iron plate, and pinched it for a neck, they take and blow it into a brass mould until it fits out the shape of the thing. Then they open the mould, and the bottle comes free, but stuck to the pipe, until a touch with a cold iron snaps the two apart. That's the way; but this bottle, you'll say, has a neck like a retort. I'll tell you why, Mr. Deering. Ellis had just blown the thing complete, when the policeman put a hand on his shoulder. The pipe was at his mouth. He gave a last gasp into it and went down, the soft bottle-neck bending and sealing itself as the falling pipe dragged it over. Very well; I'd known the man and something of his story, and I brought away the green bottle, just as he'd left it, for a memento. But, Mr. Deering, I brought away that in it that I hadn't bargained for. Can't you guess what it was?"

"No."

"Why, Ellis's soul, Mr. Deering, that passed into it with that last gasp of his, and was sealed up for anyone that likes to let it out."

I got to my feet, driven beyond endurance.

"You ass!" I cried. "Have you drivelled to an end?"

"Oh, dear no!" he whispered, with a little nervous but defiant chuckle. "Now, you know, don't you, Mr. Deering, that there's something uncommon about—about that out there? Perhaps you'll be able to explain it. It was in the hope that I asked you (who've made such a study of psychological phenomena) to endure my company for a night. And, to tell you the truth, there's something more and worse. Wouldn't you like to hear about it, Mr. Deering?"

"Oh, go on!" I said, with a groan. "I've accepted my company, as you say, and—"

"Won't you come further from the door?" he asked, truckling to and hating me, as I believed. "I can see you aren't comfortable, and no wonder."

I ground my teeth on a curse, and slouching to the mantelpiece, put my back against it. A bluebottle, droning heavily in labour, whirled about the room and settled with a buzzing flop on the pie. The cessation of its fulsome chaunt seemed to embolden unseen things to stir and giggle in the dark corners of the room.

"*Aren't* you going on?" I said desperately.

"Yes," he answered; "I'm going on. From first to last I'll tell you everything, and then you can form your own conclusions. Mr. Deering, I'd got to know, as I said, the man Ephraim Ellis. How, don't particularly matter. I'm fond of prowling about at night. I make acquaintances, and pick up things that interest me. This man did. There was something suggestive about him—something haunted, as I'd like to put it. He kept company at one time with a slavey of mine that died of fits (I've seen her in 'em), and perhaps that led to my following him up to his work-place and getting into talk with him. He was a glass-blower, and on night duty. A queer customer he was, and dark and secret as sin. Sometimes I'd look at him, red and shifty in the glow, and I'd think, 'Are you calculating the consequences, my friend, of braining me with a white-hot bottle?' He may have been, more than you'd fancy; for I believe the man took me for an unclean spirit sent to goad him to further desperations. 'Further,' I say; but, mind you, I only go by report. It would never do, would it, Mr. Deering, for you and me to be certain, or they might claim us for accessories?"

I broke into a hoarse, angry exclamation.

"No, no," he interrupted me hurriedly, "of course they couldn't. It was only my fun. But the truth is, Ellis's fellow-workmen were fully persuaded that Ellis had murdered Riddick, who had been found one morning, after he'd relieved Ellis at solitary night duty, with his head melted and run away against the door of a furnace. I don't know; and I don't know what they went upon, seeing the trunk was all right, and that there was no head to examine for trace of injuries. But they made out their suspicions—on technical grounds, I suppose; and, as to the moral—why, Riddick, by their showing, had been a taunting devil, a regular bad lot, who'd made a game of baiting Ellis till he drove the man almost to madness. Anyhow, Ellis was marked down by them, and given the cold shoulder of fear; and so he worked apart (for he was too valuable a hand to be dismissed)—he worked apart—with only me, I really believe, in the wide world to speak to him, until the police, acting upon rumours, or the shadows of 'em, came to lay hands on him.

"But now, I must tell you, before that happened there was something else occurred that was more intimate to the moral, if not to the circumstantial, point. Ellis took to having fits, or seizures, in which he'd rave that Riddick hadn't been got rid of after all, but that he'd all of a sudden be there again, and burrowing into him, and hanging on inside like a bat under ivy, while he'd whisper into his soul blasphemies not fit to be mentioned. He'd not lose his senses—what he'd got of 'em—in these states; but he'd sit down staring, with a face on him as if he'd swallowed a live eel. Sometimes I could have burst with laughter at the sight. And then, once upon a time, Mr. Deering, he took me all in a moment into his confidence, as I may say. And it was like a deathbed confession, for that night the police came and finished him.

"I had been standing by, watching him at work, when he broke off for a drink of water. The common tap was in a little yard at the back of the premises, and as he went out to it I fancied he beckoned me to follow him. Anyhow, I did, and faced him there under the starlight. I'm only speaking of three nights ago, so you may believe the whole thing sticks pretty vividly in my memory.

"He glanced up as I stood before him.

"'Why do you follow me?' he says in a low voice. 'Why do you come and stand there and look at me? Are you Riddick? My God, I'll melt your head like wax if you are!' says he.

"'Why, Mr. Ellis,' says I, taken aback, till I jumped to the humour of the thing, 'if Riddick grips you, as he has done, while I'm looking on, I can't be Riddick, can I?'

"'No, that's true,' he says. 'What do you want with me, then?' And, 'Oh, my God!' he says, in such a Hamlet's ghost voice as would have set you sniggering, 'can you stand by and see a soul raving in the grip of damnation and not offer to help it?'

"'Mr. Ellis,' I answered, 'does Riddick really come to you like that?'

"'He comes and clutches me,' he said, 'as he clutched me when he was alive. He holds me and claims me to his own wickedness, and I must listen and listen, and can't get away. I want to escape, and he clings on and whispers. And if I strike him down, and melt his bloody battered face into glass, there he is in a little while up and at my soul again, struggling with it in my throat, lest it get away from him and fly free with some last breath I put into my work.'

"He looked at me in a death's-head kind of manner, and I had a business, as you may guess, Mr. Deering, not to explode in his face.

"Well, after a minute he turns round, with a groan, and goes back to his work. And I followed, as you may suppose.

"Now, he was at his bottles once more, and me standing by him, when all of a sudden he put down his pipe, and his face was like soapy pumice-stone.

"'He's entered into me! He's got me again!' he whispered in a voice like choking.

"'Go on with your work, as if you didn't know,' says I, choking too, though for a different reason. 'Then you'll be able to take him off his guard and blow him out into a bottle.'

"I thought that was too tall, even for *his* reach. But, Mr. Deering—would you believe it?—the mug actually made a run and scramble to do as I told him. Only I suppose Riddick was holding on so tight that, when he blew, the two, himself and the other, came away together. Anyhow, there's the consequences in the next room—sealed and untouched, as it was left from the corpse's mouth; for the police took him while he was near bursting himself over that, the very last bottle he was ever to mould."

He brought himself to a stop with a feculent chuckle. Then: "What you'll judge it to be, I can't tell," he went on. "It's as funny as fits, whatever it may mean. I know, for myself, I'd sooner sit and watch it—on the right side of the glass—than I would a little fish in an aquarium setting himself to catch, and lose, and catch again, and suck down by fractions a huge, wriggling worm."

I came away from the mantelpiece. The room seemed a swimming vortex. I have a notion that I cursed Sewell for any unnamable carrion. But, if I did, my loathing and horror hit him without effect. I can only remember that we were in the museum again, that dusk had gathered there heavy and opaque; and then suddenly Sewell had lit a candle, and was holding it behind the thing on the table, while he invited me with a gesture to advance and inspect.

It was an ordinary claret bottle, but distorted at the neck. The light struck into and through it. And I looked, and saw that its milky-greenness was in never-ceasing motion.

"There they are!" whispered Sewell gluttonously. "Look, Mr. Deering, mightn't it be the worm and the fish, now!"

A little palpitating, shuddering blot of terror, human and inhuman; now distended, as if gasping in a momentary respite; now crouching and hugging itself into a shapeless ball, and always steadily, untiringly followed and sprung upon by the thing that had the appearance, through the semi-opaque glass, of a shambling, fat-lidded . . . .

Something gave in me, and with a sobbing snarl I caught the bottle up in my hand.

"Mr. Deering!" cried Sewell, "Mr. Deering! what are you going to do?"

"Stand back!" I shrieked, "stand back!"

He ran round at me, with a little nervous gobble of laughter.

"Don't!" he cried. "Let's take it away and bury it."

He caught at my arm, but I flung him aside madly, and with all my force dashed the horror to the floor.

A moment's silence succeeded the ringing crash.

"Oh," whispered Sewell, giggling, "listen! It's going up the stairs after the other—there's something beating on the skylight!"

I tore on to the landing. There was a sound as if some sprawling, bloated body were climbing the bare treads in a series of scrambling flops. Higher, it might have been a great moth that fluttered frenziedly against the glass.

The cord of the light hung down to my hand. I wrenched at it demoniacally, and the glass above swung open with a scream.

A whir, receding into the faint stinging whine of a distant organ, vibrated overhead and was gone. Something on the upper stairs—something unseen and shocking—turned, and began to descend towards me. And at that I wheeled, and rushed staggering for escape and release, leaving Sewell to finish conclusions with what remained.

A GHOST-CHILD
(1906)

In making this confession public, I am aware that I am giving a butterfly to be broken on a wheel. There is so much of delicacy in its subject, that the mere resolve to handle it at all might seem to imply a lack of the sensitiveness necessary to its understanding; and it is certain that the more reverent the touch, the more irresistible will figure its opportunity to the common scepticism which is bondslave to its five senses. Moreover one cannot, in the reason of things, write to publish for Aristarchus alone; but the gauntlet of Grub Street must be run in any bid for truth and sincerity.

On the other hand, to withhold from evidence, in these days of what one may call a zetetic psychology, anything which may appear elucidatory, however exquisitely and rarely, of our spiritual relationships, must be pronounced, I think, a sin against the Holy Ghost.

All in all, therefore, I decide to give, with every passage to personal identification safeguarded, the story of a possession, or visitation, which is signified in the title to my narrative.

Tryphena was the sole orphaned representative of an obscure but gentle family which had lived for generations in the east of England. The spirit of the fens, of the long grey marshes, whose shores are the neutral ground of two elements, slumbered in her eyes. Looking into them, one seemed to see little beds of tiny green mosses luminous under water, or stirred by the movement of microscopic life in their midst. Secrets, one felt, were shadowed in their depths, too frail and sweet for understanding. The pretty love-fancy of babies seen in the eyes of maidens, was in hers to be interpreted into the very cosmic dust of sea-urchins, sparkling like chrysoberyls. Her soul looked out through them, as if they were the windows of a water-nursery.

She was always a child among children, in heart and knowledge most innocent, until Jason came and stood in her field of vision. Then, spirit of the neutral ground as she was, inclining to earth or water with the sway of the tides, she came wondering and dripping, as it were, to land, and took up her abode for final choice among the daughters of the earth. She knew her woman's estate, in fact, and the irresistible attraction of all completed perfections to the light that burns to destroy them.

Tryphena was not only an orphan, but an heiress. Her considerable estate was administered by her guardian, Jason's father, a widower, who was possessed of this single adored child. The fruits of parental infatuation had come early to ripen on the seedling. The boy was self-willed and perverse, the more so as he was naturally of a hot-hearted disposition. Violence and remorse would sway him in alternate moods, and be made, each in its turn, a self-indulgence. He took a delight in crossing his father's wishes, and no less in atoning for his gracelessness with moving demonstrations of affection.

Foremost of the old man's most cherished projects was, very naturally, a union between the two young people. He planned, manoeuvred, spoke for it with all his heart of love and eloquence. And, indeed, it seemed at last as if his hopes were to be crowned. Jason, returning from a lengthy voyage (for his enterprising spirit had early decided for the sea, and he was a naval officer), saw, and was struck amazed before, the transformed vision of his old child-playfellow. She was an opened flower whom he had left a green bud—a thing so rare and flawless that it seemed a sacrilege for earthly passions to converse of her. Familiarity, however, and some sense of reciprocal attraction, quickly dethroned that eucharist. Tryphena could blush, could thrill, could solicit, in the sweet ways of innocent womanhood. She loved him dearly, wholly, it was plain—had found the realization of all her old formless dreams in this wondrous birth of a desire for one, in whose new-impassioned eyes she had known herself reflected hitherto only for the most patronized of small gossips. And, for her part, fearless as nature, she made no secret of her love. She was absorbed in, a captive to, Jason from that moment and for ever.

He responded. What man, however perverse, could have resisted, on first appeal, the attraction of such beauty, the flower of a radiant soul? The two were betrothed; the old man's cup of happiness was brimmed.

Then came clouds and a cold wind, chilling the garden of Hesperis. Jason was always one of those who, possessing classic noses, will cut them off, on easy provocation, to spite their faces. He was so proudly independent, to himself, that he resented the least assumption of proprietorship in him on the part of other people—even of those who had the best claim to his love and submission. This pride was an obsession. It stultified the real good in him, which was considerable. Apart from it, he was a good, warm-tempered fellow, hasty but affectionate. Under its dominion, he would have broken his own heart on an imaginary grievance.

He found one, it is to be supposed, in the privileges assumed by love; in its exacting claims upon him; perhaps in its little unreasoning jealousies. He distorted these into an implied conceit of authority over him on the part of an heiress who was condescending to his meaner fortunes. The suggestion was quite base and without warrant; but pride has no balance. No doubt, moreover, the rather childish self-depreciations of the old man, his father, in his attitude towards a match he had so fondly desired, helped to aggravate this feeling. The upshot was that, when within a few months of the date which was to make his union with Tryphena eternal, Jason broke away from a restraint which his pride pictured to him as intolerable, and went on a yachting expedition with a friend.

Then, at once, and with characteristic violence, came the reaction. He wrote, impetuously, frenziedly, from a distant port, claiming himself Tryphena's, and Tryphena his, for ever and ever and ever. They were man and wife before God. He had behaved like an insensate brute, and he was at that moment starting to speed to her side, to beg her forgiveness and the return of her love.

He had no need to play the suitor afresh. She had never doubted or questioned their mutual bondage, and would have died a maid for his sake. Something of sweet exultation only seemed to quicken and leap in her body, that her faith in her dear love was vindicated.

But the joy came near to upset the reason of the old man, already tottering to its dotage; and what followed destroyed it utterly.

The yacht, flying home, was lost at sea, and Jason was drowned.

I once saw Tryphena about this time. She lived with her near mindless charge, lonely, in an old grey house upon the borders of a salt mere, and had little but the unearthly cries of seabirds to answer to the questions of her widowed heart. She worked, sweet in charity, among the marsh folk, a beautiful unearthly presence; and was especially to be found where infants and the troubles of child-bearing women called for her help and sympathy. She was a wife herself, she would say quaintly; and some day perhaps, by grace of the good spirits of the sea, would be a mother. None thought to cross her statement, put with so sweet a sanity; and, indeed, I have often noticed that the neighbourhood of great waters breeds in souls a mysticism which is remote from the very understanding of land-dwellers.

How I saw her was thus:—

I was fishing, on a day of chill calm, in a dinghy off the flat coast. The stillness of the morning had tempted me some distance from the village where I was staying. Presently a sense of bad sport and healthy famine "plumped" in me, so to speak, for luncheon, and I looked about for a spot picturesque enough to add a zest to sandwiches, whisky, and tobacco. Close by, a little creek or estuary ran up into a mere, between which and the sea lay a cluster of low sand-hills; thither I pulled. The spot, when I reached it, was calm, chill desolation manifest—lifeless water and lifeless sand, with no traffic between them but the dead interchange of salt. Low sedges, at first, and behind them low woods were mirrored in the water at a distance, with an interval between me and them of sheeted glass; and right across this shining pool ran a dim, half-drowned causeway—the sea-path, it appeared, to and from a lonely house which I could just distinguish squatting among trees. It was Tryphena's home.

Now, paddling dispiritedly, I turned a cold dune, and saw a mermaid before me. At least, that was my instant impression. The creature sat coiled on the strand, combing her hair—that was certain, for I saw the gold-green tresses of it whisked by her action into rainbow threads. It appeared as certain that her upper half was flesh and her lower fish; and it was only on my nearer approach that this latter resolved itself into a pale green skirt, roped, owing to her posture, about her limbs, and the hem fanned out at her feet into a tail fin. Thus also her bosom, which had appeared naked, became a bodice, as near to her flesh in colour and texture as a smock is to a lady's-smock, which some call a cuckoo-flower.

It was plain enough now; yet the illusion for the moment had quite startled me.

As I came near, she paused in her strange business to canvass me. It was Tryphena herself, as after-inquiry informed me. I have never seen so lovely a creature. Her eyes, as they regarded me passing, were something to haunt a dream: so great in tragedy—not fathomless, but all in motion near their surfaces, it seemed, with green and rooted sorrows. They were the eyes, I thought, of an Undine late-humanized, late awakened to the rapturous and troubled knowledge of the woman's burden. Her forehead was most fair, and the glistening thatch divided on it like a golden cloud revealing the face of a wondering angel.

I passed, and a sand-heap stole my vision foot by foot. The vision was gone when I returned. I have reason to believe it was vouchsafed me within a few months of the coming of the ghost-child.

On the morning succeeding the night of the day on which Jason and Tryphena were to have been married, the girl came down from her bedroom with an extraordinary expression of still rapture on her face. After breakfast she took the old man into her confidence. She was childish still; her manner quite youthfully thrilling; but now there was a new-born wonder in it that hovered on the pink of shame.

"Father! I have been under the deep waters and found him. He came to me last night in my dreams—so sobbing, so impassioned—to assure me that he had never really ceased to love me, though he had near broken his own heart pretending it. Poor boy! poor ghost! What could I do but take him to my arms? And all night he lay there, blest and forgiven, till in the morning he melted away with a sigh that woke me; and it seemed to me that I came up dripping from the sea."

"My boy! He has come back!" chuckled the old man. "What have you done with him, Tryphena?"

"I will hold him tighter the next time," she said.

But the spirit of Jason visited her dreams no more.

That was in March. In the Christmas following, when the mere was locked in stillness, and the wan reflection of snow mingled on the ceiling with the red dance of firelight, one morning the old man came hurrying and panting to Tryphena's door.

"Tryphena! Come down quickly! My boy, my Jason, has come back! It was a lie that they told us about his being lost at sea!"

Her heart leapt like a candle-flame! What new delusion of the old man's was this? She hurried over her dressing and descended. A garrulous old voice mingled with a childish treble in the breakfast-room. Hardly breathing, she turned the handle of the door, and saw Jason before her.

But it was Jason, the prattling babe of her first knowledge; Jason, the flaxen-headed, apple-cheeked cherub of the nursery; Jason, the confiding, the merry, the loving, before pride had come to warp his innocence. She fell on her knees to the child, and with a burst of ecstasy caught him to her heart.

She asked no question of the old man as to when or whence this apparition had come, or why he was here. For some reason she dared not. She accepted him as some waif, whom an accidental likeness had made glorious to their hungering hearts. As for the father, he was utterly satisfied and content. He had heard a knock at the door, he said, and had opened it and found this. The child was naked, and his pink, wet body glazed with ice. Yet he seemed insensible to the killing cold. It was Jason—that was enough. There is no date nor time for imbecility. Its phantoms spring from the clash of ancient memories. This was just as actually his child as—more so, in fact, than—the grown young figure which, for all its manhood, had dissolved into the mist of waters. He was more familiar with, more confident of it, after all. It had come back to be unquestioningly dependent on him; and that was likest the real Jason, flesh of his flesh.

"Who are you, darling?" said Tryphena.

"I am Jason," answered the child.

She wept, and fondled him rapturously.

"And who am I?" she asked. "If you are Jason, you must know what to call me."

"I know," he said; "but I mustn't, unless you ask me."

"I won't," she answered, with a burst of weeping. "It is Christmas Day, dearest, when the miracle of a little child was wrought. I will ask you nothing but to stay and bless our desolate home."

He nodded, laughing.

"I will stay, until you ask me."

They found some little old robes of the baby Jason, put away in lavender, and dressed him in them. All day he laughed and prattled; yet it was strange that, talk as he might, he never once referred to matters familiar to the childhood of the lost sailor.

In the early afternoon he asked to be taken out—seawards, that was his wish. Tryphena clothed him warmly, and, taking his little hand, led him away. They left the old man sleeping peacefully. He was never to wake again.

As they crossed the narrow causeway, snow, thick and silent, began to fall. Tryphena was not afraid, for herself or the child. A rapture upheld her; a sense of some compelling happiness, which she knew before long must take shape on her lips.

They reached the seaward dunes—mere ghosts of foothold in that smoke of flakes. The lap of vast waters seemed all around them, hollow and mysterious. The sound flooded Tryphena's ears, drowning her senses. She cried out, and stopped.

"Before they go," she screamed— "before they go, tell me what you were to call me!"

The child sprang a little distance, and stood facing her. Already his lower limbs seemed dissolving in the mists.

"I was to call you 'mother'!" he cried, with a smile and toss of his hand.

Even as he spoke, his pretty features wavered and vanished. The snow broke into him, or he became part with it. Where he had been, a gleam of iridescent dust seemed to show one moment before it sank and was extinguished in the falling cloud. Then there was only the snow, heaping an eternal chaos with nothingness.

Tryphena made this confession, on a Christmas Eve night, to one who was a believer in dreams. The next morning she was seen to cross the causeway, and thereafter was never seen again. But she left the sweetest memory behind her, for human charity, and an elf-like gift of loveliness.

POOR LUCY RIVERS
(1906)

The following story was told to a friend—with leave, conditionally, to make it public—by a well-known physician who died last year.

I was in Paul's type-writing exchange (says the professional narrator), seeing about some circulars I required, when a young lady came in bearing a box, the weight of which seemed to tax her strength severely. She was a very personable young woman, though looking ill, I fancied—in short, with those diathetic symptoms which point to a condition of hysteria. The manager, who had been engaged elsewhere, making towards me at the moment, I intimated to him that he should attend to the new-comer first. He turned to her.

"Now, madam?" said he.

"I bought this machine second-hand of you last week," she began, after a little hesitation. He admitted his memory of the fact. "I want to know," she said, "if you'll change it for another."

"Is there anything wrong with it, then?" he asked.

"Yes," she said; "No!" she said; "Everything!" she said, in a crescendo of spasms, looking as if she were about to cry. The manager shrugged his shoulders.

"Very reprehensible of us," said he; "and hardly our way. It is not customary; but, of course—if it doesn't suit—to give satisfaction—" he cleared his throat.

"I don't want to be unfair," said the young woman. "It doesn't suit *me*. It might another person."

He had lifted, while speaking, its case off the type-writer, and now, placing the machine on a desk, inserted a sheet or two of paper, and ran his fingers deftly over the keys.

"Really, madam," said he, removing and examining the slip, "I can detect nothing wrong."

"I said—perhaps—only as regards myself."

She was hanging her head, and spoke very low.

"But!" said he, and stopped—and could only add the emphasis of another deprecatory shrug.

"Will you do me the favour, madam, to try it in my presence?"

"No," she murmured; "please don't ask me. I'd really rather not." Again the suggestion of strain—of suffering.

"At least," said he, "oblige me by looking at this."

He held before her the few lines he had typed. She had averted her head during the minute he had been at work; and it was now with evident reluctance, and some force put upon herself, that she acquiesced. But the moment she raised her eyes, her face brightened with a distinct expression of relief.

"Yes," she said; "I know there's nothing wrong with it. I'm sure it's all my fault. But—but, if you don't mind. So much depends on it."

Well, the girl was pretty; the manager was human. There were a dozen young women, of a more or less pert type, at work in the front office. I dare say he had qualified in the illogic of feminine moods. At any rate, the visitor walked off in a little with a machine presumably another than that she had brought.

"Professional?" I asked, to the manager's resigned smile addressed to me.

"So to speak," said he. "She's one of the 'augment her income' class. I fancy it's little enough without. She's done an occasional job for us. We've got her card somewhere."

"Can you find it?"

He could find it, though he was evidently surprised at the request—scarce reasonably, I think, seeing how he himself had just given me an instance of that male inclination to the attractive, which is so calculated to impress woman in general with the injustice of our claims to impartiality.

With the piece of pasteboard in my hand, I walked off then and there to commission "Miss Phillida Gray" with the job I had intended for Paul's. Psychologically, I suppose, the case interested me. Here was a young person who seemed, for no *practical* reason, to have quarrelled with her unexceptionable means to a livelihood.

It raised more than one question; the incompleteness of woman as a wage earner, so long as she was emancipated from all but her fancifulness; the possibility of the spontaneous generation of soul—the *divina particula aurae*—in man-made mechanisms, in the construction of which their makers had invested their whole of mental capital. Frankenstein loathed the abortion of his genius. Who shall say that the soul of the inventor may not speak antipathetically, through the instrument which records it, to that soul's natural antagonist? Locomotives have moods, as any engine-driver will tell you; and any shaver, that his razor, after maltreating in some fit of perversity one side of his face, will repent, and caress the other as gently as any sucking-dove.

I laughed at this point of my reflections. Had Miss Gray's typewriter, embodying the soul of a blasphemer, taken to swearing at her?

It was a bitterly cold day. Snow, which had fallen heavily in November, was yet lying compact and unthawed in January. One had the novel experience in London of passing between piled ramparts of it. Traffic for some two months had been at a discount; and walking, for one of my years, was still so perilous a business that I was long in getting to Miss Gray's door.

She lived West Kensington way, in a "converted flat," whose title, like that of a familiar type of Christian exhibited on platforms, did not convince of anything but a sort of paying opportunism. That is to say, at the cost of some internal match-boarding, roughly fitted and stained, an unlettable private residence, of the estimated yearly rental of forty pounds, had been divided into two "sets" at thirty-five apiece—whereby fashion, let us hope, profited as greatly as the landlord.

Miss Gray inhabited the upper section, the door to which was opened by a little Cockney drab, very smutty, and smelling of gas stoves.

"Yes, she was in." (For all her burden, "Phillida," with her young limbs, had outstripped me.) "Would I please to walk up?"

It was the dismallest room I was shown into—really the most unattractive setting for the personable little body I had seen. She was not there at the moment, so that I could take stock without rudeness. The one curtainless window stared, under a lid of fog, at the factory-like rear of houses in the next street. Within was scarce an evidence of dainty feminine occupation. It was all an illustration of the empty larder and the wolf at the door. How long would the bolt withstand him? The very walls, it seemed, had been stripped for sops to his ravening—stripped so nervously, so hurriedly, that ribbons of paper had been flayed here and there from the plaster. The ceiling was falling; the common grate cold; there was a rag of old carpet on the floor—a dreary, deadly place! The type-writer—the new one—laid upon a little table placed ready for its use, was, in its varnished case, the one prominent object, quite healthy by contrast. How would the wolf moan and scratch to hear it desperately busy, with click and clang, building up its paper rampart against his besieging!

I had fallen of a sudden so depressed, into a spirit of such premonitory haunting, that for a moment I almost thought I could hear the brute of my own fancy snuffling outside. Surely there was something breathing, rustling near me—something—

I grunted, shook myself, and walked to the mantel-piece. There was nothing to remark on it but a copy of some verses on a sheet of notepaper; but the printed address at the top, and the signature at the foot of this, immediately caught my attention. I trust, under the circumstances (there was a coincidence here), that it was not dishonest, but I took out my glasses, and read those verses—or, to be strictly accurate, the gallant opening quatrain—with a laudable coolness. But inasmuch as the matter of the second and third stanzas, which I had an opportunity of perusing later, bears upon one aspect of my story, I may as well quote the whole poem here for what it is worth.

Phyllis, I cannot woo in rhyme,
  As courtlier gallants woo,
With utterances sweet as thyme
  And melting as the dew.

An arm to serve; true eyes to see;
  Honour surpassing love;
These, for all song, my vouchers be,
  Dear love, so thou'lt them prove.

Bid me—and though the rhyming art
  I may not thee contrive—
I'll print upon thy lips, sweetheart,
  A poem that shall live.

It may have been derivative; it seemed to me, when I came to read the complete copy, passable. At the first, even, I was certainly conscious of a thrill of secret gratification. But, as I said, I had mastered no more than the first four lines, when a rustle at the door informed me that I was detected.

She started, I could see, as I turned round. I was not at the trouble of apologizing for my inquisitiveness.

"Yes," I said; "I saw you at Paul's Exchange, got your address, and came on here. I want some circulars typed. No doubt you will undertake the job?"

I was conning her narrowly while I spoke. It was obviously a case of neurasthenia—the tendril shooting in the sunless vault. But she had more spirit than I calculated on. She just walked across to the empty fireplace, collared those verses, and put them into her pocket. I rather admired her for it.

"Yes, with pleasure," she said, sweetening the rebuke with a blush, and stultifying it by affecting to look on the mantelpiece for a card, which eventually she produced from another place. "These are my terms."

"Thank you," I replied. "What do you say to a contra account—you to do my work, and I to set my professional attendance against it? I am a doctor."

She looked at me mute and amazed.

"But there is nothing the matter with me," she murmured, and broke into a nervous smile.

"O, I beg your pardon!" I said. "Then it was only your instrument which was out of sorts?"

Her face fell at once.

"You heard me—of course," she said. "Yes, I—it was out of sorts, as you say. One gets fancies, perhaps, living alone, and typing—typing."

I thought of the discordant clack going on hour by hour—the dead words of others made brassily vociferous, until one's own individuality would become merged in the infernal harmonics.

"And so," I said, "like the dog's master in the fable, you quarrelled with an old servant."

"O, no!" she answered. "I had only had it for a week—since I came here."

"You have only been here a week?"

"Little more," she replied. "I had to move from my old rooms. It is very kind of you to take such an interest in me. Will you tell me what I can do for you?"

My instructions were soon given. The morrow would see them attended to. No, she need not send the copies on. I would myself call for them in the afternoon.

"I hope *this* machine will be more to the purpose," I said.

"*I* hope so, too," she answered.

"Well, she seems a lady," I thought, as I walked home; "a little anaemic flower of gentility." But sentiment was not to the point.

That evening, "over the walnuts and the wine," I tackled Master Jack, my second son. He was a promising youth; was reading for the Bar, and, for all I knew, might have contributed to the "Gownsman."

"Jack," I said, when we were alone, "I never knew till to-day that you considered yourself a poet."

He looked at me coolly and inquiringly, but said nothing.

"Do you consider yourself a marrying man, too?" I asked.

He shook his head, with a little amazed smile.

"Then what the devil do you mean by addressing a copy of love verses to Miss Phillida Gray?"

He was on his feet in a moment, as pale as death. "If you were not my father"—he began.

"But I am, my boy," I answered, "and an indulgent one, I think you'll grant."

He turned, and stalked out of the room; returned in a minute, and flung down a duplicate draft of *the* poem on the table before me. I put down the crackers, took up the paper, and finished my reading of it.

"Jack," I said, "I beg your pardon. It does credit to your heart—you understand the emphasis? You are a young gentleman of some prospects. Miss Gray is a young lady of none."

He hesitated a moment; then flung himself on his knees before me. He was only a great boy.

"Dad," he said; "dear old Dad; you've seen them—you've seen her?"

I admitted the facts. "But that is not at all an answer to me," I said.

"Where is she?" he entreated, pawing me.

"You don't know?"

"Not from Adam. I drove her hard, and she ran away from me. She said she would, if I insisted—not to kill those same prospects of mine. My prospects! Good God! What are they without her? She left her old rooms, and no address. How did you get to see her—and my stuff?"

I could satisfy him on these points.

"But it's true," he said "and—and I'm in love, Dad—Dad, I'm in love."

He leaned his arms on the table, and his head on his arms.

"Well," I said, "how did you get to know her?"

"Business," he muttered, "pure business. I just answered her advertisement—took her some of my twaddle. She's an orphan—daughter of a Captain Gray, navy man; and—and she's an angel."

"I hope he is," I answered. "But anyhow, that settles it. There's no marrying and giving in marriage in heaven." He looked up.

"You don't mean it? No! you dearest and most indulgent of old Dads! Tell me where she is."

I rose.

"I may be all that; but I'm not such a fool. I shall see her to-morrow. Give me till after then."

"O, you perfect saint!"

"I promise absolutely nothing."

"I don't want you to. I leave you to her. She could beguile a Saint Anthony."

"Hey!"

"I mean as a Christian woman should."

"O! that explains it."

The following afternoon I went to West Kensington. The little drab was snuffling when she opened the door. She had a little hat on her head.

"Missus wasn't well," she said; "and she hadn't liked to leave her, though by rights she was only engaged for an hour or two in the day."

"Well," I said, "I'm a doctor, and will attend to her. You can go."

She gladly shut me in and herself out. The clang of the door echoed up the narrow staircase, and was succeeded, as if it had started it, by the quick toing and froing of a footfall in the room above. There was something inexpressibly ghostly in the sound, in the reeling dusk which transmitted it.

I perceived, the moment I set eyes on the girl, that there was something seriously wrong with her. Her face was white as wax, and quivered with an incessant horror of laughter. She tried to rally, to greet me, but broke down at the first attempt, and stood as mute as stone.

I thank my God I can be a sympathetic without being a fanciful man. I went to her at once, and imprisoned her icy hands in the human strength of my own.

"What is it? Have you the papers ready for me?" She shook her head, and spoke only after a second effort.

"I am very sorry."

"You haven't done them, then? Never mind. But why not? Didn't the new machine suit either?"

I felt her hands twitch in mine. She made another movement of dissent.

"That's odd," I said. "It looks as if it wasn't the fault of the tools, but of the workwoman."

All in a moment she was clinging to me convulsively, and crying—

"You are a doctor—you'll understand—don't leave me alone—don't let me stop here!"

"Now listen," I said "listen, and control yourself. Do you hear? I have come *prepared* to take you away. I'll explain why presently."

"I thought at first it was my fault," she wept distressfully, "working, perhaps, until I grew light-headed" (Ah, hunger and loneliness and that grinding labour!); "but when I was sure of myself; still it went on, and I could not do my tasks to earn money. Then I thought—how can God let such things be!—that the instrument itself must be haunted. It took to going at night; and in the morning"—she gripped my hands— "I burnt them. I tried to think I had done it myself in my sleep, and I always burnt them. But it didn't stop, and at last I made up my mind to take it back and ask for another—another—you remember?"

She pressed closer to me, and looked fearfully over her shoulder.

"It does the same," she whispered, gulping. "It wasn't the machine at all. It's the place—itself—that's haunted."

I confess a tremor ran through me. The room was dusking—hugging itself into secrecy over its own sordid details. Out near the window, the type-writer, like a watchful sentient thing, seemed grinning at us with all its ivory teeth. She had carried it there, that it might be as far from herself as possible.

"First let me light the gas," I said, gently but resolutely detaching her hands.

"There is none," she murmured.

None. It was beyond her means. This poor creature kept her deadly vigils with a couple of candles. I lit them—they served but to make the gloom more visible—and went to pull down the blind.

"O, take care of it!" she whispered fearfully, meaning the typewriter. "It is awful to shut out the daylight so soon."

God in heaven, what she must have suffered! But I admitted nothing, and took her determinedly in hand.

"Now," I said, returning to her, "tell me plainly and distinctly what it is that the machine does."

She did not answer. I repeated my question.

"It writes things," she muttered— "things that don't come from me. Day and night it's the same. The words on the paper aren't the words that come from my fingers."

"But that is impossible, you know."

"So *I* should have thought once. Perhaps—what is it to be possessed? There was another type-writer—another girl—lived in these rooms before me."

"Indeed! And what became of her?"

"She disappeared mysteriously—no one knows why or where. Maria, my little maid, told me about her. Her name was Lucy Rivers, and—she just disappeared. The landlord advertised her effects, to be claimed, or sold to pay the rent; and that was done, and she made no sign. It was about two months ago."

"Well, will you now practically demonstrate to me this reprehensible eccentricity on the part of your instrument?"

"Don't ask me. I don't dare."

"I would do it myself; but of course you will understand that a more satisfactory conclusion would be come to by my watching your fingers. Make an effort—you needn't even look at the result—and I will take you away immediately after."

"You are very good," she answered pathetically; "but I don't know that I ought to accept. Where to, please? And—and I don't even know your name."

"Well, I have my own reasons for withholding it."

"It is all so horrible," she said; "and I am in your hands."

"They are waiting to transfer you to mamma's," said I.

The name seemed an instant inspiration and solace to her. She looked at me, without a word, full of wonder and gratitude; then asked me to bring the candles, and she would acquit herself of her task. She showed the best pluck over it, though her face was ashy, and her mouth a line, and her little nostrils pulsing the whole time she was at work.

I had got her down to one of my circulars, and, watching her fingers intently, was as sure as observer could be that she had followed the text verbatim.

"Now," I said, when she came to a pause, "give me a hint how to remove this paper, and go you to the other end of the room."

She flicked up a catch. "You have only to pull it off the roller," she said; and rose and obeyed. The moment she was away I followed my instructions, and drew forth the printed sheet and looked at it.

It may have occupied me longer than I intended. But I was folding it very deliberately, and putting it away in my pocket when I walked across to her with a smile. She gazed at me one intent moment, and dropped her eyes.

"Yes," she said; and I knew that she had satisfied herself. "Will you take me away now, at once, please?"

The idea of escape, of liberty once realized, it would have been dangerous to balk her by a moment. I had acquainted mamma that I might possibly bring her a visitor. Well, it simply meant that the suggested visit must be indefinitely prolonged.

Miss Gray accompanied me home, where certain surprises, in addition to the tenderest of ministrations, were awaiting her. All that becomes private history, and outside my story. I am not a man of sentiment; and if people choose to write poems and make general asses of themselves, why—God bless them!

The problem I had set *my*self to unravel was what looked deucedly like a tough psychologic poser. But I was resolute to face it, and had formed my plan. It was no unusual thing for me to be out all night. That night, after dining, I spent in the "converted" flat in West Kensington.

I had brought with me—I confess to so much weakness—one of your portable electric lamps. The moment I was shut in and established, I pulled out the paper Miss Gray had typed for me, spread it under the glow and stared at it. Was it a copy of my circular? Would a sober "First Aid Society" Secretary be likely, do you think, to require circulars containing such expressions as "*William! William! Come back to me! O, William, in God's name! William! William! William!*"—in monstrous iteration—the one cry, or the gist of it, for lines and lines in succession?

I am at the other end from humour in saying this. It is heaven's truth. Line after line, half down the page, went that monotonous, heart-breaking appeal. It was so piercingly moving, my human terror of its unearthliness was all drowned, absorbed in an overflowing pity.

I am not going to record the experiences of that night. That unchanging mood of mine upheld me through consciousnesses and sub-consciousnesses which shall be sacred. Sometimes, submerged in these, I seemed to hear the clack of the instrument in the window, but at a vast distance. I may have seen—I may have dreamt—I accepted it all. Awaking in the chill grey of morning, I felt no surprise at seeing some loose sheets of paper lying on the floor. "*William! William!*" their text ran down, "*Come back to me!*" It was all that same wail of a broken heart. I followed Miss Gray's example. I took out my match-box, and reverently, reverently burned them.

An hour or two later I was at Paul's Exchange, privately interviewing my manager.

"Did you ever employ a Miss Lucy Rivers?"

"Certainly we did. Poor Lucy Rivers! She rented a machine of us. In fact—"

He paused.

"Well?"

"Well—it is a mere matter of business—she 'flitted,' and we had to reclaim our instrument. As it happens, it was the very one purchased by the young lady who so interested you here two days ago."

"The first machine, you mean?"

"The first—*and* the second." He smiled. "As a matter of fact, she took away again what she brought."

"Miss Rivers's?"

He nodded.

"There was absolutely nothing wrong with it—mere fad. Women start these fancies. The click of the thing gets on their nerves, I suppose. We must protect ourselves, you see; and I'll warrant she finds it perfection now."

"Perhaps she does. What was Miss Rivers's address?" He gave me, with a positive grin this time, the "converted" flat.

"But that was only latterly," he said. "She had moved from—"

He directed me elsewhere.

"Why," said I, taking up my hat, "did you call her 'poor Lucy Rivers'?"

"O, I don't know!" he said. "She was rather an attractive young lady. But we had to discontinue our patronage. She developed the most extraordinary—but it's no business of mine. She was one of the submerged tenth; and she's gone under for good, I suppose."

I made my way to the *other* address—a little lodging in a shabby-genteel street. A bitter-faced landlady, one of the "preordained" sort, greeted me with resignation when she thought I came for rooms, and with acerbity when she heard that my sole mission was to inquire about a Miss Lucy Rivers.

"I won't deceive you, sir," she said. "When it come to receiving gentlemen privately, I told her she must go."

"Gentlemen!"

"I won't do Miss Rivers an injustice," she said. "It was *ha* gentleman."

"Was that latterly?"

"It was not latterly, sir. But it was the effects of its not being latterly which made her take to things."

"What things?"

"Well, sir, she grew strange company, and took to the roof."

"What on earth do you mean?"

"Just precisely what I say, sir; through the trap-door by the steps, and up among the chimney-pots. *He'd* been there with her before, and perhaps she thought she'd find him hiding among the stacks. He called himself an astronomer; but it's my belief it was another sort of star-gazing. I couldn't stand it at last, and I had to give her notice."

It was falling near a gloomy midday when I again entered the flat, and shut myself in with its ghosts and echoes. I had a set conviction, a set purpose in my mind. There was that which seemed to scuttle, like a little demon of laughter, in my wake, now urging me on, now slipping round and above to trip me as I mounted. I went steadily on and up, past the sitting-room door, to the floor above. And here, for the first time, a thrill in my blood seemed to shock and hold me for a moment. Before my eyes, rising to a skylight, now dark and choked with snow, went a flight of steps. Pulling myself together, I mounted these, and with a huge effort (*the bolt was not shot*) shouldered the trap open. There were a fall and rustle without; daylight entered; and, levering the door over, I emerged upon the roof.

Snow, grim and grimy and knee-deep, was over everything, muffling the contours of the chimneys, the parapets, the irregularities of the leads. The dull thunder of the streets came up to me; a fog of thaw was in the air; a thin drizzle was already falling. I drove my foot forward into a mound, and hitched it on something. In an instant I was down on my knees, scattering the sodden raff right and left, and—my God!—a face!

She lay there as she had been overwhelmed, and frozen, and preserved these two months. She had closed the trap behind her, and nobody had known. Pure as wax—pitiful as hunger—dead! Poor Lucy Rivers!

Who was she, and who the man? We could never learn. She had woven his name, his desertion, her own ruin and despair into the texture of her broken life. Only on the great day of retribution shall he answer to that agonized cry.

THE GHOST-LEECH
(1906)

Kelvin, not I, is responsible for this story, which he told me sitting smoking by his study window. It was a squalid night, I remember, wet and fretful—the sort of night which seems to sojourners in the deep country (as we then were) to bring rumours of plashy pavements, and the roar of rain-sodden traffic, and the wailing and blaspheming of women lost and crying out of a great darkness. No knowledge of our rural isolation could allay this haunting impression in my mind that night. I felt ill at ease, and, for some reason, out of suits with life. It mattered nothing that a belt of wild wood land separated us from the country station five miles away. That, after all, by the noises in it, might have been a very causeway, by which innumerable spectres were hurrying home from their business in the distant cities. The dark clouds, as long as we could see them labouring from the south, appeared freighted with the very burden of congregated dreariness. They glided up, like vast electric tramcars, and seemed to pause overhead, as if to discharge into the sanctuary of our quiet pastures their loads of aggressive vulgarity. My nerves were all jangled into disorder, I fear, and inclining me to imaginative hyperbole.

Kelvin, for his part, was very quiet. He was a conundrum, that man. Once the keenest of sportsmen, he was now for years become an almost sentimental humanitarian—and illogical, of necessity. He would not consent to kill under any circumstances—wilfully, that is to say; but he enjoyed his mutton with the best of us. However, I am not quarrelling with his point of view. He, for one—by his own admission, anyhow—owed a life to "the blind Fury with th' abhorred shears," and he would not, from the date of his debt, cross her prerogatives. The same occasion, it appeared, had opened in him an unstanchable vein of superstition, which was wont to gush—bloodily, I might say—in depressing seasons of the mind. It provoked me, on the evening of the present anecdote, to a sort of peevish protest.

"Why the devil," I said, "are spectral manifestations—at least, according to you fellows—everlastingly morbid and ugly? Are there no gentle disembodied things, who, of their love and pity, would be rather more anxious than the wicked, one would think, to communicate with their survivors?"

"Of course," said Kelvin; "but their brief sweet little reassurances pass unnoticed. Their forms are insignificant, their voices inarticulate; they can only appeal by symbol, desperately clinging to the earth the while. On the other hand, the world tethers its worldlings by the foot, so that they cannot take flight when they will. There remains, so to speak, too much earth in their composition, and it keeps 'em subject to the laws of gravitation."

I laughed; then shrugged impatiently.

"What a rasping night it is! The devil take that moth!"

The window was shut, and the persistent whirring and tapping of a big white insect on the glass outside jarred irritably on my nerves.

"Let it in, for goodness' sake," I said, "if it will insist on making a holocaust of itself!"

Kelvin had looked up when I first spoke. Now he rose, with shining eyes, and a curious little sigh of the sort that one vents on the receipt of wonderful news coming out of suspense.

"Yes, I'll open the window," he said low; and with the word threw up the casement. The moth whizzed in, whizzed round, and settled on his hand. He lifted it, with an odd set smile, into the intimate range of his vision, and scrutinized it intently. Suddenly and quickly, then, as if satisfied about something, he held it away from him.

"*Ite missa est!*" he murmured, quoting some words of the Mass (he was a Catholic); and the moth fluttered and rose. Now, you may believe it or not; but there was a fire burning on the hearth, and straight for that fire went the moth, and seemed to go up with the smoke into the chimney. I was so astonished that I gasped; but Kelvin appeared serenely unconcerned as he faced round on me.

"Well," I exploded, "if a man mayn't kill, he may persuade to suicide, it seems."

He answered good-humouredly, "All right; but it wasn't suicide."

Then he resumed his seat by me, and relighted his pipe. I sat stolidly, with an indefinable feeling of grievance, and said nothing. But the silence soon grew unbearable.

"Kelvin," I said, suddenly and viciously; "what the deuce do you mean?"

"You wouldn't believe," he answered, at once and cheerily, "even if I told you."

"Told me what?"

"Well, this. There was the soul of little Patsy that went up in the smoke."

"The village child you are so attached to?"

"Yes; and who has lain dying these weeks past."

"Why should it come to you?"

"It was a compact between us—if she were summoned, in a moment, without time for a good-bye. We were close friends."

"Kelvin—excuse me—you are getting to be impossible."

"All right. Look at your watch. Time was made for unbelievers. There's no convincing a sceptic but by foot-rule. Look at your watch."

I did, I confess—covertly—in the instant of distraction caused by Kelvin's little son, who came to bid his father good night. He was a quiet, winning little fellow, glowing with health and beauty.

"Good night, Bobo," said Kelvin, kissing the child fondly. "Ask God to make little Patsy's bed comfy, before you get into your own."

I kissed the boy also; but awkwardly, for some reason, under his frank courteousness. After he was gone, I sank back in my chair and said, grudging the concession—

"Very well. It's half-past eight."

Kelvin nodded, and said nothing more for a long time. Then, all of a sudden, he broke out—

"I usen't to believe in such things myself, once upon a time; but Bobo converted me. Would you like to hear the story?"

"O, yes!" I said, tolerantly superior. "Fire away!"

He laughed, filling his pipe—the laugh of a man too surely self-convinced to regard criticism of his faith.

"Patsy," he said, "had no Ghost-Leech to touch her well. Poor little Patsy! But she's better among the flowers."

"Of Paradise, I suppose you mean? Well, if she is, she is," I said, as if I were deprecating the inevitably undesirable. "But what is a Ghost-Leech?"

"A Ghost-Leech," he said— "the sort, anyhow, that I've knowledge of—is one who has served seven years goal-keeper in the hurling-matches of the dead."

I stared at him. Was he really going, or gone, off his head? He laughed again, waving his hand to reassure me.

"You may accept my proof or not. Anyhow, Bobo's recovery was proof enough for me. A sense of humour, I admit, is outside our conception of the disembodied. We lay down laughter with life, don't we? You'd count it heresy to believe otherwise. Yet have you ever considered how man's one great distinctive faculty must be admitted into all evidence of his deeds upon earth, as minuted by the recording angel? It must be admitted, of course, and appreciatively by the final assessor. How could he judge laughter who had never laughed? The cachinnatory nerve is touched off from across the Styx—wireless telegraphy; and man will laugh still, though he be damned."

"Kelvin! my good soul!"

"The dead, I tell you, do not put off their sense of humour with their flesh. They laugh beyond the grave. They are full of a sense of fun, and not necessarily the most transcendent."

"No, indeed, by all the testimony of spiritualism."

"Well; now listen. I was staying once in a village on the west coast of Ireland. The people of my hamlet were at deadly traditional feud with the people of a neighbouring hamlet. Traditional, I say, because the vendetta (it almost amounted to one) derived from the old days of rivalry between them in the ancient game of hurling, which was a sort of primitive violent "rugger" played with a wooden ball. The game itself was long fallen into disuse in the district, and had been supplanted, even in times out of memory, by sports of a gentler, more modern cast. But it, and the feud it had occasioned, were still continued unabated beyond the grave. How do I know this? Why, on the evidence of my Ghost-Leech.

"He was a strange, moody, solitary man, pitied, though secretly dreaded, by his neighbours. They might have credited him with possession—particularly with a bad local form of possession; to suspect it was enough in itself to keep their mouths shut from questioning him, or their ears from inviting confession of his sufferings. For, so their surmise were correct, and he in the grip of the hurlers, a word wrung from him out of season would have brought the whole village under the curse of its dead."

I broke in here. "Kelvin, for the Lord's sake! you are too cimmerian. Titillate your glooms with a touch of that spiritual laughter."

Agreeably to my banter, he smiled.

"There's fun in it," he said; "only it's rather ghastly fun. What do you say to the rival teams meeting in one or other of the village graveyards, and whacking a skull about with long shank-bones?"

"I should say, It doesn't surprise me in the least. Anything turning upon a more esoteric psychology would. What pitiful imaginations you Christmas-number seers are possessed of!"

"I dare say. But I'm not imagining. It's you practical souls that imagine—that common sense, for instance, is reason; that the top-hat is the divinely inspired shibboleth of the chosen; and so on. But you don't disappoint me. Shall I go on?"

"O, yes! go on."

"The hurlers meet under the full moon, they say, in one or other of the rival graveyards; *but they must have a living bachelor out of each parish to keep goal for them.*"

"I see! 'They say'? I see!"

"The doom of the poor wretch thus chosen is, as you may suppose, an appalling one. He must go, or suffer terrors damning out of reason. There is no power on earth can save him. One night he is sitting, perhaps, in his cabin at any peaceful work. The moor, mystic under the moonlight, stretches from miles away up to his walls, surrounding and isolating them. His little home is an ark, anchored amid a waste and silent sea of flowers. Suddenly the latch clinks up, advances, falls. The night air breathing in passes a presence standing in the opening, and quivers and dies. Stealthily the door gapes, ever so little, ever so softly, and a face, like the gliding rim of the moon, creeps round its edge. It is the face, he recognizes appalled, of one long dead. The eyeplaces are black hollows; but there is a movement in them like the glint of water in a deep well. A hand lifts and beckons. The goal-keeper is chosen, and must go. For seven years, it is said, he must serve the hurling-matches of the dead."

"State it for a fact. Don't hedge on report."

"I don't. This man served his time. If he hadn't, Bobo wouldn't be here."

"O? Poor Bobo!"

"This man, I say, survived the ghastly ordeal—one case out of a dozen that succumb. Then he got his fee."

"O, a fee! What was that? A Rachel of the bogs?"

"The power to cure by touch any human sickness, even the most humanly baffling."

"Really a royal reward. It's easy to see a fortune in it."

"He would have been welcome to mine; but he would take nothing. He made my little boy whole again."

"Kelvin! I dare say I'm a brute. What had been the matter with him?"

"Ah, what! He simply moaned and wasted—moaned eternally. Atrophy; meningitis; cachexy—they gave it a dozen names, but not a single cure. He was dying under slow torture—a heavy sight for a father.

"One day an old Shaman of the moors called upon me. He was ancient, ancient—as dry as his staff, and so bent that, a little more, and he had tripped over his long beard in walking. I can't reproduce his brogue; but this is the substance of what it conveyed to me:—

"Had I ever heard speak of Baruch of the lone shebeen—him that had once kept an illicit still, but that the ghosts had got hold of for his sins? No? Well, he, the Shaman, was come too near the end of his own living tether to fear ghoulish reprisals if he told me. And he told me.

"Baruch, he said, was suspected in the village of keeping the dead's hurling-goal—had long been suspected—it was an old tale by now. But, och, wirrastrue! if, as he calculated, Baruch was nearing the close of his seven years' service, Baruch was the man for me, and could do for my child what no other living man, barring a ghosts' goalkeeper, could do likewise.

"I humoured him when he was present; laughed at him when he was gone; but—I went to see Baruch. It's all right: you aren't a father."

"You went to see Baruch. Go on."

"He lived remote in such a little cabin as I have described. Lord! what a thing it was!—a living trophy of damnation—a statue inhabiting the human vestment! His face was young enough; but sorrow stricken into stone—unearthly suffering carved out of a block. It is astonishing what expression can be conveyed without a line. There was not a wrinkle in Baruch's face.

"All scepticism withered in me at the sight—all the desperate effrontery with which I had intended to challenge his gift. I asked him simply if he would cure my child.

"He answered, in a voice as hoarse and feeble as an old man's, but with a queer little promise of joy in it, like a sound of unborn rain, 'Asthore! for this I've lived me lone among the peats, and bid me time, and suffered what I know. In a good hour be it spoken! Wance more, and come again when the moon has passed its full.'

"I went, without another question, or the thought of one. That was a bad week for me—a mortal struggle for the child. The dead kept pulling him to draw him down; but he fought and held on, the little plucked one. On the day following the night of full moon, I carried him in my arms to the cabin—myself, all the way. I wouldn't let on to a soul; I went roundabout, and I got to Baruch unnoticed. I knew it was kill or cure for Bobo. He couldn't have survived another night.

"I tell you, it was a laughing spirit that greeted me. Have you ever seen Doré's picture of the 'Wandering Jew,' at the end of his journey, having his boots pulled off? There is the same release depicted, the same sweet comedy of redemption—the same figure of fun, if you like, that Baruch presented.

"He put his hands on Bobo's head, and—"

"Well?"

"Bobo walked home with me, that's all."

Kelvin got up from his chair to relight his pipe at the fire. As he moved, the door of the room opened, and a decent woman, his housekeeper, stood, with a grave face, in the entrance.

"Patsy's dead?" said Kelvin.

"Ah, the poor mite!" answered the woman, with a burst of tears. "She passed but now, sir, at half after eight, in her little bed."

THE JADE BUTTON
(1906)

The little story I am about to tell will meet, I have no doubt, with a good deal of incredulity, not to say derision. Very well; there is the subject of it himself to testify. If you can put an end to him by any lethal process known to man, I will acknowledge myself misinformed, and attend your last moments on the scaffold.

Miss Belmont disapproved of Mrs. John Belmont; and Mrs. John Belmont hated Miss Belmont. And the visible token of this antagonism was a button.

It was of jade stone, and it was a talisman. For three generations it had been the mascot of the Belmont family, an heirloom, and symbolizing in its shining disk a little local sun, as it were, of prosperity. The last three head Belmonts had all been men of an ample presence. The first of them, the original owner of the stone, having assigned it a place in perpetuity at the bottom hole of his waistcoat (as representing the centre of his system), his heirs were careful to substantiate a tradition which meant so much to them in a double sense.

Indeed, the button was as good as a blister. It seemed to draw its wearer to a head in the prosperous part of him. It was set in gold, artfully furnished at its back with a loop and hank, and made transferable from waistcoat to waistcoat, that its possessor for the time being might enjoy at all seasons its beneficent influence. In broad or long cloth, in twill or flannel, by day and by night, the button attended him, regulating indiscriminately his business and his digestion. In such circumstances, it is plain that Death must have been hard put to it to find a vulnerable place; and such was the fact. It has often been said that a man's soul is in his stomach; how, then, could it get behind the button? Only by one of those unworthy subterfuges, which, nevertheless, it does not disdain. The first Belmont lived to ninety, and with such increasing portliness that, at the last, a half-moon had to be cut, and perpetually enlarged, out of the dining-room table to accommodate his presence. Practically, he was eating his way through the board, with the prospect of emerging at the other end, when, in rising from a particularly substantial repast one night, he caught the button in the crack between the first slab (almost devoured) and the second, wrenched it away, and was immediately seized with apoplexy. He died; and the Destroyer, after pursuing his heir to threescore years and ten, looking for the heel of Achilles, as unworthily "got home" into him. He was lumbering down Fleet Street one dog-day when, oppressed beyond endurance by the heat, he wrenched open—in defiance of all canons of taste and prudence—his waistcoat. The button—*the* button—was burst from its bonds in the act, though, fortunately—for the next-of-kin—to be caught by its hank in the owner's watch-chain. But to the owner himself the impulse was fatal. A prowling cutpurse, quick to the chance, "let out" full on the old gentleman's bow-window, quenching its lights, so to speak, for ever; and then, having snatched the chain, incontinently doubled into the arms of a constable. The property was recovered—but for the heir; the second Belmont's bellows having been broken beyond mending

The third met with as inglorious an end, and at a comparatively early age; for the button—as a saving clause to whatever god had thrown it down, for the fun of the thing, among men—was possessed with a very devil of touchiness, and always instant to resent the least fancied slight to its self-importance. Else had Tithonus been its wearer to this day, as—but I won't anticipate. The third Belmont, then, in a fit of colossal forgetfulness, sent the button, *in* a white waistcoat, to the wash. The calamity was detected forthwith, *but not in time to avert itself.* After death the doctor. Before the outraged article could be restored to its owner and victim, he had died of a rapid dropsy, and the button became the property of Mrs. John Belmont, his relict and residuary legatee, who—

But, for the history of the button itself? Why, in brief, as it affected the Belmont family, it was this. Mr. Adolphus Belmont had been Consul at one of the five treaty ports of China about the troublous years of 1840-42. During the short time that he held office, a certain local mandarin, Elephoo Ting by name, was reported to Peking for high treason, and honoured with an imperial ukase, or invitation to forestall the headsman. There was no doubt, indeed, that Elephoo Ting had been very strenuous, in public, in combating the intrusion of the foreign devil, while inviting him, in private, to come on and hold tight. There is no doubt, too, that in the result Elephoo and Adolphus had made a profitable partnership of it in the matter of opium, and that the mandarin had formed a very high, and even sentimental, opinion of the business capacities of his young friend. Young, that is to say, relatively, for Adolphus was already sixty-three when appointed to his post. But, then, of the immemorial Ting's age no record actually existed. The oldest inhabitant of Ningpo knew him as one knows the historic beech of one's district. He had always been there—bland, prosperous, enormous, a smooth bole of a man radiating benevolence. And now at last he was to die. It seemed impossible.

It *was* impossible, save on a condition. That he confided to his odd partner and confidant, the English Consul, during a last interview. He held a carving-knife in his hand.

"Shall I accept this signal favour of the imperial sun?" he said.

"Have you any choice?" asked the Consul gloomily. "The decree is out; the soldiers surround your dwelling."

Elephoo Ting laughed softly.

"Vain, vain all, unless I discard my talisman." He produced the jade button from his cap. "This," he said, "I had from my father, when the old man sickened at last of life, desiring to be an ancestor. It renders who wears it, while he wears it, immortal; only it is jealous, jealous, and stands upon its dignity. Shall I, too, part with it, and at a stroke let in the light of ages?"

He saw the incredulity in his visitor's face, and handed him the carving-knife.

"Strike," he said, "I bid thee."

"You take the consequences?"

"All."

With infinite cynicism, Mr. Belmont essayed to tickle, just to tickle, the creature's infatuation with the steel point. It bent, where it touched, like paper. He thrust hard and ever harder, until at last he was thrashing and slicing with the implement in a sort of frenzy of horror. The mandarin stood apathetic, while the innocuous blade swept and rustled about his huge bulk like a harmless feather. Then said he, as the other desisted at length, unnerved and trembling: "Art thou convinced?"

"I am convinced," said the Consul.

Elephoo Ting handed him the button in exchange for the knife.

"Take and wear it," he said, "for my sake, whom you have pleased by outwitting, on the score of benefiting, two Governments. You have the makings of a great mandarin in you; the button will do the rest. Would you ever escape the too-soon satiety of this stodgy life, pass it on, with these instructions which I shall give you, to your next-of-kin. Be ever deferential to the button and considerate of its vanity, for it is the fetish of a sensitive but undiscriminating spirit. So long as you cherish it, you will prosper. But the least apparent slight to itself, it will revenge, and promptly. As for me, I have an indigestion of the world that I would cure."

And with the words he too became an ancestor.

Then riches and bodily amplitude came to Adolphus Belmont, until the earth groaned under his importance. He was a spanker, and after him Richard Belmont was a spanker, and after him John Belmont was a very spanker of spanks, even at thirty-two, when he committed the last enormous indiscretion which brought him death and his fortunes almost ruin. For the outrage to the button had been so immeasurable that, not content with his obliteration, it must manoeuvre likewise to scatter the accumulations of fortune, which it had brought him, by involving in a common ruin most of the concerns in which that fortune was invested, so that his widow found herself left, all in a moment, a comparatively poor woman.

And here Mrs. John Belmont comes in.

She was a little woman, of piquancy and resource, and a very accomplished angler of men. She could count on her pink fingertips the ten most killing baits for vanity. And, having once recovered the button, she set herself to conciliating it with a thousand pretty kisses and attentions. It lived between the bosom of her frock and the ruff of her dainty nightgown. Yet for a long time it sulked, refusing to be coaxed into better than a tacit staying of its devastating hand. And so matters stood when the Assembly ball was held.

Miss Emma Belmont and Mrs. John Belmont lived in the same town, connexions, but apart. Their visits were visits of ceremony—and dislike. Miss Emma was Mr. John's sister, and had always highly disapproved of his marriage with the "adventuress." Her very name, she thought, bordered on an impropriety! How could any "Inez" dissociate herself from the tradition of cigarette-stained lips and white eyeballs travelling behind a fan like little moons of coquetry? This one, in fact, took no trouble to. Her reputation involved them in a common scandal; and it was solely on this account, I think, that she so resented her sister-in-law's appropriation of the button. She herself was devoted to good works, and utterly content in her mission. She did not want the button; but, inasmuch as it was a Belmont heirloom, and Mrs. John childless, she chose to symbolize in it the bone of contention, and to use it as a convenient bar to amenities which would, otherwise, have seemed to argue in her a sympathy with a mode of life with which she could not too emphatically wish to disconnect herself.

They met at the Assembly ball. Miss Belmont, though herself involved in the financial ebb, had considered it her duty to respect so respectable an occasion, and even to adorn it with a silk of such inflexibility that (I tremble as I write it) one could imagine her slipping out of it through a trap, like the vanishing lady, and leaving all standing. Presently Mrs. John Belmont, with a wicked look, floated up to her.

"*You* here, Inez!" exclaimed Miss Emma, affecting an amazement which, unhappily, she could not feel.

The other flirted and simpered. When she smiled, one could detect little threads drawn in the fine powder near the corners of her mouth. There was no ensign of widowhood about her. She ruffled with little gaudy downs and feathers, like a new-fledged bird of paradise.

"Yes, indeed," she said. "And I've brought Captain Naylor, who's been dining with me. Shall I introduce him to you?"

Miss Belmont's sense of decorum left her speechless. Inez, on the contrary, rippled out the most china-tinkling laugh.

"You dear old thing," she tittered. "Don't look so shocked. I knew you'd be here to chaperon me, and—" She came a step closer. "Yes, the button's there, Emma. You may stare; but make up your mind, I'm not going to part with it."

Miss Belmont found herself, and responded quietly—

"I hope not indeed, Inez. I don't ask or expect you. You might multiply it to-night by a dozen, and only offend me less."

Mrs. John laughed again, rather shrilly.

"O, fie!" she said. "Why, even you haven't a high-necked dress, you know."

And then a very black and red man, in a jam-pot collar and with a voice like a rook, came and claimed her.

"Haw, Mrs. Belmont! Aw—er, dance, I think."

Miss Belmont, to save appearances, rigidly sat out the evening. When at last she could endure no more, she had her fly called and prepared to go home. She was about to get into it, when she observed a familiar figure standing among the few midnight loafers who had gathered without the shadow of the porch.

"Hurley!" she exclaimed.

The man, after a moment, slouched reluctantly forward, touching his hat. He had once been her most favoured protégé—a rogue and irreclaimable, whom she had persuaded, temporarily, from the devil's service to her own. He had returned to his master, but with a reservation of respect for the practical Christian. Miss Belmont was orthodox, but she had a way with sinners. She pitied and fed and *trusted* them. She was a member of the Prisoners' First Aid Society, with a reverence for the law and a weakness for the lawless. Her aim was to reconcile the two, to interpret, in a yearning charity, between the policeman and the criminal, who at least, in the result, made a common cause of honouring *her*. Inez asserted that, living, as she did, very nervously alone on the outskirts of the town, she had adopted this double method of propitiation for the sake of her own security. But, then, Inez had a forked tongue, which you would never have guessed from seeing the little scarlet tip of it caressing her lips.

Well, Miss Belmont had once coaxed Jim Hurley into being her handy man, foreseeing his redemption in an innocent association with flowers and the cult of the artless cabbage. He proved loyal to her, gained her confidence, knew all about the button and other matters of family moment. But the contiguity of the kitchen-garden with Squire Thorneycroft's pheasant-coops was too much for hereditary proclivities. He stole eggs, sold them, was detected, prosecuted, sentenced to a short term of imprisonment, and disappeared. Miss Belmont herself met him on his discharge from the jail gates, but he was not to be induced to return. The wild man was in his brain, and off he had gone, with Parthian shots of affection, in quest of fun. And for two years she had not seen him again until to-night, when his scratch of red hair and beard—which always looked as if he had just pulled his head out of a quickset—suddenly blew into flame before her. And then there followed a shock of distress.

"Jim! Why, what's happened? What's the matter with you?"

There was no need to specify. The man was obviously going off his tramp—nearing the turn of the dark road. He was ghastly, and constantly gave little spasmodic wrenching coughs during the minute he stood beside her.

"Well," he gasped, "I dunno. The rot has got into my stummick. I be all touchwood inside like an old ellum."

"Will you come and see me?"

"'Es. By'm-by."

"Why not now? Where are you going to sleep?"

He grinned, and coughed, half suffocated, as he backed.

"I've got my plans, Missis. You—leave me alone."

It did not sound gracious. One would not have guessed by it his design, which was nothing less than a jolly throw against the devil in the teeth of death. Miss Belmont, a little hurt, but more sad, got into her fly and was driven home. Arrived there, she sat up an hour contemplative. She was just preparing to go to bed in the grey dawn, when she heard the garden-gate click and footsteps rapidly traverse the path to the front door. Her heart seemed to stop. She stole trembling into the hall. "*Who's there?*" she demanded in a quavering voice. The answer came, with a clearness which made her start, through the letter-box.

"Me, Missis—Jim Hurley."

Amazed, and a little embarrassed, she opened. The man burst, almost fell in, and, staggering, recovered himself.

"'Ere!" he said, with eager manipulation trying to force something upon her. "I've done 'er! I've got it for yer! Take it—make 'aste—they're arter me. It's yourn as by rights, and she's got to crow on the wrong side of 'er woundy little mouth."

But Miss Belmont, with instinctive repulsion, had put her hands behind her back and retreated before him.

"Jim!" she said sickly. "*What* have you got? What do you mean? I'll take nothing from you."

"O, go along!" he insisted. His cough was gone. He seemed animated with a new masterfulness. "Ain't I in the know? It's yourn, anyhow, and"—his eye closed in an ineffable rapture— "I done the devil out of his own when I heard I be booked to go to him. He'll pay me, I reckon; but I don't care. You take it. It's your dooty as a good woman."

"No, no," cried Miss Belmont, beating him away with her hands. "Don't let me even see it to know. How could you suppose such a thing? Take it back while you've time."

B's 33 and 90 wore their list-footed boots; but Jim's ear was a practised one. Swiftly summoned, they had raced on his tracks from the Assembly Rooms. He had known it, and had laboured merely to keep his start of them by three minutes—two—one. Now, while their sole was yet on the threshold, he darted into the dining-room and was under the table at a dive. They had him out and handcuffed, of course, in a jiffy; and then they stood to explain and expostulate.

"Well, you ain't a checked one neither, Hurley! To run up here of all places for cover! Don't you mind him, Miss." (She stood pale and shivering. "The shock!" she had murmured confusedly.) "Why," said 33, "the man was heard by plenty proposing of hisself to visit you; and looked to your hold kindness to him to take and shelter, is supposed."

She found voice to ask: "What's he done?"

"Done!" said 33. "Why, bless you, Miss! Treating of you as if you was in collusion, ain't I?" (She shivered.) "Why, he grabbed a jewel—a gold button, as I understand—out o' the buzzim o' your own late brother's good lady as she was a-stepping into her broom, and bolted with it. It'll be on 'im now if we're lucky."

"It ain't then, old cock," said Jim, with a little hoarse laugh and choke.

"Chuck it!" said 90, a saturnine man.

"That's what I done, Kroojer," said Jim. "You go and 'unt in the bloomin' 'edges if you don't believe me."

"It's my duty to tell you," said 33, "that whatever you says will be took down in evidence agen you."

"Not by you," said Jim. "Why, you can't spell."

They carried him off dispassionately, with some rough, kindly apologies to Miss Belmont for the trouble to which they had put her. She locked and bolted the door when they were gone; mechanically saw to the lamps, and went upstairs to bed in a sort of stunned dream. So she committed herself to the sheets, and so, in a sort of waking delirium, passed the remaining hours of slumber. She felt as if the even tenor of her way, her stream of placid days, had been suddenly dammed by a dead body, the self-destroyed corpse of her own character. Sometimes she would start from a suffering negation to feel B 90's hand upon her shoulder. "What have I done—O what have I done?" she would moan in anguish; and B 90 would glower from under his helmet like a passionless Rhadamanthus—

"What have you done? What, but, like our second Henry, meanly, by inference and innuendo, imposed upon your wretched tool the responsibility for a deed which you dared not seek to compass by the open processes of the law. Did you dispute the right ownership of the button? Then why choose for your confidant an ex-thief and poacher? No use to say you designed no harm. By the flower be known the seed. Come along o' me!"

She rose late, ate no breakfast, and sat awaiting, pinched and grey, the inevitable ordeal. It opened, early enough, with the advent of Mrs. John. The little widow came sailing in, with a face of floured steel. When she saw, the edge of her tongue seemed to whet itself on her lips. Miss Emma broke out at once in an unendurable cry—

"Inez! You can't think I was a party to this!"

"Who said so, dear? Though the man was a protégé of yours, and was known to have remained where he encountered me by your instructions."

"It is not true."

"Isn't it? Well, at least, the plan miscarried. Now, give me the button, and I promise, to the best of my power, to hush the matter up."

"I haven't got it, indeed; O, you must believe me! He told the policeman himself that he had thrown it away while escaping."

Yes, yes. I give him credit for his loyalty to you. But, Emma—you know I never put much faith in your sanctimoniousness. Don't be a fool, and drive me to extremities."

"You can't mean it. I blame my covetous heart. I envied you—I admit it—this dear fetish of our family. But to think me capable of such a wickedness! O, Inez!"

Then Mrs. John Belmont exploded. I muffle the report. It left Miss Belmont flaccid and invertebrate, weakly sobbing that she would see Hurley; would try to get him to identify the exact spot where he had parted with the bauble; would move heaven and earth to make her guiltless restitution. Yet all the time, remembering the scene of last night, she must have known her promise vain. Jim had sought to thrust no shadow of a fact upon her. He had not thrown the button away. He alone knew where it now was; but would he so far play into the hands of her enemy as to tell? She felt faint in the horror of this doubt; and Mrs. John perceived the horror.

As for her, she was utterly hateful and incredulous. She had friends, she screamed—one in particular—who would act, and unmercifully, to see her righted. She hardly refrained from striking her sister-in-law, as she rushed out in a storm of hysterics.

And at this point I was called in—by Miss Belmont, that is to say.

I found her utterly prostrated—within step of the brink of the final collapse.

I coaxed her back, foot by foot; won the whole truth from her; laughed her terrors to scorn, and staked her my professional credit to have the matter put right, or on the way to right, by our next meeting.

And I meant it, and was confident. For that very day—though of this she did not know—I had officially ordered Jim Hurley's removal from the cell in which he had been lodged to the County Hospital. The man was dying, that was the fact; and a fact which he had known perfectly when he staked at one throw for an easy bed for himself, and a repayment of his debt to his old benefactress.

He was ensconced in a little ward by himself, when I visited him and sat down to my task. He cocked an eye at me from a red tangle, and grinned.

"Now, Hurley," I said, "I come straight from Miss Emma, by her authority, to acquaint you with the results of your deed."

"O!" he answered. "Hev the peelers been a-dirtyin' of their pore knees lookin' for it in the 'edgerows? I 'opes as they found it."

"You know they couldn't. You've got it yourself."

"S'elp me, I haven't!"

Then I informed him, carefully and in detail, of the awful miscarriage of his intentions. He was patently dumbfounded.

"Well, I'm blowed!" he whispered, quite amazed. "Well, I *am* blowed!"

"You must undo this," I said. "There's only one way. Where *is* the button?"

He gauged me profoundly a moment.

"On a ledge under the table," he said. Then he thrust out a claw. "Don't you go lettin' *'er* 'ave it back," he said, "or I'll 'aunt you!"

I considered.

"You must undo what you've done," I repeated. "Don't you see? Unless you can prove that it's been in your possession all the time, *and is now*, her character's gone for ever. Mrs. John will see to that."

He did not, professionally, lack wits. He understood perfectly. "You're 'er friend?" he asked.

I nodded.

"All right," he said, "you get 'old of it private, and smuggle of it 'ere, and I'll manage the rest."

"But, my good fellow! You've been overhauled, I suppose, and pretty thoroughly. How can you convince—*convince*, you understand—that you've kept the thing snug through it all?"

"You go and smuggle of it 'ere," he repeated doggedly.

It needed only a very little manoeuvring. I hurried back to Miss Belmont's, heard the lady was still confined to her room, forbade the servant to report me, and claimed the privacy of the dining-room for the purpose of writing a prescription. The moment I was alone, I made an excited and perfectly undignified plunge under the table, found the ledge (the thing, in auctioneer's parlance, was a "capital set," in four leaves), and the button, which in a feverish ecstasy I pocketed. Then, very well satisfied, I hurried back to Mr. Hurley.

I found him, even in that short interval, changed for the worse; so much changed, that, in face of his condition, a certain sense of novel vigour, an overweening confidence in my own importance which had grown up, and lusty, in me during my return journey, seemed nothing less than an indecency. However, curiously enough, this mood began to ebb and sober from the very moment of my handing over the *pièce de conviction* to its purloiner. He "palmed" it professionally, cleared his throat, and took instant command of the occasion. "Now," he said, "tell 'em I've confessed to you, and let 'em all come."

His confidence mastered the depression which had overtaken me. I returned, with fair assurance, to Miss Belmont, who received my news with a perfect rapture of relief. What she had suffered, poor good woman, none but herself might know.

"Did he own to you where he had hidden it?" she asked. And "Yes," I could answer, perfectly truthfully.

By my advice, she prepared at once to go and fetch her sister-in-law to the hospital—with a friend, if she desired it—that all might witness to the details of the restitution.

In the meanwhile I myself paid a visit to the police station, and thence returned to my post to await the arrival of my company.

It came in about an hour: Miss Belmont, tearfully expectant; Mrs. John Belmont, shrill and incredulous; an immaculate tall gentleman, Captain Naylor by name, whose chin was propped on a very high collar, that he might perpetually sniff the incense of his own superiority; and, lastly, and officially to the occasion, B 90.

I lost no time in conducting them to the bedside of the patient. He had rallied wonderfully since our last encounter. He was sitting up against his pillow, his red hair fluffed out like the aureole of a dissipated angel, an expression on his face of a quite sanctimonious relish. I fancy he even winked at me.

"Now, Hurley," I said gravely, "as one on the threshold of the grave" (which, nevertheless, I had my doubts about), "speak out and tell the truth."

He cleared his throat, and started at once in a loud voice, as if repeating a lesson he had set himself—

"'Earing as 'ow my rash hact 'ave brought suspicion on a innercent lady, I 'ereby makes affirmation of the fac's. I stole the button, and 'id it in my boot, where it is now."

"No, it ain't," said B 90 suddenly. "Stow that."

Mr. Hurley smiled pityingly.

"O, ain't it, sir?" he said. "Ow do you know?"

"Because I searched you myself," said B 90 shortly.

The patient, infinitely tolerant, waved his hand.

"'E searched me, ladies and gentlemen! Ho, lor! Look at 'im; I only arsks that—look at 'im! Why, he doesn't even know as there's a smut on his nose at this moment." (B 90 hastily rubbed that organ, and remembering himself, lapsed into stolidity once more.) Mr. Hurley addressed him with exaggerated politeness— "*Would* you be so good, sir, as to go and fetch my boots?"

B 90 thought profoundly, and officially, a minute; wheeled suddenly, withdrew, and returned shortly with the articles, very massive and muddy, which he laid on the counterpane before the prisoner. The latter, cherishing the ineffable *dénouement*, deliberately took and examined the left one, paused a moment, smilingly canvassing his company, and then quickly, with an almost imperceptible wrench and twirl, had unscrewed the heel bodily from its place and held it out.

"'Ere!" he said; and, with his arm extended, sank back in an invertebrate ecstasy upon his pillow.

The heel was pierced with a tiny compartment on its inner side, and within the aperture lay the button.

They all saw it, but not as I, who, standing as I did at the bedhead, and being something of an amateur conjurer myself, was conscious in a flash of the rascal "passing" the trinket into its receptacle even as he exposed it.

There followed an exclamation or two, and silence. Then Captain Naylor said "Haw!" and Miss Belmont, with a gasp, turned a mild reproachful gaze upon her sister-in-law. But Mrs. John had not the grace to accept it. She gave a little vexed, covetous laugh, and stepped forward. "Well," she said to Miss Emma, "you must go without it still, dear, it seems." Then, coldly, to Hurley: "Give it me, please."

Now, so far so good; and, though I was enraged with, I could not combat the decision. But truly I was not prepared for the upshot.

Jim, at Mrs. John's first movement, had recovered possession of the button.

"No, you don't!" he said quite savagely. "I know all about it, and 'tain't yourn by rights."

"Jim, Jim," cried Miss Belmont in great agitation; "it is hers, indeed; please give it up. You don't think what you make me suffer!"

But the man was black with a lowering determination.

"'Tain't," he said. "Keep off, you! I've not thrown agen the devil for nothing. It's goin' to be Miss Emma's or nobody's."

"Not mine," cried the poor lady again. "I don't want it. Not for worlds. I wouldn't take it now!"

And then Mrs. John Belmont, in one discordant explosion of fury, gave away her case for ever.

"Insolent! Beyond endurance!" she shrieked, and whirled, with a flaming face, upon her cavalier.

"Archibald! why do you stand grinning there? Why don't you take it from him?"

Thus prompted, Archibald, in great confusion, uttered an inarticulate "Haw!" explained himself in a second and clearer one, and strode threateningly towards the bed. Watching, with glittering eyes, the advance, Jim, at the last moment, *whipped the button into his mouth and swallowed it!*

The case, as a pathological no less than as a criminological curiosity, was unique. I will state a few particulars. The button lodged in the pancreas, in which it was presently detected, comfortably ensconced, by means of the Röntgen rays. And it is a fact that, from the moment it settled there—*never* apparently (I use the emphasis with a full sense of my responsibility) to be evicted—Mr. Hurley began to recover, and from recovering to thrive—on anything. Croton-oil—I give only one instance—was a very cream of nourishment to him. Galvanic batteries but shook him into the laughter which makes fat, but without stirring the button. It was ridiculous to suggest an operation, though the point was long considered. But in the meanwhile the button had continued piling up over itself such impenetrable defences of adipose tissue that its very locality had become conjectural. The question was dropped, only to give rise to another. How could one any longer detain this luxuriant man in hospital as an invalid? He was removed, therefore, beaming, to the police court; received, for some inexplicable reason, a nominal sentence, dating from the time of his arrest (everything, in fact, was henceforward to prosper with him), and trundled himself out into the world, where he disappeared. I have seen him occasionally since at years-long intervals. He grows ever more sleek and portly, till the shadows of the three dead Belmonts together would not suffice to make him a pair of breeches. He has a colossal fortune; he is respectable, and, of course, respected—a genial monster of benevolence; and he never fails to remind me, when we meet, of the time when I could pronounce his life not worth a button.

I have, can only have, one theory. The button, after many cross adventures, "got home" at last—fatally for Mrs. John Belmont, who fell into a vicious decline upon its loss, and, tenderly nursed by her sister-in-law, departed this sphere in an uncertain year of her life. And, unless the button itself comes to dissolve, Jim, I fear, is immortal.

JOHN FIELD'S RETURN
(1913)

John Field's father had been a man of considerable business acumen, a forceful, wide-grasping figure, one of the most noticeable of his time in Capel Court. It will be admitted, I suppose, that luck is a foremost factor in the success of a stockbroker; but why do some men habitually command it and others fail to? Putting aside the Buddhistic theory of pre-existence, with its demised rewards and atonements, it would seem as if luck were no other than the definite sum in certain human entities of a multitude of inherited qualities. One is not lucky because one is virtuous, or has been virtuous in a former life, but because there happens to have come together in one a cluster of ancestral propensities, each congenial to each, and all together forming the character most apt to command luck.

It is not for me or for anyone to analyse these constituents; yet somehow, I think, we are instinctively conscious of the lucky man when we meet him. Maybe it is that same instinctive recognition which partly makes for the lucky man's luck, inasmuch as we are naturally inclined to invest our trust in such a child of Fortune; so that after all, perhaps, it is not so much his definite qualities that we are to search for the reason of his success as our own confident sympathies towards that in him which virtually ensures success.

Anyhow, John Field the elder did possess the indefinable something, and he prospered greatly on the strength of it. He was physically big and strong enough to have illustrated the Spanish proverb that 'Good luck gets on by elbowing'; but indeed, though a certain genial arrogance characterised his operations, his effective strength lay much more in an infinite foresight and grasp of opportunity.

He lived well and long and died without fuss, leaving his fortune and his business to his only son and partner, John Field the younger.

Now this John was a man of a very different constitution. With no congenital equipment like his father's, he was yet not so much a fool as a failure. While existing and surviving within that protective shadow, he had had no particular reason to suspect the fact; it was only when he succeeded to his inheritance that certain doubts in him grew gradually from misgiving to conviction.

He was already a man of forty-seven when left alone in the world, by temperament a sybarite and a confirmed bachelor. He was rather a retiring soul, home-loving, and inclined to the solitary discussion of costly wines and meats. Gastronomy, indeed, may have been called his favourite study, though he indulged it with the secrecy of a shy man. So long as his father lived he had accepted unquestioningly, or without apparent criticism, the provisions of an abounding table; when committed to his own resources, he began to experiment, tentatively and timidly at first, on the fruits of his private observation. He had unobtrusively accumulated in his time quite a little Epicurean library, from *The Cook's Oracle* of Dr. Kitchener to the *Please, m'm, the Butcher* of our own day, and this he now disinterred from its omnigenous lurking-holes, and allotted the dusk end of a shelf in the dining-room bookcase. With some nervous diffidence, also, he effected a reform in his *ménage*, and substituted for the capable cook of his father's reign a veritable *chef de cuisine*—an artist trained in the dietetic studios, so to speak, of Voisin's and the *Boeuf à la Mode*. These temples of gastronomy, with others of their distinguished kind, had always been among John junior's most quietly favoured resorts during his rare trips abroad.

John Field had been well educated. Perhaps, after all, since some sort of mental employment is almost imposed upon one who has been, he simply developed, in cultivating the art of the palate, along his line of least resistance. Education makes us aspire, but it fails in teaching us to what. That, in order to the satisfaction of a vague intellectual hunger, we must find out for ourselves. Some resolve the problem through the eyes, and collect pictures; some through the ears, and study Wagner; others through the nose, and grow carnations. There is food for taste in each of these, and surely there is also food for taste in a taste for food. Indeed, epicurism may be said to command all tastes, since a good dinner enhances the aesthetic values of all art, whether musical, spectacular, or literary. In the respect of his hobby, therefore, John Field might have claimed distinction as a virtuoso. He had as fine a collection of cooking recipes as anyone in the kingdom.

In person, Mr. Field was a short meagre man, one of those starveling figures whose dimensions of capacity seem hopelessly inadequate to the strain put upon them, and who yet can absorb a gargantuan repast without a sign, moral or physical, of inconvenience. Such paradoxes, however, have their exact antitheses in the minute appetites that amass flesh; and both, I suppose, turn upon constitution. It takes more dressing to recruit a poor soil than a rich one. In any case, there is nothing more certain than that a glutton is not to be known by his waist.

Small side-whiskers, large blind-looking blue eyes, an habitual smile, more wistful in suggestion than humorous, a shrinking manner—such in John Field comprised the negative features of an uneventful personality. He could not look people in the face, he seemed nervous, timid, and as if always groping among problems whose solution eluded him. Yet, underneath all the shy commonplace and reserve there was something—some little blot on the man's soul, a rather appalling little thing it was—of whose existence no one even guessed.

John Field was forty-seven, I say, when he succeeded to his father's coffers and business; and, despite the fact that he had been for long years a partner in the firm, the latter statement is made advisedly. He had been a partner, indeed; but for all practical purposes no more than a sleeping one. Within the protecting shadow of that vast personality he had played at speculation, rather, in truth, as children used to play at the game with cards and counters. But, during the whole period of the association, he had never once originated, or dreamed of originating, or been invited to originate a move of his own. He had been just the passive instrument in a despotic hand.

He had been hardly aware, even, of his subservience. Those who are bred in the shadow of power assume, naturally, something of its hue. It was only when stripped of his borrowed covering that he realised his own anaemic nakedness. That he himself, and no other, was John Field and Son came upon him with something the shock of a sleep-walker's sudden awakening to a consciousness of his own lost isolation.

A friend once told me of an experience he had had. It was on the roof of a crawling omnibus, and the night was dense with fog. Suddenly there was a swerve, a crash, a desperate reining-in. The driver, utterly bemused, had taken the footpath for the road, and had pulled up only timely against a wall of shadowy brick. My friend, thinking it his best policy to alight, descended, and stood a moment to consider his way in the obscurity. During that moment, the driver, recovering his course, drove off, leaving my friend stranded at what, it occurred to him, was a curious elevation. And then he discovered the reason. He was standing on the parapet of a bridge which crossed some railway at a giddy height. A single step backwards, and he had gone crashing into eternity.

Now something of the shock and horror of that experience was John Field's, when the jog of his life's easy routine was exchanged in a moment for a consciousness of terrific poising on the verge of an unguessed-at abyss. He got off the parapet, so to speak; but his wits from that hour were never perhaps wholly at his command. A constitutional inability in him to think things out increased, until, from dread of itself, it became quite morbid in its character. This, however, was only the case as regarded his official responsibilities. Privately, he remained quite rational in the pursuit of his hobby.

Unfortunately the two could not be entirely dissociated, since the official had to supply the substance of the domestic. The firm of John Field and Son had never identified itself with the gilt-edged method of business. It took huge risks and built on huge profits. Wars, loans, taxes, monetary abundance or monetary scarcity, the fluctuations occurring in all human affairs from the fall of a ministry to the rise of a Mahdi—where safer firms cautiously exploited the legitimate accidents of such, Fields plunged and won through, as through the waters of Pactolus, breathless but dripping with gold. It was just a question of the Head's genius—or of his constitutional luck. He had an inspired way with him which carried daring to a triumphant finish. The thing was personal and not transmissible; that was its fatal flaw. Its genius once departed, the House remained committed to a policy of brilliancy which it had no exceptional light left to supply; and in consequence it fell, and swiftly, upon dark times. By quick and quicker process the luck that had habitually characterised its ventures under the old regime came to be not so much diluted, or even ended, as reversed. The fortunes of Fields began steadily to decline, to roll down—presently to the accompaniment of a heavy crash or two. And, suddenly, John Field the younger found himself staring aghast at the prospect of ruin. He only, perhaps, began fully to realise his own inadequacy when he realised that amazing fact. He had had so little need hitherto to think for himself that he had failed utterly to grasp his incapacity for effective thought of any sort.

One morning he sat at his office table, his right hand supporting his chin, his left toying with a pen, his round eyes vaguely contemplating a vision of the things he ought to have done to have reversed the disastrous order of a late settlement. Already he saw himself in imagination "posted" in the great hall, a "lame duck." And then his mind wandered away to a recipe he had just secured for the *Docce Piccante* of Florence—a peculiarly delectable dish which he had long coveted. Had he any right at last to indulge himself in these ruinous extravagances? The thought was prostration. He had no more power to forgo his hobby than a drunkard his whisky, a millionaire his free libraries, a magistrate his joke, though he had to pawn his hat to achieve his desire. As he sat, he spoke wistfully, without raising his eyes, to Harding, his chief clerk, who stood near by silently regarding him.

"This is very bad, Harding. Everything seems to go wrong with us since my father's death. And yet the character of the business remains unaltered."

The clerk uttered a sound that might have signified protest or assent. In point of fact he could have qualified the statement by a reminder that, though the business remained the same, the Head was different. A fleeting impulse, also, to cite an instance, from Aesop's Fables, of the injury that might be caused to certain members through a disagreement with their principal, he abandoned as too suggestively personal. And yet it would have been a telling illustration. They, the establishment to wit, were being threatened with a loss of livelihood through the gastronomic obsessions of this—well, one of the many names that Prince Hal called Falstaff.

Harding, a man of mature age and solid conservative principles, had risen to his position more through worth than brilliancy. John Field senior had not desired brilliancy in his employés; he had provided that in himself; it was the solid reliable qualities he had sought. This chief clerk was, as regarded speculative business, almost as incompetent as his present master himself to take the initiative—only with a difference. He could not advise where to venture; but he could tell where not to. That, however, was only a negative instinct, and little in request. While being as much in the confidence of John Field as was possible with so shy a man, he neither imposed nor was asked his opinion on momentous matters. But he saw, had for long seen, how things were going, and, in anticipation of the end, he was putting out cautious feelers towards problematic berths. He did this, to give him his just dues, with no unkind motive. He had a liking for his thewless employer—even a respect, though tempered with the business man's contempt for a visionary; but he felt no conscious capacity in himself for setting the wrong right, and he had the interests of a growing family to consult. There was never any invitation to human sympathy, moreover, on the part of this dull reserve. It was impossible to fathom it, whether for depth or shallowness.

"Does it not?" continued John Field, "or does anything strike you as different?"

"Only the driving force behind the machinery, sir," said Harding impulsively. The words were out before he could temper them.

John Field glanced up and down—an instant of startled intelligence; then resumed, more busily than ever, that idle scratching with his pen.

"O!" he murmured; "yes. I think I know what you mean. And yet the rules of heredity, Harding. It ought to be in me somewhere."

The clerk was silent, and the restless fingers scratched on, "blind tooling" with an inkless pen on blotting-paper, the empty hieroglyphics of an expressionless soul. Presently he began to murmur again, as if in self-communion:

"Perhaps I have been trying—all this time—to keep something from myself—the fact that others guessed the secret which I trusted to luck to hold inviolate. But where is luck—what has become of it?—that is just the question. I know it at home—sometimes—but not here. Not mental incompetency, but mental limitations—yes, that is it, mental limitations. And why?" His head bowed lower, as if in conscious incoherence, and his lips whispered on: "I don't understand; yet I foresee; I follow; but always on the threshold the footsteps die away. You don't guess what it is to hunt eternal chimeras, and then to find something tangible, gross, on which one's intellect can fasten tooth and nail—a certainty—yes, literally, tooth and nail."

He ceased, and not knowing where else to look, the clerk's eyes sought the floor. He was taken completely by surprise in the shock of this unwonted, this unexpected self-revelation. There was something wrong here, he thought; some congenital aberration hitherto unsuspected by him, and which might account for much.

And, as he stood, he heard a sudden violent sound, and started to the vision of his employer transformed, translated—a little suffering agitated figure, sprung upon its feet and apostrophising Destiny in a torrent of emotion:

"Why is it not in me, my father's genius? But I say it is, it is, only plugged in—stifled behind some monstrous obstruction. I feel it struggling for vent—bursting to rend the darkness; only the barrier is too dense. If I could once force it, once tear a way, my mind would be free to follow its own clues to ends as triumphant as his. They are there, those clues—I see them, touch them—and they lead me always, always up to the impenetrable wall and there stop. Why will it refuse to be pierced—why will it not let me through to the things I follow—Harding, why will it not? It keeps my intellect a prisoner, and doomed eternally to feed on the husks it can gather for its hunger? Harding!"

His vacant eyes were alight, his lean chest heaved, his voice was broken with emotion. It was like the bursting of some immured mental reservoir, never suspected until overflowing. Greatly shocked and concerned, the chief clerk took a step towards him.

"There, Mr. Field, sir," he said. "Come, come. You are overwrought; you imagine things; we shall see our way to an improvement by and by. We have a great deal of prestige to build upon, and we will be more circumspect in the future. Try to command yourself, sir."

His words, a long habit of self-obliteration, wrought their effect upon the sufferer. Gradually his voluble distress subsided, and he came to speak in a calmer tone.

"Yes, yes, Harding. I think I am unduly upset, perhaps. Only I understand what no one else does. It is here, all the time" (he put a hand to his forehead); "but something intervenes and closes the outlet. If I could only break a way through; if I could only gather how to do it—"

The other interrupted him: "What you want, sir, is a complete rest for your brain. It is bad for that to force conclusions. Let it vegetate, and they will come of themselves. The green shoot, you know, if watered and not disturbed, will make its way up through the hardest ground."

"That is very true, Harding—very comfortingly put. What shall I do?"

"If you take my advice, sir, you will cut the office for a week or two. We can manage without you. Go away to some quiet restorative place, and leave no address with anyone. No correspondence, no worry of any sort."

"I think I will do as you say. If I do not turn up to-morrow, you will understand I have taken your advice. God bless you, Harding."

The clerk, leaving the room, shut himself into his own, sat down, and shook his head. "Mad," he thought. "Not totally unexpected, either; but its suddenness took me off my feet. I must accept this breathing-space to look round me. I'm sorry; but, whatever the block in his brain, it's likely to stick there. We shall go from bad to worse. If I had dared to let him know, there's another crash imminent—those B Annuities—smoke and ashes. He'll be best away from it all." He hummed awhile, softly tapping his fingers on the table as he pondered. "What can be the psychologic explanation? That starting on a clue—to nothing; and yet the feeling of a goal? I wonder if it's true; I wonder if he really inherits so much of his father as to get on the track of great things that he's unable to develop? And then his mental refuge—if I read him right—the intellectual occupation of the table, good Lord! To 'epicurise' oneself into oblivion of one's abortive aspirations! It seems an odd way; but every man knows his own resources best, I suppose."

It will be observed that, for all his retiring disposition, John Field had not succeeded in hiding his foible from the world. But Harding was really distressed and perplexed. He foresaw fresh disaster, without having a conception of any means possible to avert it; and he prayed only that his employer, did he decide to take his advice and a holiday, would read of his loss in the papers, and so spare him, Harding, the pain of having to announce it to him.

Well, at least, it appeared, John Field had adopted his recommendation and withdrawn into some pastoral obscurity; for, for the next week, his place at the office did not know him, nor did he vouchsafe any message or communication whatsoever to give a clue to his whereabouts. And then came the expected debacle. A mortgage bank, largely propped by speculative financiers, stopped payment, and the house of Field was shaken to its foundations.

Harding steered through the mad waters as well as he was able, but he knew it was only a temporary escape, and that they must end on the rocks. He felt exhausted, hopeless, and he longed for some strong capable hand to take the tiller and the responsibility out of his own. On the morning of the ninth day of his chief's absence, on going into the latter's room for some papers, he saw John Field sitting in his accustomed chair.

To say that he was startled would express indifferently the shock that this unexpected apparition gave him. He had heard nothing of his employer's arrival; had neither expected him nor been warned by him of his intended return. And then the thought of the inevitable discussion between them made his heart turn suddenly sick.

"God bless me, sir!" he exclaimed, falling back a step. "This is a surprise—they never told me. Are you better—recovered?"

"Yes—well."

There was a tone in the voice which answered that Harding had never heard before. It suggested somehow the clearer cleaner enunciation which an operation for adenoids might have induced. And then suddenly John Field turned round in his chair, with a gesture as quick and peremptory as it was unusual. He looked pale; but the habitual vagueness of his blue eyes was replaced by an odd alertness, which seemed positively to scintillate as if in the glow of some inner fire.

"Shut the door," he said; "shut the door, and lock it."

Harding obeyed mechanically. He felt himself somehow on the threshold of a stupendous revelation.

"Something has happened," said John Field, as the chief clerk turned to face him again. "I am through, Harding—I am through with it."

"Through, sir?"

"The obstruction—you know what—it is gone."

"Gone? But how?"

"It was organic, as I always supposed it to be. Never mind the process—more successful than I ever dared to hope. The question now is one of time. We must hurry, hurry, Harding."

"Demented, at last and completely," thought the clerk. "I understand." Then he pressed out with his hand the trembling of his lips.

"Mr. Field," he said, "I must say it, I am afraid. No hurry will ever overtake what is gone beyond redemption. Have you not heard?"

"Yes, of course, I saw it in the papers. But you talk foolishly when you speak of 'beyond redemption.' Nature, Harding, abhors a vacuum. We cannot lose but she compensates—often with disproportionate riches. Cut out the killing canker, and earn life of her tenfold renewed. I have been with her and studied her methods. Let the bank go with the rest. They were the buds sacrificed to divert all growth into the perfect blossom. I have a hundred schemes, understood at last, to bring us gold. Only the time is short—or may be. We must hurry if we want to reap the harvest. There are plans to formulate—arrears of long months to make up. Come here to me."

All amazed, yet conscious of some compelling force, or atmosphere, the chief clerk obeyed. He still believed his master mad, yet he had no power to resist his will. As he approached, John Field, already bent over his desk, looked up.

"They never told you," he said, "that I had returned. I wished to enter unobserved. I desire the knowledge of my presence to be withheld from all but yourself. These enterprises I have in view—they are vast and absorbing, and they need the utmost concentration of my mind upon them. I appoint you my instrument and mouthpiece in them all. Say nothing of my initiative; say nothing of my return; but be secret and trustworthy. When you seek me I shall be here—locked in and alone. Wait upon me quietly, and never concern yourself as to my coming and going. Ruin will ensue upon any failure of yours to respect my confidence. Be faithful, and golden days are in store for us all."

Harding, scarcely able to articulate, murmured his assent to the compact. His brain felt giddy. Surely, if here was a confirmation of his suspicion, madness expressed itself in a lucidity, a force of decision, which had never characterised the normal being. Moreover, being but human, that confident promise of wealth rang in his head like a golden clarion. How could he believe it other than a sane promise? So are we constituted. In the light of potential gain, all extravagance becomes reason to us. Like one in a dream, he bent above the sitting figure.

An hour later he issued from the room, closed the door softly, gave a little stagger, and made crookedly on tiptoe for his own sanctum, into which he shut and locked himself. He then deposited a sheaf of papers he carried upon his desk, and sank giddily into a chair.

"Who could have believed it possible?"—so his thoughts careered. "It has happened—it has actually happened—and here is the genius of the old man returned upon the house. What did it: what brought it about—the bursting of some mental ligature; some internal explosion, like the purging of a foul tobacco-pipe with fusées; or some operation was it? Will he ever tell me; shall I ever know? Only it has come to pass—that is the astounding thing. These schemes"—he put a hand, fondly, tremulously, upon the papers—"there is wealth in every one of them—foresight, certain calculation, brilliancy. They restore the odour of the past; they are the John Field and Son of my first knowledge."

Presently he rose and went about his business. For a week he went about it, and always like a man in a dream. In the markets, while the schemes matured, he trod, confident and victorious, the pavements of a golden past; back in the office he was like one entering the portals of some hushed terrific temple. It felt so to him, he could not have explained why. There seemed always a tremendous atmosphere brooding within the familiar place—an atmosphere which transformed all things into unreality, and weighed upon the spirits of the most flippant clerks. And during the whole time John Field remained shut up in his room, accessible to him alone, going and coming—if, indeed, he ever went—unguessed at and unobserved, directing operations, and planning out the harvest for his reaping.

One day—it was the day of all others to witness the first garnering of the ripened crop—Harding, coming out from a whispered consultation with his chief, and hearing the door, as usual, locked softly behind him, was aware, as he stood with his fingers yet on the handle, of a clerk advancing hastily towards him down the corridor with a newspaper in his hand. There was a look of terror in the boy's eyes, a scared pallor on his face that arrested the other instantly.

"What is it, Jessel?" he said, as the intruder came near. "Good God! why do you look like that?"

"Read, Mr. Harding. See, there, sir."

He held out the paper, an early evening edition; his voice shook; he cleared his throat nervously. Harding, conscious of a vague panic at his heart, took the paper from his hand, glanced at the heading signified, and stood suddenly rigid.

"Half-way down the last column, sir," whispered the boy; and Harding, clinching himself to the effort, read:

> "Tragic end of a well-known stockbroker. Early this morning a gamekeeper, while making his round of Lord Pamplin's Stanbury estate, discovered the body of a well-dressed man lying in a copse within a few hundred yards of the main road. A revolver was grasped in the deceased's right hand, and every evidence pointed to its being a case of suicide. The body had evidently lain where it was found a considerable time, probably a week or longer. At present it remains unidentified.
>
> "Later: The body has been identified, from papers discovered upon it, as that of a Mr. John Field, a well-known stockbroker in the City. Mr. Field had latterly been staying at the Clayton Arms in Stanbury, from which hostelry he disappeared, without giving notice, some eight or nine days ago. It is believed that financial difficulties were responsible for the unfortunate gentleman's rash act, to which he was driven on the receipt of newspaper information as to the failure of certain gigantic operations on the Stock Exchange. Mr. Field is supposed to have

> gone straight from the inn to the spot where the corpse was discovered, and there to have shot himself through the head. Jewellery and money were found intact upon the body, which, according to medical testimony, must have lain undisturbed where it had fallen for at least a week. The inquest is fixed for to-morrow."

The paper rustled and fell from Harding's hand.

"That's non—," he said thickly; "look—you—Jes—loo—" like a man with incipient lockjaw. And then, clutching first at his throat, he threw himself on the door with a thin scream.

"Mr. Harding," cried the boy aghast. "What are you doing? It's fastened. He can't be in there."

Harding snarled round.

"Did I say he was, you fool? What—have you felt it too? Are you suggesting? What if I heard something. I must get in here—Jessel, I must. Come and put your shoulder to it."

Scared, the youngster obeyed. But first he turned the handle.

"Why, it's not locked!" he gasped, and opened the door.

Harding staggered, and came erect. He looked round the room. His face was like chalk, his eyes like grey flints in it.

"No, it's empty," he said, in a crowing whisper. "Of course it is. It was jus' my fancy—jus'—my fancy."

THE CORNER HOUSE
(1913)

Some three years ago two men, both preoccupied in thought, went by one another on Vauxhall Bridge. The next instant, the one making for the Surrey side halted on a subconscious recognition, wheeled about, and, returning hurriedly on his tracks, accosted the back of the retreating figure:

"Is that you, Gethin?"

The other started, turned round, and uttered a pleased exclamation:

"O, Acheson! I didn't see you. What good luck!"

"Eh? O, yes, of course!"

"I'm on my way to look for lodgings. You can come and advise me."

The first speaker hesitated, glanced at his watch, and raised a lean anxious face, the lenses of whose spectacles, catching the just kindled lamplight at an angle, looked suddenly like dead, upturned eyes.

It was a dripping, sodden November evening. Rain fell drearily; every buttress and lamp-post had its fibrous reflection underfoot, as if the pavement had grown transparent, revealing the deep roots of the things embedded in it. The heavy air floated with umbrellas, like a last swarming of antediluvian bats; labouring omnibuses were packed to suffocation; to anyone looking over the parapet, the barges slowly forging through the arches below appeared like submarines crawling dim and phantom-like in abysmal waters. A dull depressing squalor characterised everything—the faces of passers-by, the sordid brick of the houses, the streaming windows of the cheap shop-fronts. In the dropping mist of the rain one could see myriads of blacks being slowly precipitated to the pavement. It seemed impossible that a feeling of solidity could ever be restored to the texture of things.

Acheson looked at his watch again before he returned it to his pocket.

"Why, the fact is," he said, "I—I was going home to tea."

He was a small spare man, more callow than clean-shaved, with a sensitive neurotic face and a hungry expression. He looked older than his friend, though, as a matter of fact, the two were much of an age, young men of twenty-five or thereabouts. He was as boneless as the other was compact and strong-ribbed. Friendship could not have offered a greater physical contrast. The handbag which Gethin carried with ease would have weighed Acheson to the earth. Holding that in one hand, and his umbrella in the other, the former had nothing but a foot to kick out in invitation.

"Come and have tea with me?" he said. "You won't abandon an ancient chum, unassisted, to these wildernesses?"

A vision of a cosy fireside in the Wandsworth Road, of a singing kettle, and a dish of hot poached eggs, to be discussed over a volume of Myers's *Human Personality*, passed wistfully for one moment before Acheson's consciousness. He yielded it, the next, with a sigh. Curiosity, after all, was a dominant factor in his being; and he wanted to hear what had brought Gethin so unexpectedly from his native Woking to seek lodgings in this unattractive quarter of London. He succumbed, with a feeble grace.

"O, certainly!" he said. "Where shall we go?"

The other shrugged his shoulders.

"Where?" he said. "I am a stranger—a country cousin. I leave myself in your hands."

Crossing to the Middlesex shore, and chatting somewhat spasmodically under the general weight of things, they soon found a humble caravanserai, which was at least good enough to offer them warmth, dryness, and a sufficiency of creature comfort. But they were both men of small means, and accustomed to accept the amenities of existence as they could afford them.

It had been in the mind of each, perhaps, to postpone all intimate discussion until they were thus snugly ensconced and isolated; but, now that the moment was come, a mutual consciousness of something difficult and rather barren in the situation stepped between. They talked, after the first brief exchange of enthusiasms, in that rather forced galvanic way which often characterises the re-meetings of once intimate friends, whose interests and sympathies have long ceased to be one. Goodwill could not quite restore a confidence which had been largely due to circumstance and environment; nor could the fire of an ancient devotion penetrate through this distance of time with more than a very qualified warmth. As they secretly recognised the shadow, Gethin and Acheson yielded themselves a little sarcastically to its chill.

They had once been fellow-draughtsmen in a local architect's office, and Acheson had been the first to break away. That was some five years since, when a measure of interest, together with his own personal tastes and qualifications, had procured him the post of free-librarian in an important London centre. That was the best he had coveted, or ever intended to covet. He had no ambitions, but a vast psychologic curiosity, and the post assured him a perpetual sufficiency of the means to feed his intellect, and keep his body going. Years of study had not tended, perhaps, to qualify him for the continued friendship of the athletic, somewhat grim young giant by his side. He was painfully conscious of the fact as he glanced furtively from time to time at Gethin's face, and calculated the effect upon it should he suddenly rise and declare the necessity of his getting on homewards.

"You haven't told me yet," he said presently, in his high, rather strained voice, "what has brought you from home, looking for lodgings in this particular part of London?"

"Why not this as well as any other, Acheson?"

"O, well, if you put it that way, really I don't know."

Gethin laughed.

"As far as I know my London geography, it's handy for me."

"What!" said Acheson. "Why is it?"

Gethin laughed again annoyingly. He was rather inclined to that form of humour which sees fun in perfectly natural ignorances.

"Isn't Victoria Street in this neighbourhood?" he said.

"Yes; but—"

"And isn't Wrexham's in Victoria Street? That's to be my office for the future—I hope."

"Architects?"

"Yes, architects."

"You've left Pettigrews, then?"

"Yes, I've left them. What was there to keep me, when a better berth offered? I've had to wait longer for one than you."

"Well, I can only hope it's as satisfactory, now it's come."

"O, as to that, old man, my ambitions always widen with my prospects! But I'm only on probation for the moment. It's an opportunity, and—well, I've got to find lodgings for a month."

"If you want an inexpensive quarter—"

"I do."

"Then this is certainly as good as any."

"So I supposed. But there was just one other reason—ridiculous, but enough to influence me."

"What was that?"

Gethin leaned over the table, his arms crossed, a curious smile on his face.

"Acheson," said he, "do you still make a hobby of all that supernatural business?"

"I don't know what you mean by a hobby. I assume the necessary interest of the subject to any intelligent mind."

"I see. You are still a corresponding member of the Psychical Research Society?"

"O, yes!"

"Well, do you know you gave me quite a turn, meeting me on the bridge like that."

"Did I? Why?"

"Because, as it happens, a friend and neighbour was the last person who met my father before he disappeared for ever—and it was on Vauxhall Bridge."

Acheson nodded surprisedly, but he was patently not much impressed by the coincidence.

"O, I don't say there's anything in it," said Gethin; "only it struck me. It was the memory of that first meeting, in point of fact, which led me, absurdly enough, perhaps, to seek this way round to my improved fortunes. He was going to look for work, too. I dare say you remember something of the story."

"Something. Tell it me again."

"There's not much to tell. It's fifteen years ago, and I was a boy at the time—a boy at school. We had been in fair circumstances, and then it all stopped suddenly. Canstons, the big Army contractors, smashed up, and my father was in it, and his savings were in it. We were near ruined, in fact, and I don't think my mother took it very well. Between ourselves, there were scenes at home. He left that, at last, on the chance or offer of work in London—went off one day after tiffin, and never turned up again. From that moment to this we have never set eyes on him, or gathered by so much as a word a clue to his whereabouts. He just disappeared from mortal ken."

He paused, and there followed a short silence.

"They vanish sometimes," said Acheson presently. "There have been authentic cases."

"Relations came forward," continued Gethin, as if he had not heard him; "I had to put my young shoulder to the wheel, and we scraped along. But it was funny."

"Was he—have you any reason—" began the librarian; but the other took him up.

"The last man in the world to commit suicide—a cheery soul, like his son; indomitable, I might call him, without conceit. Besides, the neighbour who saw him, who met him on that bridge, testified to his buoyant, hopeful mood. He was on his way then, like myself, to look for lodgings. Acheson"—he bent forward very earnestly, and touched his friend on the arm— "it was a wet November evening, like this."

He waited for the inevitable comment, a little surprised that his friend did not immediately respond, as expected. Acheson chewed the offered coincidence again, reflective; and his verdict once more was that it was untenable.

"If my studies teach me anything," he said, "it is the folly of jumping in such matters to hasty conclusions. A tempered scepticism is the first equipment of your rational psychist. Coming from Woking, if you don't go on to Waterloo, you must get out at Vauxhall. In electing deliberately to do so, you made your own coincidence."

"But the date and the weather, man?"

"Both suggested that course to you. Now, if some accident had turned you out at—"

"And the meeting on the bridge?"

"No analogy whatever. You have asked me to help you to find lodgings, you see; and, if you are serious—"

"You bet I am. *I* don't want to vanish, like the baseless fabric of a what-d'ye-call-it."

"You see? localised from the outset. No; depend upon it, Gethin—you'll forgive my saying it—there was some perfectly human and natural explanation of your father's conduct."

"O, of course, you mean some discreditable attachment. I shouldn't have believed it of him, but I confess that that's the view my mother took."

"H'm, I take it for granted that every enquiry—"

"Yes, yes. O, yes; of course!"

He answered a little impatiently, and sat frowning, and drumming his fingers on the table.

"Well, if you are ready," he said suddenly, looking up.

"Quite ready," said Acheson, with a sigh of relief, and got to his feet.

Gethin paid the reckoning, lifted his bag thoughtfully, and they passed out into the street together. Swift darkness had descended while they loitered, and the rain was falling more hopelessly than ever. There was no wind, but the air was opaque with a very fog of water, through which the flare of the shops and the jets of the lamps burned with a dull miasmatic glow, which, in the light of passing vehicles, seemed to be constantly throwing off from itself a multitude of little travelling globes, which sped on like fen-candles into the murk, and were one by one extinguished. The houses looked gigantically tall and unreal; there was little human in suggestion about the shapes of the few foot-passengers, as they hurried past them, muffled, grey and dripping, into their dreary selves. Gethin gave a gasp of disgust.

"Look here," he said; "I'm lost. I hold by you to convoy me into some harbour of refuge."

Acheson considered a moment.

"There are plenty enough of every sort," he said, "both right and left. It's a heterogeneous quarter. Mansions rub shoulders with dosshouses hereabouts. But we must strike a line and take our chance. Your first point is a lodging for the night. If it doesn't suit, you can look again to-morrow. Supposing we turn down here for an experiment. It's sure, by its looks, to reveal a harvest of lodging-cards as thick as blackberries. Shall we go?"

"O, anywhere!" said Gethin, in a depressed voice.

They turned into a blank little street, making in the Horseferry Road direction. Quiet and dismality swallowed them almost on the instant. The sound of traffic died down behind them; their own footsteps spoke louder; the rain and the fog claimed them to complete isolation. Not a creature seemed to be abroad here; and the squalid ranks of houses they passed were, for the most part, lightless and lifeless in suggestion. They plodded along, painstakingly scrutinising the fronts. The crop of cards, if it had ever existed, was gathered or rotted away. Not a casual invitation greeted their groping eyes; but, one by one, as they advanced, the recurrent lamps brightened to a nucleus, made dismally emphatic the meanness of their surroundings, and drowsed and dulled again as they fell behind. They turned off at an inviting angle, and again turned, and yet once more.

"Where are we?" said Gethin suddenly.

His companion stopped.

"Why, that's the funny part of it," he said, in a most unhumorous voice.

"You don't know?"

"The rain and this obscurity are so very confusing," pleaded Acheson. "If we could only find a policeman, now—"

They stood, as he spoke, at the corner opening of a frowsy, melancholy little square, with a patch of degraded garden in its midst—at least, so it looked. Opposite them was the blank side-wall of a house—the first, it seemed, of a terrace. A street-lamp diffused its melancholy halo at the kerb of the pavement hard by.

"Perhaps the name's written up there," said Gethin. "I'll go and look."

He crossed the splashy road, and went round to the front of the house.

"Here we are," he called across to Acheson. "Come over. A chance, anyway."

Acheson followed and stood beside him.

"Where?" he said.

The light from the lamp fell full upon the corner house. It was one of a four-square terrace, as they had supposed. A shallow flight of steps led up to its door; the sill of its ground-floor window stood about level with the tops of the area-railings in front.

"'Lodgings for a single gentleman,'" said Gethin, "and a reassuring light behind the blind. It doesn't look too pretentious. Shall I try?"

"Lodgings!" said Acheson stupidly. "There?"

"Can't you see it?" answered Gethin impatiently. "Shall I try, I say?"

"O, there's no harm in trying," said Acheson. His voice sounded quite strange to himself.

With something of a flounce, Gethin ran up the steps. As he did so, Acheson backed to the lamp-post, and put an arm involuntarily about it. Standing thus, the falling curtain of light dazzled his eyes, and blinded them for the moment to what followed. He was aroused by hearing his friend speak close beside him.

"It's all right. She can take me in provisionally, anyhow. I'm about done, and I shall chance it. What's the matter with you? Has the tea got into your head?"

Acheson came away from his support, reeling a little.

"No, no," he said. "I'm glad—I won't detain you." And he fairly bolted away into the darkness.

Gethin looked after him a moment; then shrugged his shoulders, and turned to his new quarters. "Poor old Peter," he muttered. "What's come to him? I don't believe he's quite all there."

His landlady was waiting for him at the door. She was a little lean woman, haggard to deathliness. The wolf of hunger, it was evident, had gnawed her ribs and nozzled in the blue places of her eyes. She was all spoiled and drawn in appearance, and her voice was as lifeless as her face. She motioned him into the hall, coughing in a small distant way.

He entered, with a cheery stamp. Half-perished oilcloth was on the floor, and a cheap paraffin-lamp burned sickly on the wall.

"A beastly night," he said. "Which way, Mrs. Quennel?"

She took the lamp from the wall, and, holding it high, revealed the foot of a squalid stairway going up into darkness.

"On the first floor, Mr. Gethin," she said, holding her other hand before her mouth to cough.

He followed her up, commanding his nerves with an effort. Fatality had evidently appropriated to him a refuge in the last stage of decline. But it was a refuge, and cheap.

He was satisfied so far. The room was poor, and its appointments refined to attenuation. But the linen on the little iron bedstead was fresh, and the small grained washing-stand scrubbed to barrenness. There were a cane-bottomed chair or two, and some dingy lithographs on the walls.

"A sittin'-room?" said the landlady weakly, behind her hand.

"We'll discuss that to-morrow," answered Gethin.

"Meals?"

"Not now," said the lodger. "I'm going to turn in and go to sleep, early as it is. I've had a tiring day."

She went to strike a light and kindle a candle on the little dressing-table. Her movements were as bodiless as her voice. Gethin, watching her blankly, was urged to ask a question:

"Any other lodgers?"

She turned, with the lamp again in her hand. Her fragment of a face appeared, in its glow, to jerk and waver in the oddest way.

"One, Mr. Gethin," she said. "But he keeps to his room when he's at home, and locks it when he goes out. You won't be troubled by him."

He was about to disclaim any *arrière-pensée* in his enquiry, but desisted in sheer depression. He wanted somehow to get rid of her, and be alone. She chilled him.

And, almost before he realised it, she was gone, and the door shut.

He undressed wearily, extracted his nightshirt from the bag, and dived under the sheets. They were thin but innocuous. Then, leaving, for some unconfessed reason, his candle burning by his side, he settled himself to sleep, and opened his eyes again suddenly, with a start.

"She called me by my name," he whispered, "and I'll swear I never told it her!"

In the discussion of that amazing problem, his mind swayed, flickered, and suddenly went out. Health and bodily fatigue were on his side, and he sank into a profound sleep.

He was awakened suddenly—it might have been after many hours—by a consciousness of voices murmuring in his neighbourhood. Alert on the instant, he sat up, in immediate possession of his full faculties, and waited, listening. Two people, he was convinced, were talking just outside his room door—one, his landlady; the second, by his full hoarse intonation, a man. Gethin held his breath.

"My God," the deep voice was saying, as he first realised it, "I daren't do it!"

"Be a man!" answered the other, shrill and sibilant, fearful in its tenseness. "Break it in before it's too late, and save us from death and ruin!"

"I daren't," repeated the former speaker. "It might happen on the moment. I'll go for the police. Come away, Martha, in God's name!"

"And leave the new lodger?"

"I'll wake him first."

Gethin sprang out of bed, as the door was flung wide; and there was the figure of a great, white-faced, shadowy man standing in the opening. Wild fear was in his eyes, entreaty in his shaking hands. The lodger had only time to notice that he was bulky in his build, in suggestion something like a respectable ex-butler, and that he was in hat and overcoat, when the figure had withdrawn, and was appealing to him from the outer darkness.

"Come along, sir, in God's name, and run for it!"

On the instant Gethin was out, and in the passage. Breathing, sobbing, palpitating forms seemed to urge and shoulder him this way and that.

"What is it?" he cried. "What's the matter? I don't know where I am—I don't know what you are talking about!"

"You'll soon know unless you hurry up," said the man's quavering voice in the darkness.

Gethin, groping out, felt the wall, and put his back against it.

"I'll not move," he said loudly, "until I know what all this means!"

The woman's thin hurried voice took up the tale, small and toneless, as if she were speaking the other side of glass:

"It's Danby, the lodger, sir. He's one of those dynamiters, it seems. We never knew or guessed—he kept himself so secret in his room, and locked it when he went out. He was arrested this very evening, with an infernal machine in his possession. George, my husband here, saw him taken with his own eyes."

The wall felt suddenly cold against Gethin's back.

"What dynamiters?" he said. "I didn't know there were any of them about now." He set his teeth. "But in any case," he added, "if he's taken, he's taken, and there's an end of him."

The woman trembled on:

"The thing, it seems, sir, went by clockwork—and there's a ticking going on in his room now. You can hear it quite plain if you put your ear to the door."

Gethin laughed—on a rather hollow note.

"Is that all? Why, you don't suppose, even if it was true, that he would go out and leave one of those things maturing in his absence?"

"Some accident may have started it, sir—a rat or a mouse. There's plenty hereabouts."

"Come," said Gethin decidedly; "we'll break in. That's nonsense, you know. If he was such a fool—"

"They're all fools, sir."

"We'll break in, I say. Where's that big husband of yours? Now, Mr. Quennel?"

"I won't go near it!" said the hoarse frightened voice from the stairhead.

"Then, here goes," said Gethin. "Where's the room?"

He came away from the wall—felt himself quickly and softly induced, rather than directed, towards a door. Touching it, he bent his ear, and listened. Sure enough, a little sharp regular pulsation came from within, indefinite in quality, but quite appreciable in that still fog-ridden house.

"It's inconceivable," he whispered, "but we'll soon solve the mystery."

The lock was a cheap affair; the door, which opened inwards, of the flimsiest; the lodger muscular. He put his broad shoulder to the essay, and, getting purchase with his bare feet, bore on the wood with one mighty heave. There followed a crack, a ripping sound, and, to Gethin, a sudden wink of light and a jerk—nothing more. But the sensation was so instant, and so physically and mentally disintegrating, that, for the moment, he could conceive no thought of himself but as a sort of pyrotechnic bomb, which had been shot into mid-air, had burst, and was slowly dropping a multitude of coloured stars. These, as they fell, went out one by one, and, with the quenching of the last, consciousness in him ceased altogether.

Somebody was speaking to him; some application, distinctly physical in its nature, was being made to his body. It felt like a boot. He opened his eyes languidly, and encountered the vision of a face bent above him. It was an official face, and mature, surmounted by a blue helmet, and the expression on it was unsympathetic, not to say threatening.

"Come, sir, what are you doing here?" said the police sergeant. "You must get up, please, and give an account of yourself."

Gethin, accepting the offer of a proffered arm like a bolster, scrambled to his feet in a hurry. He understood on the instant what had happened. The bomb had actually exploded as he broke in the door, and he had been knocked insensible. A mercy, at least, that it was no worse. He clung on to his support a little, feeling somewhat dazed and shocked. It occurred to him, then, with a thrill of gratification, that he must have the constitution of a cat, not only to have survived that appalling experience, but to be standing, as he was, in his normal condition of body. And then something tickled him suddenly, and he lapsed into a shaking giggle. To have been asked to give an account of himself sounded so inexpressibly funny under the circumstances. It was as if he had manufactured the bomb. But, in the midst, the element of tragedy in the business struck and sobered him. He backed, and shook himself into reason.

"What about the other two?" he said. "Are they hurt?"

"Eh?" said the officer blankly.

"The others," persisted Gethin— "the landlord and his wife, who were with me when I broke open the door? Are they maimed—mutilated? Good God, man! they aren't killed?"

The sergeant, curiously contemplative of the speaker, stood, one thumb hooked into his belt, the other hand slowly fondling his chin.

"If I was you," he said at length, thoughtfully and oddly irrelevantly, "I'd take a red-herring and soda-water for my breakfast."

Gethin stared, flushed, and put the question a second time:

"I ask you, are they killed?"

"O, yes! They're dead all right—dead and buried, too."

"Buried!"

Gethin clapped a hand to his head. Had he been insensible longer than he supposed? But, in that case—

"When?" he asked faintly.

"It will have been in '85," said the officer, watchful of him.

Gethin's brain seemed to stagger, and recover itself with a crick. For the first time a sense of something unspeakable in his surroundings was beginning to penetrate it. Weak dawn, while he lay, had come into the house, revealing its structure. Now, in a moment, he understood that there was more of that visible than was compatible with decency or reason. The whole interior of the building, seen from his place in the passage, seemed a shattered ruin. Walls were broken, ceilings torn, doors sprawling dismembered, lights blown out of windows, stair-rails snapped, black abysses formed in the flooring. All that, in itself, was comprehensible. The odd thing was that an indescribable air of antiquity seemed to characterise the wholesale dilapidations.

"This house was blown to pieces," was all he could think of saying.

"Blown to pieces," echoed the sergeant; and added remonstrantly: "Come now, sir, pull your wits together!"

"When?" said Gethin.

"Fifteen years ago, to a day."

"To a day?"

"To a day. I ought to remember. I was on duty hard by at the time."

Gethin felt suddenly sick. He leaned back against the wall.

"I suppose I got muddled up in the fog," he said faintly, "and took refuge in this house, and went to sleep and had a dream."

"That was it, sir, no doubt," said the sergeant encouragingly.

"Untenanted, eh?" said Gethin.

"Avoided like," said the sergeant. "It's never got cured of its bad name."

"For fifteen years? Great God!"

He came away from the wall.

"I think I should like to get out of it—into the air," he said.

"There's your bag and umbrella," said the officer, "at the door of that room. Ain't you going to take them?"

He accompanied Gethin down the stairs. In the lower quarters, age-long dust and grime showed visible on all sides. The very edges of the shattered panes were green with decay; canopies of cobweb festooned the ceilings. Gethin breathed out a volume of relief as he found himself in the square, looking up awestruck at the blackened deserted building.

"How did you suspect me?" he asked the sergeant.

"Saw the front door ajar, and muddy footsteps going through the hall and up the stairs."

"You think I was drunk, don't you?"

"We'll call it a bit taken, sir."

"A small offence?"

"Very like," said the officer drily. "I hope you enjoyed yourself."

Gethin, biting his lip, looked at him a little pallidly.

"I wish you'd tell me," he said. "Who was it blew that up?"

"Name of Danby," said the sergeant promptly, relieving his throat and coming erect again: "a dynamiter, one of the 'eighties lot. He was the cause of it, anyway—left a charged machine working in his room there, while he went out to deposit another, a blind one, which he'd picked up by mistake. They arrested him with it on him."

Gethin found a momentary difficulty in asking his next question: "Any lives lost—here, I mean?"

"They accounted for three," said the sergeant; "those two Quennels that you spoke of, and a third, unidentified. He was supposed a chance lodger; but he was mutilated beyond recognition, and none ever claimed him. They say you can see the marks of his blood on the wall now. I don't know; I never had the curiosity to look."

"Thanks," said Gethin. He turned away, quite white. "I don't know where I am," he said. "I suppose you won't mind taking half a crown to put me on my way, and in recognition of your services?"

Weeks later, Gethin ran across Acheson in Victoria Street, and accosted him. Acheson had a queer look to greet him with, guilty and anxious in one.

"Probation satisfactorily over?" he asked.

"That's all right," said Gethin. "I stopped you to tell you something, and to ask a question. I've found out what became of my father."

Acheson gasped, and murmured something inarticulate.

"Acheson," said his friend, "what was the matter with that corner house the other night?"

The large spectacles seemed to disc as Acheson looked up.

"Don't you know, Gethin?"

"What did you see in it, I say?"

"Why—why, I didn't see what you saw, that's all."

"Not the lights and the bill? Well, good-bye, Acheson."

The librarian ran after him.

"Gethin! Would you mind telling me? The P.R.S.—I'm a corresponding member—I—"

Gethin shook him off good-humouredly:

"Not a bit of it, my friend. You lost a rare chance of securing evidence at first-hand when you deserted me so basely that time. You're not a practical psychist, Acheson—too much of the tea-and-crumpet ghost-seer about you. You prefer to take your spirits on trust. Besides, you libelled my father. Good-bye!"

THE HAMADRYAD
(1913)

I

Just outside Winton in Hampshire, if you leave the town due west, you come, climbing all the way, to a scarce noticeable bifurcation of the road, the right prong of which is nothing less than the original Roman thoroughfare to old Sarum. Making straight, after its kind, for its destination, this antique track (for it is little more at this date) conducts you from the outset into an immense solitude of downs, over which it passes in a long series of dips and rises, now by grass, now by hedgerows, until, at some three miles distant, it runs into timber very quiet and remote. Here is the wood of Lamont, notable for its strange flowers and insects, for its grassy glades and tangled coverts. These are nowadays jealously 'preserved'; but in the time of which I write—which was many years ago—a kindly tolerance admitted to their peaceable enjoyment all who were indisposed to abuse the privilege accorded them. But, even then, the place was so removed, and so devoid of attraction to the commonplace wayfarer, that few came to take advantage of its liberties, and those few mostly botanists or entomologists.

One September evening, in a year long past, a young man—an aurelian, to use the older and prettier term—came trudging over the downs to spend a ghostly vigil in Lamont. He carried in his pockets a dark lantern, a bottle of beer and sugar mixed, a brush, a nest of specimen boxes, and a little phial of chloroform, with a square or two of blotting-paper to finish. Such was the necessary paraphernalia of a moth-trapper by night, when the rarest and most beautiful species are to be secured. Young Mirvan had no other equipment about him but a hazel stick, which he swung regularly as he strode along.

It was a still and lovely night, with an autumnal keenness in the air which was both sweet and bracing. Low in the sky hung a full moon, so radiant and so large in seeming, that it appeared like the glowing sail of some fairy craft, just risen above the horizon of billowing hills, and reflected in their milky greenness as in water. Nearer, the undulating spaces were all sown with shadowy furrows and dense clumps of gloom, with here and there the spark of some distant homestead starring the slopes. No sound, but the occasional short bay of a dog, faint and far, broke the stillness. The lonely road and the lonely moon-drowned country possessed, and were possessed by, the solitary walker.

So detached from the world, his heart should have beat with a corresponding serenity. He was engaged in a pursuit which he loved, both for its environments and its curious interests. He had already one of the finest collections of lepidoptera in the county, and he asked nothing better than to be left in peaceable enjoyment of his hobby. But, alas! that was no longer to be. For family reasons he was to make, in a few days' time, a *mariage de convenance* with a cousin whom he did not love, and who regarded him merely as a necessary step to affluence and a position. Between the young mystic, the half-recluse and self-sufficer, and the near soulless girl of the world there could never be anything in common, and Mirvan felt that his days of irresponsible dreaming were numbered. This was to be his last night-visit, he felt, to the ghostly woods of Lamont, and, so far as that side of him was concerned, the thought was like a death-bed sorrow. The mystery and the loneliness of things had never before appeared to him so beautiful.

At the bottom of a long slope, so filled with misty greenness that it seemed to him as if he were walking into the sea, he turned into a close lane, which, at a few hundred yards' distance, brought him to the skirts of the wood, into which he passed with a sure knowledge, and was soon fathoms deep in foliage. Finding and traversing a silent glade or two, he presently, always easily ascending, came out into a clear grassy space, beyond which stretched the high woods all bathed in moonlight. And here, conscious even in his depression of some return of the accustomed glow, he felt for his brush and bottle, and stole in among the broken shadows. Selecting some likely trees, he painted their trunks here and there with patches of his mixture, and afterwards, having so treated as many as his memory might retain, withdrew to a neighbouring oak, and, seating himself among its roots, gave himself over, while he waited, to wistful meditation.

He was in a singularly emotional mood. His isolation in this world of leaf and moonlight; his passionate sense of strange delights, half hidden, half recognised, to be forgone; his dread of the bondage to come, all wrought upon him to a moving degree. He had never before so felt the haunting mystery of trees—their high-whispered secrets, the strange things they harboured, the way they disposed themselves to screen from mortal eyes the movements of things still stranger. He could have imagined the woods, for some reason, busy with unseen life; have imagined that an inarticulate giggle of voices, now hushed, now faintly audible, was whispering somewhere in their recesses. A silent white thing rushed past him, and it was only when it stooped, and rose again, that he recognised it, or thought he recognised it, for an owl. Once his eyes, unconsciously fixed upon a curious luminous halo in the grass a little distance away, were astonished into a belief that the thing undulated—was in movement. He was startled into rising and seeking the place; but discovered for his pains no more than a ring of white funguses, on whose surface the moonbeams seemed to boil and quiver. As he returned to his seat, tiny travelling sparks appeared to run from him in all directions, like glow-worms suddenly galvanised into activity. He rubbed his eyes, bewildered and a little agitated.

"I am a bit overstrung," he thought, "and my fancy is playing tricks with me. I must rouse myself and do something. It is time I examined the trees."

Taking his nerves resolutely in hand, he lit his dark-lantern, and, directing the light in front of him, advanced towards the trunk most nearly in his path. As he approached it, a drift of floating gossamer seemed to interpose itself within the glow, and, wreathing fantastically a moment, display a little shadowy face and disappear. To say that he was not conscious of a shock and thrill would be to underrate his sensibility; but, though, in the sudden start he gave, he nearly dropped the lantern, his feeling was one of astonishment rather than of fear. And, in the same instant, all supernatural tremors were lost in the excitement of the collector, for the light of the bull's-eye had fallen full upon a great moth resting drunk and stupefied upon the wet bark of the tree.

It was a rare specimen of the rarest of all moths, the Clifden Nonpareil, which covers with fore-wings of marbled silver-grey the most beautiful under-wings of banded black and violet. The prize was a splendid one for a lepidopterist, and, as Mirvan dropped softly to his knees to make ready his box with a fragment of chloroformed blotting-paper, his heart was thumping as if it would suffocate him. He was hardly breathing, indeed, as he rose again prepared, and saw the big moth still motionlessly awaiting its capture. Holding the light steadily focused on his prey, he advanced his right hand with the box in it—and instantly another little hand slipped in between.

It was like a flower, as soft, as semi-transparent—hardly more than a child's in size, but moulded to a ripe perfection. As Mirvan advanced the lantern, it disappeared.

He stood for some moments quite motionless; then, with a sigh, softly closed the shutter, and let the sense of moonlight regather about him. Even now he was so far from panic-struck that he could think with some vexation of his arrested deed. With the quenching of the light the silver moth had become one with the silver bark on which it lay.

And then, suddenly again, came the web of gossamer, drifting between with its fantastic convolutions, until it seemed to catch and wind itself about the tree. And, in the same instant, Mirvan was aware of the shadowy shape of a girl, standing by the trunk, and clinging to it as she regarded him.

At the first, he could separate her no more than the moth from the bark against which she rested; but presently the sense of a bewitching child-face, half shy, half alluring, of a faint glow-worm mist of hair, of limbs like rounded stones gleaming through dark water, grew upon him from doubt to certainty and from certainty to rapture. His inquietude from the outset had never approached fear nearer than its boundaries in a fearful joy. Now, at a leap, it had become an overmastering emotion of desire, a passion to absorb and possess. He forgot himself; or, rather, himself was gone—the thing of prescriptive conduct and staid conventions. All sorts of primitive impulses raced in his veins; long-buried impressions of hills and woodlands, of sweet midnight pursuits and thymy contacts glimmered in his brain. Melodious voices seemed to whisper from the thickets, only to become, when he turned to answer them, the murmur of far-running waters, or the rapture of bird song in some distant copse. He knew it, he thought. This was life in its heyday of joy and mystery. His heart throbbed with a delirious ecstasy; and in the midst he heard her speak.

"Spare my pretty moth!"

Was it a voice, a dream, a breath of music on the night? Quite overcome, he extinguished his lantern, and, throwing it on the grass, leaned towards the vision.

"It is the spoil of my life," he whispered. "At what price, you lovely thing?"

She seemed to laugh, putting her finger to her lips. Burning all through, Mirvan advanced a step. As he did so, the shape, winding its pale arms about the tree, as if it appealed to it for protection, appeared to dissolve and vanish where it stood.

He uttered a little despairing cry. What had become of her? In the agony of that impossible loss, he leapt and ran round the tree. He trod upon his lantern, and, stumbling, caught at the trunk. It seemed soft to his hand, warm and palpitating. In an access of emotion, he threw himself upon it, gripping and striving as if he would bear it down. "Your secret!" he panted; "yield it!"

And suddenly it seemed to melt beneath him; soft arms came about his neck; a voice sighed in his ear: "Captured! O, captured! A moth for a moth, you dearest!"

Intoxicated with bliss, he set his lips in the darkness to lips as sweet as wine.

From that dream, as from a deep swoon, Mirvan awoke to find himself lying on the grass in the grey dawn. The wood was all about him, quiet as death. Not a whisper broke its silences, not a thing seemed stirring in its thickets. He got to his feet, and stood in a dazed way, thinking it was time for him to be turning homewards. Once he started, and paused and came back. And a second time he started, and checked himself, and returned to the oak, and stood looking at it with glazed eyes.

"Was it all a moonstruck dream?" he murmured. "For your part in it, thanks, anyhow, dear oak."

But the oak did not respond by so much as a quivering leaf.

II

Mirvan dutifully married, and kept to his marriage bond, found no more joy in his state than he had anticipated. His wife's was a small nature, dull and exacting, incapable of passion, save in its squalidest aspect of jealousy. The secrets of his soul were locked from her; and, though she could never have sympathised with them revealed, the thought of something withheld filled her with a perpetual sense of injury. She seemed always seeking for a proof of his hidden depravity of heart and mind.

At the end of a year a girl baby was born to them. Mirvan, after the first natural interest evoked by the knowledge of his being a father, took little notice of it. It appeared an ordinary unexciting child, and, though pretty, the farthest from precocious. When two years had passed it was still as speechless as on the day of its birth—in actual vociferation even less emphatic. He began to wonder, with only a faint stirring of curiosity rather than of concern, if it would ever come to articulate.

But on the morrow of the child's second birthday a curious change was announced. That night Mirvan had passed in a strange mood of agitation. He could not sleep; it had seemed to him that something was in the house—something not belonging to it. It was only at dawn that he had lost consciousness, under, as it appeared to him, the whispering branches of an oak tree. The nurse coming into the room, pale and startled, was the first to awake him to a sense of realities. She showed a disposition to cry. Would her master and mistress come at once, she said. Baby was sitting up in her cradle and talking.

They rose, and followed her out. That sense of estrangement between them made the mother hasten to claim the first right to her child. The best her narrow nature could exhibit was all devoted to this possession.

She stopped, with a gasp, when she entered the night-nursery. The tiny being was seated up on her pillow, taking voluble stock of all the wonderful things about her. Her speech was ludicrously pretty, but comprehensible only in fragments. It was the look of sudden intelligence in her eyes that was the oddest part. It was baby, but indescribably developed between a single sleeping and waking.

Mirvan stole a look at his wife. A certain revulsion of feeling in her was patent to his soul. He, on the contrary, felt such an attraction to the child as he had never known before. From that day she was his constant delight and companion; and from that day, as he was aware, his wife hated him.

The nurse could not be induced to stay, and another was procured. But, indeed, her post was a sinecure. The child was always with her father; her elfish prattle followed his footsteps all day long. When she came near her mother, it was to be coldly repulsed, and often to answer pertly, "Baby not love you"; to which the woman would reply: "I don't want your love. You are no child of mine."

And thus another six months passed by; and every day of it added to the infant's precocity and strange beauty.

One evening Mirvan, thinking to interest his little daughter, took her into his study to show her his collection of moths and butterflies. But the sight of the first drawer of specimens, as he pulled it out and lowered it for her inspection, had a startlingly opposite effect to that which he had anticipated. She turned pale, shrinking back a little.

"How are they made to settle so still behind the little window?" she whispered.

"They do not settle; they are dead, baby," he answered, amused.

"Dead!" her face was going white. "Who killed them?"

"Why, I did," he said. "I caught, and drugged them to death, then put pins through their bodies, and stretched out their wings, and left them to dry."

She gave a single gasp; and then her infant fury broke. She screamed at and reviled him; she beat him with her little hands. She cried that he was cruel, cruel—that he was worse than the fox and stoat, that only slew for food—that she would never, never love him or speak to him again. Finally, she ran from the room in a storm of tears, and he heard her stamping up to her nursery.

Mirvan was utterly amazed, and more than a little distressed and troubled. All that evening he was haunted with a sense of guilt; and by and by, unable to sit out his depression, he stole upstairs to visit his rebellious little girl in her cot. She was lying to all appearance fast asleep, the sheet covering her face to the hair, and, unwilling to disturb her, he just dropped a remorseful pat on the counterpane, and left the room.

It thundered all night; and the next morning he was awakened, as once before, to find the nurse in his room.

"Please, ma'am," the girl was saying, "I think there's something wrong with baby. She won't speak, and I can't seem to make her understand."

He was up before his wife this time, and out and in the nursery. As he stood staring, with a dead feeling at his heart, his wife brushed past him, and fell on her knees beside the cot.

"Baby!" she whispered in a voice of rapture. "It is mother's own darling come back again."

"She don't seem to hear or understand," said the girl; "and there's something odd-looking about her."

The mother had the child in her arms, kissing and fondling her. She looked round fiercely at the speaker. "You are a fool," she said. "You can go."

But, indeed, from that moment the child never spoke or heard or saw again; and from that moment Mirvan gave himself up, wholly, patiently, remorsefully, to her care. He knew that those who have been once borrowed and returned by the fairies must never be allowed to reveal their experiences or to recognise their playfellows in all their time to come.

THE VOICE
(1913)

The day had been wet and mellow after a longish drought. The soil sucked at the warm flood, as a thirsty horse swills at a trough, drawing in its satisfaction quietly and intently; the cottage windows twinkled under their brows of dripping thatch; the hills, misty and phantasmic, seemed to roll like leviathans in a fog of descending water. And it was under such circumstances of weather that I first saw Balmworth.

One could not conceive a village more faithful to its etymology. It saunters down a gentle slope, half a mile long, from the hills to the sea; slips without a stumble into a tiny cove—landlocked for nine-tenths of its circumference, and green as an aquamarine set in a loop of silver chalk—and elsewhere and on all sides is made comfortable in its place with cushions of velvet down. Coming from the little station-village of Flock—itself a drowsy portal to the hills—one ascends a three-mile rise, traverses a short tableland, and goes straight down, smiling, into the harbourage of the tranquil valley. What does it concern one that those slumberous green pillows which contain it are neighboured on either side by populous and popular "seaside resorts"? The hills are ramparts as well as boundaries, and the vulgar, confined to *char-à-bancs* and high roads, essay to storm them but fitfully. Their flying visits but serve, in fact, to accent the peace, as the casual rush of a motor-car outside lonely windows leaves a profounder silence in its wake.

And the inhabitants are all in keeping. Here are no sharks of landladies, hungering to feed on the inexperienced adventurer; no maximum of cost for a minimum of service; no cracked pianos at a shilling a thump; no castors estimated in the weekly bill at a figure which would keep a furrier in pepper for a year; no priceless china, cheapened from the nearest crockery store, and put up on brackets to be accidentally broken, and paid for; no charge for the attendance which is ever lacking; no suffering protests, no extortion, no inflated prices whatever. No fleas, I would fain add; but that would not be true. Yet even they feed delicately, with ever a gentle consideration for the provision of the only man in the place who sells Keating.

Balmworth, to be sure, lets lodgings (indeed, in the "season" it is so greatly affected by those who love not the swarming warrens of August that it is difficult to secure a bed there), but on an artless Arcadian plan. It is as ready to take in the houseless traveller as it would be to be taken in by him. Any Jeremy Diddler so inclined might steal his dirty week's toll of its hospitality. Its landladies tot up their bills, all wrong, with infinite travail, and finally beg the good graces of their lodgers to help them to screw and pummel the items into some correspondence with the totals. They smile; they confide; they are on pleasant personal, but not in the least self-obtrusive terms with you from the outset. Supercilious or baronial-nosed people discomfort them. Sometimes they entreat your acceptance of a basket of blackberries or rosy apples. They are mostly the wives and mothers of the boatmen, to whom appertaineth the conduct of the Cove, sailing and fishing, the letting out of craft, the exploiting, in short, of little Balmworth as a sea pleasure-garden .

It is a very quaint and pretty basin among the cliffs, is this Cove—something like Mother Carey's Peace-pool. It is just a mile in circumference; and the land's fond arms, not quite meeting round it, leave open a narrow water-way, through which pleasuring steamers can creep in in all but stormy weather. They do not trouble one much. The life of the Cove congregates all the morning about the eastern side, to which they do not come, and where cluster the little white bathing-huts which are the real lodgings of Balmworth. For this pool of translucent water, on whose floor sixteen feet down one may see the weeds swaying pale as if in moonlight, is very grateful to the bather; and there be those who will camp all day among the little huts, that they may undress and plunge at pleasure.

Opposite the water-way above mentioned sweeps up a mighty forehead of chalk, mottled like old ivory, which, descending gradually as it curves either way about the Cove, ends at the entrance in horns of stratified rock. In the western arm of this curve is gathered the business material of the place—boats, nets, lobster-pots, prawn-chests, lugworms and lumber. It is significant that never a life-belt is to be seen there, unless in the shed where the men of the coastguard keep their trim black boats with the brass fittings. Balmworth pays no tax to the white-horsed farmers of the sea, and that for a simple reason. When the wind blows enough to imperil small craft, no sailing-boat can make the outward passage of the waterway. Even in calm weather so narrow is it that the tripper-steamers have to slip in with caution. Meet that such a place, so secure, so unvexed, so child-like in its character, should be haunted, if at all, by a child's voice.

Perhaps it was the cluck of choked gutters, or the soft trample of the rain on the road, or some small, inarticulate converse of unseen talkers that deceived my hearing; but, as I walked, while the hills sunk fading about me into night and water, I could have thought, and more than once, that something ran beside me, a little thing that begged in a little voice, as a small trained mendicant might do, and sobbed and sniffed to rouse my unresponsive sympathy. The impression was so faint, so unreal, that my only wonder lay in its imposing itself on me so persistently. I sought to associate the fancy with the sights and sounds about me; but it would not so be put away. It ran and babbled, sometimes in front of me, sometimes at my side—not words, but their shadow; no face, but the uplifted glimmering blotch of one, which, when I bent to canvass it, was always a stone in the road.

I felt no distress, but a certain curiosity. That the delusion was a delusion I never had a doubt. The key to the enigma was all that lacked. But I was confident that I should find it sooner or later.

I went on placidly, descending to the Cove. The lights of an inn, of cottages, met me right and left. And then I was going down a narrow gully; and then came a pool of ashy water.

It lapped out of the mists, reaching vainly for the rank of little boats which lay thereby, drawn up on the shingle. Grey wet and desolation held all this quarter of the Cove. Not a light twinkled from the coastguard station, perched high aloft on the butt of the western horn. It was just a minute section of beach and sea, half veiled, half disclosed in the drowning fog. Not a sign of life was in evidence but the figure of a solitary boatman, roping up his craft for the night.

And then, all of a sudden, the voice had become articulate, and I saw the dark form of a little girl go bounding down the stones to the lonely figure.

"Bill, Bill!" she cried, "do let me pull! O, Bill, do let me pull!"

The tone pierced as shrill, as hollowly treble through that sodden desolation as the cry of a hawking seagull. Yet the figure among the boats took no notice of it whatever.

"Bill!" wailed the child; "do let me pull!"

The figure worked on stolidly. "Is he stone deaf? I thought.

She danced round him, crying and entreating—always in that piercing young voice. He could not fail to see, even if he had not heard her. Suddenly he rose to his height, his task finished, and came clumping up the shingle towards me. In the same moment the figure of the child seemed to go down into the waters and disappear. I uttered a shout and pounded to the spot. Not a bubble, not a ripple betrayed the place of that noiseless plunge. The tide came in, wrinkle over wrinkle, without a break. I beat back and forth, peering, calling, but with no avail. Finally I desisted, and went up the beach to the man. He, at least, though I had questioned it at first, was no ghost. I felt that I was shaking through and through as I approached him. No doubt he thought me demented.

But, if he did, he made a successful pretence of unconcern, as he stood soberly lighting his pipe. His face in the act was revealed to me, glowing and shadowing, as he pulled at the match. It was the face, indisputably, of a kindly, rugged soul, humane, earnest, unguileful—an expression of that spirit of simple gravity which comes of long association with the awe and mystery of the sea.

"I thought I heard a child calling down there," I said, commanding my voice with difficulty. "But there wasn't one, of course?"

"Bless you, see," he said, in a curiously small, indrawn way for such a bushy man, "this isn't no night for children."

"No," I replied, "a black night—no sort of weather for one's first visit to your Cove."

"I've never known the like," he answered, looking up at the sky. (They never have.)

His atmosphere invited frankness.

"What's your name?" I asked. He told me. "And your Christian name?"

"Bill, see," he said. So he pronounced "Sir," quite mincingly.

He was going up the village, and I was suddenly anxious for his company. I refrained, even, from looking over my shoulder as we left the boats and the whispering crescent of beach.

"Ah!" I said; "that was the name I thought I heard the child call—Bill."

"Yes, see," he responded heartily.

"'Bill,' I thought I heard her say, 'do let me pull, Bill.'"

"Ah!" he said; "that'll be little Miss Vera."

"Little Miss—but you said you didn't hear her?"

"No, see," he answered simply. "I can't do it; but others can. She visits us time and again by their showing—the little drownded sperit of her."

"How was she drowned?" My voice seemed something apart from me.

"Had set her heart," he said soberly, "on pulling of a boat all by herself—was always a-crying on me to let her. But I had my orders. She was a bit what you'd call wilful, see; and one evening—it might have been like this" (he had forgotten his former statement)— "she give her lady mother the slip, and run down to the boats, and had one out, all with her own hands, before a soul knew she was gone." He stopped a moment, blowing at his pipe till it scattered a very shower of sparks into the wet. "I picked up her little body myself," he said. "There it was in the water, as quiet as sleep. She'd just run the boat off of the beach, and herself with it. So she'd never had her pull after all. God rest her pretty sperit!"

I saw him later, in the tap of The Pure Drop. He was having his temperate pot and pipe before turning in, and was taking his earnest share in a political discussion. The visitation lay, if it lay at all, quite simply and unharmfully on his mind. Surely that was the right unsophisticated way to accept it. The responsibility for haunting lies with the haunter. As for myself, I have not learned to appreciate Balmworth at a figure less than its due because of that infinite weirdness of my introduction to it. It is a rare haven on a noisy coast; its voices murmur either out of sleep or death. But that one shrill small voice I have never heard again.

TONY'S DRUM
(1913)

I

Somewhere on the heights of Malplaquet a bugle sang out in the dead exhausted evening. Sergeant Garrow, kneeling in the brushwood below, cursed the whine of it with picturesque vehemence:

"Why don't ye come and give us a haul, ye braying jackass," he panted, "instead of standing up there and boasting of your wind?"

The wail, in its passing, seemed to release the babel of mournful sounds it had for the moment subdued—sobbing of wounded horses, crying of wounded men, all flowing over the lip of the plateau above, and mingling confusedly with the wind in the leaves and the rush of a little river, vocal in the thickets deep below.

It was the evening following that day of dreadful battle which had cost us twenty thousand lives for the gain of a position not worth negotiating. Our troops could boast that they had won his camp from the enemy for the sake of a night's lodging; and there they lay in it, their fires spotting the heath, their anguish testifying to their gain. The woods of Lanière and Taisnière under the hill were spilled full of dead men, and sentries almost as torpid watched the captured entrenchments.

Sergeant Garrow, staggering up the ravine-side with a little smitten drummer-boy in his arms, had fought to within hail of the plateau of Malplaquet, when he found that his endurance had reached its limit. He put his burden gently down against a tree, and, half falling beside it, squatted haggardly, his chest labouring.

"Lad," he whispered presently, "I'm spent. I can carry thee no farther, lad!"

The boy was beyond answering. He lay huddled among the roots, his drum still slung at his side, his wounded chest exposed. It had been smashed by a round-shot, and his friend's rough surgery had been able to make nothing of the injury. But the doctors were all at work above.

The sergeant panted as if he would never get his heart again. He could only squat and gasp, praying for help. Presently there came up through the wood an officer, taking the steeps in his torn galligaskins as vigorously as if he had never fought all day. It was Captain Hugomort of the 4th King's Own, a soldier who had the reputation for possessing the toughest rind and the softest heart in all Her Majesty's army. His strength was as prodigious as his humanity, and his cheery ugliness as prepossessing as either. He stopped, leaning one hand against a tree, and breathed himself. The sergeant rubbed his fingers in the grass before saluting.

"Only a woundy drummer-boy, sir," he said apologetically, in answer to the unspoken query. "A bit of a thing; but beyont me."

The other nodded comprehendingly.

"What is he doing on this bloody hill-side of Flanders? He should have been in bed by rights, miles away in old England."

He stooped, and peered into the lad's white face; then, as gently as a mother, lifted the little broken body in his arms, and carried it up to the plateau. It was cold September weather, and the camp-fires, after the false heat of the day, were welcome. Hugomort, motioning for room, laid the child down in the heather by one, and bent over him. The sergeant, wearily following, came and stood beside.

"Dying!" he said. "No need for a doctor, sir."

"Who is it?"

"Truelove, sir. A main spirited lad."

Again, far away over the heath, a bugle sounded—ineffably mournful—the Last Post. The drummer-boy's eyes opened; his lips moved. Hugomort put out his hand, commanding silence.

"What is it, my child?"

"The drum—give it to daddy."

He could hardly hear the bodiless whisper. There was not a moment to lose. He stooped low, and spoke his faithful promise:

"Before God I will, manny—and with my own hands, if God wills."

A smile, like a faintest ripple, crossed the boy's face; his shattered chest rose once, and fell; his eyes rolled back, and Hugomort got to his feet.

"Unbuckle it, sergeant," he said, in a subdued voice. "He's gone."

II

The Hugomorts were a race of strong men, but this Captain Roger was an Anak among the Anakim. He was so huge and gristly, it was said, that bullets rebounded from him like peas, and bayonets pricked him no more than thorns. He fought through the Marlborough wars, receiving many wounds of a kind, and, after the capture of Douay, accompanied his chief back to England, where, standing enrolled of the heroes, he had to suffer a siege on his own account, the missiles being feminine and multifarious. In the end, to the scandal of his name and of society, he made a ruinous mésalliance; but that offence, so far as it affects posterity, has long mellowed into the distinction conferred by dead and gone romance. Disgraces, once poignant, become in their remoteness the pride of race, and Mrs. Roger's portrait owns at this day a distinguished position to itself on the walls of the great gallery at Hugomort. It is in an oval frame, and exhibits, at half-length, the figure of a very fresh and blooming young woman, having the brown curls and humid artless eyes of the Kneller convention. She wears loosely on her head a little stone-blue hood surmounted by a straw *paysanne*, a trifle 'raked,' which sports a primrose-coloured ribbon; and her right hand presses a bunch of lavender to her bosom, as to the white and fragrant shrine of innocence. Her darker blue bodice is laced and square-cut, showing a frill of smock, and there is a suggestion of pretty wistfulness about the whole picture which is curiously winning.

Well, that is the portrait of Betty Truelove, the lavender-girl, who was married to the Captain, when—being only a younger son of the younger branch of Hugomort—he had little more than his commission to justify his folly. But of that he never repented, claiming, even, a sort of supernatural sanction for the happiness that came to him with the love of his beautiful wife. And this is how the thing happened.

After his return, the Captain, as may be supposed, was too much occupied for a long time to think of discharging his commission to the dead drummer-boy's father. But he had by no means forgotten his promise; and so it chanced that he started at length to vindicate it within a few days of the anniversary of the battle of Malplaquet. He had already ascertained, from the regimental rolls, the address of the home he sought; and he now rode forth from London, with the drum in a bag at his saddle-bow, bound for the little village of Mitcham in Surrey where the Trueloves lived. He had dressed himself soberly, as befitted the sad occasion; but indeed it wanted more than the dark blue riding-coat, with its deep cuffs and skirts turned back with buff, than the little plain hat and heavy military jackboots which he wore, more, even, than his strong companionable face, to mislead the world as to his natural distinction. He looked the fine gentleman, and was not to be mistaken for a lesser because he was riding with a drum at his knee to fulfil a big man's vow to a trumpery little soldier-thing.

His way took him by fields, and long rolls of common haunted by Egyptians, and again by fields, to the pleasant village of Tooting, five miles south-west of the City; and thence a branch road to Reigate brought him at the end of a couple more miles to the place he sought.

It was a mellow and a glowing day, and Hugomort's soul felt one with the quiet sunshine. How, in the Low Countries, had not these characteristic English sights and sounds haunted him!—the deep pastures, the sweet-breathed cattle, the maidens with skins like apple-blossom and soft merry voices. He drank in the scene as if it were fresh warm milk; he expanded his huge chest, and took enjoying draughts of the air, which was as fragrant as if the very pillowy clouds had been stored in lavender. Lavender! The whole place smelt of it. He remembered now that Mitcham was the lavender-garden of England. Destiny could not have allured him to a sweeter spot.

At a reputable inn, The Old House at Home, standing about midway in the single long street, he dismounted, and, dismissing his horse to the ostler, entered, carrying his bag with the drum in it, to bespeak a meal and make an enquiry or so. He found the landlord properly communicative, and, over a good rib of beef, asked his simple question as to the habitat of the Truelove family. The answer sounded the first note of a complication. He looked up explanatory:

"I speak of the drummer-boy's father."

The landlord nodded his head. Every particular of village sayings and doings was docketed and pigeon-holed in that enormous knowledge-box. Even the way he held his hands clasped under his apron suggested his possession of secret evidences.

"Of Tony the drummer-boy's father," he repeated. "It was Tony, the naughty lad, that broke his daddy's heart a'running away to the wars."

Hugomort's eyes opened.

"Dead?"

"Strook dead," said the landlord. "He never rightly got over it."

The Captain paused in his eating, and sat back.

"Let us be clear on that point," he said. "The father Truelove is dead?"

"Six months gone," said the landlord.

"Tony the drummer-boy's father?"

"Tony the drummer-boy's father."

"He died of grief?"

"Of grief, sir. A wild boy was Tony, but dear to his daddy's heart. He run away and joined the red-coats. But, a month before they Marlborough wars begun, back he comes, with his fine laced frock and his drum, to say good-bye to his daddy and his sister Betty."

"Well?"

"His daddy was away, sir, over to the great sheep-fair at Dorking, and he never saw him. But that Tony filled out his furlough as befitted him. How he kep' us alive, to be sure—a young spark! I call to mind," said the landlord, looking out of the window, with a glassy contemplative eye, "his thrashing young Jakes, twice his size, to within an inch of his reason, for breaking in his drumhead with an ash stick. Lord, what a boy!"

The Captain had resumed his eating.

"He was killed at Malplaquet," he said. "And his father died of the news?"

"It finished him," said the landlord. "He'd been ailing sore, ever since he'd learnt how the boy had come and gone without his seeing him."

Hugomort cut another slice of beef.

"Well," he said; "is there anyone to represent the family at this day?"

The landlord gave a snort, sudden and alarming.

"Charles Truelove, the eldest," he said shortly.

The guest glanced up, surprised.

"Why do you speak of him in that tone?"

"A devil," said the landlord briefly.

Hugomort asked for information. He learned, to his interest, the following facts: that the father Truelove, early left a widower, had been a prosperous wool-stapler in the village, and that, of his three children, Charles, Betty and Tony, the eldest had turned out reprobate, a gambler and falsifier of books, while the youngest, a born adventurer, had slipped from the parental control to follow a recruiting sergeant. Now, it appeared that, the moment the wool-stapler was dead, his banished first-born had turned up from nowhere, dropping from the sky like a vulture, to claim his share of the spoil (which was considerable), and that, to the astonishment of everybody, a Will had been found, dated before Tony's birth, which, barring a trifling provision for the daughter, left everything, all the profits of which the testator might die possessed, to the black sheep. It was a stunning fact, but indisputable, and Charles, whom all had supposed disinherited by a later Will, was in possession of the property. Nor was that the worst.

"The daughter?" said Captain Hugomort.

"Was offered a provision by her brother," said the landlord indignantly, "on terms that would have disgraced a poplolly; but she preferred her independence with poverty, and none to blame her. She bides with a cook-maid, once her father's servant, in a cottage nigh to the common, and they eke out a hard living with selling of lavender brooms and sweet water to the travelling folk."

The Captain, a satisfied man, put down his knife and fork.

"I fancy she is the one for my money," he said.

"Anan?" quoth the landlord.

"Never mind," said Hugomort. "Bring me a pipe, and a glass of right Nantes."

He pondered over the story, lazily, while he smoked. It appeared to him that his commission, defeated in the male direction, could not be better discharged than in the feminine. Betty should have the drum.

He was in a curiously impressionable mood, full of fancies sweet and warm. Perhaps the good beef and brandy had something to do with it; but in addition, it seemed, the spirit of the lavender had got into his senses, and was throbbing there towards some emotional expression or demonstration. His brain was steeped, his heart muffled in lavender; some fragrant personification of the flower appeared to hover on the threshold of his soul, like a little butterfly Psyche with trembling wings. And then suddenly he looked up, and there outside the window stood the very substance of his vision.

There was a great waggon halted there—one of those tilted huge-tyred farm-carts, drawn by six horses, with bell-hung yokes to the hames of their collars, which catered for the humbler class of travellers—and, pleading softly hither and thither among the alighted passengers, was a young girl, with a basket on her arm and a little phial of sweet water in her hand. She was dressed even as in the picture, and her face was a garden of pinks and roses, a *parterre* which seemed to astonish into sudden violence a big semi-military ruffian, in enormous boots, and with a sword hanging from a greasy shoulder-strap, who had alighted with the rest.

"Curse me pretty," cried this fellow, "if I ever saw a kiss more sweetly invited!"

Hugomort did not hear the words; but he understood their import through the little panic scuffle that followed, and hurried out just as the bully had got his arm about the child's waist. He caught the fellow by the neck, as a dog catches a rat, and flung him to the ground.

The swaggerer, half-stunned for the moment, rose the next, with a howl of fury, and felt for his sword-hilt. But the Captain, forestalling him, wrenched away the blade, and, snapping it across his knee, took the ruffian fairly by his scruff and breeches, and lifting him high, rolled him into the waggon, and bade him, on pain of being broke, dare again to lift his hand to an officer and gentleman. Then, leaving the man quite cowed and whimpering, he strode back through the obsequious admiring throng, and, lifting his hat, with the grand air, to the subject of his protection, says he:

"You are upset, my child, and no wonder. Pray accept of Captain Hugomort's escort to your home."

And she looked up into his strong ugly face, with her wet eyes blinking, and hung her pretty head and went with him.

III

And that was how Captain Hugomort found his wife; but not all at once. At the sweet beginning of things he imposed himself as a lodger on the two women, Betty and cook-maid Hunston, with the professed view of showing them a new way to self-help. They lived in a little old cottage on the skirt of the common where the turn of the road took it, and spent all their working-time in expressing oil from *lavandula vera*, and distilling it, and treating it with spirits of wine until it sparkled into crystal perfume. Also they made brooms in season of the blossoming heads, and, a little later, sachets of the dried ones; and out of these, when all was done, they squeezed a margin of profit, sufficient, with Betty's small provision, to keep them going.

This was, in fact, an idyll of lavender, having, for its central figure, it seemed, the very Chloris of sweet flowers. So she appeared to Hugomort, all fragrant, all soft, all endearing. He lived in an atmosphere of lavender and loving witchery. But she meant no arts, and was in truth at his mercy. It was a perilous time for her. This god who had come to her in her need!—she might have resisted his noble condescension; it was his Herculean strength that took her, and at once, by storm. She never thought for a moment of questioning his assumption of a right to protect her. Fortunately for her romance's happy consummation, nobility, drugged and drowned as it was in sweet sensuousness, kept its instinct for cleanness. Maybe, also, superstition helped to support it through a temptation or so.

Well, the Captain, as I say, took a lodging with the two women, and from that moment some curious things began to happen. He did not on the first day mention anything as to the object of his visit; but he hung the drum in its bag from a nail on the wall of the tiny room allotted him, and slept that night in lavender-scented sheets, and dreamed of lavender eyes, and of lavender-shadowed arms coming about him. And in the morning he woke up, and saw the drum on a chair at his bed-foot.

He was surprised, of course. He was as sure as sure could be that the thing had been ensconced in its bag when he went to bed. Someone must have entered his room unheard during the night, and removed it. But, why? It seemed a senseless act. He dismissed, however, for the moment the subject from his mind, and got up and dressed. His tiny quarters delighted him, seen in the fresh morning.

They looked over a little garden, lush with dewy flowers; and thence flowed the common in grassy billows. And even sweeter and more lovely than remembered dreams appeared his nymph, velvety from slumber. His soul began to throb to her with a sensation it had never yet experienced.

That day he entered himself into the confidence of both these girls—there was something in him that invited women's trust—and presently he went out and returned with the drum.

"What is there about this to invite curiosity?" he said, holding it forth with a smile.

They shook their heads guilelessly.

"Has either of you seen it before?"

They looked one at the other enquiringly, and answered, "No," with obvious bewilderment. He was convinced, but puzzled. And then his eyes softened, and his voice, as he approached Betty Truelove.

"Nay, little mistress," he said; "but your heart must rally itself to the pain it is my hard fate to inflict. You have seen it, indeed, for it was your brother's."

She did not move; but her face flushed, and her throat swelled. Perhaps she had already half anticipated the truth. "Little Tony," she whispered, and that was all.

In gentle vein, then, he told them of the battle, of its fortunes and its heroisms, among which he counted very kindly the little drummer-boy's uncomplaining death. "He thought only of his daddy," he said, "and of his sorrowful pride in receiving this last token of his boy's patriotism and affection. Alas! it was not destined that I should vindicate my promise to the letter; but to thee, my child, as to love's trustee, do I make over its reversion. Take the drum, and cherish it."

She received the soldierly toy from his hands, like one half blind; and, as she so held it, he left her.

Later in the day, confident in his own true sympathy, he ventured to touch upon the subject again, and she opened her heart to him, like a flower to the sun.

"He was ever his father's love," she said. "He could dare with him as might none else. It was a bitter thing they might not meet when he came to say good-bye—bitterest for the elder. The child, like children, was thoughtless, and gloried, as well he might, in his importance. He was always a righting nature, and resourceful as he was bold. Well I remember how, the day before he left, he had his drum broke in some quarrel; but he found means to restore it, the wild clever child. He was a little thing to be killed."

Hugomort dared to enclose the young scented hand in his. She shook slightly, but submitted.

"I marvel," he said, like one pondering. "I marvel."

"At what?" she whispered.

"How one," he said, "so infatuated as your father, could so have sinned against the darling of his heart?"

She understood him, and hung her head.

"O! not sinned," she pleaded. "He must have meant the best. Who could have foreseen the cruel stroke that bereft us in an hour?"

"Himself," he answered sternly, and looked at her. "Tell me; did you never hear talk of a later Will?"

She shook her head; and he passed to other subjects.

That night he went to bed in love. His passion was like a fever, and kept him awake and tossing. He knew that he had discharged his task, and that no reason remained to him to stop. Yet the very thought of going was a torture. She slept, he knew, in the little room against his. O, that the frail wall would mist away and reveal her to his arms! Yet he cherished her sweet innocence too well to wish it his at any price but the lawful. And what had he to offer her there? Just his own ugly self and his commission, supplemented by a sorry small allowance. But he must have her somehow—he must, or die.

He hardly slept all night; not a thing stirred in the little quiet house; and when the morning stole into his hot eyes, there was the drum standing on the chair at his bed-foot.

He uttered an ejaculation; he leapt to the floor and stood staring. Then he went and touched the thing gingerly. Tony's drum—not a doubt about it.

Presently, while he was dressing as in a dream, he heard voices in the garden, mingled of angry and pleading. He looked from the window, and saw his soft goddess bending before the wrath of a lowering, dissipated-looking young man, who reviled and threatened her. His heart flamed; but, guessing the truth, he forbore for the moment to interfere. But by and by, making an opportunity, he questioned cook-maid Hunston as to the brother. He learned enough to fire his soul with indignation—too much and too offending to be set down here in detail. But, briefly, it seemed, the provision originally offered by young Truelove to his sister had been made conditional on her becoming the price of silence to a brother-blackleg, who knew enough of Master Charles's past to make his tenure of the present particularly insecure. So it was rumoured, and so believed; and now, it appeared, the persecution was acquiring a fresh virulence through the entry of the Captain himself upon the scene, and the girl had been taunted and insulted on the score of her supposed protector. Indeed, Mrs. Hunston, with weeping eyes, begged him to spare her mistress by going.

"I shall do nothing of the sort," he said. "I am going to marry your mistress myself."

"Dear heart alive!" cried the girl, and sat down plump upon a chair.

He saw Betty, who had been avoiding him hitherto, in the garden, and ran out to her. She was making a show of unconcern; but her lids were swollen with weeping. Yet his first thought was a diversion.

"What of the drum?" he said.

She glanced up at him, astonished, and so away.

"Was it you brought it to my room last night?" he demanded.

She stared at him again, going as pale as a lily, then suddenly began to run. He followed and caught her.

"It was there this morning," he said.

"I never put it."

"Didn't you?"

"O! how could you believe it of me?"

"It must have been your friend, then?"

"She slept with me. She never moved. I know."

"What! were you awake too?"

"Let me go. I cannot keep from crying."

He lifted her in his arms, making nothing and everything of her in a breath, and carried her into the cottage parlour. And there he sat down with her, holding her close.

"Child, isn't this sudden—this love of yours and mine?"

She wept, and whispered without coquetry: "You give me no chance."

"You shall be taken away from here, Betty, from the struggle and the shame."

"Alack!" she said; "the shame will go with me."

"You think it shame, then, to be my wife?" She stopped her breath, listening, all at once. "That was settled," he said, "the moment I saw you in the street. You threw lavender in my eyes, child. It is all a pastoral of lavender, and I have gone into the sweetest garden in all the world for my flower-wife.

"We have forgotten the drum," he said presently. "It is a strange thing."

She looked up at him, trembling.

"You are sure you did not come and fetch it yourself?"

"Betty, Mistress!"

"In your sleep, I mean?"

"Even in my sleep if I had come I could not have gone. Make it sure to-night, at least."

"If I could be sure it was not you."

"I have said what I have said. Put it in its bag and sleep safe."

IV

Into the warm ecstasy of Hugomort's dreams crept a strange sound, the far-distant roll of a drum. It seemed to come from a vast remoteness, to swell gradually into a low thunder, and so to fade out and cease. Now, sleeping as he was, it came to him suddenly that this very night was the anniversary of that on which, a year before, he had climbed the hill of Malplaquet to find a little dying drummer-boy stretched among the trees. And the scene rose so vividly before him that in a moment he was there again, toiling up and up, making for the plateau. And even as he reached it, he saw that its heath, far and near, was all sown with blossoms of fire, thick and melancholy as corpse-candles. But not a solitary form of all the wounded and dying remained on the plateau. The place was one vast sepulchral emptiness; the souls of the fallen were fled; only the sound of the flames, flapping and reverberating, broke the desolate silences. But, little by little as he gazed, another sound crept into his brain, at first hardly to be distinguished from the fluttering of the fires—a throb, a mere pulse beating in the deep heart of stillness. It waxed and grew; its hurried tremor was resolved into a definite crepitation; it swelled out of the black distances nearer and louder—the roll of a drum. For the second time! Whence and with what purpose was it making towards him? The fires had died down. Standing in that blind oblivion, a fear, such as he had never yet felt, stole into his heart. The drum came on. Its voice by now was overmastering, hollow and resonant as if sounded in an empty room.

A room! With a shock he leapt to instant realisation of the truth. It was a room. He was lying in the cottage all the time, and the sound was in the house—in the adjoining chamber—outside his door, furious, triumphant, deafening! God in heaven! How could they be sleeping through that appalling racket? It seemed to shake the building; it increased in volume; yet he lay as if spellbound, unable to move limb or lid. It came on—it was upon him—with a final thundering crash it passed into his room—and at once ceased in a flurry of soaring vibrations.

In that instant light seemed to flash into the sleeper's eyes, and, with a cry, he broke the spell that held him, and leapt into consciousness. Bright dawn was stealing through the window, and there on the chair stood the drum.

Wild-eyed, his skin still wet with the terror of his dream, Hugomort leapt from his bed, and approached the thing. Its batter-head appeared as if still palpitating from the blows rained upon it—it seemed to heave and writhe with pain. Merciful Christ! was something imprisoned within? In an access of horror, touched with fury, the waker seized his sword, and, severing the straps and cords, wrenched off at a blow the upper hoop, and let it drop to the floor. The drum was empty; but on the under side of the head revealed ran lines of legal script, footed by a signature. Hugomort dropped on his knees to read. A Will!

A Will, drawn, signed and attested in London, revoking all former Wills and codicils, and leaving everything of which the testator might die possessed, conjointly, and with sole reversion to the survivor should either child die unwedded, to Elizabeth and Anthony Truelove, the testator's beloved only daughter and his youngest son.

And so Tony the marplot made restitution. Fishing among his father's papers, he had found and appropriated the opportune parchment, to replace that burst by Master Jakes. He knew quite well what he had done; hence his dying concern to have the document returned.

The sequel is to be found in the Hugomort Memoirs. Mrs. Roger, it is related, made a handsomer provision for her scoundrel brother than he had ever designed for her; but luckily he did not live long to enjoy it. As to the drum, I have told the story as the Captain authenticated it; but the supernatural business was, of course, discredited by his relations, who attributed the discovery of the Will simply and solely to their kinsman's native shrewdness. In the marriage which followed, he was considered, as inevitably, to have disgraced himself; but he outlived all that, and quadrupled the small fortune his wife brought him, and made otherwise a big name for himself. But, from first to last, he never, to his renown, addressed his wife on paper but as his sweetest fondest lavender-girl. He had her painted by Sir Godfrey in the dress she had worn outside The Old House at Home, and to this day a bunch of lavender figures in the family crest.

A DANSE-MACABRE
(1915)

Carleon and I had been talking fitfully, as the train sped on, of things suggested, perhaps, by that sense of volant instability with which a rapid journey in a third-class brake-van is calculated to possess one—the mysteries of Life and Death, and the greater mystery of Life-in-Death, to wit. I had lately been reading Myers's "Human Personality," and my mind was full of Individualism, and Hypnotic Suggcstion, and thosc fathomlcss strata of sub-consciousness which he under a man as the forty mattresses lay under the True Princess, without obliterating the sensation of the single pea which, placed at the bottom, made its irritation felt through all. Whence, perhaps, that state of mental excitation which was responsible for the illusion that followed.

Silence had fallen between us when, about sunset time, the train entered into a long, deep-sunk valley. I looked up, and saw the ridges all crested with a running fire of rays, as in some titanic battle, the drifted smoke from which hung in the hollows like blue water. Carleon swept his hand through the sunbeam which came in at the window, thereby setting its motes gyrating as if they boiled.

"The fourth dimension," he said, smiling— "imagination. We live upon it all the time, and never know, except when some chance ray like this reveals it to us."

I nodded indulgently, but did not answer. Something in the twilight peace of the valley was beginning to hypnotise me. The slope of it on which I looked went up in a luminous haze, through which the purple swell of trees, the dim gold of quarries, the milky greenness of the grass showed all distinct, but subdued to a phantasmal loveliness. Somehow there stole into my spirit a strange sense, born of that dreamy mental detachment, of its all being antiquely familiar to me—not in the local meaning alone. I might or might not have travelled that way before; the impression borrowed from infinitely remoter distances. Absorbed by it, absorbed into it, I passed beyond my surroundings—forgot myself; forgot Carleon. I was roused by feeling the quick touch of his hand on my knee.

"Look!" he said.

He was gazing fixedly from his window; I followed the direction of his eyes. We were running at the moment past a scattered line of trees—slender birches inter-thronged with darker thorns—which stood on the hillside; and wreathing itself around and about the congregated trunks in a glimmering fantastic dance was a number of pallid forms.

Mystic, infinitely graceful, but at first indeterminate, they took shape to my enthralled imagination as I stared—and were spirit girls, beckoning, alluring, with white arms raised, and white robes, shot with faint iridescences, clinging and floating.

I struggled to dismiss the illusion, or to seek its correlation in Carleon's eyes; but my own would not forego their fascination for an instant.

And still, as we passed, the white shapes wove their paces—in and out, in and out—in silent loveliness. I began, I thought, to distinguish, like roses seen through mist, the unearthly sweetness of their faces—a gleam of smiling teeth, a least flush of pink, the phantom blue of eyes that laughed and faded. But as they came they went, witcheries proffered only to be withdrawn. I seemed to hear old music sounding in my brain; somehow I was approaching a bourne of hills and grooves long foundered in the deeps of memory; there was wonder in my heart and a great ecstasy of expectation—the train ran beyond the trees, and in an instant the dancers were gone.

Ceased; snatched out of being in a moment. I sat as if stunned; and then, as before, Carleon's voice awakened me:—

"Look there!"

I flung myself beside him, and stared back the way we had come.

A little darkling church stood on the hillside, and all between it and the lower belt of trees was a crowded graveyard. The stones stood up or leaned awry in every arrested pose—erect and sharp white, or tumbled and moss-grown—hundreds of them, and each stiffened to "attention," after that Danse-Macabre, at the ghostly word of command. It was the tree trunks and those innumerable memento-moris which had woven between them as we sped past that fantastic optical illusion.

At least, so we were bound to suppose.

Or one may suppose, if one prefers it, that Imagination is the parent of being, and the true begetter of all visualised Manifestation.

A QUEER CICERONE
(1915)

I had paid my sixpence at the little informal "box-office," and received in exchange my printed permit to visit the Castle. It was one of those lordly "show-places" whose owners take a plain business view of the attractions at their disposal, while ostensibly exploiting them on behalf of this or that charity. How the exclusive spirits of eld, represented on their walls in the numerous pictured forms they once inhabited, regard this converting of their pride and panoply to practical ends, is a matter for their descendants to judge; but no doubt the most of them owed, and still owe, a debt to humanity, any liquidation of which in terms of charity would be enough to reconcile them to the indignity of being regarded like a waxworks. For my part, I am free to confess that, did I see any profit in an ancestor, I should apply it unequivocally to the charity that begins at home.

I discovered, when I entered, quite a little party waiting to be personally conducted round the rooms. Obviously trippers of the most commonplace type (and what was I better?), they stood herded together in a sort of gelid ante-chamber, pending the arrival of the housekeeper who was to act as cicerone. A hovering menial, in the nature of a commissionaire, had just disappeared in quest of the errant lady, and for the moment we were left unshepherded.

Assuming the nonchalant air of a chance visitor of distinction to whom palaces were familiar, I casually, while sauntering aloof from it, took the measure of my company. It was not in the least unusual or interesting. It comprised a couple of rather sickly 'gents' of the haberdashery type; two flat ladies in pince-nez, patently in search of culture and instruction; a huge German tourist, all bush and spectacles, with a mighty sandwich-box slung over his shoulder, and a voice of guttural ferocity; an ample but diffident matron, accompanied by a small youth in clumping boots and a new ready-made Norfolk suit a size too large for him, and, finally, a pair of tittering hobble-skirted young ladies, of the class that parades pavements arm-in-arm. All whispered in their separate groups, each suspicious of the other, but with voices universally hushed to the sacred solemnity of the occasion. Only the German showed a disposition to truculent neighbourliness, proffering some advances to the hobble-skirted damsels, which were first haughtily, and then gigglingly, ignored. Whereat the flat ladies, though intellectually addicted to his race, showed their sense of his unflattering preference by turning their backs on him.

The room in which we were delayed was the first of a suite, and very chill and melancholy in its few appointments. There were some arms, I remember, on the walls, and a sprinkling of antlers—of all mural decorations the most petrifyingly depressing. They offered no scope to my assumption of critical ease, and—conscious of an inquisition, a little derisive, I thought, in its quality, on the part of the company—I was gravitating towards the general group, when we were all galvanised into animation by hearing the sound of a light, quick footfall approaching us from the direction of the room we were about to traverse. It tripped on, awaking innumerable small echoes in its advance, and suddenly materialised before us in the form of a very elegant gentleman, of young middle-age and distinguished appearance.

"Permit me," he said, halting, hand on heart, with an inimitable bow. "I make it my pleasure to represent for the nonce the admirable but unctuous Mrs. Somerset, our valued housekeeper, who is unfortunately indisposed for the moment."

I could flatter myself at least that my manner had so far impressed the party as to cause it to constitute me by mute agreement its spokesman. I accepted, as they all looked towards me, the compliment for what it implied, though with a certain stiffness which was due as much to surprise as to embarrassment. For surely courtesy, in the person of this distinguished stranger, was taking a course as unusual as the clothes he inhabited were strange. They consisted of a dark blue, swallow-tailed coat, with a high velvet collar and brass buttons, a voluminous stock, a buff waistcoat, and mouse-coloured tights, having a bunch of seals pendent from their fob and ending in smart pumps. His hair, ample and dusty golden, was brushed high from his forehead in a sort of ordered mane; the face underneath was an ironically handsome one, but so startlingly pale that the blue eyes fixed in it suggested nothing so much as the "antique jewels set in Parian marble stone" of a once famous poem. He bowed again, and to me, accepting the general verdict.

"It is most good of you," I said. "Of course, if we had known, if we had had any idea—"

He interrupted me, I thought, with a little impatience:—

"Not at all. It is, as I informed you, a pleasure—a rare opportunity. I fancy I may promise you a fuller approximation to the truth, regarding certain of our family traditions, than you would ever be likely to attain through the lips of the meritorious but diplomatic Somerset."

He turned, inviting us, with an incomparable gesture, into the next room. He was certainly an anachronism, a marvel; yet I was willing to admit to myself that eccentrics, sartorial and otherwise, were not confined to the inner circle of society. As to the others, I perceived that they were self-defensively prepared to accept this oddity as part of the mysterious ritual appertaining to the sacred obscurities of the life patrician.

"The first two rooms," said our guide, halting us on the threshold, "are, as you will perceive, appropriated to family portraits. The little furniture that remains is inconsiderable and baroque. It is what survives from the time of the fourth marquis. We observe his portrait here" (he signified a canvas on the wall, representing a dull, arrogant-looking old gentleman in an embroidered coat and a bobwig), "and can readily associate with it the tasteless ostentation which characterised his reign. He was really what we should call now a complete aristocratic bounder."

His tone suggested a mixture of flippancy and malice, which was none the less emphatic because his voice was a peculiarly soft and secret one. Somehow, hearing it, I thought of slanders sniggered from behind a covering hand. The young ladies tittered, as if a little shamefaced and uneasy, drawing his attention to them. He was obviously attracted at once. Their smart modernity, piquant in its way, proved a charm to him that he made no pretence of discounting. He addressed himself instantly to the two:—

"Sacred truth, ladies, upon my honour. He was a 'throw-back,' as we say of dogs. The mark of the prosperous cheesemonger was all over him."

"Ach!" said the German, vibratingly asserting himself, "a dror-back? Vot is dart?"

"A Teutonic reaction," said the stranger, taking the speaker's measure insolently, with his chin a little lifted, and his eyes narrowed; "or rather a recrudescence of barbarism in a race or line that has emerged from it. Your countrymen, from what I hear, should afford many illustrations of the process."

The flat ladies exchanged a little scornful laugh, which they repeated less disguisedly as the German responded: "I do not ondorrstand."

The common little boy, holding to his mother's skirts, urged her on to the next picture, a full-length portrait of a grim Elizabethan warrior in armour.

"Look at his long sword, mothre!" he whispered.

"He didn't wear corsets—not much," said one of the haberdashery youths facetiously, in an audible voice to the other; and the nearest spinster, with a sidelong stare of indignation at him, edged away.

"A crusader?" said the second flat lady, as if putting it to herself. "I wonder, now."

The stranger smiled ironically to the hobble-skirts, one of whom was emboldened to ask him: "Was he one of the family, sir?"

"By Heraldry out of Wardour Street," answered our guide. "Very dark horses, both of them." And then he added, going a few steps: "You do us too much honour, sweet charmer—positively you do." He tapped the portrait of a ponderous patrician: "The first marquis," he said, "created in 1784 out of nothing. The King represented the Almighty in that stupendous achievement. God save the King!"

"Let's go, mothre," whispered the small common boy, pressing suddenly against the ample skirts. "I don't like it."

"Hush, 'Enery dear," she returned, in a whispered panic. "There ain't nothing to be afraid of."

"Wasn't there none of you before that, sir?" asked the second haberdashery youth.

The stranger sniggered.

"I'll let you all into a little secret," he said confidentially. "The antiquity of the family, despite our ingenious Mrs. Somerset, is mere hocus-pocus. The first marquis's grandfather was a Huntingdonshire dairy-farmer, who amassed a considerable fortune over cheeses. He came to London, speculated in South Sea stock, and sold out at top prices just before the crash. We don't like it talked about, you know; but it was his grandson who was the real founder of the house. He was in the Newcastle administration of '57, and was ennobled for the owlish part he took in opposing the reconquest of India under Clive. And, after that, the more fat-headed he became, the higher they foisted him to get him out of the way. Fact, I assure you. Our crest should be by rights a Stilton rampant, our arms a cheese-scoop, silver on a trencher powdered mites, and our motto, in your own admirable vernacular, 'Ain't I the cheese!'"

The young ladies tittered, sharing a little protesting wriggle between them. Then one urged the other, who responded sotto voce: "Ask him yourself, stupid."

"Charmed," said the stranger. "Those roguish lips have only to command."

"We only wanted to know," said number two blushfully, "which is the wicked lord—don't push so, Dolly!"

"Ah!" The stranger showed his teeth in a stiffly-creased smile, and shook a long forefinger remonstrantly at the speaker. "You have been studying that outrageous guide-book, I perceive. What is the passage—eh? 'Reputed to have been painted by a mysterious travelling artist of sinister appearance, who, being invited in one night to play with his lordship, subsequently liquidated the debt he incurred by painting his host's portrait.'"

He turned on his heel and pointed into the next room. Full in our view opposite the door appeared a glazed frame, but black and empty in seeming—an effect I supposed to be due to the refraction of light upon its surface.

"A most calumniated individual," he protested, wheeling round again. "There is his place; we shall come to it presently; but only, I regret, to find it vacant. A matter of restoration, you see, and much to be deplored at the moment. I should have liked to challenge your verdict, face to face with him. These libels die hard—and when given the authority of a guide-book! Take my word for it, he was a most estimable creature, morally worth dozens of the sanctimonious humbugs glorified in the Somerset hagiology. Pah! I am weary, I tell you, of hearing their false virtues extolled. But wait a minute, and you shall learn. The 'wicked lord,' young misses? And so he is the flattered siderite of your regard. Well, it is well to be sought by such eyes on any count; but I think his would win your leniency. Only excess of love proved his undoing; and I am sure you would not consider that a crime."

We were all struck a little dumb, I think, by this outburst. The two girls had linked together again, both silent and somewhat white; the gaunt spinsters, rigid and upright, exchanged petrified glances; the fat woman was mopping her face, a tremulous sigh fluttering the hem of her handkerchief; the two young shopmen dwelt slack-jawed; even the German tourist, glaring through his spectacles, shook a little in his breathing, as if a sudden asthma had caught him. But our host, as though unconscious of the effect he had produced, motioned us on smilingly; and so, mechanically obeying, we paused at the next canvas—the uncompleted full-length of a beautiful young woman with haunting eyes.

"The Lady Betty," he said, "as she sat for 'Innocence' to Schleimhitz. The portrait was only finished, as you see, as far as the waist. He was a slow worker, and not good at drapery."

The German cleared his throat, and pushing his way past the flat ladies (I thought for the moment one was near furiously hooking at him with her umbrella), glanced with an air of amorous appropriation at the hobble-skirts, and spoke:—

"Schleimhitz wass fery goot at drapery. There wass a reason berhaps—"

"Ah—tut—tut!" exclaimed the stranger, with a little hurried smile; and led us on.

"Portrait," he said, "by Gainsborough, of a boy—unidentified. There was a story of his having been mislaid by his father, the second marquis, on the occasion of that gentleman's first marriage, and never discovered again."

"Poor little chap," murmured one of the hobble-skirts. "I wonder what became of him? Isn't he pretty?"

"An ancestress," said our cicerone, at the next canvas, "who married an actor. He played first gentleman on the stage, and first cad off it. I believe he broke her heart—or her spirit; I forget which. She kept them both in one decanter." He sniggered round at the two girls. "No, 'pon honour," he said, "I vow to the truth of it. You must trust me above Mrs. Somerset."

"A collateral branch this," he said, passing on. "He buried three wives, who lie and whisper together in the family vault. He himself was buried, by his own direction, at sea. They say the coffin hissed as it touched the water."

The little common boy suddenly began to cry loudly.

"I'm frightened, mothre!" he wailed. "Take me away."

The stranger, bending to look for him, made as if to claw through the group. I saw a most diabolical expression on his face.

"Ah!" he said, "I'll have you yet!"

The child screamed violently, and beat in frantic terror against his mother. I interposed, an odd damp on my forehead.

"Look here," I said; "leave the boy alone, will you?"

They were all backing, startled and scared, when there came a hurried, loud step into the room from behind us, and we turned in a panic huddle. It was the commissionaire, very flustered and irate.

"Now, then, you know," he said, "you'd no right to take it upon yourselves to go round like this unattended."

"Pardon me," I said, resuming my charge of spokesman; "we did nothing of the sort. This gentleman offered himself to escort us."

I turned, as did all the others, and my voice died in my throat. There was no gentleman at all—the room was empty. As I stood stupidly staring, I was conscious of the voice of the commissionaire, aggrieved, expostulatory, but with a curious note of distress in it:

"What gentleman? There's nobody has the right but Mrs. Somerset, and she's ill—she's had a stroke. We've just found her in her room, with a face like the horrors on her."

Suddenly one of the women shrieked hysterically:

"O look! He's there! O come away!"

And, as she screamed, I saw. The empty picture frame in the next room was empty no longer. It was filled by the form of him, handsome and smiling, who had just been conducting us round the walls.

SUB SPECIE
(1915)

Courage is a perverse quality. I think there are no men actually fearless, and there is none actually a coward; but always the coward in one respect has it in him to be the hero in another, and vice versa. There was an individual once who, when volunteer assistance was called for to man a lifeboat in a great emergency, came forward and took an oar, and acquitted himself heroically in the face of imminent death. That person, some time afterwards, betrayed the most abject cowardice in the matter of having a tooth drawn. The incident was related to me at first hand, and I thought of it on the occasion when I was present at Carleon's hypnotising of Thewlis.

Thewlis was an extreme example of the neurotic—physically no craven, while a prey to infinite qualms in the abstract—yet he unhesitatingly dared an ordeal which nothing would have induced me to undergo. For its purpose was no less than to unearth, by way of the successive strata of sub-consciousness, the root origin of his malady. He had an idea himself that the process would prove terrifying; he faced the test unflinching, nevertheless.

The experiment was conducted at night in Carleon's sitting-room—a shabby, ill-furnished apartment, but so acoustically arranged, like a torture-chamber, as to consume all sound within itself. The light from a single shaded lamp fell quietly upon Thewlis's closed lids and upturned face, whose repose—for it appeared quite restful in that initiatory trance—gave its meanness an aspect of dignity which it was far from possessing normally. Carleon, with his lank, exhausted look and belying seer's vision, stood above, debating, as it were, like a skilled operator, where first to get his knife in. And at last he spoke:

"Do you know me, Thewlis?"

"Yes, you are Carleon." The voice was strangely still and toneless; but it was Thewlis's voice without any question.

"Speak to him, will you?" said Carleon, turning to me.

Much against the grain I complied with: "Hullo, Thewlis! know me too?"

Not a response of any sort; not a flicker of acknowledgment on the white, impassive face. It was clear I did not exist for him. Carleon bent towards the motionless figure.

"Who is that sitting near you to your left?"

"I don't know."

"It is Hendon."

"Yes, it is Hendon."

Carleon motioned to me to rise and walk apart, a direction which I obeyed rebelliously.

"Go and shake hands with Hendon sitting in that chair, and then return to your seat," said Carleon to the figure.

Thewlis rose, made a step to the chair I had vacated, went through the process of shaking hands with its imaginary occupant (I observed that his fingers actually remained unclosed in the act, as though they grasped something tangible between them), and reseated himself. Carleon, with a gesture, bade me approach.

"Now speak to him again," he said to me.

"Hope I didn't hurt you, Thewlis," I said. "You know I always forget your flabby paw."

Silence again; no consciousness whatever, it appeared, of my voice or presence.

"We are *en rapport*," said Carleon, addressing me. "I only desired to convince you. He sees nothing, feels nothing, but through this medium." He tapped his own forehead; then took Thewlis's right arm, and held it out horizontally. "You cannot lower that," he said.

"No," answered Thewlis.

"Bear on it," said Carleon to me, "and see if you can force him."

I responded reluctantly. The arm remained stiff, but a slight spasm of pain seemed to twitch the features of the sleeper.

"Curse it!" I muttered: "that was beastly."

"No, no," said Carleon. "Don't take it in that spirit." He made a pass or two above the face of the seated figure. "Now," he said.

I bore on the arm again; the only effect was to lever the figure slightly forward. I quitted my hold, and it returned to its former position. But there was no least suggestion this time of wincing.

"I have deepened the trance," said Carleon. "He has sunk below the region of physical sensation."

It was odd that he might talk to me freely about Thewlis without eliciting any more comment from him than my own words could evoke. He had to switch on, as it were, the connection between them to make a full circuit of the hypnotic current.

"Lower your arm," said Carleon; and the arm dropped and subsided.

Carleon dwelt a moment, considering, his long fingers grating at his chin.

"Thewlis," he said, "do you hear me?"

"Yes, I hear."

Something indescribably different in the tone struck me. It was thicker—adenoidy, if I might so express it.

"Are you happy, Thewlis?"

"No. I am very unhappy."

"Try to explain to me why."

"I am leading the double life—a ghastly, whited sepulchre; a mask of hypocrisy veiling filth and corruption."

I made a violent gesture of protest.

"Hush!" said Carleon, his eyes alight. "Don't be a fool, Hendon; don't mistake me. He is down in a former existence—the one immediately precedent. Didn't you hear his voice?"

His hands were busy once more. I half started to my feet.

"I have had enough of this," I said. "Set the man free."

"No," said Carleon, "no. That spent fire explains much, but not all. It is not quite the demon we seek. We must go yet a stage lower."

Thewlis looked like death; but it was useless for me to protest. The operator knew what he was about.

"Thewlis," he said suddenly; "you are to answer me."

He was answered—and in such manner as to make me leap and the hair prickle on my scalp. A torrent of blasphemy and derision, uttered in a shrill woman's voice, broke from the unsealed lips. I cannot repeat it; I cannot explain the inevitable moral of ruin and degradation which it conveyed. It all ended as abruptly as it had begun.

I looked aghast at Carleon; he looked at me. We were both silent. Then suddenly he cried out, "Good God, Hendon! Two generations back Thewlis was a woman—and that explains it all!"

THE ACCIDENT
(1915)

I had never been in the town before, he said, and I have no desire to visit it again. It is the sort of place that exists to be forgotten by the casual stranger as soon as possible—modern, tawdry, commercial, having the stamp of municipal vulgarity all over it. Its very ghosts are mechanic, as I had the best reason for discovering—poisonous, petrol-animated things, that leave an exhaust of oil fuel in their wake in lieu of the good old-fashioned brimstone.

I came into this undesirable town at sunset, after a long day's tramp. The outskirts of any properly-constituted borough are commonly but the uncommendable prelude to warmths and hospitalities mellowing as one advances: this seemed all outskirts. To a dreary monotony of grey brick, flaring pothouses, pinchbeck emporiums, exhibiting, in dingily-lighted sections, parks of cheap perambulators, rolls of linoleum and suites of colourable furniture tart with French polish, succeeded more grey brick only more pretentious, flaunting gin-palaces, co-operative stores like barracks, and that was all—not a crevice with so much as a scrap of antique moss in it; not a curio shop in all the place.

Somewhere about the depressing midmost of this town I struck a casual trail for bed and dinner. There was an hotel, so-called, which suggested an ostentatious mean between champagne and swipes, and made no appeal either to my taste or my pocket: my destiny gravitated towards a quieter and more melancholy hostelry whose name caught my eye at a point where the High street took a sudden half-turn to the left, as if it shied from the very neighbourhood of a thing so dull and joyless.

It was a dismal inn, there was no denying; its very name, "The Ark," suggested desolation, a lonely stranding in the back-waters of life, its use past, its custom staled. And yet it was obviously new, raw, a destined failure from its inception. It stood spiritlessly aloof from the main stream of traffic, blinking dim eyes at the throng that would not be diverted its way—a common thing, but even tragic in its excommunication. I entered through its dingy portals without fervour.

The coffee-room was of a piece with the rest, long, gaunt and empty, its cruets tarnished, its table-cloths, for all I knew, "filthy dowlas," its knives and forks black-handled, the smoky, featureless wall paper blistered at the seams and peeling from the corners. And the single waiter appeared the right sexton for this mortuary—an old-young, unearthly-eyed creature of the resuscitated corpse type, wax-faced and blue-chinned, apparelled in the mouldy livery of festivity, as if he had been erroneously buried after some debauch of second-hand hope, and dug up at the last moment prematurely aged and earth-stained. His very presence imparted a funeral flavour to the baked meats—or to the meat, for there was but one, a cold, a deathly cold, sirloin of beef.

The room was as quiet as a church at midnight. In all its hollow emptiness, the shuffle of the waiter's pulpy shoes, the soft intimate crunch of my own jaws, were the only sounds to disturb the small dust of its silence. I ate as noiselessly as possible, yet my teeth seemed to snap like castanets. I grew nervous, oppressed; I longed for some other sound, some cheery entry to break the intolerable stillness of things; it was like the proverbial hush before the storm. And then quite suddenly I had my wish.

The waiter was away at the sideboard, cutting me a second helping; I was aware of a quick stop in his operations, of an odd little cough, of his gaping furtively round at me, the carving knife and fork poised in his hands. And then my ears were pricking.

It was very small and remote at first, a mere pattering throb, beating as if from a vast distance, hardly to be associated with any definite cause. But rapidly, as I listened, it grew, as it were, into focus, and was the detonating pulse of a motorcycle, flurried, mad, recording a speed which in that time and place appeared nothing less than insane. The thing, at the pace it was advancing, must be past the windows in a moment; involuntarily I held my breath, awaiting the approach, the crashing diapason, the closing swell and the subsequent receding into silence. It was near—within fifty yards: at the bend of the road it must swerve to the left, giving "The Ark" a wide berth—I jumped to my feet, with a gasp, upsetting my chair behind me. It had not taken the bend; it was coming straight on, through the wall, into the room, right upon me, a rushing indefinite shadow. There was a crash, one thin, agonised scream, a slam of light like the flap of a great ghostly wing—

"Beef, sir," said the waiter.

He was standing there with the plate, waiting placidly for me to resume my seat.

"God Almighty!" I muttered, looking stupidly down. Was I mad, over-tired, delirious? He had put the chair softly on its feet again, and mechanically I dropped into it. I had taken up my knife and fork, when I heard his whisper at my ear: "It's all right, sir. Some will hear it, and some won't."

I clapped down the implements again and leaned back. "Hear it!"—my voice was thick and trembling. "It wasn't my fancy, then? What was it, in God's name?"

"He ran away with her," he said, "just stopped at the garden gate, and she jumped behind him pillion, and off they went harum-scarum. Polly Truelove was her name—a handsome bit of flesh, I've been told; but the parents wouldn't permit it; and so they eloped together like that. It was neck or nothing; but the odds were against them; the street was too narrer, and what with dodging—they had a slip at the lamp-post, and crashed right into it." He backed a step or two, and stamped with his foot on the floor. "Here it stood," he said, "as near as you might guess. They were both killed on the spot—smashed to a pudden; and burnt, too."

"Here!" I exclaimed.

"Ah!" said the waiter; "you see in them days the High Street run straight through where this house stands now. They deflected it when they built the new Municipal Offices. Here on this very spot stood the lamp-post. It's always on a Friday it comes; and some will hear it and some won't. Sleeping in the house, sir?"

"No," I said. "I'm not sure I'm sleeping anywhere to-night."

THE APOTHECARY'S REVENGE (1915)

Prominent, under the shadow of the projecting gable the little gilded bason and lancet above the door reflected back the light from a single dismal lantern, burning a cotton wick, which hung from a bracket over the archway opposite. It was nearing sundown, and the few pedestrians abroad walked hurriedly and stealthily, keeping in the middle of the street as if they feared some lurking ambush. One of these, a tall, muffled figure of a man, with a drawn, agitated countenance, wheeled suddenly, and, pushing without a pause through the unlocked doorway under the gilded sign, mounted the flight of complaining stairs which rose before him in the gloom beyond. Evidently familiar with the place, the visitor, on reaching the landing, knocked fearfully but resolutely on a dark oblong in the obscurity which betokened where a closed door broke the panelled surface of the wall.

A groan or sigh, some sound indefinite but sufficient, responding, he turned the handle, his long fingers clouding it with a clammy moisture, and, edging round the door, closed it softly behind him and stood looking eagerly towards the end of the room. Its sole occupant, the learned Quinones, that miserly apothecary whose wisdom, nevertheless, served him for a perennial harvest, was, he knew well enough, notoriously chary of speech, grudging it to others as though, like the fairy-gifted maiden's, there were a present of a jewel in every word he let drop. Saturnine, austere, caustic in his few utterances, he was wont to vouchsafe small comment on the catalogues of ills and vapours that were perpetually laid before him; but a phrase with him, so famous was he, took all the force of a prescription. Thus regarded, it was little likely that he would forego the principles of a lifetime for the sake of him who had now broken in upon his solitude.

He was seated at a table in the window opposite the door, his back to the intruder, his left ear turned a little, as if in some listening irascibility over the interruption. The fading alchemy of the sunset, dropping in flakes and dust through the diamond-paned casement, rimmed the hunched silhouette of him with a faint aura, and made an amber mist of the dry thin hair on his scalp, and turned the narrow section of cheek visible from lead to gold. It was to this strangely-crowned and indeterminate shadow that the visitor addressed himself, in hurried, fluttering speech, the true purport of which only gathered form as desperation lent it eloquence:

"You know me, Quinones—yes, you know me, learned master—as I know you. No need to waste a look on recognition. My voice is stored in your memory, with other debts to be liquidated. You do not forget these things."

He took an impulsive step forward, and the board creaked and jumped under his foot. It seemed as if the figure in the chair started slightly, and then settled again to its listening. The visitor held out his hands with an imploring gesture.

"I did you an ill deed in the past, Quinones, and it is written against me in your books. What is the use to tell you that I have repented it since in sack-cloth and ashes? And yet let it be of use. O, in these mortal times, when all the world should be in one brotherhood of help and sympathy, let your resentment sleep—forgive, and prove by that nobility your true title to the greatness that all men allow you. I have bitten the hand, I confess it, that cherished me: let that hand retaliate in the finest spirit by ministering to the wound I inflicted, not first on you, but on my own miserable nature. Be generous to me, Quinones, for I have lived to know and suffer."

He paused; and in the pause there rose a melancholy cry from the darkening street: "Bring out your dead; bring out your dead!" The sound seemed to goad him to a frenzy.

"Listen, Quinones; I have learned to know, I say. Love, that in its purity can redeem the worst, has been my teacher. For love I would live—I, who until it transformed me, feared no death, refused no risks. Now, for its sake, I am a coward; I shrink in terror that this mortality may claim me—me, who have learned at last the glory and the fruitfulness of life. O save me, Quinones! You alone among all the Galenical masters can do so, if you will. Fortify my blood; render me immune; give me the secret of your plague-water, the one specific, as all admit, quite certain in its results. Give it to me and mine, and earn for evermore the name of saint, the gratitude of hearts that wait upon your bounty not to break."

The seated figure seemed, in the uncertain light, to stir and chuckle—or was it a sound of water gurgling in the basement. Still no response came from it; and, hearkening vainly through the thick silence, the mood of the man roared up in a moment from submission to deadly fury:

"Inhuman, unforgiving! Not for you to forget, in your God-feigned aloofness, the least, the most paltry hurt to your vanity. You hear, but you will not answer. Answer to this, then. I came to appeal to the great in you, as other blind fools have certified it; but I came prepared with sharper weapons than entreaty, should, as I foresaw in my heart, the fools prove fools indeed. I am a desperate man, Quinones, and you are alone—quite alone with me, I do believe. It is either the secret yielded, or your life. Make your choice, and quickly. A poor revenge, will you not think it, to lie there in your blood while I am ranging free and unsuspected in this welter!"

He half crouched, peering through the deepening twilight, a sudden blade in his hand, the tumult in his brain grown rabid—then, with a shriek, "Let your plague-water save you now!" leapt on the unresponsive figure.

It swayed, swung, and rolled stiffly to the floor, revealing a livid face, blotched and plague-stricken, and fangs—good Lord, they grinned!

Quinones mortal had not half the sinister significance of Quinones dead and rigid. He had sat there, waiting his age-delayed but never-forgotten revenge—sat there a stiffening corpse, long after the rest of his household had fled.

With a scream, the other rushed from the room, into the street—and so in a little for the cart and the plague-pit. Quinones was quits with him at last.

THE BLUE DRAGON
(1915)

I ran across Gilroy in Christie's show rooms one view day before a sale of heterogeneous china. That had been formerly a not uncommon encounter; but of late years the keen edge of Gilroy's virtuosity seemed to have dulled, and though, as I understood, he still collected, friends spoke of an abatement of enthusiasm in him, at least in a certain marked direction. Rather to test that report than from any desire to ask his opinion on a coveted object, I got him to come and look at a Ming saucer, a green dragon on a mustard-yellow ground, which stood with other exhibits in a case in a corner of the room. He acquiesced, though I thought unwillingly, and stood a little aloof regarding the thing, but without a sign of that minute particular interest he would once have displayed in it. I fancied even I detected a hint of repulsion, of contemptuous dislike in the long, white face with its set, thin lips. And that amused me and tickled my curiosity.

"Don't you take an interest any longer," I said, "in Oriental ware?"

He wore habitually gold pince-nez, with a broad black ribbon, and his eyes, naturally contracted, but absurdly magnified by the lenses, now regarded me with an exaggerated inquisition.

"Not much, to tell the truth. Why do you ask?"

"Why not? You used to be an enthusiast."

"Eclectic, I flatter myself. I never specialised. Old Bow and Chelsea are my present fancy. I'm not a rich man, you know."

"I've known prices paid for Old Bow and Chelsea."

"Not by this child. And they're so clean and wholesome, innocent of the least hint of latency—Shamanism—whatever you like to call it. There's something rather bestially suggestive, to my mind, in much Mongolian art—a sort of pervading demonism which infects even its representations of inanimate objects."

I laughed. "But didn't Chelsea borrow something from the Orient?"

"The innocent may touch pitch without being denied, the Apocrypha despite. Think of the baby who shared his milk-sop, unharmed, with the venomous serpent."

"Gilroy; is it that you've had an experience?"

He stood looking at me silently a moment; and then suddenly took my arm.

"Come into the open air," he said, "away from that—and I'll tell you. Yes, I've had a sort of experience."

We went down the sunny Mall together, and he spoke as follows:—

"It was the last piece of Oriental ware I ever bought, or shall buy; and I picked it up at, of all places in the world, a marine store-dealer's in Deptford, a queer old cabin with a black rag doll hanging over the doorway. How it, the thing, got there I don't know; probably brought by some Chinese sailorman; but anyhow I saw it, and bought it—for a trifle too—a blue and white cylindrical brushpot, a Yung Ching period, about five inches high, and closed with a wooden lid that fitted it like a plug. There was a beastie, of the usual grotesque type, painted on its side; but I made no particular examination of my 'find' until I got it home, when, in the growing dusk, I sat me down before the fire and took it from its paper. It was quite an acquisition at the price; but there seemed nothing remarkable about it, unless, perhaps, in the anatomy of the little sit-up monstrosity, dog or dragon or devil, which struck me as unusual. The skeleton, in short, or certain articulated indications of it, appeared either on the outside of the animal—like that of Hartley Coleridge's imaginary chimera—or showed through—it was impossible to tell which—from the inside, as if the thing had been X-rayed. Its jaw was a compromise between a beak and a snout, and its body displayed a pelt of fine long hair.

"Now I was moved to take the lid off, because, oddly, there seemed a sort of faint shifting bias to the pot, as if it contained some small soft object. But the lid would not be induced to move, and I could get no purchase on its sloping edge. I grew impatient at last, and tried to lever it up with a penknife; when the thing happened that any ass might have foreseen. There was a crack, and off flew the lid, carrying with it a triangular wedge of china from the lip. The 'piece,' from the virtuosic point of view, was ruined.

"Utterly disgusted with myself, I threw the pot into a soft easy chair close by, and damned to all eternity the folly of the collector in investing his capital in fragile articles which a misplaced touch could render comparatively valueless. Then I sat sulking and glowering into the fire, until its soft reverberations, and the twilight stillness of the room, began to weigh upon my lids and senses, and I found myself nodding. I did not go to sleep; but I dozed; and, as I dozed, a consciousness of intense depression gradually came to overwhelm me. I neither knew nor troubled about its cause or constitution: it was there, and threatening swiftly to master my power of resistance—a sense of the weary futility of life, and of a desire to end it. Death was in my soul, a scarce resistible longing—and at that instant something tickled my ear. I put up my hand impatiently to brush away the irritation; and felt nothing. But a second time it occurred, and my fingers touched something pulpy and hairy, which leaped from under them. I don't think I'm feminine enough in general to scream at a mouse—but a mouse on one's neck! I shot up into a sitting posture; and—I'm not a self-destroying man—and in that moment I knew my own morbid folly. But I was sickeningly scared—shaking all over; and I sat staring about me. There was something going down me at a soft, scrambling rush—something that traversed my leg and reached the carpet. A little spurt of coal gas was momentarily illuminating the room and—I don't know what made me go for it—but I jumped and snatched up the Ching pot. And there was nothing on it, not a sign of beast or painting, only the smooth white glaze. Nothing, I say; and why? Because it was on the floor, blue and in movement—a tiny thing that ran round and round, and then made for my leg as if to remount it and reach what was in my hands. With a gasp I threw the pot away from me into the easy chair; and, as I did so, the running thing seemed to make a spring for it and disappear. I was sick, I tell you, but with nerve to snatch up the wooden stopper and clap it in place. And as I jammed it down, I saw the dragon come out on the surface of the pot again as wicked and fantastic as ever. That was the experience."

"H'm! What did you do with it?"

"Why, I took it as it was, gripping on the lid like death, and stopping the fracture with my thumb (I could feel it there inside, nuzzling and palpitating all the time), and, my landlady being out, put it into the kitchen fire. There was an explosion that cracked the range—a close one; and for days afterwards a horrible smell of burnt fur about the house."

"Seems as if the beast appeared on the pot inside out, and your taking oft the lid pulled him right way round again."

"Doesn't it?"

"Well, I'm afraid, in spite of your experience, I shall go for the Ming saucer."

"That's all right; only—no, it really wasn't an Oriental variety of the blue crocodile and pink oyster genus."

THE CLOSED DOOR
(1915)

The Wanderer, the water squelching in his broken boots at every step, splashed his way across the melancholy estate. A drenched moon, seeming to pitch at its moorings as the running clouds lifted it, glazed with a lamentable light the wet roofs and palings of the surrounding houses. Those, scattered loosely over a wide area of swampy ground, illustrated the latest word, in one direction, of suburban expansion. They would close up some day and become part of the city of which they were now only the advanced outposts; at present they stood in their pretentious instability for nothing better than the smart foresight of a speculative builder. So much, in the flying moonshine, was evident to the Wanderer. He marked the little barren, stony gardens, the rows of forlorn saplings, the weedy wastes—dumping-grounds for pots and broken crockery—the unmade roads scarred with their wildernesses of soggy ruts; and his soul yearned for the flare of city slums, whose squalor was still the sweltering over-ripened fruit of exotic ages. A lonely gas-lamp here and there blinked testily, like a lightship in a waste of waters, whenever the wind smote its solitary eye; for the rest, scarce ten o'clock as it was, drab dejection seemed on all sides to have extinguished its tapers and gone drearily to bed.

The Wanderer, going forward with that stoic, hunch-shouldered aspect which is common to those long familiar with shrunk vitals and the filter of rain into coat-collars, raised his head suddenly and looked about him. A sound of universal running and dripping had succeeded on the passing of the last brief hammering storm.

"The Laurels," he muttered: "That was the name the old woman told me—The Laurels! Curse these bally houses! When shall I reach the one I want? Uncle Greg, like all the rest of them, will have gone to bed, if I'm not quick."

He had not, after all, much to hope of the sinister old man; but anyhow he was Uncle Gregory's own sole sister's child, and any chance was worth risking in this deadly pass to which he had come. If he could only induce Uncle Greg to ship him off somewhere abroad—just to be rid of his intolerable importunities! Surely, for his own sake, he would not drive him to desperation. Uncle Greg was a wicked old Pharisee and humbug, but respectability was the breath of his nostrils. He lived by it and prevailed by it, witness this very estate exploited by him, and on which he himself was established, the crowning expression of its social orthodoxy. It would be ruinous business to have a profligate and pauperised nephew haunting its decent preserves. Yes, his case was strong enough to warrant a descent on Uncle Greg, much as in his heart he feared the malefic old man.

He had come to an abrupt stop in the houses; beyond seemed to stretch a moon-dappled hiatus of broken ground. But, looking intently across this, he perceived distinctly enough a solitary house, standing remote and lone on the limits of the estate. Towards that house, since he had investigated all others, it was necessary for him to make his way. He distinguished a track of some sort, and followed it.

As he approached the building, apprehension stiffened in him to fury. It was dark and lifeless like the others. Not the gleam of a light twinkled anywhere from its windows; the household, to all appearance, was a-bed.

Cursing between his teeth, he came up to the gate, and read without difficulty its inscription. The Laurels, safe enough. He had reached his goal at last, and to what end?

One moment he stood, deliberating the prospect before him; the next, in a rage of decision, he had opened the gate and walked in. A black shrubbery, of the nature to justify the name, appeared to accept him into its yawning arms. There was a gloom of trees about the house, in whose shadow the white shutters in the windows seemed to open and stare at him secretively. Not a sound proceeded from the building anywhere; yet its vulgarity, its raw newness, were enough to allay any sensation of eeriness which its silence, its ghostly isolation in the moonlight, might otherwise have conveyed.

The Wanderer, standing before the hall door, held his breath to consider. His feet had crunched on the gravel path; yet it seemed to him that to breathe were more certainly to betray himself. To betray himself to what?

Yes, to what? Why should he fear or hesitate? Desperate men need dread no ambushes. There was no lower than the bottom of things, and he lay there already, bruised and broken. To turn now were to turn for shelter to the booming wind, the rain-swept waste. There was none other possible to him, save through the door of crime. He might open that yet; Uncle Greg should decide for him. He had one negotiable asset—himself. There was a positive value in self-obliteration; it was worth money. The lesson could not be better conveyed than through self-assertion. He lifted his hand to the knocker.

The blow sounded startlingly through the silent house; and yet he had knocked but timidly at the outset—too timidly, it appeared. He raised his hand again; louder this time; and still no one answered.

Then anger grew in him; he refused to be ignored; if he had to wake the whole household he would stay and not desist until he was admitted. The reverberations, violently continued, gave him heart and courage, gave him confidence. Conversely with his own determination must be rising the palpitations of the silent listeners within. It was impossible that they could not hear him. He rained at last a very battery of blows upon the door. Still there followed no response. Then, in a sort of derisive perversity, he took to delivering second taps with the knocker, regular, monotonous, up to fifty or so. That must goad the most resolute inmate to rebellion.

Suddenly, quite suddenly, he paused.

"If you knock too long at a closed door, the devil may open to you."

Where had he heard that—read that? Superstitious drivel, of course; and yet, the spectral night, the lonely house, and this silence! Pooh! It was Uncle Greg he demanded and was resolute to arouse. Uncle Greg was devil enough for anyone. Let him appear, to vindicate the proverb if he liked; he asked nothing better.

He had raised his hand once more, when he fancied he heard the faintest echo of a response within the house. It might have been a faint call or a footstep. "Ah!" he breathed to himself, "the old devil at last!"

The sound increased—came on. Unquestionably it was the stealthy tread of a footstep in the hall. A tiny ray of light shot through the keyhole. The Wanderer clutched the rags upon his chest and stood rigid. In the very act of steadying himself, he saw that the hall door was open and Uncle Greg standing motionless on the threshold.

The same heavy, sly figure as of old, beaming hairless self-complacency in its every slab feature. He wore a shawl dressing-gown of a flamboyant pattern; his stumpy feet were encased in gorgeous carpet slippers; in one hand he held a lighted candle, in the other a revolver. He betrayed no astonishment, but only a sort of furtive glee.

"Charlie!" he said, in his whispering chuckle: "poor Charlie, is it, that has been knocking fit to wake the dead."

"I was desperate to get in—to make you hear," muttered the Wanderer. "Look at my state, Uncle Greg."

"And you made me hear," said the old builder. "What a determined fellow, to be sure. There was nothing for it at last but to get up and come. I have brought my pistol with me, you see."

"Not to use it on me, I hope, Uncle Greg?" said the Wanderer, with a ghastly jocularity.

"No," said Uncle Gregory; "no. It's not the kind of weapon for your sort. I've a better way of retaliating on you."

The visitor, in this visible presence, was stung to wordy violence on the instant.

"O, a better way, have you?" he said sneeringly. "We'll see about that. I know where I'm not wanted, and the value to be put on my undesirability. If you wish to hoof me out of this precious dovecot of yours, you'll have to pay for the privilege, you know, Uncle Greg."

"Shall I?" said the old man. "Why, how you go on, Charlie. There are Christian ways of retaliating, ain't there? Suppose in my old age, I have come to that."

"Come to that!" The Wanderer drew in his breath as if to a sudden pang. Was it conceivable that out of such ineffable slyness and hypocrisy as he remembered of old had blossomed this aftermath of Christian charity and forgiveness? He tried to read the change in the familiar face, but the swaying candle-light distorted it absurdly.

"I can't make out if you're getting at me or not," he said. "Anyhow my misery is plain enough. May I come in, Uncle Greg?"

"Why not?" said the old man. "It's the very thing I want."

He turned and went silently along the hall. The Wanderer, following half dazed, observed stupidly how the candle-light seemed to have awakened a very phantasmagoria of shadows on the walls and ceiling. They jerked and frolic'd above and around; they tumbled over the stair-rails as if in some fantastic scramble for place and precedence. The effect was so bewildering, that it came as a quick shock to him to notice suddenly, through the thick of their gambolling, the echoing emptiness of the passage he trod. It was without carpet or furniture—bare to its limits.

And so it was with the room into which Uncle Gregory preceded him. From door to shuttered window it was void as death; only a faint, sickly odour pervaded it; only a very little litter of damp straw was scattered about its boards. The Wanderer stopped, petrified, staring before him—staring hither and thither, and then at Uncle Gregory. The old man stood, swaying the candle high, swaying it to and fro so that his own shadow, obeying its motions, danced and leapt and dilated on the walls and floor.

"Damn it!" cried the Wanderer, finding his breath in a gasp; "stop that—stop it, will you! What is the meaning of this? What trick are you playing on me?"

"Trick, Charlie!" The old builder bent in a soundless chuckle. "It's all right; it's all right, you know. If I'd known you were coming, I'd have delayed the bankruptcy proceedings."

"What! Sold up?"

"That's the word, Charlie. Nothing left—only this."

He held out the revolver, balancing it in his hand.

"A heavy bullet," he said— "fit to splash a man's brains all over the shop. What a curse you intended to make of my life, didn't you? A mean, squalid ruffian—you were always that, you know. I hated you, Charlie, my dear; I always hated you, you poisonous prodigal. Now I'm going to have my turn with you at last. You'd come here, would you, to bleed the old man? You shall bleed for him, hang for him, you hound! They'll think you did it, and you shall answer with the red witness on your hands."

The Wanderer's face was white as drained veal; he had thought for an instant that the other meant to murder him; and then he saw in a flash his more terrific purpose. He gave a scream like a run-over woman, and leapt forward—but it was too late. The pistol crashed, and Uncle Gregory's brains flew all about the room.

Or so they appeared to as, on the moment, darkness rang down. He staggered back, with a sob that was wrenched from him like a hook from a fish's throat. He put his hand to his forehead, and it seemed to adhere there with a little treacly suggestion, and a more overpowering sense of that odour which had already nauseated him. And then he turned and fled. The hall door was still open, revealing a livid oblong of watery moonshine. Into that he fell, rather than plunged, as a man leaps from the side of a burning ship. He had no thought or care for his direction, so long as it bore him from that horror. Once, as he tore along, he stumbled and fell, his hands in a pool of water. That suggesting something to him, frantically, hurriedly, he rinsed his palms and bathed his forehead before he rose again and sped on. He had only one purpose in his mind—to reach the city lights and find shelter from himself in their glare.

Little by little he had come to recognise that the doom imposed upon him was unavoidable and irrevocable. What insidious pressure, intimate and satanic, had persuaded him to that necessity, gradually enveloping his mind until escape from its torture seemed possible in only one direction, he knew well enough, while he was helpless to resist it. There was a limit to the endurances of reason; better the condemned cell and the rope and the pinioned arms than this long-drawn-out agony of apprehension. After all, if he were to die, a self-accused though innocent man, perhaps the sacrifice might be accepted by the Unknown in some sort as an atonement, and he might be spared in the hereafter that company which alone he unspeakably dreaded. But a man could not continue for ever with that shadow at his shoulder, which no word of his—he believed it truly—could conceivably dissipate. He might have washed his flesh and his clothes: the stains of blood were indelible. So surely as he confessed his visit to the house on that night of terror, so surely, viewing his antecedents and the purpose for which he had come, would he place the noose about his own neck. He could not resist his impulse the less for that; the diabolical thing which inspired it was more powerful than himself. He was so weary, so nerve-worn in the end, that even the thought of temporising with the truth seemed an intolerable ordeal. Better to confess at once that he was guilty of murder, and get it over. Only that way lay peace from it all.

During all these three days, so haunted, so marked as he was, his immunity from arrest had not ceased to astonish him. It was inconceivable that he had not been observed on his way either to or from the fatal house; it was incredible that that persistent knocking of his had failed to find its echo in some panic heart. He had dared no attempt to leave the place; he had possessed no means to lie hidden in it. On the contrary, some little dawn of luck, which had found him out since that night, had brought him more prominently than usual into the open. Was not that the common irony of Fortune—to bestow her grudging favours at the moment when for all moral purposes they had become valueless? So now, though she was represented by no more than a job to distribute circulars, that respite from starvation was gained at the expense of bitter bread to eat.

On each of the three days he had bought and feverishly perused a halfpenny paper; but never one had contained any mention of the tragedy. No shouting headline rushed into his ken; no report of discovery or inquest appeared to confirm him in his sickest apprehensions. Was it possible that the police, for their own purposes, were lying low? That were an unusual course, at least in these days of sensational publicity. And then there flashed into his mind another explanation of this silence, and the most hideously plausible of them all. The bankruptcy; the emptied house; its unsuspected inmate. Of course the body was lying there yet, undiscovered; and the crisis, in the prolonged expectation of which he had been lingering out the exquisite torment of these days, were merely postponed.

To the madness of that thought his reason succumbed, and finally. He could endure no more. One morning he walked into the local police-station and addressed the inspector on duty.

"I have come to give myself up for the murder at The Laurels."

The inspector, immovable, grizzle-bearded, with overhanging eyebrows, betrayed no least hint of emotion; but he just signed to a subordinate to keep the door.

"Yes," he said evenly. "What is your name?"

The Wanderer confessed it; as also his relationship to the dead man, the purpose for which he had called upon him and, more excitedly, the measure of his own worthlessness and iniquity.

The inspector stopped him, with official aplomb, in mid-career.

"This occurred three nights ago, you say? I want you to give an account of your movements up to that time."

"That is easily done," said the Wanderer, with a little panting laugh, now that the horror was off his mind. "I had been discharged only a week before from B Hospital, where I had been an inpatient for two months and more. You won't expect me to tell you for what."

"No," said the Inspector; and "Exactly," he said.

"Well, I shall have to detain you for inquiries."

The magistrate, a precise, benevolent man, with a certain soldierly compactness about his attire, ended some remarks he had been making on the advisability of contriving some punishment for those who increasingly took up the time of the Court with unfounded self-accusations, the result commonly of drink

"Your statement about the hospital," he said, addressing the prisoner, "has been confirmed. It is possible that some mental distemper, induced by your recent condition, was responsible for this wild appropriation of a crime which, amounting as it did to an unquestionable case of self-destruction, occurred quite a month ago, when you were lying ill. Not less can excuse you for this wanton imperilling of your own life. What is that you say?"

His words had to be interpreted to the magistrate, so thickly inarticulate they came from his lips.

"I knocked, and knocked, and he opened to me at last. He had a pistol in his hand, and I saw him do it."

"Come," said the magistrate kindly: "you must forget all that. Leave closed doors alone for the future, is my advice. Remember what is said—that the devil lays snares for the importunate; only not being omniscient, he sometimes overreaches himself on the question of an alibi. Nevertheless, it is not safe to count upon his anachronisms. He has succeeded once or twice, I am afraid, in getting innocent men hanged. The best thing for all of us is to avoid knocking him up when we find him asleep.

"I think, for your own sake, I shall remand you for a week into the hands of the prison doctor."

THE DARK COMPARTMENT
(1915)

I remember once, when hunting for a seat in a crowded train, finding unexpectedly an empty compartment, the door of which, when I came to try it, was locked. Holding on to the handle, I looked about for the guard. At that moment another hurrying passenger halted beside me, peered over my shoulder into the carriage, and went quickly away. Something in the man's manner striking me, I also investigated, and saw that the floor of the compartment was sprinkled thick with sawdust. Incontinently I let go the handle, and hastened to find a seat elsewhere.

There cannot be many engines, after all, which do not trail the ghosts of past tragedies in their wake. That was an experience unforeseen enough to give one a sharp little qualm; but I would not willingly exchange it for Manby's. In his case—but let him tell his own story:

"I had been visiting the old Hampshire Abbey town, and a run thence of thirty minutes by rail would take me to the next stopping-place on my itinerary, where there were barracks, and a cathedral, and a public school, and a gaol—not to speak of cosy hotels. It was a dark November evening, and soppingly wet, so that, dawdling over my tea-board comforts at the inn, I came near in the end to missing my train altogether. It was actually starting when I gained the platform, and I had to make a dash for it, and scramble into the first compartment that offered.

"The light in the roof burned so dim that, what with that and the momentary flurry of my entrance, I did not recognise at once whether I were alone or had broken into company. As my eyes, however, accustomed themselves to the obscurity, I saw that there were two men sitting together opposite me at the further end of the compartment.

"The lamp, I say, was so down—a mere night-light in suggestion—that it was difficult to distinguish the character of my travelling companions. Moreover, as one of them seemed thickly bearded, and the other wore a dark felt hat slouched over his eyes, their faces, or the section of each of them visible to me, appeared nothing but featureless white maps, hung up, as it were, in the gloom. The two sat very quiet, close together, but without exchanging the least communication that I could see; and presently, from under cover of my own hat-brim, I took to scrutinising the silent shapes. I was the more emboldened to that inquisition by the utter indifference with which they had accepted my abrupt invasion. They seemed now, even, to be wholly unconscious of my presence.

"The deathliness of that disregard, rigid and motionless; the huddled cohesion of the twin shadows, with those blots of white representing their faces, affected me strangely and uneasily after a while. I wanted one or the other of them to stir, to resolve himself into a detached human entity—and quite suddenly I had my wish. How it happened I don't know; but there came a sort of local shifting of the gloom, a sense of a quick gleam in its midst, and in that moment I understood. The man with the slouched hat had handcuffs on his wrists, and he was travelling in charge of a prison warder.

"And almost as I realised the truth the prisoner began to speak:—

"'I'm sick; I want air.'

"I say he spoke, and I might say the other answered. A sense of those words, anyhow, throbbed in my brain, and they had their instant corollary in his rising and standing at the window unopposed. I felt the rush of wet air, and saw the wing-like filling of the dark Inverness cape he wore. And then suddenly there was a tiny snap, and he went out of the window like a flying crow. I saw the warder snatch at him, and follow the way he had gone, pulled off his feet by the wrench and jerk. And there was I alone in the dark compartment, with only the window guard, broken and bent askew, to witness to the stunning tragedy which had passed in a moment before my eyes.

"Even as I leapt to my feet I grasped what had happened. Under cover of his cloak, and the roar of wheels and rain, the prisoner, though manacled, had managed rapidly to file through the bar to breaking point.

"I tore at the alarm communication cord, and stood gasping and shaken. Almost against my expectation, the train slowed down within a few seconds and came to a stop. I put my head out of the window on my side, and beckoned frantically to the shape I saw beating towards me along the blown track-side. The guard came below, looking up with the staring, rather combative, expression of the official summoned against his own better faith. 'What is it?'

"'For God's sake, come here! Two men have just gone out of the window.'

"He climbed grudgingly to the footboard, and so into the carriage. 'Yes, sir,' he said. 'Where were they sitting?'

"His cool, incredulous tone maddened me.

"'There, by that open window,' I said. 'Isn't it plain enough?'

"He crossed the carriage, pressed his hand on the seat, turned to me again. 'That won't do. No one's been sitting here. The cushion's cold. Feel for yourself.'

"'God in heaven, man!' I cried. 'Do you take me to be mad or drunk? They sat there, I tell you—a warder and his charge; and the prisoner stood up on some pretext and went clean out, dragging the other after him. There's the broken window rail to witness.'

"'Is there?' He had had his back to it; but moved now, just glancing over his shoulder, so that I might see. And there was the window-rail whole and sound, and the window itself closed.

"Presently, after I don't know what brief interval, I found myself giggling hysterically.

"'Look here,' I said, 'I think I'll change my carriage.'

"'I would,' said the guard, 'if I were you.'

"Both his tone and his look were odd; but he formally took my name and address, with an intimation that the minimum penalty was five pounds. It was, on the face of it, a serious offence, you will agree. Yet, curiously, I received no summons from the company, or ever heard another word on the matter."

THE FOOTSTEPS
(1915)

Twice she had heard them, she told me, and on each occasion with indescribable terror: if she were to hear them a third time, it must surely mean death.

It was this way. Like some other people, she had her dream-house—a place which she was convinced existed in fact, and which some day she would chance upon and instantly recognise. She was able to describe it to me minutely—with an exactness of detail which I cannot aim at reproducing. It was a Victorian house, substantial, standing in its own grounds, and with nothing in the least ghostly about its aspect. Entering up the drive, one passed a block of blind-fronted stables to reach a long conservatory, by way of which, for no explained reason, one entered the building. A large drawing-room, sumptuously furnished and carpeted, succeeded; and thence one passed up a couple of shallow steps, extending almost the width of the room, into a second considerable chamber, crowded this one with china, having all an odd suggestion of something wrong and rather horrible about it, and leading in its turn into yet a third room, which was peculiar only for its gloomy panelling and the door fast shut at its further end. She knew that the whole vast house was empty of life; that its chambers and corridors throughout were open, if she wished it, to her inspection. Only this one closed door was forbidden—impossible. She had an awful desire to penetrate its secret; and yet with a sickness of terror for what it might reveal to her should she succeed. But she dared not try. And then came the footsteps—of some one, of something, moving within the hidden room. They rustled and spoke, now receding, now approaching; and suddenly they stopped, while horror breathed through the keyhole, as if in the very crisis of some terrific decision. And at that she woke.

Such was her dream—the paralysing nightmare which she had twice experienced, and lived in mortal fear of suffering for a third, and final, time.

She was young, and she spoke her fancy playfully, as if to deprecate any serious acceptance of her mock-heroics. Yet I could see plainly enough that a real apprehension lay behind her pretence.

"Take it this way," I said. "You feel positively convinced that that house exists in fact somewhere?"

"Yes, positively," she answered.

"Well, I don't doubt it. Too many authentic instances of dream-houses proving real are on record to permit me to. And you haunt it in some astral or sub-conscious form. Well, how are you to know that that other sub-conscious form, represented by the footsteps, is not as terrified about you as you are about it? You may be the walking ghost in its fancy."

"O, I hope not!" she said. But it was evident that my suggestion had opened up in her a train of reflection unmorbid, by contrast with the other, and even, strangely, a little pitiful and emotional.

Well, I did not re-encounter my young lady for years after that; and, when I did meet her again, she was a mature lady, married and with children. But she knew me at once, and greeted me with a fervour which I hardly understood until, chancing on one occasion to be alone with her, she opened out her heart to me.

"I have always so wished to renew our acquaintance. Do you remember that time we met when I told you about my dream-house?"

"Certainly I do; and about my own efforts to reassure you."

"I wanted to tell you—I have always wanted to; and you have the best right to know, because you gave me the true clue to my riddle. The footsteps I heard were the footsteps of fear, and *I* was the unconscious ghost that caused it."

I nodded, in no whit surprised. "Go on, if you will," I said.

"You must keep my confidence," she answered; "but I want you to know—you alone of all people. It was so very strange, so very tragic. He, the owner of the house, used to dream that he was down in that room, his own study, and that silence and an awful emptiness closed him in, so that he had to walk, walk, to forget. And then came the footsteps—in the panelled room—right up to the door; and horror would seize him—horror of the thing that waited there outside—it might be death, or something unspeakable, but he had not the courage to open and face it.

"We had not met then, he and I; and when at last we did, in another place, it was the familiar story of a spoilt girl, and slanderous tongues, and a great heart slighted and abused. I am not going to palliate or defend, but only to relate. He was wounded to the soul; he was alone in the world, and his life was his own. There came a time at last when he stood—in that room—and his hand was not empty—"

I begged her not to go on; but she was resolved.

"The girl, the wretched girl, had learned the truth late—the vindication of the name she had loved and honoured in her heart before all the world. She was passionate and wilful, and she flew at once to make atonement—"

She stopped. "You must not," I said. "Besides, it is unnecessary; I can guess the sequel. You saw it, with your living eyes, for the first time—the house of your dreams."

"Yes, I saw it: it was all exactly as I had pictured—the silence, the emptiness, for the household had long been dismissed. And I knew where I had to go; what I had to do. At the last it was opened, and—and it was not Death."

She ended, gave a little sigh, as of a soul unburdened, and after that a little laugh.

"It is the children's play-room now," she said; "and is not that wonderful? Not many people, I expect, come to be the mistresses of their own dream-houses."

THE GLASS BALL
(1915)

It happened in the winter of 1881 (said my friend). You remember that winter? It began to freeze hard early in November, and the frost never fairly broke until the second or third week in March. I had come up to town by the South-Western Railway, travelling through a white and windless country; and the cold was stupefying. I lay most of the way in a sort of torpor, gelid from toe to brain, and only just sensible of the still and silent flow of things outside the window. A desolate day, with hardly a human shape abroad to emphasise its loneliness. I don't know if I slept at all. I was alone in my compartment, and in a sort of mental stupor, as I say. And then suddenly I was awake and staring. It was snowing outside, and something had spoken to me—or tried to speak. There was an impression in my brain as of a little, black, leaning figure, infinitely small as if infinitely distant—a mere oblique accent on the sheeted immensity of things—of a staggered white face, of a loud, sub-conscious voice. And here, without and within, were only void and running silence. I shook, as one shakes escaping by a hair's-breadth the insidious clutch of a nightmare. It had been a nightmare, I supposed, of the kind that discovers a minute rent in the veil over the unseen, synchronously with some malefic horror on the further side. And, as always, the rent had been closed, only just timely for me. Such dreams are momentarily demoralising: oddly enough the fear of this one dwelt with me for days. I could not shake off its memory, in the tremor of which was mingled, nevertheless, a strange emotion like pity. Imagine some lone survivor in the Arctic wastes uttering instinctively, as he sinks to his death, that call for human aid which none, even the most daring, may forego at the last. For some nameless reason that image, or its like, hung constantly in my mind, until presently it wrought in me an only half-reluctant desire to have my dream again. What, I thought, if that dreadful approaching face seen through the rent had been addressed to me not in malignity, but in an agony of supplication?

That was a morbid fancy, resolutely to be dismissed. A few strenuous days in London promised to see the last of it. Christmas was near, and with it an engagement to a family of young relatives, who would certainly expect seasonable presents. I prepared for the sacrifice.

It was then that the name of John Trent swam suddenly into my field of mental vision, and with a click, stood focused there. Who was John Trent? I knew no more than that he was a lost gentleman, whose whereabouts his family, or lawyers, or natural representatives were daily seeking through advertisement in the papers and police-stations. It was only one case like fifty others, and there was no known reason why it should suddenly absorb my attention. Yet quite unaccountably it did. Each morning I turned for first news to that reiterated paragraph in the agony column offering money for whatsoever information as to the movements of the vanished John Trent. He had last been seen, it appeared, on the afternoon of my journey to London (perhaps it was that slight coincidence which attracted me), when he had left his lodgings at Winchfield for a walk; and thereafter he had been seen no more. Some later particulars gave his age as forty, his disposition as solitary, his temper as peculiar and inclined to rashness. He had been something wont, in the past, to self-obliterations, it seemed; yet hardly after this senseless fashion. And there the tale of him ended.

One afternoon I walked down to the Lowther Arcade, then drearily existent, to effect my purchases. It was all a long medley of toys and fancy stuff from which to select; but I chose with an eye to meetness and economy, even down to the baby, on whose behalf I had the inspiration to buy a glass snowing-ball. You know the sort? I hadn't seen one since I was a child myself, and I was delighted. There is a man inside, with a little wintry landscape, and a Swiss chalet, and when you turn the ball upside down and round again, thick snow is falling. That is the rule, but I observed at once that the specimen I received from the superior young lady was an exception to the rule. It had inside it only the solitary figure of a man, and the man was skating. Yes, he skated actually, moving in little swoops and circles over a sheet of ice which seemed to dissect the ball; and as he skated the snow fell.

I stood staring stupidly and, as I stared, the man went through the ice and disappeared.

"That's different from the others," I said loudly to the girl. I suppose my tone startled her; I'm sure it startled me. "Is it?" she said. "I don't think so." And no more it was. When I looked again at the thing in my hand, there were the peasant and the chalet, and the little landscape, all correct and all motionless in their places.

I didn't buy the ball, but something else; and from the Arcade I went straight to the nearest police-station where, among the posted bills, figured that relating to the disappearance of John Trent. "I think," I said to the inspector, "I can tell you where he is. He is under the ice in Fleet pond."

And so he was; and thence they dragged him when the bitter frost came to an end. The little oblique accent on the whirling white sheet half seen, half dreamt, by me, the mortal expression, the loud cry—they had all represented the fate of John Trent skating, like a madman, solitary and unsuspected, on that vast plane of ice beside the track.

He had gone insanely to his doom, on that stark, inhuman day, without a word to, and unseen by, a solitary soul save myself, and by me only in that exchange of sub-conscious recognitions which obliterates intervening space. To mine alone, in all that running, close-shut train, had his been able to appeal—yet with what purpose from such a man?

I think I know. He had a young child—one—legitimately and wholly dependent on him. Until they could produce certain evidence that he, John Trent, was dead and not merely disappeared, that child would be a beggar. And that was why he had wanted his fate to be definitely known—why, to my still deficient understanding, he had turned its little inmates out of their glass snowing-house, and had taken their place.

THE MARBLE HANDS
(1915)

We left our bicycles by the little lych-gate and entered the old churchyard. Heriot had told me frankly that he did not want to come; but at the last moment, sentiment or curiosity prevailing with him, he had changed his mind. I knew indefinitely that there was something disagreeable to him in the place's associations, though he had always referred with affection to the relative with whom he had stayed here as a boy. Perhaps she lay under one of these greening stones.

We walked round the church, with its squat, shingled spire. It was utterly peaceful, here on the brow of the little town where the flowering fields began. The bones of the hill were the bones of the dead, and its flesh was grass. Suddenly Heriot stopped me. We were standing then to the northwest of the chancel, and a gloom of motionless trees over-shadowed us.

"I wish you'd just look in there a moment," he said, "and come back and tell me what you see."

He was pointing towards a little bay made by the low boundary wall, the green floor of which was hidden from our view by the thick branches and a couple of interposing tombs, huge, coffer-shaped, and shut within rails. His voice sounded odd; there was a "plunging" look in his eyes, to use a gambler's phrase. I stared at him a moment, followed the direction of his hand; then, without a word, stooped under the heavy, brushing boughs, passed round the great tombs, and came upon a solitary grave.

It lay there quite alone in the hidden bay—a strange thing, fantastic and gruesome. There was no headstone, but a bevelled marble curb, without name or epitaph, enclosed a gravelled space from which projected two hands. They were of white marble, very faintly touched with green, and conveyed in that still, lonely spot a most curious sense of reality, as if actually thrust up, deathly and alluring, from the grave beneath. The impression grew upon me as I looked, until I could have thought they moved stealthily, consciously, turning in the soil as if to greet me. It was absurd, but— I turned and went rather hastily back to Heriot.

"All right. I see they are there still," he said; and that was all. Without another word we left the place and, remounting, continued our way.

Miles from the spot, lying on a sunny downside, with the sheep about us in hundreds cropping the hot grass, he told me the story:

"She and her husband were living in the town at the time of my first visit there, when I was a child of seven. They were known to Aunt Caddie, who disliked the woman. I did not dislike her at all, because, when we met, she made a favourite of me. She was a little pretty thing, frivolous and shallow; but truly, I know now, with an abominable side to her. She was inordinately vain of her hands; and indeed they were the loveliest things, softer and shapelier than a child's. She used to have them photographed, in fifty different positions; and once they were exquisitely done in marble by a sculptor, a friend of hers. Yes, those were the ones you saw. But they were cruel little hands, for all their beauty. There was something wicked and unclean about the way in which she regarded them.

"She died while I was there, and she was commemorated by her own explicit desire after the fashion you saw. The marble hands were to be her sole epitaph, more eloquent than letters. They should preserve her name and the tradition of her most exquisite feature to remoter ages than any crumbling inscription could reach. And so it was done.

"That fancy was not popular with the parishioners, but it gave me no childish qualms. The hands were really beautifully modelled on the originals, and the originals had often caressed me. I was never afraid to go and look at them, sprouting like white celery from the ground.

"I left, and two years later was visiting Aunt Caddie a second time. In the course of conversation I learned that the husband of the woman had married again—a lady belonging to the place—and that the hands, only quite recently, had been removed. The new wife had objected to them—for some reason perhaps not difficult to understand—and they had been uprooted by the husband's order.

"I think I was a little sorry—the hands had always seemed somehow personal to me—and, on the first occasion that offered, I slipped away by myself to see how the grave looked without them. It was a close, lowering day, I remember, and the churchyard was very still. Directly, stooping under the branches, I saw the spot, I understood that Aunt Caddie had spoken prematurely. The hands had not been removed so far, but were extended in their old place and attitude, looking as if held out to welcome me. I was glad; and I ran and knelt, and put my own hands down to touch them. They were soft and cold like dead meat, and they closed caressingly about mine, as if inviting me to pull—*to pull.*

"I don't know what happened afterwards. Perhaps I had been sickening all the time for the fever which overtook me. There was a period of horror, and blankness—of crawling, worm-threaded immurements and heaving bones—and then at last the blessed daylight."

Heriot stopped, and sat plucking at the crisp pasture.

"I never learned," he said suddenly, "what other experiences synchronised with mine. But the place somehow got an uncanny reputation, and the marble hands were put back. Imagination, to be sure, can play strange tricks with one."

THE MASK
(1915)

"Le masque tombe, l'homme reste."

There are mental modes as there are sartorial, and, commercially, the successful publisher is like the successful tailor, a man who knows how timely to exploit the fashion. Is it for the moment realism, romance, the psychic, the analytic, the homely—he makes, with Rabelais, his soup according to his bread, and feeds the multitude, as it asks, either on turtle or pease-porridge.

It was on the crest of a big psychic wave that Hands and Cumberbatch launched their "Haunted Houses"—a commonplace but quite effective title. It was all projected and floated within the compass of a few months, and it proved a first success. The idea was, of course, authentic possessions, or manifestations, and the thing was to be done in convincing style, with photogravure illustrations. The letter-press was entrusted to Penn-Howard, and the camera business to an old college-friend of his selection, J. B. Lamont. The two worked in double harness, and collected between them more material than could be used. But the cream of it was in the book, though not that particular skimming I am here to present, and for whose suppression at the time there were reasons.

I knew Penn-Howard pretty intimately, and should not have thought him an ideal hand for the task. He was a younger son of Lord Staveley, and carried an Honourable to his name. A brilliant fellow, cool, practical, modern, with infinite humour and aplomb, he would yet to my mind have lacked the first essential of an evangelist, a faith in the gospel he preached. He did not, in short, believe in spooks, and his dealings with the supernatural must all have been in the nature of an urbane Pyrrhonism. But he was a fine, imaginative writer, who could raise terrors he did not feel; and that, no doubt, explained in part his publishers' choice. What chiefly influenced them, however, was unquestionably his social popularity; he was known and liked everywhere, and could count most countable people among his friends, actual or potential. Where he wanted to go he went, and where he went he was welcome—an invaluable factor in this somewhat delicate business of ghost-hunting. But fashion affects even spirits, and, when the supernatural is *en vogue*, doors long jealously shut upon family secrets will be found to open themselves in a quite wonderful way. Hence, the time and the man agreeing, the success of the book.

I met Penn-Howard at Lady Caroon's during the time he was collecting his material. There were a few other guests at Hawkesbury, among them, just arrived, a tall, serious young fellow called Howick. Mr. Howick, I understood, had lately succeeded, from a collateral branch, to the Howick estates in Hampshire. His sister was to have come with him, but had excused herself at the last moment—or rather, had been excused by him. She was indefinitely "ailing," it appeared, and unfit for society. He used the word, in my hearing, with a certain hard decisiveness, in which there seemed a hint of something painful. Others may have felt it too, for the subject of the absentee was at once and discreetly waived.

Hawkesbury has its ghost—a nebulous radiance with a face that floats before one in the gloom of corridors—and naturally at some time during the evening the talk turned upon visitations. Penn-Howard was very picturesque, but, to me, unconvincing on the subject. There was no feeling behind his imagination; and, when put to it, he admitted as much. Some one had complimented him on the gruesome originality of a story of his which had recently appeared in one of the sixpenny magazines, and, quite good-humouredly, he had repudiated the term.

"No mortal being," he said, "may claim originality for his productions. There are the three primary colours, blue, red and yellow, and the three dimensions, length, breadth and thickness. They are original; it would be original to make a fourth; only we can't do it. We can only exploit creation ready-made as we find it. Everything for us is comprised within those limits—even Lady Caroon's ghost. It is a question of selection and chemical affinities, that is all. There is no such thing here as a supernature."

He was cried out on for his heresy to his own art—for his confession of its soullessness.

"Soul," he contended at that, "is not wanted in art, nor is religion; but only the five unperturbed and explorative senses. Pan, I think, would have made the ideal artist."

I saw Howick, who was sitting silently apart, suddenly hug himself at these words, bending forward and stiffening his lips, as a man does who mutely traverses a sentiment he is too shy or too superior to discuss. I did not know which it was with him; but inclined to the latter. There was something bonily professorial in his aspect.

While we were talking Lamont came in. He had not appeared at dinner, and I had not yet seen him. He was a compact, stubby man, in astigmatic glasses, and very dark, with a cleft chin, and a resolute mouth under a moustache in keeping with his strong, thick eyebrows. He gave me somehow in the connection a feeling of much greater fitness than did Penn-Howard. There was no suggestion of the *esprit-fort* about him, and I got an idea that, though only the technical collaborator, the right atmosphere of the book, if and when it appeared, would be due more to him than to the other. He spoke little, but authoritatively; and I remember he told us that night some queer things about photography—such, for instance, as its mysterious relation to something in light-rays, which was not heat and was not light, and yet like light could reveal the hidden, as a mirror reveals to one the objects out of sight behind one's back. Thence, touching upon astral charts and composite portraits by the way, he came to his illustration, which was creepy enough.

He had once for some reason, it appeared, taken a post-mortem photograph. The man, the subject, had cut in life a considerable figure in the parliamentary world as an advanced advocate of social and moral reform, and had died in the odour of political sanctity. In securing the negative, circumstances had necessitated a long exposure; but accident had contrived a longer and a deadlier, in the double sense. The searchlight of the lens, being left concentrated an undue time on the lifeless face, had discovered things hitherto impenetrable and unguessed-at. The nature of the real horror had been drawn through the super-imposing veil, and the revelation of what had been existing all the time under the surface was not pleasant. The photograph had not appeared in the illustrated paper for which it was intended, and Lamont had destroyed the negative.

So he told us, in a forcible, economic way which was more effective than much verbal adornment; and again my attention was caught by Howick, who seemed dwelling upon the speaker's words with an expression quite arresting in its ungainly intensity. Later on I saw the two in earnest conversation together.

That was in October, and I left Hawkesbury on the following day. Full ten months passed before I saw Penn-Howard again; and then one hot evening towards dusk he walked into my chambers in Brick Court and asked for a cigarette.

He seemed distraught, withdrawn, like a man who, having something on his mind, was pondering an uncompromising way of relief from it. Quite undesignedly and inevitably I gave him his cue by asking how the book progressed. He heaved out a great, smoke-laden sigh at once, stirred, drew up and dropped his shoulders, and looked at the fiery point of his cigarette before replacing the butt between his lips.

"O, the book!" he said. "It's ready for the press, so far as I'm concerned."

"And Lamont?"

"Yes, and J. B."

He got up, paced the width of the room and back, and stood before me, alternately drawing at and withdrawing his cigarette.

"There's one thing that won't go into it," he said, his eyes suggesting a rather forced evasion of mine.

"O! What's that?"

Again, as if doubtful of himself, he turned to tramp out his restlessness or agitation; thought better of it, and sat resolutely down in a chair against the dark end of the bookcase.

"Would you care to know?" he said. "Truth is, I came to tell you—if I could; to ask your opinion on the thing. There's the comfort of the judicial brain about you: I can imagine, like a client, that simply to confide one's case to such is to feel relieved of a load of responsibility. It won't go into the book, I say; but I want it to go out of me. I'm too full of it for comfort."

"Of it? Of what?"

"What?" he said, as if in a sudden spasm of violence. "I wish to God you'd tell me."

He sat moodily silent for some minutes, and I did nothing to help him out. A hot, sour air came in by the open window, and the heavy red curtains shrank and dilated languidly in it, as if they were the lungs of the stifling room. Outside the dusty roar of the traffic went on unceasingly, with a noise like that of overhead machinery. I was feeling stale and tired, and wished, in the Rooseveltian phrase, that Penn-Howard would either get on or get out.

"It's a queer thing, isn't it," he said suddenly, with an obvious effort, "that of all the stuff collected for that book you were speaking of, the only authentic instance for which I can personally vouch is the only instance to be excluded? All the rest was on hearsay."

"Well, you surprise me," I said, quietly, after a pause. "Not because any authentic instance, about which I know nothing, is excluded, but because, by your own confession, there is one to exclude."

"I know what you mean, of course," he answered; and quoted: "'But, spite of all the criticising elves, those who would make us feel must feel themselves.' Quite right. I never really believed in supernatural influences. Do I now? That is what I want you to decide for me."

He laughed slightly; sighed again, and seemed rather to shrink into his dusky corner.

"I'm going to tell you at a run," he said. "Bear with me, like an angelic fellow. You remember that man Howick at Lady Caroon's?"

"Yes, quite well."

"It seemed, when he learnt our business, Lamont's and mine, that there was something he wished to tell us. He pitched upon J. B. as the more responsible partner; and I'm not sure he wasn't right."

"Nor am I."

"O! you aren't, are you? Well, Jemmy was my choice, anyhow, and for the sake of the qualities you think I lack. He has a way of getting behind things—always had, even at Oxford. Some men seem to know the trick by instinct. He is a very queer sort, and the featest with the camera of any one I've ever seen or heard of. It was for that reason I asked him to come—to get the ghostliest possible out of ghostly buildings and haunted rooms. You remember what he told us that night? I've seen some of his spirit photographs, though without feeling convinced. But his description of that dead face! My God! I thought at the time he was just improvising to suit the occasion; but—"

He stopped abruptly. There was something odd here. It was evident that, for an unknown reason, the thought of that time was not the thought of this. I detected an obvious emotion, quite strange to it, in Penn-Howard's voice. His face, from our positions and the dusk, was almost hidden from me. I made no comment; and thenceforth he spoke on uninterruptedly, while the room slowly darkened about us as we sat.

"Howick wanted us, at the end of our visit, to go with him to his house. Something was happening there, he said, for which he was unable to account. We could not, however, consent, owing to our engagements; but we undertook to include him sooner or later in our ghostly itinerary. He was obliged; but, being so put off, would give us no clue to the nature of the mystery which was disturbing him. As it turned out, we had no choice but to take Haggarts the very last on our list."

"That is the name of his place?"

"Yes. It sounds a bit thin and eerie, doesn't it? but in point of fact, I believe, Haggart is a local word for hawthorn. We went there last of all, and we went there intending to stay a night, and we stayed seven. It was a queer business; and I come to you fresh from it.

"The estate lies slap in the middle of Hampshire. To reach it you alight at a country station which might serve roughly on the map for the hub of the county wheel. The train slides from a tunnel into a ravine of chalk, deep and dazzling, and you have to get on a level with the top of that ravine; and there at once you find immeasurable silence and loneliness. Nothing in my home peregrinations has struck me more forcibly than the real insignificance of urban expansion in its relation to the country as a whole. Towns, however they grow and multiply, remain but inconsiderable freckles on that vast open countenance. Outside the City man's possible radius, and excepting the great manufacturing centres, two miles, one mile beyond the boundary of ninety-nine towns out of a hundred will find you in pastoral solitudes apparently limitless. Here, with Winchester lying but eight miles southward, it was so. From the top of the tunnel we had just penetrated came into view, first a wilderness of thorn-scattered downs, dipping steeply and ruggedly into the railway-cutting, then an endlessly extended panorama of wood and waste and field, seemingly houseless and hamletless, and broken only by the white scars of roads, mounting few and far like the crests of waves on a desert sea. Howick had sent a car to meet us, and we switch-backed on monotonously, by unrailed pastures, by woody bottoms, by old hedges grey with dust and draggled with straw. We saw the house long before we headed for it—a strange, ill-designed structure standing out by itself in the fields. It was an antique moat-house, disproportionately tall for its area, and its front flanked by a couple of brick towers, one squat, one lofty. One wound about the lanes to reach it, having it now at this side, now at that, now fairly at one's back, until suddenly it came into close view, a building far more grandiose and imposing than one had surmised. There was the ancient moat surrounding it, and much water channelling the flats about. But there was evidence too, at close quarters, of what one had not guessed—rich, quiet gardens, substantial outbuildings, and a general atmosphere of prosperity.

"An odd, remote place, but in itself distinctly attractive. And Howick did us well. You remember him? A tall stick of a fellow, without a laugh to his whole anatomy, and the hair gone from his temples at thirty; but with the grand manner in entertaining. We had some '47 port that night—a treat—one of a few remaining bottles laid down by his grand-uncle, Roger Howick, of whom more in a little. And everything was in mellow keeping—pictures, furniture, old crusted anecdote. Only our host was, for all his gracious unbending, somehow out of tone with his environments—in that connection of fruitiness, like the dry nodule on a juicy apple. Constitutionally reserved, I should think, circumstance at that time had drained him of the last capacity for spontaneity. The little fits of abstraction and the wincing starts from them; the forced conversation; the atmosphere of brooding trouble felt through his most hospitable efforts—all pointed to a state of mind which he could neither conceal nor as yet indulge. Often I detected him looking furtively at J. B., often, still more secretively, at his sister, who was the only other one present at the dinner-table."

For a moment Penn-Howard ceased speaking; and I heard him shift his position, as if suddenly cramped, and slightly clear his throat.

"I mention her now for the first time," he went on presently. "She came in after we were seated, and there was the briefest formal introduction, of which she took no notice. She was a slender, unprepossessing woman—her brother's senior by some ten years, I judged—with a strange, unnatural complexion, rather long, pale eyes in red rims, and a sullen manner. Responding only after the curtest fashion to any commonplaces addressed to her, she left us, much to my relief, before dessert, and we saw her no more that evening.

"'Unfit for society'? Most assuredly she was. I remembered her brother's words spoken ten months before, and concluded that nothing had occurred since then to qualify his verdict. A most disagreeable person; unless, perhaps—

"It came to me all at once: was she connected with the mystery, or the mystery with her? A ghost seer, perhaps—neurotic—a victim to hallucinations? Well, Howick had not spoken so far, and it was no good speculating. I turned to the pious discussion of the '47.

"After dinner we went into the gardens where, the night being hot and still, we lingered until the stars came out. During the whole time Howick spoke no word of our mission; but, about the hour the household turned in, he took us back to the hall—a spacious, panelled lounge between the towers—where we settled for a pipe and nightcap. And there silence, like a ghostly overture to the impending, entered our brains and we sat, as it were, listening to it.

"Presently Howick got up. The strained look on his face was succeeded all at once by a sort of sombre light, odd and revealing. All sound in the house had long since ceased.

"'I want you to come with me,' he said quietly.

"We rose at once; and he went before, but a few paces, and opened a door.

"'Yes, here,' he said, in answer to a look of J. B.'s, 'quite close, quite domestic; no bogey of rat-infested corridors or tumble-down attics—no bogey at all, perhaps. It lies under the east tower, this room. When we first came here I thought to make it my study.'

"He seemed to me then, and always, like a man whose strait concepts of decency had suffered some startling offence, as it might be with one into whose perfectly-planned tenement had crept the insidious poison of sewer-gas. Sliding his hand along the wall, he switched on the electric light ('Haggarts' had its own power station), and the room leapt into being. We entered, I leading a little. You must remember I was by then a hardened witch-finder, and inured to atmospheres concocted of the imagination.

"It was not a large room, and it was quite comfortable. There was a heavily-clothed table in the middle, a few brass-nailed, leather-backed and seated Jacobean chairs, a high white Adams mantelpiece surmounted by a portrait, a full Chippendale bookcase to either side of it, and on the walls three or four pictures, including a second portrait, of a woman, half-length in an oval frame, which hung opposite the other.

"'Miss Howick, I see,' I murmured, turning with a nod to our host. He heard me, as his eyes denoted: but he gave no answer. And then the portrait over the mantelpiece drew my attention. It was in a very poor style of art; yet somehow, one felt, crudely truthful in an amateurish way. There is a class of peripatetic painters, a sort of pedlars in portraiture among country folk, which, having a gift for likenesses, often succeeds photographically in delineating what a higher art inclines to idealise—the obvious in character. Such an one, I concluded, had worked here, painting just what he saw, and only too faithfully. For the obvious was not pleasant—a dark, pitiless face, with a brutal underlip and challenging green eyes, that seemed for ever fixed on the face on the wall opposite. It was that of a middle-aged man, lean and thin-haired, and must have dated, by the cut of its black, brass-buttoned coat, from the late Georgian era.

"I turned again questioningly to Howick. This time he enlightened me. 'Roger Howick,' he said, 'my great-uncle. It is said he painted that himself, looking in the glass. He had a small gift. Most of the pictures in this room are by him.'

"Instinctively I glanced once more towards the oval frame, and thought: 'Most—but not that one.' Unmistakably it was a portrait of our host's sister—the odd complexion, the sullen, fixed expression, the very dress and coiffure, they were all the same. I wondered how the living subject could endure the thought of that day-long, night-long stare focused for ever on her painted presentment.

"And then silence ensued. We were all in the room, and not a word was spoken. I don't know how long it lasted; but suddenly Lamont addressed me, in a quick, sharp voice:

"'What's the matter, Penn-Howard?'

"The shock of the question took me like a blow out of sleep. I answered at once: 'Something's shut up here. Why don't you let it out?'

"Howick pushed us from the room, and closed the door. 'That's it,' he said, and that was all. I felt dazed and amazed. I wanted to explain, to protest. A most extraordinary sensation like suppressed tears kept me dumb. I felt humiliated to a degree, and inclined to ease all my conflict of emotions in hysterical laughter. Curse the thing now! It makes me go hot to think of it.

"Howick showed me up to my bedroom. 'We'll talk of it to-morrow,' he said, and he left me. I was glad to be alone, to get, after a few moments, resolute command of myself. I had a good night after all, and awoke, refreshed and sane, in the clear morning.

"I learned, when I came downstairs, that J. B. and our host were gone out together for an early stroll in the cool. Pending their return, I came to a resolution. I would go and face the room alone, in the bright daylight. Both my pride and my principles were at stake, and I owed the effort to myself. There was nothing to prevent me. I found the door unlocked, and I went in.

"There was some sunlight in the room, penetrating through a thickish shrubbery outside the two windows. I thought the place peculiarly quiet, with an atmosphere of suspense in it which suggested the inaudible whisperings of some infernal inquisition. Nothing was watching me: the green eyes of the man were fixed eternally on the face opposite; and yet I was being watched by everything. It was indescribable, maddening. Determined not to succumb to what I still insisted to myself was a mere trick of the nerves, I walked manfully up to the oval portrait to examine it at close hand. A name and date near the lower margin caught my eye—T. Lawrence, 1828. I fairly gasped, reading it. A 'Lawrence,' and of that remoteness? Then it was not our host's sister! I turned sharply, hearing light breathing—and there she was behind me.

"'What are you doing here?' she said, in a small, cold voice. 'Don't you know it is my room?'

"How can I convey the impression she made upon me by daylight? I can think only of one fantastic image to describe her complexion—the hands of a young laundress, puffed and mottled and mealily wrinkled after many hours' work at the tub. So in this face was somehow spoilt and slandered youth, subdued, like the dyer's hand, to 'what it worked in.' And yet it was the face of the portrait, even to the dusty gold of the hair.

"I made some lame apology. She stamped her foot to end it and dismiss me. But as I passed her to go, she spoke again: 'You will never find it. It is only faith that can move such mountains.'

"I encountered J. B. in the morning-room, and we breakfasted alone together. Howick did not appear—purposely, I think. I felt somehow depressed and uneasy, but resolved to hold fast to myself without too many words. Once I enlightened Lamont: 'That portrait,' I said, 'is not of Howick's sister.' J. B. lifted his eyebrows. 'O!' said he, 'you have been paying it a morning visit, have you? No, it is a portrait of Maud Howick, daughter to Roger, the man who hangs opposite her.' It was my turn to stare. 'Howick has been giving you his family history?' I asked. J. B. did not answer for a minute; then he said: 'I hope you won't take it in bad part, Penn-Howard; but—yes, he has been talking to me. I know, I think, all there is to know.' I had some right to be offended; and he admitted it. 'Howick would put it to me,' he said. 'He was struck, it seemed, by something I said that night at Lady Caroon's; and he thinks you at heart a polite sceptic' 'Well,' I said, 'have you solved the mystery, whatever it is?' He answered no, but that he had a theory; and asked me if I had formed any. 'Not a ghost of one,' I replied; 'and so Howick was certainly right in confiding first in you—first and last, indeed, if I am to be kept in the dark.' 'On the contrary,' said J. B.; 'I am going to repeat every word of Howick's story to you—only in a quiet place.'

"We found one presently, out in the fields in the shadow of a ruined byre. It stood up bare and lonely, like a tattered baldachin, and far away under the stoop of its roof we could see the walls of the moat-house rising lean and brown into a cloudless sky. Lamont began his narration with a question: 'How old would you suppose this Miss Ruth Howick, the sister, to be?' I was about to answer promptly, recalled my perplexity, and hesitated. 'Tell me, without more ado,' I responded. 'Nineteen,' he said, and shut his lips like a trap. Something caught at me, and I at myself. 'Go on,' I said;

'anything after that.' And J. B. responded, speaking in his abrupt, incisive way:

"'This James Howick came into his own here some year and a-half ago. There were only himself and his sister—to whom he was and is devoted—the sole survivors of a once considerable family. Their father, Gilbert Howick,—son of Paul, who was younger brother to the Roger of the portrait—married one Margaret (a beautiful ward of Paul's, and brought up by him as a member of his own family) about whose origin attached some mystery, which was only made clear to her husband on the occasion of their marriage. Margaret, in brief, was then revealed to Gilbert for his own first-cousin once removed, being the natural daughter of his cousin Maud, one of the two children of Roger. I know nothing about the liaison which necessitated this explanation, nor do we need to know. Its results are what concern us. Roger, it is certain, took his daughter's dereliction in a truly devilish spirit. He was an evil, dark man, it was said, pledged to the world and its pride, and once a notorious liver. There is none so extreme in fanaticism as a convert from irreligion; none so damnably righteous as a rake reformed. Having committed the fruits of her sin to the merciful custody of his younger brother—a very different soul, of a humane and pious disposition—Roger turned his attention to the moral and physical ruin of the sinner. He swore that she should forfeit the youth she had abused; and he was as good as his word. No one knows how it happened; no one knows what passed in that dark and haunted house. But Maud grew old in youth. She had been spoiled and petted for her beauty; now the spirit broke in her, and she seemed to shrink and disappear behind the wrinkled, crumbling veil of what had been—like a snake, Penn-Howard, that struggles and cannot cast its dead skin. She grew old in youth. That portrait of her was painted when she was nineteen.'

"I cried out. 'It was impossible!' 'It would seem so,' said Lamont. 'By what infernal arts he held her to his will—holds her now—it is sickening to conjecture.' I turned to look at him. 'Holds her now!' I repeated. 'Then you mean—' 'Yes,' he said; 'it is her imprisoned youth that is for ever trying to escape, to emerge, like the snake, from its dead self. That is the secret of the room. At least, such is my theory.'

"I sat as in a dream, awed by, yet struggling to reject, a conclusion so fantastic. 'Well, grant your theory,' I said at length, with a deep breath; 'how does it affect this woman—or girl—this Ruth?'

"'Think,' said Lamont. 'She is actually that erring child's granddaughter. It seems wonderfully pitiful to me. Her own mother died in that house, during a visit, in giving birth to her. At the time, the son, Roger's son, was master of Haggarts. He was a poor-witted creature, Howick tells me; but he lived, as the imbecile often will, to a ripe old age. Ruth was born prematurely. Her mother, it was said, fell under the cursed influence of the place, and withered in her prime. Maud herself, according to the story, had already died in that very room—was found dead there, little more than a child still in years, a poor, worn ghost of womanhood in seeming. Since then, the room has always had an evil reputation—with what justice Howick never knew or regarded, until the death of his uncle put him, a year and a-half ago, in possession of the place.'

"'But this Ruth—'

"'It came upon her, it seems, gradually at first, then more rapidly. She lost her health and vivacity; she was for ever haunting the room. When we first met Howick, she was already horribly changed. Ten months have passed since then. He has tried to hide it from the world; has made practically a hermit of himself. The servants of that date have been changed for others, and changed again. She feels, it must be supposed, what we felt—a ceaseless anguish to release something—nothing—a mere pent shadow of horror. And more than that: the sin of the mother is being visited on the child of the child—and through the same diabolical agency.'

"Lamont paused a moment, staring before him, and knotting his fingers together till they cracked. 'Penn-Howard,' he said, 'I believe—I do believe, on my soul, that the secret, whatever it is, lies at the hands of that devil portrait.'

"'Then why, in God's name, not remove and burn the thing?'

"'He has offered to. It had a dreadful effect upon her. She cried that so the clue would be lost for ever. And so it affects her to be excluded from the room. He has had to give it all up as hopeless.'

"He rose, and I rose with him, not in truth convinced, but oddly agitated.

"'Well,' I said, 'what do you propose doing?'

"He seemed deep in thought, and did not answer me. At the house door we parted. Entering alone, I met Howick in the hall. He looked at me searchingly in his lank, haggard way, then suddenly took my hand. 'You know?' he said. 'He has told you? Mr. Penn-Howard, she was such a bright and pretty child.' I saw tears in his eyes, and understood him better from that moment.

"Lamont was absent all day, and returned late from a prolonged tramp over the hills. The poignant subject was tacitly shelved that night, and we went to bed early.

"The next morning, after breakfast, J. B. turned upon our host. 'I want,' he said, 'that room to myself, possibly for the whole morning, possibly for longer. Can you secure it to me?' Howick nodded. I could detect in his eyes some faint reflection of the strong spirit which faced him. Somehow one never despairs in J. B.'s presence. 'I will say you are looking for it,' he said. 'She will not disturb you then.' 'There is a closet,' said Lamont, 'in my bedroom which will do very well for a dark room.'

"He disappeared soon after with his camera. It was his business, and I seldom disturbed him at it. We left him alone, and tried to forget him, though I could see all the morning that Howick was in a state of painful nervous tension. Not till after lunch did we hear or see anything of my colleague, and then he came in, descending from his improvised dark room. He held a negative in his hand, and he shut the door behind him like a man who had something of moment to reveal. 'Mr. Howick,' he said, straight out and at once, 'I am going to ask you to let me destroy that portrait of your great-uncle.'

"The words took us like a smack; and, as we stood gaping, J. B. held out his negative. 'Look at this,' he said, and beckoning us to the window, let the light slant upon the thing so as to disclose its subject. 'The secret stands revealed, does it not?' said he, quiet and low. 'A long, a very long exposure, and the devil is betrayed. O, a wonderful detective is the camera.'

"I heard Howick breathing fast over my shoulder. For myself, I was as much perplexed as astonished. 'It is the portrait,' I muttered, 'and yet it is not. There is the ghost of something revealing itself through it.' 'Exactly,' said J. B. drily—and went and put the negative behind the clock on the mantel-piece. 'Well, shall we do it?' he asked, turning to our host. Howick's face was ghastly. He could hardly get out the words, 'In God's name, do what you will! Better to dare and end it all than live on like this.' J. B. stood looking at him earnestly. 'No,' he said. 'You go to her. Penn-Howard and I will manage the business.'

"We left him, and went to the room and locked ourselves in. I confess my blood was tingling. So shut in with it, the unspeakable atmosphere of that place seemed to intensify to a degree quite infernal. I seemed to realise in it a battle of two wills, Lamont's and another's. My friend's face was a little pale; but the set of its every feature spoke of an inexorable purpose. As we handled the portrait to lower it, it fell heavily and unaccountably forward, an edge of the massive frame just missing J. B.'s skull by an inch. 'That miscarriage does for you, my friend,' he said, showing his teeth a little, like a dog. Portrait and frame lay apart on the floor; the shock had disunited them. Lamont knelt, and went over the former unflinchingly. The green eyes, caught from their age-long inquisition of the face on the wall opposite, seemed to glare up into his in hate and fury. 'Get out your knife!' I cried irresistibly, 'and slash the cursed thing to pieces.' 'No,' he answered; 'that is not at all my purpose.'

"What was his purpose? I knew in a moment. He fetched out his knife indeed, and, hunting over the surface of the thing, found a blister in the paint, cut into it, seized an edge between thumb and finger, and, flaying away a long strip, uttered a loud, jubilant exclamation. 'Look at this, Penn-Howard.' I bent over—and then I understood in a flash. It was but a strip exposed; but it was like a chink of dazzling daylight let through. There was another portrait painted underneath.

"Artists tell me that when one oil-painting is superimposed on another within a few years of the production of the first, only exceptional circumstances can render their successful separation possible. I know nothing about the technical difficulties; I know only that in this case we were able to remove the over-lying skin, strip by strip, almost without a hitch, until the whole of the upper portrait lay in flakes of rubbish upon the floor—to be delivered within a few minutes to consuming fire. And the thing revealed! I cannot describe the beauty of that vision, bursting into flower out of its age-long Cimmerian darkness. It was the personification of youth—a young girl (she might have been sixteen), laughing and lovely, the most wilful, bewitching face you could imagine—Maud Howick."

Once more Penn-Howard fell silent. The room by now was dark; his figure was indistinguishable, and his voice, when he spoke again, seemed a shadow borne out of the shadows:

"While we gazed, fascinated, there came a knock on the door. It was Howick. His face was transfigured—his eyes glowed. 'She has fallen asleep,' he said; 'and that is not all. My God, what has happened?' We took him in and showed him the portrait. He broke down before it. 'The little grandmother!' he said, 'the poor, erring child! And it was of that, and by that damnable method, that that fiend incarnate robbed her! To imprison her youth within his wicked soul, drawn by him out of the mirror to stand for ever at sentry over her lest she escape. And she pined and withered in that hideous bondage, until he could show her, in that other, what his hate had wrought of her. But she is free at last—her soul is free to fly for ever this dark house of its captivity.'

"J. B. looked at him searchingly. 'And your sister?' he said. Howick did not answer; but he beckoned us to follow him, and he led us into the drawing-room where she lay. Fast in dreamless slumber as the sleeping beauty. But the change! God in heaven; she was already a child again!"

The speaker halted for the last time. It was minutes before he took up the tale, in a constrained and hesitating way:

"I saw all this, I tell you—saw it with these eyes. We stayed there yet a week longer; and I left her in the end a radiant, laughing child, a joyous, captivating little soul, who remembered, or seemed to remember, nothing of the fearful months preceding. And yet, now I am away, I doubt. It is the curse of my disposition. What, for instance, if one were to yield her one's soul and discover, too late, that one had succumbed to some unreal glamour, to the arts of a veritable and most feminine Lamia. I believe it is not so; I know it is not so—and yet, the incredible—"

His voice died out. I saw how it was, and answered, I am afraid, brutally:

"You aren't really in love with her, of course. That is as clear as print."

He rose at once. "That decides it," he said. "I shall go back and ask her to be my wife."

But he did not do so. Two days later I met him in the street. His manner was quite breezy and insouciant. "O, by the by!" he said, in a break of our conversation, "did I tell you that I had heard from J . B .? He and Miss Howick are engaged."

THE PÉTROLEUSE
(1915)

The house stood alone, and quite isolated, on the edge of a piece of waste suburban ground. Magnified by the dark, it was yet of proportions obviously sufficient to supply a Latimer-Ridley blaze, enough, to a fanatic imagination, to flood all England with the fierceness of its illumination. The flat-chested, hectic-cheeked young woman looking up at it felt herself already an acclaimed heroine and, in some fantastic way, martyr.

The gaining an entrance was a laughably easy matter—just the lifting of a latch in a side-door, and a cautious step within. The house was simply deserted, simply unoccupied—a remote and lifeless shell. It might be unletable; it might be potentially profitable; it might again represent a chief asset in the income of a sympathiser with the cause. It was convenient, that was the main point. The incendiary paused, breathing hurriedly, to deliver a handbag she carried of its compressed load of newspapers, fire-lighters, turpentine and a small dark lantern. Then, detaching from the pile, for subsequent use, a copy or two of the periodical which voiced her views, she stealthily kindled the lantern, and prepared, as stealthily, to examine her ground.

It gave her a little thrill and shock at the outset to discover that the place was not so wholly unfurnished as she had been inclined to suppose. There were signs of some late occupation, not substantial or many, but enough to imply an abandonment only as yet provisional. A rickety kitchen table, one or two drunken chairs, a torn jack-towel behind the door—these and other discarded litter confessed themselves leeringly to the little misty eye of the lantern. But a hasty half scrutiny revealing the things all thick with dust, the woman turned from them, reassured, to pursue her purpose and design.

Ordinarily, the mere thought of a solitary night-vigil in an empty house would have been enough to fill her with unspeakable terrors; now the ecstasy of the exaltée had uplifted her above all such temporal weaknesses. Going forward, she saw the bare hall, the white slope of the carpetless stairs and, as if irresistibly impelled, mounted to the room above.

Here, also, were some attenuated relics of occupation—tattered window curtains, a half-disembowelled easy chair spilling flock, a broken packing-case or two. Congratulating Providence on its foresight, the intruder began at once and hastily to dispose her materials in the most effective places. She went round the large room by the wall, taking advantage of each combustible object. When all was prepared she would re-make the circuit, firing each little heap in its turn.

Suddenly she started, and her skin crept from crown to heel. What was that in the room with her? She flashed the lantern-light from wall to wall—over the floor—even over the ceiling. No sight, no sound whatever: only the constriction and expansion of dark palpitating emptiness. With a gasp, which spoke her half-way already on the road to collapse, she hurried to make an end of her task. Lantern and matches in hand, she crouched to ignite the first heap of inflammable rubbish. It was gone.

It was gone; the second was gone—the third—the fourth. More noiselessly than she had disposed them, each had been removed behind her back as she passed on, and carried—whither? She reeled; then made like a mad woman for the door, found it, and began to descend the stairs. And instantly she understood. The soaked paper, the firelighters had been transferred by unseen hands to places more cunningly meet than hers to produce a wholesale conflagration. Fire a house from the ground floor if you would wholly consume it; it is half measures to start half-way. And so the little heaps, like peering demons, winked up at her from hall wainscot, and partition corner, and stair-foot. Yes, the deadliest there. It seemed to smoke already, emitting a phosphorescent light, which was horribly contorted. The woman sat down upon the stairs because her knees would no longer support her. But she was up again in a moment, with a screech. For in that moment the smoke had burst like a shell, and the whole well of the house was a storm of spouting flame. She turned and fled before it—up, up, while it followed in crackling breakers. Was ever fire so insistent and so hellish! Up, up, until only the unattainable skylight stood between her and freedom. The fire was coming in at the door: a tunnel of blackness seemed to open before her, and she fell into it—and into instant deep unconsciousness.

With the growth of morning came a little crowd about the place. Two policemen were engaged within the walls of a long-blackened ruin, endeavouring to persuade thence a raving white-faced woman, who persisted in frantically defying their efforts.

"Whoth that?" asked a curious, thick-nosed newcomer, with a pack on his back.

"One of them crazy militants," was the answer. "She's been caught a trying to set fire to a burnt-out house."

"Burned-out, thay?"

"This three year and more, old man. Arson, it was supposed; and him that did it caught in the trap he'd set for the insurance companies—caught and burnt himself, before he could make his escape. A bloomin' ass, I call 'im!"

The Jew stared, and went into a noiseless chuckle.

"Thertainly, thir," he said. "The man must have been a fool. But thith woman must be a greater, thince there is no policy at all in question?"

"That's just it," answered the other; "though they call it one, poor misguided creeturs. And here it is nat'rally ended in the madness it promised."

THE QUEER PICTURE
(1915)

It was standing with its face to the wall in a dark corner of the dingy old shop in Beak Street, whose miscellaneous litter had peered at me through a window so dirty as to make its owner appear rather to wish to baffle custom than to court it. Nor in that respect was its owner's manner reassuring. His eyes peered dimly out of an unwashed face, like the pale blue oriental saucers through the window. He seemed to regard me with indifference and a little weariness, as if the profit of chaffering were hardly worth its trouble. "O, yes!" he said, in a weak, hoarse voice, to my appreciations of this or that, as I edged my way through the labyrinth of Chippendale chairs, bureaux, coffin-stools, and gate-legged tables piled with Staffordshire figures, brass door-knockers, candlesticks, and "genuine antiques" of every sort, description and plausibility.

A little nettled by the creature's apathy, I stooped, somewhat truculently, and turned the picture round for myself. It showed a landscape, pretty dark and mellow in tone, of, I fancied, the Crome or Nasmyth period. A woodland road, receding from the middle foreground of the canvas, presently took a curve round some palings to the left, and disappeared into greenery. Prominent over the near palings towered a huge oak; on the other side was a close medley of foliage gradually dimming into blue distances. The whole was feelingly painted and composed, the large oak tree, quite superbly rendered, forming its predominant feature. It all only suffered slightly to my mind as a composition from the white emptiness of the road and the absence of figures. I said so to the dealer. "O yes!" he answered, with a dry cough, and I shrugged my shoulders.

I have had one or two "finds" in my time—enough to stimulate my adventurous nerve. This thing seemed to me good: there was power in it, and knowledge. The time was evidently near twilight, still and darkling—a lonely, solemn place. The atmosphere was unmistakably suggested. Its canvas measurement was some 34 by 28 inches, and it possessed a frame, a little dingy and battered, but of the right sort. "Whom is it by?" I said.

The dealer made as if to bend, cleared his thin old throat and stood up again. "It's unsigned," he said.

"But don't you know?"

"If you were to ask me," he answered, "I should say—no more than that, mind you—that it was Urquhart's work." Then, in response to my mute inquiry, "He was a follower of John Constable, you know."

I didn't know; I knew nothing about the man; but, whoever he was, his capacity was plain. I decided to risk it. "Well, how much?" I said.

"Twenty pounds," said the dealer.

As a matter of principle I protested— "Unsigned; of disputable origin; preposterous!" "O yes!" he said, in his indifferent way. "Twenty pounds is the price. It's a greatly admired piece. If you change your mind, I will take it back any time within a week, less ten per cent."

That seemed a fair offer, and I ended by carrying the picture home with me in a cab. Alone, I cleared the mantelpiece of my sitting-room, and stood the treasure up on it. I thought it distinctly an admirable piece of work, and so far rejoiced in my bargain. It seemed to reflect the very spirit of the twilight which was even now creeping over my room, to assimilate and conform to it. As I gazed I grew penetrated, possessed, by what I gazed on. I was on the wide, white road, standing or crouching somewhere down here out of the picture, and staring into its diminishing distances. The great oak was motionlessly alive; there seemed "a listening fear in its regard." An expectation, an indescribable awe, held me amazedly entranced. And then my breath caught in a quick gasp. Round by the bend of the road, far away, there occurred a minute stirring, and something came into the picture that was not there before. The thing came on, increasing in regular progression as it advanced—and it was the figure of a young man, in a bygone costume, swinging airily towards me. I sat petrified, dumb-stricken; and all in an instant there arose between me and the illusion, blotting it out, a vague, shadowy shape. That receded quickly, shrinking as it withdrew, until it also was the figure of a man going away from me along the road to meet the other. The two encountered, and had passed, when the second wheeled suddenly in his tracks, and struck the first on the neck, so that the young man fell into the road. I saw something—a running stain of red, and simultaneously broke, with a cry, from my stupefaction and, leaping to the mantelpiece, turned the horror with its face to the wall. As I did so I saw that the canvas was empty of figures.

The old dealer made no demur whatever about my returning the picture. "It always comes back," he said impassively, as he paid me in cash eighteen pounds out of the twenty I had given for it. "It stands me in well, you see, as an investment. It's a fine work. I dare say you'll be the dozenth or more who's been struck by it, and carried it away with the same result. Twilight's the time, they say."

"Don't you know it is?" I responded warmly. "Haven't you seen it yourself?"

"No," he said, with a thin cough, "no." (He had returned the picture to its former place and position.) "I don't bother to look. It wouldn't be policy, and it wouldn't be fair, you know, for me to sell it if I had. I'm not bound to go upon hearsay; and it doesn't trouble me where it stands."

"But"—I turned on my heel indignantly, and came back— "you said it was an Urquhart."

"On its intrinsic evidences," he responded; "not in the least because it happens that Urquhart was hanged for the murder of his wife's paramour on a country road he was engaged in painting at the time. He stuck him in the neck with a palette-knife. That may have been the very picture—or it may not—before the figures were filled in. Urquhart generally used sheep and countrymen. But all that's no concern of mine. I say it's an Urquhart because of the style. No one but him, in my opinion, could have painted that oak."

THE SHADOW-DANCE
(1915)

"Yes, it was a rum start," said the modish young man.

He was a modern version of the crutch and toothpick genus, a derivative from the "Gaiety boy" of the Nellie Farren epoch, very spotless, very superior, very—fundamentally and combatively—simple. I don't know how he had found his way into Carleon's rooms and our company, but Carleon had a liking for odd characters. He was a collector, as it were, of human pottery, and to the collector, as we know, primitive examples are of especial interest.

The bait in this instance, I think, had been Bridge, which, since some formal "Ducdame" must serve for calling fools into a circle, was our common pretext for assembling for an orgy of talk. We had played, however, for insignificant stakes and, on the whole, irreverently as regarded the sanctity of the game; and the young man was palpably bored. He thought us, without question, outsiders, and not altogether good form; and it was even a relief to him when the desultory play languished, and conversation became general in its place.

Somebody—I don't remember on what provocation—had referred to the now historic affair of the Hungarian Ballet, which, the rage in London for a season, had voluntarily closed its own career a week before the date advertised for its termination; and the modish young man, it appeared, was the only one of us all who had happened to be present in the theatre on the occasion of the final performance. He told us so; and added that "it was a rum start."

"The abrupt finish was due, of course," said Carleon, bending forward, hectic, bright-eyed, and hugging himself, as was his wont, "to Kaunitz's death. She was the bright particular 'draw.' It would have been nothing without her. Besides, there was the tragedy. What was the 'rum start'? Tell us."

"The way it ended that night," said the young man. He was a little abashed by the sudden concentration of interest on himself; but carried it off with sang-froid. Only a slight flush of pink on his youthful cheek, as he flicked the ash from his cigarette with the delicate little finger of the hand that held it, confessed to a certain uneasy self-consciousness.

"I have heard something about it," said Carleon. "Give us your version."

"I'm no hand at describing things," responded the young man, committed and at bay; "never wrote a line of description in my life, nor wanted to. It was the Shadow-Dance, you know—the last thing on the programme. I dare say some of you have seen Kaunitz in it."

One or two of us had. It was incomparably the most beautiful, the most mystic, idyll achieved by even that superlative dancer; a fantasia of moonlight, supported by an ethereal, only half-revealed, shimmer of attendant sylphids.

"Yes," said Carleon eagerly.

"Well, you know," said the young man, "there is a sort of dance first, in and out of the shadows, a mysterious, gossamery kind of business, with nobody made out exactly, and the moon slowly rising behind the trees. And then, suddenly, the moon reaches a gap in the branches, and—and it's full moon, don't you know, a regular white blaze of it, and all the shapes have vanished; only you sort of guess them, get a hint of their arms and faces hiding behind the leaves and under the shrubs and things. And that was the time when Kaunitz ought to have come on."

"Didn't she come on?"

"Not at first; not when she ought to. There was a devil of a pause, and you could see something was wrong. And after a bit there was a sort of rustle in the house, and people began to cough; and the music slipped round to the beginning again; and they danced it all over a second time, until it came to the full moonlight—and there she was this time all right—how, I don't know, for I hadn't seen her enter."

"How did she dance—when she did appear?"

The young man blew the ash from his cigarette. "Oh, I don't know!" he said.

"You must know. Wasn't it something quite out of the common? You called it a rum start, you remember."

"Well, if you insist upon it, it was—the most extraordinary thing I ever witnessed—more like what they describe the Pepper's Ghost business than anything else I can think. She was here, there, anywhere; seemingly independent of what d'ye call—gravitation, you know; she seemed to jump and hang in the air before she came down. And there was another thing. The idea was to dance to her own shadow, you see—follow it, run away from it, flirt with it—and it was the business of the moon, or the limelight man, to keep the shadow going."

"Well?"

"Well, there was no shadow—not a sign of one."

"That may have been the limelight man's fault."

"Very likely; but I don't think so. There was something odd about it all; and most in the way she went."

"How was that?"

"Why, she just gave a spring, and was gone." Carleon sank back, with a sigh as if of repletion, and sat softly cracking his fingers together.

"Didn't you notice anything strange about the house, the audience?" he said— "people crying out; girls crouching and hiding their faces, for instance?"

"Perhaps, now I think of it," answered the modish youth. "I noticed, anyhow, that the curtain came down with a bang, and that there seemed a sort of general flurry and stampede of things, both behind it and on our side."

"Well, as to that, it is a fact, though you may not know it, that after that night the company absolutely refused to complete its engagement on any terms."

"I dare say. They had lost Kaunitz."

"To be sure they had. She was already lying dead in her dressing-room when the Shadow-Dance began."

"Not when it began?"

"So, anyhow, it was whispered."

"I say," said the young man, looking rather white; "I'm not going to believe that, you know."

THE THING IN THE FOREST
(1915)

Into the snow-locked forests of Upper Hungary steal wolves in winter; but there is a footfall worse than theirs to knock upon the heart of the lonely traveller.

One December evening Elspet, the young, newly wedded wife of the woodman Stefan, came hurrying over the lower slopes of the White Mountains from the town where she had been all day marketing. She carried a basket with provisions on her arm; her plump cheeks were like a couple of cold apples; her breath spoke short, but more from nervousness than exhaustion. It was nearing dusk, and she was glad to see the little lonely church in the hollow below, the hub, as it were, of many radiating paths through the trees, one of which was the road to her own warm cottage yet a half-mile away.

She paused a moment at the foot of the slope, undecided about entering the little chill, silent building and making her plea for protection to the great battered stone image of Our Lady of Succour which stood within by the confessional box; but the stillness and the growing darkness decided her, and she went on. A spark of fire glowing through the presbytery window seemed to repel rather than attract her, and she was glad when the convolutions of the path hid it from her sight. Being new to the district, she had seen very little of Father Ruhl as yet, and somehow the penetrating knowledge and burning eyes of the pastor made her feel uncomfortable.

The soft drift, the lane of tall, motionless pines, stretched on in a quiet like death. Somewhere the sun, like a dead fire, had fallen into opalescent embers faintly luminous: they were enough only to touch the shadows with a ghastlier pallor. It was so still that the light crunch in the snow of the girl's own footfalls trod on her heart like a desecration.

Suddenly there was something near her that had not been before. It had come like a shadow, without more sound or warning. It was here—there—behind her. She turned, in mortal panic, and saw a wolf. With a strangled cry and trembling limbs she strove to hurry on her way; and always she knew, though there was no whisper of pursuit, that the gliding shadow followed in her wake. Desperate in her terror, she stopped once more and faced it.

A wolf!—was it a wolf? O who could doubt it! Yet the wild expression in those famished eyes, so lost, so pitiful, so mingled of insatiable hunger and human need! Condemned, for its unspeakable sins, to take this form with sunset, and so howl and snuffle about the doors of men until the blessed day released it. A werewolf—not a wolf.

That terrific realization of the truth smote the girl as with a knife out of darkness: for an instant she came near fainting. And then a low moan broke into her heart and flooded it with pity. So lost, so infinitely hopeless. And so pitiful—yes, in spite of all, so pitiful. It had sinned, beyond any sinning that her innocence knew or her experience could gauge; but she was a woman, very blest, very happy, in her store of comforts and her surety of love. She knew that it was forbidden to succour these damned and nameless outcasts, to help or sympathize with them in any way.

But— There was good store of meat in her basket, and who need ever know or tell? With shaking hands she found and threw a sop to the desolate brute—then, turning, sped upon her way. But at home her secret sin stood up before her, and, interposing between her husband and herself, threw its shadow upon both their faces. What had she dared—what done? By her own act forfeited her birthright of innocence; by her own act placed herself in the power of the evil to which she had ministered. All that night she lay in shame and horror, and all the next day, until Stefan had come about his dinner and gone again, she moved in a dumb agony. Then, driven unendurably by the memory of his troubled, bewildered face, as twilight threatened she put on her cloak and went down to the little church in the hollow to confess her sin.

"Mother, forgive, and save me," she whispered, as she passed the statue. Now for a break from the story. Where do you think that this came from? Another site, that's where. Sorry if you find this annoying, but you might want to find a site that does the work instead of stealing someone else's work.

After ringing the bell for the confessor, she had not knelt long at the confessional box in the dim chapel, cold and empty as a waiting vault, when the chancel rail clicked, and the footsteps of Father Ruhl were heard rustling over the stones. He came, he took his seat behind the grating; and, with many sighs and falterings, Elspet avowed her guilt. And as, with bowed head, she ended, a strange sound answered her—it was like a little laugh, and yet not so much like a laugh as a snarl. With a shock as of death she raised her face. It was Father Ruhl who sat there—and yet it was not Father Ruhl. In that time of twilight his face was already changing, narrowing, becoming wolfish—the eyes rounded and the jaw slavered. She gasped, and shrunk back; and at that, barking and snapping at the grating, with a wicked look he dropped—and she heard him coming. Sheer horror lent her wings. With a scream she sprang to her feet and fled. Her cloak caught in something—there was a wrench and crash and, like a flood, oblivion overswept her.

It was the old deaf and near senile sacristan who found them lying there, the woman unhurt but insensible, the priest crushed out of life by the fall of the ancient statue, long tottering to its collapse. She recovered, for her part: for his, no one knows where he lies buried. But there were dark stories of a baying pack that night, and of an empty, bloodstained pavement when they came to seek for the body.

THE VAN ON THE ROAD
(1915)

Concanon had taken the train to Farnborough, on the South-Western main line, and thence walked to view the "House to Let." The house, according to the agents, had appeared the very thing to suit him. It was small, isolated, the rent was low, and there was a garden. Its reported solitude was what had most appealed to him. He had just completed a labour involving perpetual research and application, and his brain-exhaustion coveted an utter pastoral vacancy—for months, for years, for a lifetime if need be. As yet freedom and idleness filled him with only a dim rapture.

His direction soon took him off the highways into remote quietudes. Trees and fields were all about him; and then came a little village. It was a grave, sunless day, with only the tiniest breeze that blew in ghostly spasms, and danced in little eddies of dust before his feet, and in a moment was gone. Suddenly, at a half mile beyond the village in a flat country, he came upon a horseless furniture van standing in the middle of the road.

It struck him as odd, and no more. As he passed, he observed that the back doors were open, and that an oak chest of an antique pattern was slightly protruded through them. But no sign of men or cattle was visible anywhere.

He went on, assuming that, according to his directions, he must be very near his destination. Somehow his thoughts reverted to a story recently told him. It was of a deserted house, into which nobody could penetrate. So surely as one tried, some force, invisible, unaccountable, ejected him. Then once a scandalised and indignant mob had essayed to storm the place. They threw stones, they were prepared to fire on it; when suddenly there had appeared at a window a presence so hideous that the boldest screamed and fled. And thenceforth the house was accursed and abandoned.

Concanon was wondering what had recalled the weird thing to his mind, when he came upon a little lane leading off the road; and at the end was the House to Let. He would have known it at once from the particulars given him, without the advertising board to confirm. Alert on the instant, he turned down the lane, and, approaching, saw at once the explanation of the van. The tenants were in actual process of leaving.

He was surprised, as he had certainly understood from the agent that the house was empty; yet here were evidences enough of active removal. Straw strewed the short drive; articles of furniture, placed ready for porterage, stood about the steps.

Yet still not a living soul appeared to attest the fact.

Lonely of the loneliest the house undoubtedly appeared; yet, in its position, its embowered quiet, its rusted antiquity, restfully potential of promise. Concanon went on and entered the hall, assuring himself, he knew not why, that here anyhow was no repelling malignity. Rather some emotion, vaguely sympathetic, seemed to lure him on from room to room. They were all littered with unremoved furniture. Obviously the British workman, claiming his prescriptive right to thirst, had adjourned to the neighbouring village for beer, leaving his task unfinished.

Now it seemed to Concanon all of a sudden that the thing he had considered and repudiated was actually happening to him—he was being softly, invisibly, propelled towards the door. The conviction was so strong that, to test it, he leaned slightly backwards, enough to throw him normally off his balance. The next moment he was out in the garden and walking rapidly away from the house, his heart thumping and his brain in a fume. He went up the lane, and coming out into the road, saw the deserted van still in its place. The oak chest appeared, if anything, a thought more protruded.

An hour later he walked into the agent's office in Farnborough.

"You never told me," he said, "that the house was occupied."

The agent stared at him.

"It isn't occupied, sir."

"Was, then, until recently. I found the removal going on."

"It hasn't been let, I assure you, for over a year."

It was Concanon's turn to stare.

"Will you come back there with me?" he said. "We'll get a trap and drive over."

There was something wrong here, it appeared. Could it be possible that tenants unbid had taken advantage of the remoteness of the place to put in a year's occupation rent-free? Yes, the agent would come with him.

They drove over. Nearing the lane, Concanon observed that the furniture-van was no longer in evidence. It had been removed during the interval. That was a plausible hypothesis, but no hypothesis could account for the utter desertion and emptiness of the house when they reached it. The men on their return must have worked with a superhuman activity. There was no trace anywhere of straw, of furniture, of human occupation. It was all dust and echoing loneliness.

The agent, taking his client for the second time over the premises, was a little curt in his manner. Probably he thought Concanon drunk or possessed. He looked at him covertly from time to time, but hardly alluded to the mare's nest which had brought him afield to the utter waste of his afternoon.

Back in his office, he could scarcely command the professional blandishment meet for the netting of a customer. He spoke with a minute show of impatience, barely troubling to suggest alternatives.

"Well, sir," he said, "are you satisfied with the place or not?"

"Who were the last tenants?" said Concanon, answering the question with a question.

The agent shrugged his shoulders.

"A family, name of Darrel," he said shortly.

"An ordinary family; I mean there was nothing unusual about them?" asked the customer, he himself hardly know why.

"They paid their rent," said the agent. "That was all I needed to know about them."

"Of whom did they consist?"

"Father, mother, and a daughter of the mother, who had been married before. The mother died during their tenancy. Well, sir, about the house?"

Concanon rose, and stood with his back to the empty fireplace.

"I wish you'd tell me," he said, "what sort of people they were."

His nervous insistence impressed the agent despite his commonplace self.

"Really, sir," he said, "I knew nothing definite against them."

"Definite?

"The man hadn't, perhaps, a first-class reputation. He was, in fact, rather a domestic tyrant, and unpopular with his neighbours."

"There was no suggestion of—"

"Foul play? Good heavens, no! What are you hinting at? The poor woman died of some internal complaint. Though certainly—"

"Well, what?"

"Why, it simply occurred to me that the money was hers. But you mustn't accept that for any suggestive admission. Everything was perfectly straight and above-board."

"And they left a year ago, you say?"

"Rather more."

"Do you know where they went?"

"No, I don't. I know only that the furniture was stored."

"Where?"

"That I can't recall. Now, sir, I must really trouble you for an answer."

"Leave that open," said Concanon. "The place suits me and it doesn't. If I decide to take, I'll let you know."

He left the office in an odd mood. He seemed to himself to have been impelled to these questions. He returned to town in a state of queer mental perturbation, which did nothing but increase during the next day or two. Clearly, unless he could devise some means to quiet it, his search for repose had exchanged him merely Scylla for Charybdis.

One night he saw in a dream once more the deserted furniture van. It stood on the empty road, as it had stood to his waking vision; only there was a difference—the oak chest was so protruded that it seemed to shoot towards him. He woke trembling and in a violent sweat; and by the morning he had made up his mind. He must do his utmost to trace the thing.

Now, at the time of his first experience, he had noted plainly enough, with no ulterior purpose, yet somehow compelled to the observation, the inscription on the van. It was that of a well-known Pantechnicon at Southampton; and his one obvious recourse was to visit the place. Necessarily his mission must be a blind one; nor could he conceive what was to be its upshot. But go he must, if only as a first step towards resolving a very haunting psychical problem. He took an early opportunity to run down.

As he approached the place, he saw that a quantity of furniture and household effects was in process of being removed from it at the moment. A couple of tilted vans, heavily laden, issued from the yard as he approached, and prominent on the tail board of the second lay the oak chest. He believed he recognised it with certainty, and his heart gave an odd twist. Then, turning, he followed the van through the streets. It led him to the rear quarters of some auction rooms, where it stopped to unload. He waited to see the chest carried in, then walked round to the front offices and inquired as to forthcoming furniture sales. The one they were about to catalogue, he learned, was to take place in a week.

He would wait for it, he told himself. He was, happily, an idle man, and weather and water were attractive. Calling at the auction rooms in due course, he procured a catalogue and, having ascertained from it that the goods were to be sold by the direction of a Mr. Darrel, their owner, he passed in to view the lots. The chest, on examination, proved to be a sound antique piece; but it was completely, and naturally, empty. On the day of the sale he attended, and, having bought the thing at a fair price, had it carried home to his lodgings.

At night he examined his purchase. It was to reveal to him for once and for all the actuality of the ghostly influence which had mastered him, or his own unfounded superstition. It was with a thrill, quite momentarily sickening in its intensity, that he found his minute investigation rewarded at last by the discovery of a secret panel which, sliding apart, betrayed the fact of a document hidden behind it. Concanon disinterred his prize with shaking fingers, and spread it open.

It was a Will, duly attested, and signed by one Kathleen Darrel (*née* Brewer) making her only surviving daughter, Lucy Allingham, her sole residuary legatee, after the payment of a certain bequest to John Darrell, the testator's husband.

The next day Concanon returned to town, where he made it his first business to visit the probate office at Somerset House. The will in his possession, he discovered, post-dated another, proved by John Darrell, in which the whole of Kathleen Darrel's property and effects were left unconditionally to her husband.

Concanon promptly transferred the further conduct of the matter to the hands of his lawyers, who, discarding all evidences of supernatural agency, proceeded to work, like plain business men, to find the girl, Lucy Allingham. A series of advertisements was successful at length in producing her, and then the story, such as it was, came out. Darrel had been a brute, both to his wife, whose fortune he had married, and to his step-daughter. The complete control he had effected over the former had resulted in the will by which he alone profited; but remorse of conscience, it seemed, had driven the mother, when stricken to her death, to remedy the injustice done her child by executing a later will—that hidden away in the oak chest. It was duly witnessed by a couple of ignorant and illiterate laundry hands, who had been sworn to secrecy, and the girl supposed that some frantic, inarticulate efforts made by her mother, when actually dying, to explain something to her, had related to the secret deposit. The two had lived in mortal terror of Darrel; the mother had postponed her revelation, with fatal results, to the very last. The moment she was dead and buried, the miscreant had driven the girl from home, with an intimation that she was to expect nothing more from him. She, delicately reared and educated, had been eking out a miserable existence as a skirt hand, when the solicitors' advertisement at length reached her.

The law did the rest, and effectively; and a scoundrel was duly checkmated. But there was a postscript, proper to the singularity of the occasion. The emotional experience, operating on a somewhat debilitated constitution; the impulse to a certain intimacy, supernaturally encouraged; the communion in a secret very sweet and pitiful in its essence—how could these result but in a craving for closer relations? The girl was desirable, the man, in his then condition, wholly susceptible. When at length Concanon moved into a country cottage—not that one in question, but another and a fairer, far away—he took a wife with him for love's sake.

THE WHITE HARE
(1915)

You know the Mendips or you don't know them—their beauty, their savagery, their wide-flung loneliness sweeping miles down into the haunted valley called the moors, where, in the moonlit nights, strange craft come floating from Glastonbury on mystic waters long since sunk and lost. There may be trippers in this place and that to vulgarise the brooding hours, and if you see with their eyes you see nothing; but they are local, after all—mere profaners of places already profaned to show. One may leave them behind, to resettle like flies disturbed from carrion, and, entering into the fastnesses of the hills, forget them in a moment. The place belongs to legend and the past; it murmurs with inarticulate voices, drums and rustles under visionary footfalls. Once, long ago there stood a little ruined church, difficult to strangers to find, among the high, far thickets, and there the dead lay tumbled and neglected, because the building had been desecrated of old, and never since reconsecrated; so that it was avoided by the people, and the fence surrounding the graveyard rotted piecemeal and grew choked with fungus and brier.

There was an evening when young Modred, abroad with his gun, found himself benighted, a little cold, but curious, near that thicket—and suddenly a white hare slipped from the palings, and ran before him like a jumping snowball. He fired on the instant, and could have sworn his unerring eye had not failed him; but the hare ran on and melted, verily like snow, into the glooms. He was startled, awed, but not to be browbeaten by puss or devil. Another evening he sought the place, sighted his quarry, and again failed inexplicably to bring her down. Then he remembered—white hare, white witch—silver alone could prevail against the cursed thing. On the third evening therefore he loaded with a silver button from his coat, a keepsake from his maiden love, and, biding his time, let fly at the loping succuba. There was a scream like a woman's—and the hare sped on and vanished. But she was hit at last.

The next day Modred learned that his love was dead. She had taken down her father's gun, not knowing it was loaded, to clean, and by some means the charge had been exploded into her breast.

Hideous the tragedy; hideous the moral to be drawn from it. From that time the man went like a mad thing, his heart broken, his soul an alien from earth and heaven. That it should have been she, and her gift to him her death! But most he raved against the cynic God, who might have ordered things differently, but would have them thus and thus to make sport for himself.

And then the dead girl's mother came to die; but she could not die; and she screamed and stormed on life to let her go; but life held her still fast in her agony. Then one day she sent for Modred.

"Cut the cursed thing from my shoulder," she said, "and let me pass."

"What thing?" he asked stupefied.

"Your silver button," she said, "that mauled, but could not end me. It has lain there ever since, keeping me from the churchyard and my friends the outlawed dead. I killed the innocent girl myself to mislead you, and I bore the pain of this, until now I cannot bear it. Cut it out."

Her shoulder was bare, and the button stood under the skin of it like a little blue plum. Modred, with a howl of fury, took it in his fingers and tore it away.

At that the woman screeched and fell, and out of the window leapt a white hare and vanished up the hill.

Coachwhip Publications

CoachwhipBooks.com

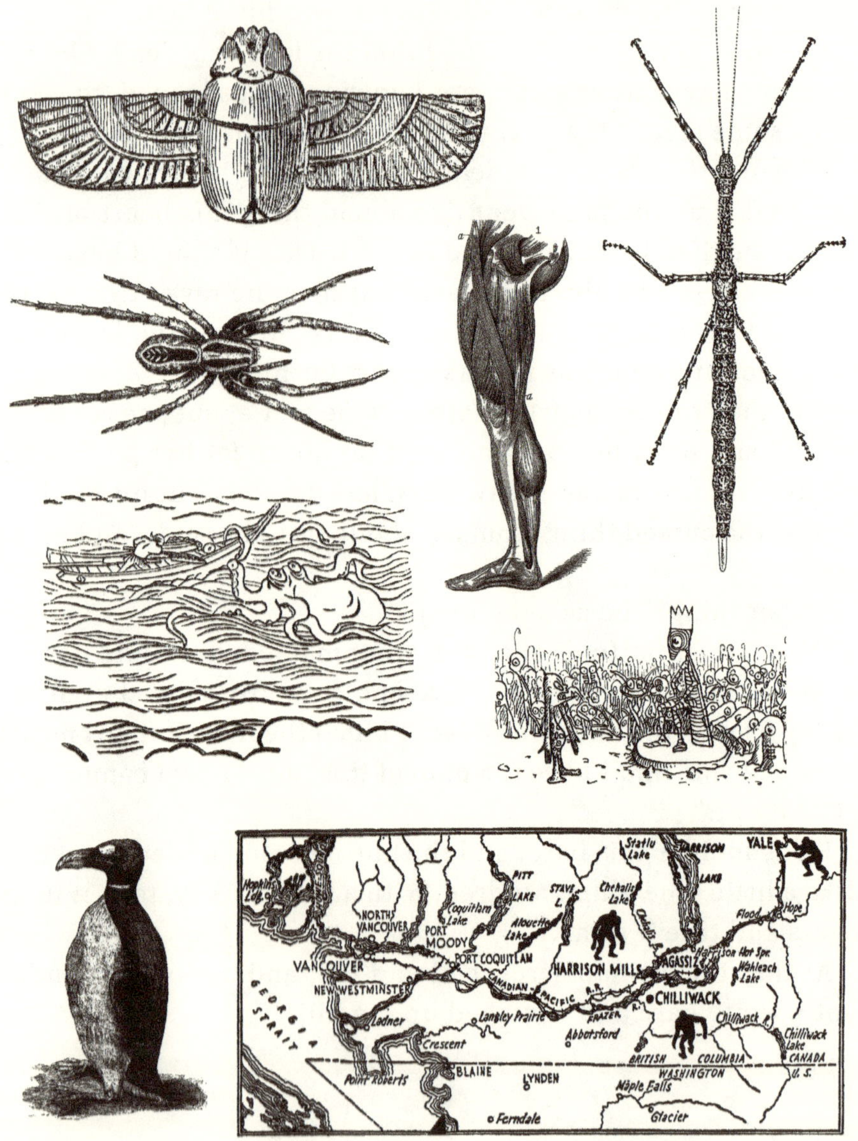

Coachwhip Publications

CoachwhipBooks.com

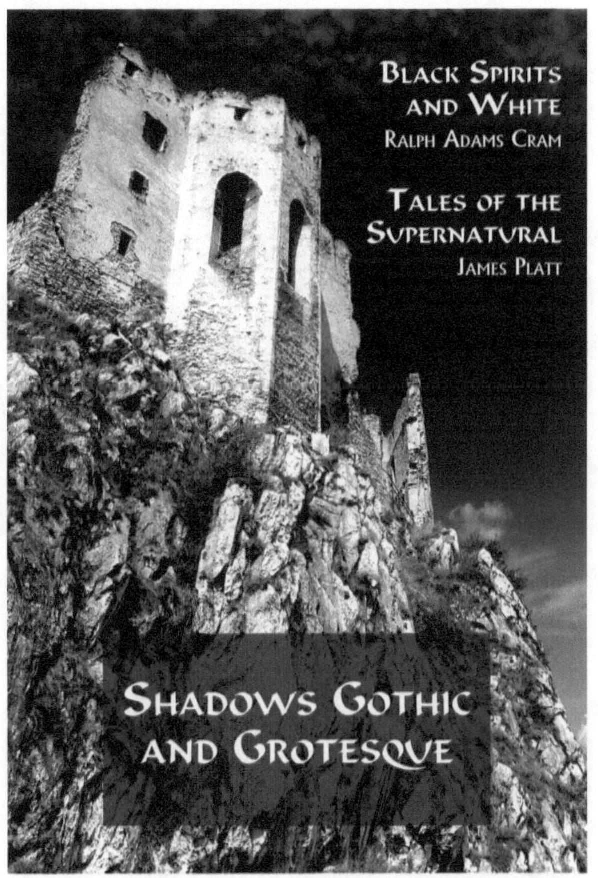

Shadows Gothic and Grotesque

ISBN 1-61646-059-8

Coachwhip Publications

Also Available

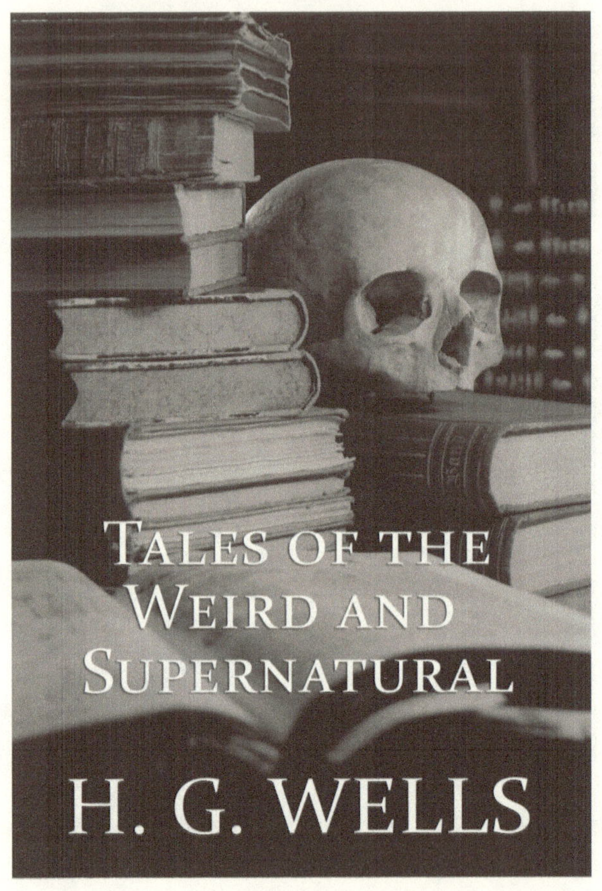

H. G. Wells:
Tales of the Weird and Supernatural
ISBN 1-61646-072-5

Coachwhip Publications

Also Available

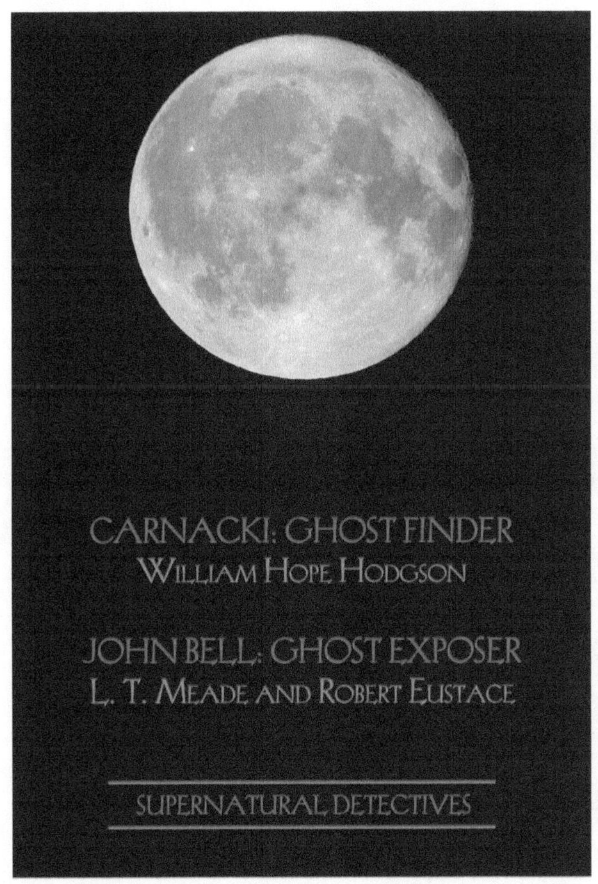

CARNACKI: GHOST FINDER
William Hope Hodgson
JOHN BELL: GHOST EXPOSER
L. T. Meade and Robert Eustace
SUPERNATURAL DETECTIVES

Supernatural Detectives 1:
Carnacki & John Bell
ISBN 1-61646-086-5

Coachwhip Publications

Also Available

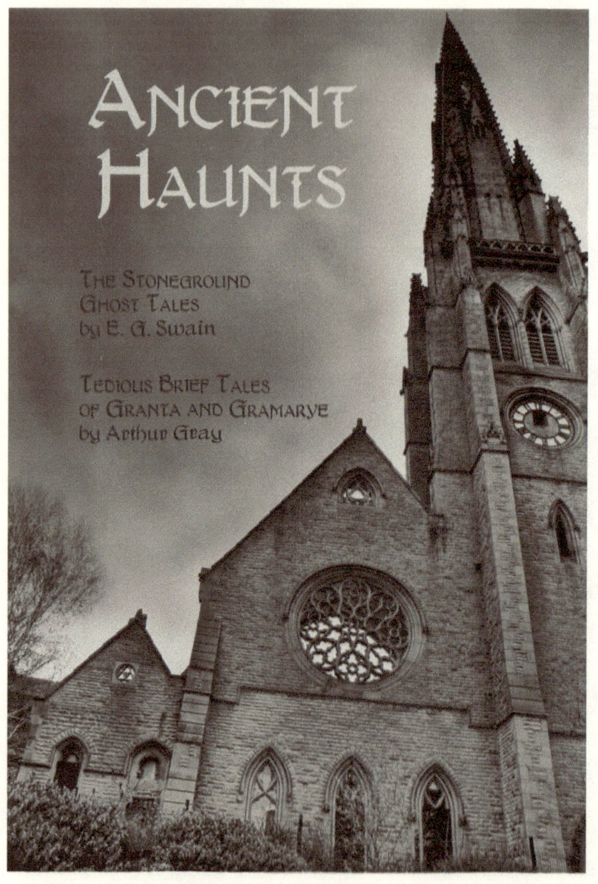

Ancient Haunts:

Stoneground Ghost Tales / Tedious Brief Tales

ISBN 1-61646-005-9

Coachwhip Publications

Also Available

Strange Haunts:
F. Marion Crawford & H. B. Marriott Watson
ISBN 1-61646-091-1

Coachwhip Publications

Also Available

The Uncle Abner Mysteries

ISBN 1-61646-016-4

Coachwhip Publications

Also Available

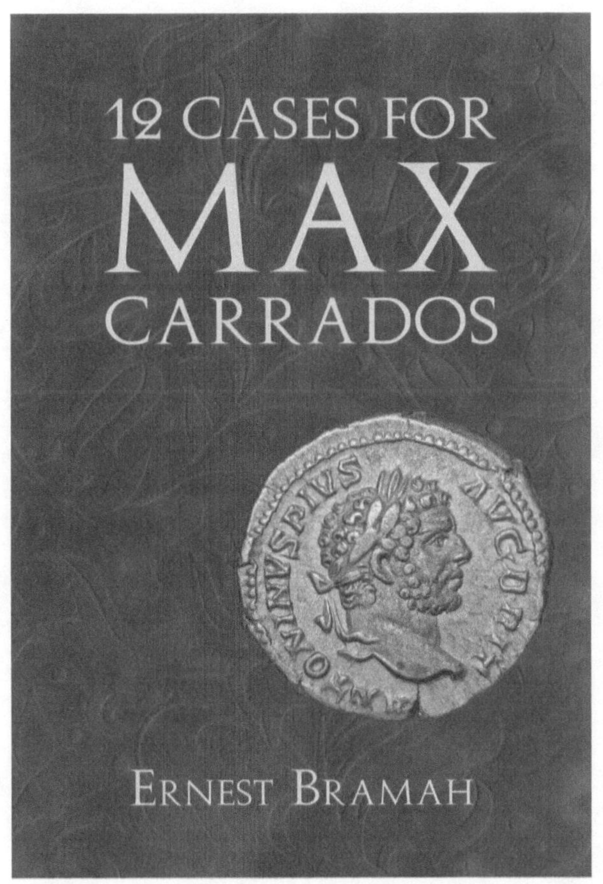

12 Cases for Max Carrados

ISBN 1-61646-018-0

www.ingramcontent.com/pod-product-compliance
Lightning Source LLC
Chambersburg PA
CBHW030549020726
47494CB00005B/1548